I0830734

ORAL LITERARY WORLDS

Oral Literary Worlds

Location, Transmission and Circulation

Edited by Sara Marzagora and Francesca Orsini

OpenBook Publishers

https://www.openbookpublishers.com

Any digital material and resources associated with this volume will be available at https://doi.org/10.11647/OBP.0405#resources

ISBN Paperback: 978-1-80511-311-9
ISBN Hardback: 978-1-80511-312-6
ISBN Digital (PDF): 978-1-80511-313-3
ISBN Digital eBook (EPUB): 978-1-80511-314-0
ISBN HTML: 978-1-80511-315-7

DOI: 10.11647/OBP.0405

Cover image: Woman playing Nyatiti during School Cultural Day in Tanzania. Photo by Onesmo Daniel (22 September 2017), https://commons.wikimedia.org/wiki/File:African_local_music_instrument_-Nyatiti_01.jpg

Cover design: Jeevanjot Kaur Nagpal

The Multilingual Locals and Significant Geographies (MULOSIGE) project received generous funding from the European Research Council (ERC) under the European Union's Horizon 2020 research and innovation programme (grant agreement No. 670876)

Contents

Acknowledgements

We would like to thank the European Research Council (ERC) for funding the MULOSIGE (Multilingual Locals and Significant Geographies) project under the European Union's Horizon 2020 Programme (grant agreement no. 853051). The project, based at SOAS, University of London, aimed to explore and compare the literary cultures of Northern India, the Maghrib, and the Horn of Africa in order to propose a located and multilingual approach to world literature and to foster South-South conversations and comparisons. The project, led by Francesca Orsini, consisted of three strands: Karima Laachir was Senior Researcher and leader of the Maghrib strand, Sara Marzagora was a Postdoctoral Researcher and leader of the Horn of Africa strand, and Ayele Kebede Roba was the Doctoral Researcher on the Horn of Africa strand. The project involved workshops in London, in Europe (Paris and Naples), and in the three regions covered by the project. The present volume developed out of the workshop on "Oral Traditions and World Literature" co-organized by Sara, Ayele and Prof Assefa Tefera Dibaba of Addis Ababa University in Addis Ababa on 17–18 December 2019. The workshop was held in a hotel (and we are grateful to the manager and staff at Hotel Regency, Addis Ababa, for their flexibility and generous help with all the arrangements) because multilingualism remains a contentious and contested issue in Ethiopia. We are grateful to the ERC for funding the workshop and allowing participants from the other project countries (Morocco and India) to join us. We would also like to thank Paige Harris for her editorial assistance, for copy-editing some of the chapters and preparing a substantial literature review that helped us write the Introduction. Finally, we would like to thank Alessandra and our copy-editors at OPB, and Mark Turin for his Foreword and for welcoming this book in his wonderful series.

Francesca Orsini & Sara Marzagora
Pollino & London, July 2024

Notes on Contributors

Adugna Barkessa Dinsa is Associate Professor in Applied Linguistics and Development at Addis Ababa University, a post he took up in 2008. Adugna teaches courses in applied linguistics, semantics, pragmatics, dialectology and language standardisation. He is the author of seven books: *Terminology Related Problems in Teaching Afaan Oromoo* (2009), *Introduction to Afaan Oromoo Grammar* (2010), *Basics to Teaching Afaan Oromoo and Literature* (2011), *Introduction to Applied Linguistic Research* (2011), *Afaan Oromoo Word and Its Structure* (2012), *Arra Gurba* 'Novel' (2017) and *Afaan Oromoo Textbooks* (grade 3, 6, 11 and 11). His PhD research was on "The Discursive Construction and Representations of the Waata Identity: A Critical Discourse Analysis of the Oral Texts". His articles include "Discursive Strategy of Orommara: A Critical Discourse Analysis of Abiy Ahmed's Political Rhetoric" (*Ethiopian Journal of the Social Sciences and Humanities*, 2010), "Back to or Away from the Glorious Past: A Critical Discourse Analysis of Abiy Ahmed's Political Talk" (*East African Journal of Social Sciences and Humanities*, 2021), "Oath in Oromia Courtroom: A Critical Discourse Analysis" (*Oromia Law Journal*, 2020) and "A Critical Discourse Analysis of Gendered Representations in Afaan Oromoo Textbook" (*East African Journal of Social Sciences and Humanities*, 2020).

Assefa (aka Asafa) Tefera Dibaba is a poet, educator and researcher based at Addis Ababa University (2019 to the present). He is the author of several anthologies of poems in Oromo, including *Anaany'aa* (1998, 2006, 2022), *Edas-Edanas* (1997, 2022), and *Finfi (Ilyaada)* (2014), and in English: *Decorous Decorum* (2006), *The Hug* (2011), *Symposia* (2018), and *Ate-Loon* (2020), and he has published works of prose, including *Danaa* (2000), *Eela* (2009), and *Theorizing the Present* (2004). Faced with persecution in Ethiopia because of his writing, Assefa relocated to the US in 2010 thanks to the Institute of International Education's Scholar Rescue Fund, and subsequently completed a PhD in Folklore and Anthropology at Indiana University (2011-2015). He presented his research in ethnoecology and ecopoetics at SOAS University of London in November 2019 as part of the MULOSIGE research project. Assefa's latest book is a 511-page ethnographic autobiography in Oromo (*Anis-Atis*, 2023), written in a poetic-prose style, which looks back at his personal and professional endeavours through the prism of the cultural, sociopolitical, and economic aspirations of the Oromo people and their movements for freedom.

Ayele Kebede Roba is Lecturer (Assistant Professor in African literatures) at the University of York. He holds a PhD in Cultural, Literary and Postcolonial Studies from SOAS University of London (2022), which was carried out as part of the MULOSIGE research project. He stayed at SOAS after his PhD to take up a Postdoctoral Fellowship in the School of Cultures, Languages and Linguistics (2022-2023) before starting his current job at York. Prior to moving to the UK for his PhD, Ayele completed a BA from Ambo University, an MA from Addis Ababa University, and worked for six years as a Lecturer in English Language and Literature at the University of Bule Hora, Ethiopia. At Bule Hora, he was the recipient of a number of research grants to study the oral literature, sociolinguistics, and cultural traditions of the Guji Oromo in Southern Ethiopia. Ayele specialises in the literatures composed in two major Ethiopian languages, Amharic and Oromo, with a particular focus on the novel, literary multilingualism, the interplay between oral literature and literary texts. His research has been published in *Critical African Studies, Comparative Literature Studies*, the *Journal of Oromo Studies*, and *The Routledge Handbook of African Literature*.

Desta Desalegn Dinege is Assistant Professor of Oral Literature in the Department of Social Science and Language Education, College of Education of Addis Ababa University. He holds a PhD in English Literature from Addis Ababa University (2015) and is the author of four books: a collection of poems in Oromo entitled *Eenyuma Amantaa?* (2008, 2012, 2013), a research book for college students in Oromo, *Bu'uura Qorannoo* (2017, 2020), a collection of short stories in Oromo titled *Waadaa* (2018), and a collection of short stories in Oromo titled

Dimimmisa (2020). He has published two articles in *Gadaa Journal* and is currently writing articles on different genres of oral literature and collaborating in several research projects, both as principal investigator and as project member.

Vanessa Paloma Elbaz is Senior Research Associate of Peterhouse at the University of Cambridge and Research Associate at its Faculty of Music. Previously a Senior Research Fulbright Fellow, a Marie Slodowska Curie Fellow, and a Posen fellow, among others, she has published extensively on the sonic histories of the Jewish diasporas from the Iberian peninsula. Her PhD is from the Université Sorbonne Paris Cité, and her MM from Indiana University Bloomington. She began her studies at the Andes University in her native Bogotá, Colombia. In 2012 she founded KHOYA: Jewish Morocco Sound Archive in Casablanca. A board member of the Jewish Music Institute, the Tangier American Institute for Moroccan Studies and the Institute for Tolerance Studies, she is the Chair of the International Council for Traditions of Music and Dance (ICTMD)'s Study Group on Mediterranean Music. Her first monograph on Sephardi women's voices in Northern Morocco is due to be published with Brill, she is editing a volume on 'Sound, Music and Memory' for the British Academy, and a special journal issue on Judeo-Spanish songbooks for Les Presses de l'INALCO.

Karima Laachir is Professor of Cultural Studies of the Middle East and North Africa and Director of Centre for Arab and Islamic Studies (Middle East and Central Asia), Australian National University, Canberra. Previously, she held tenured positions at SOAS University of London and the University of Birmingham. Karima's research focuses on the politics of culture in the Arabic-speaking world and how cultural production and practices underpin social and political movements for change. She also works on Comparative literature and Postcolonial Studies multilingually and from the perspectives of the Arabic Global South. She was the Maghreb lead of the MULOSIGE research project. Her latest publication is a Special Issue on "'Reading Together' Postcolonial Multilingual Literature in the Maghreb" in *Comparative Critical Studies* (Autumn 2024).

Sara Marzagora is a Senior Lecturer (Associate Professor) in Comparative Literature at King's College London. She previously held a four-year postdoctoral fellowship at SOAS University of London, where she led the Horn of Africa strand of the MULOSIGE research project. Sara specialises in world literature and global intellectual history, with a particular focus on Ethiopia and the Horn of Africa. Her research on Ethiopian print culture, Amharic literature, and the history of Ethiopian nationalisms has appeared, among others, in the *Journal of African History*, *Global Intellectual History*, the *International History Review*, the *Journal of African Cultural Studies*, and the *Journal of World Literature*. She is currently completing a monograph on early twentieth-century Ethiopian political thought and co-editing a volume which compares literary and policy perspectives on multilingualism in the Horn of Africa and South Asia.

Sadhana Naithani is Professor at the Centre of German Studies of Jawaharlal Nehru University in New Delhi, India, and president of the International Society for Folk Narrative Research (ISFNR). She researches Indo-European folklore and the international history of folkloristics. She is the author of *In Quest of Indian Folktales* (2006), *The Story Time of the British Empire* (2010), *Folklore Theory in Postwar Germany* (2014), and *Folklore in Baltic History* (2019). Currently she is writing on the relationship between narratives, ecology, culture and history. Her latest book *The Inhuman Empire: Wildlife, Colonialism, Culture* explores the subject. Sadhana Naithani has received many honours, among them: Fulbright Visiting Professor at the Department of Anthropology, University of California, Berkeley in the academic year 2022–23; invited to deliver the 2023 David Buchan Lecture at the University of Aberdeen, Scotland; and invited to give the keynote address at the 2024 ISFNR Congress in Riga.

Francesca Orsini is a literary historian interested in bringing a located and multilingual perspective to Indian literary history and world literature. She is the author of *The Hindi Public Sphere* (2002), *Print and Pleasure* (2009), and *East of Delhi: Multilingual literary culture and world literature* (2023). She has edited books on the history of emotions (*Love in South Asia*, 2006), the long fifteenth century (*After Timur Left*, with Samira Sheikh, 2014), oral traditions (*Tellings and Texts*, with

Katherine Schofield, OBP 2015), Hindi-English mixing (*Hinglish Live*, 2022, with Ravikant), and Cold War print cultures (*The Form of Ideology and the Ideology of Form*, OBP 2022, with Neelam Srivastava and Laetitia Zecchini). She was the Principal Investigator of the ERC-funded research project "Multilingual Locals and Significant Geographies: For a New Approach to World Literature". She co-edits with Debjani Ganguly the series *Cambridge Studies in World Literatures and Cultures*, and with Whitney Cox the forthcoming *Cambridge History of Indian Literature*. She is Professor emerita of Hindi and South Asian Literature at SOAS University of London, and a Fellow of the British Academy.

Virginia Pisano holds a BA degree in History from the Sorbonne University (Paris), a MA in Near and Middle Eastern Studies from SOAS University of London and a second MA in Cultural Management from the ESCP - Management School of Paris. She has been working as a programme coordinator for several cultural organisations focusing on the Arab world and the Mediterranean space, including the Medinea program at the Aix-en-Provence Festival, the Transcultural Music Program at the Royaumont Foundation and the Shubbak festival in London. She is currently working for Aflam, a cultural organisation based in Marseille, as program coordinator of the International Mediation Platform.

Fatima Zahra Salih is Professor of French literature in the Faculty of Arts and Humanities of the University Sultan Moulay Slimane in Morocco. Her PhD thesis was titled 'The Conquered Word of Women Novelists: A Study of the Works of Marguerite Duras, Hélène Cixous and Nathalie Sarraute'. Her main research interests are literature, intangible heritage, genre, psychoanalysis, and theatre arts. She has organised several conferences and cultural festivals, including the International Festival of the One Thousand and One Nights, and has taken part in international festivals in Belgium, Jordan, Canada, and Egypt. She worked and coordinated several international cooperation projects. She is the coordinator of the master's programme "Tangible and Intangible Heritage Studies" and vice president of the "Narration and Cultural Forms: Literature, Languages and Society" laboratory.

Tadesse Jaleta Jirata has a PhD in Interdisciplinary Child and Youth Research from the Norwegian University of Science and Technology (2013) and an MA from Addis Ababa University (2005). He worked as a researcher and lecturer at Dilla University (from 2000 to 2017) and is now an Associate Professor at Addis Ababa University (from 2018 to present). He was a postdoctoral researcher at Geneva University in Switzerland and a recipient of the Swiss Excellence Scholarship in 2016/17. He was also awarded an Open Society Scholar Award and carried out field research in South Africa in 2016. His research emphasises the dynamic relationships between folklore and young people among agro-pastoral communities in southern Ethiopia. His focus has been firstly on oral literature and intergenerational relationships, secondly on the relevance of oral literature in building young people's social competence, and thirdly on children's right to education in the context of the multilingual societies of southern Ethiopia. He has published in several high-impact peer-reviewed journals such as *Research in African Literature*; *Northeast African Studies*; the *Journal of Folklore Research*; *Global Studies of Childhood*; *Storytelling, Self, Society*; *African Studies Quarterly*; and *Africa: The Journal of the International African Institute*. He is also the author of a book titled *A Contextual Study of the Social Functions of Guji-Oromo Proverbs: The Savor and Rhetoric Power of Verbal Arts in Everyday Communications of African Peoples* (2009). He participated in several interdisciplinary research projects as a leader and principal researcher.

Clarissa Vierke is Professor of Literatures in African Languages at the University of Bayreuth. She is an expert in Swahili poetry and Islamic manuscript cultures, and has written on texts travelling the Indian Ocean to East Africa – both in Anglophone Kenya and Tanzania and Lusophone Mozambique. Her most recent publication is a poetry anthology *In this Fragile World: Swahili Poetry of Commitment by Ustadh Mahmoud Mau* (Brill, 2023), which she co-edited with Annachiara Raia (University of Leiden) and the poet. Together with colleagues working on Francophone and Lusophone literature and film, she is currently running a research project on literary entanglements in the Indian Ocean across boundaries of nations, languages, and media. She is principal investigator of the Cluster of Excellence 'Africa Multiple. Reconfiguring African Studies' and the spokesperson of the research section 'Arts and Aesthetics'. Together with colleagues from Leipzig and Cologne, she set up the project 'Recalibrating Afrikanistik' funded by the Volkswagen foundation with the aim to critically consider the future of the study of African languages and literatures.

Yenealem Aredo is Assistant Professor of Material Culture in the Department of Amharic Language, Literature and Folklore of Addis Ababa University. She teaches courses on literature and folklore and advises MA and PhD students. Yenealem has also been teaching Amharic to students from the USA, Norway, South Korea, Netherlands, and China. She holds an MA in Ethiopian Literature and Folklore and a PhD in Documentary Linguistics and Culture. Her research interests include aspects of folklore such as material culture, customary lore, oral literature, and nonverbal features. Yenealem is participating in adaptive (problem solving) and thematic research projects on the cultures of Ethiopia. Currently, she is working on a book entitled የናኦ ብሔረሰብ ፎክሎር (*Folklore of the Na'o Community*).

List of Illustrations

Foreword

Mark Turin

Oral Literary Worlds: Location, Transmission and Circulation is the twelfth publication in the World Oral Literature series with our partners, Open Book Publishers. As will become clear, this volume marks a very exciting new direction for the series as a whole.

Now running for over a decade, the World Oral Literature series was designed to preserve and promote the oral literatures of marginalized and minoritized people by publishing materials on endangered traditions in innovative, responsive, ethical and culturally-appropriate ways. Situated at the intersection of anthropology, folklore, linguistics and literary studies, the study of oral genres is a fast-developing field, and still one with few publishing outlets.

Through the timely integration of theory and practice, the editors of *Oral Literary Worlds*—Sara Marzagora and Francesca Orsini—have built a long-awaited intellectual bridge between oral literature and world literature. As they note, any possible advantages to be gained by leaving orality out of world literature 'do not offset what gets lost.' This rapprochement is extremely welcome and indeed timely. Noting that much of the scholarly writing on world literature is 'still informed by a teleological view of orature as the chronological and aesthetic antecedent of written literature,' Marzagora and Orsini seek to move the conversation forward in a manner that is productive and inclusive. The varied contributions that make up this rich volume demonstrate the timeless relevance of historical and contemporary oral traditions (or orature) to the study of world literature, and the futility of drawing disciplinary lines in the sand.

   https://doi.org/10.11647/OBP.0405.12

Growing out of a conference held in Addis Ababa in December 2019, this volume offers a sustained engagement with the longevity of oral texts and traditions, notwithstanding inevitable shift by language, form, and location. At their core, the contributions to *Oral Literary Worlds* all point in the same direction, questioning the received monodirectionality of expressive forms moving from oral to written, and challenging problematic and entrenched dichotomies that continue to exist in both scholarly and popular imaginings between "literate" and "non-literate" cultures.

Given the complicated histories of terms such as orality, literacy and tradition, the editors offer some defining principles to ground their argument. Through this discussion, readers are invited to remember that while "literature" is generally still used to refer only to cultural expressions with written form, there is no compelling reason to treat the verbal art of oral societies as fundamentally different to written traditions: oral literatures simply exist at one end of one spectrum of literary types. A bias towards the written word, combined with the tendency of anthropologists and folklorists to record and transcode oral traditions into textual form, has resulted in the misrepresentation of oral literatures as no more than verbatim transmissions of narratives across generations, and further contributes to the ill-conceived if ingrained belief that such traditions are cruder than written literature. As Marzagora and Orsini themselves ask, in a particularly vital section of their Introduction, 'Why, despite the interface between oral/written/digital platforms and so much ink spilt rejecting the reductive binary of orality/literacy, is literature in world literature only "born printed"?'

Research on oral literature has effectively challenged some of the prevailing and myopic assumptions baked into traditional theories of literacy. In addition, studies conclusively show that technologies like writing are better conceptualized as shaping, rather than determining, our collective and individual recollections. The circulation of fast-changing information technologies and media in the twenty-first century force us to consider new aspects to established questions about what it means to be "literate" in an overwhelmingly digital era. With the recent advent of generative AI, we must consider more urgently than ever whether immediate and unfettered access to vast amounts of information through the internet changes how people critically engage with texts, who ultimately owns knowledge and, most critically, what we now mean by originality, authority and creativity. The influence of the digital screen on the meaning of texts is so great that, even when it is used to render the written word, as in an e-book, the digital mediates how we encounter and interpret the text we read. And yet for scholars with a long view of the history of orality, literacy and writing, many of these transformations are old wine in new bottles.

Marzagora and Orsini, together with the authors whose wide-ranging contributions make up *Oral Literary Worlds*, assist us in navigating this complex terrain. It is encouraging to learn that even in this increasingly saturated digital landscape, the power and attraction of oral genres seems undiminished, whether in Africa, Asia or Europe. Engaging with but not limiting themselves to discussions of disembodied listeners, the editors make a compelling case for a more holistic understanding of the poetic of orality that takes into account the 'somatic, that is, physical and material elements.' With examples drawn from across the globe, Marzagora and Orsini demonstrate how embodiment, through which 'body, voice, and movement [become] part of the textual performance,' must be considered when theorizing orality. As I have reflected when observing my own children witnessing long rituals in eastern Nepal in a language and culture that was not familiar to them, 'precisely when one does not understand the words, one can appreciate the power of the voice and the body of the performer on one's somatic-physical bodily responses.' Understanding is an intellectual and cognitive process; affect, emotion and embodiment are not. We must recall that it is through repetition, reverberation and recurrence that oral genres 'become part of and shape our habitus.' Often without even realising that it's happening, orature forms 'some of our most visceral aesthetic tastes and responses.'

For literary studies to be really "worldly", then, as Marzagora and Orsini convincingly argue, 'they must account for the many oral literary worlds around us.' This is also the position of the World Oral Literature Project and this publication series that carries its name. I firmly believe that oral literature and world literature are not—and should not continue to be—two solitudes, travelling in parallel, existing side by side, and only occasionally nodding to one another from a respectful distance. Rather, they are distinct if complementary aspects of the extraordinary expressive potential that makes us human. 'What if rather than considering song, storytelling, or performance close kin but nonetheless "other" than poetry/literature, they were simply part of literature?' the editors ask. 'What if "folk" artists were just artists?' I couldn't agree more. There is so much to learn by just bending a little and adopting a posture of curiosity. Much of the dynamic creativity of literature writ large lies beyond the learned disciplinary frames in which we find comfort. Echoing Giovanni Paolini, whom the editors invoke in their introduction: *"Eccoci qua"*. Here we are. Right here, and right now. By reaching out, we are actually reaching in. In the process, we generate deeper connection and appreciation. *Oral Literary Worlds* helps us do just that.

Dr Mark Turin
Director, World Oral Literature Project
Institute for Critical Indigenous Studies
Department of Anthropology
University of British Columbia

Vancouver, Canada
April 2024

Introduction: Written and Unwritten Literary Geographies

Doing World Literature from the Perspective of Oral Texts

Sara Marzagora and Francesca Orsini

Oral Genres Are Everywhere

'Eccoci qua'. 'Here we are'. Giovanni Paolini begins his dramatic storytelling performance *Il Racconto del Vajont*, which revisits the tragic evening of October 1963, by marking a presence: the here and now and the assembled 'we'. 'Let's try and tell it together', he tells the audience, asking them to imagine how a massive landslide caused 50 million cubic meters to overflow a dam and submerge five underlying villages in north-eastern Italy, killing almost 2000 people. Packed with information and incorporating many voices and reflective loops, Paolini's narrative maintains throughout a high level of dramatic force—'started seven years earlier, the story ended in four, apocalyptic minutes'—and civic pathos.[1] Undoubtedly more powerful as a live performance, Paolini's 'teatro di narrazione'/*Vajont* remains effective even when filmed for TV (and later watched on YouTube), and it has also been published as a book.[2] Like many oral texts, it exists across multiple oral, written,

---

1   Marco Paolini, 'Vajont: 9 ottobre 1963' (Rai Due and Moby Dick Teatri della Riviera, 1997).

2   Marco Paolini, *Il racconto del Vajont* (Milan: Garzanti, 2014).

    https://doi.org/10.11647/OBP.0405.00

and digital platforms. 'In India and in Southeast Asia, no one reads the *Rāmāyaṇa* or the *Mahābhārata* for the first time', A.K. Ramanujan famously quipped: before one encounters the epics as written texts, one is already familiar with the story through oral narratives or, perhaps more likely today, audio-visual versions.[3]

A few more examples: Pakistani actor Zia Mohyuddin (1933–2023) specialized in transforming written sketches into oral narratives, bringing dialogues and poems to life with his deep, smooth voice full of irony, and helping listeners over tricky passages by means of careful stresses and pauses. For decades, audiences hung on his every word and doubled up with laughter at stage readings; cassette recordings were smuggled across the border into India, jealously held and eagerly copied.[4] By contrast, Moulay Omar Douâmi, storyteller of the square (*halqa*) of Souk Barra in Beni-Mellal in central Morocco, specialises in turning Hindi films into oral narratives in Moroccan Darija. Douami retells the story of the film he watched the day before, changing plot, characters, and places to make the story more interesting and accessible to his audience.[5] Both are examples of the interdependence and the movement between oral, written, and audiovisual modes, mediated by the performer for specific audiences but also made available to disembodied listeners through technological reproduction and digital platforms. In 2010, Francesca watched Mahmood Farooqui and Danish Husain formally sit on a stage in central Delhi dressed in starched white achkans and topis and launch into a performance of an episode of the *Dastan Amir Hamza*, in a performance style they successfully revived, virtually from scratch, from written sources (see Chapter 9 by Sadhana Naithani in this volume). Francesca does not think she was the only one in the audience missing half of what they said in highly Persianized Urdu rhymed prose, but the rhythm of their double-act and what she could understand offered a spell-binding demonstration of the power of voice and rhythm.

---

3   A. K. Ramanujan, 'Three Hundred *Rāmāyaṇas*: Five Examples and Three Thoughts on Translation' in *Many Rāmāyaṇas: The Diversity of a Narrative Tradition in South Asia*, ed. by Paula Richman (Berkeley: University of California Press, 1991), pp. 22–49 (p. 46).

4   *Zia Mohyuddin ke Saath Ek Shaam* 2022 (An Evening with Zia Mohyuddin), YouTube.

5   Fatima Zahra Salih, 'L'art de (ra)conter les films; entretien avec le conteur Moulay Omar Douâmi' (unpublished interview, 2008) and Chapter 5 in this volume.

And again: 'Ababa' Tesfaye Sahlu is known by virtually every Ethiopian who had access to a TV in the decades between the 1960s and the 1990s as *YäTärät Abbat* ('Father of the *tärät*', i.e. the fable/story). He was a multi-talented actor, singer, musician, and writer, but what made him famous is his children's TV programme *YäLəjj Gize* ('Children's Time'), a staple of Ethiopian television for decades. With consummated dramatic ability, Ababa Tesfaye played the voices of different characters and mimicked animal sounds. He often used visual illustrations to enhance the story, or sometimes broke into song, or played musical instruments, or performed magic tricks. Watched by children and adults alike, the TV show coined new catchphrases, and retained much of the style of an oral performance: Ababa Tesfaye addressed the children directly, as if he could see them through the screen ('you on the right, stop bothering your sibling'), and they indeed diligently stood up when he appeared on screen at the beginning of the show, as is customary when an old person enters the room.[6] Ababa Tesfaye died in 2017, but the recordings of his TV show are now available on YouTube, and in an internet café in Addis Ababa, Sara saw a woman dropping off her two children in front of one of these YouTube videos to keep them cared for and entertained while she went elsewhere for an errand.

These few examples—which can be multiplied *ad libitum* (slam poetry, hip hop, *jari* and *kobigaan*, etc.)—show the enduring power and attraction of oral genres in the contemporary world, in the Western world as well as in Africa and Asia. Their power lies in the expressive, affective, and somatic power of voice, rhythm, and/or melody. Liz Gunner reminds us that the:

> rendering or realizing oral works involved a body, a voice, a moment in time, and an audience. Attending to the poetics of orality must take into account the somatic, that is, physical and material elements. The possibilities and actualities these variables give rise to are vast, but the fact of a somatic rendering, where body, voice, and movement are part of the textual performance, has to be considered when theorizing orality.[7]

---

6   For a first-person account of the impact of Ababa Tesfaye on younger and older generations alike, see Rode Molla, 'Children's Experiences Matter: An Interdisciplinary Approach', *Religious Education*, 118.2 (2023), 113–118, https://doi.org/10.1080/00344087.2023.2184026

7   Liz Gunner, 'Ecologies of Orality' in *The Cambridge Companion to World Literature*, ed. by B. Etherington and J. Zimbler (Cambridge: Cambridge University Press,

Oral texts become instantiated through the bodies of performers—the timbre and artistry of their voices, their studied pauses, the quality and rhythm of their gestures, their acting out of one or more roles. Scholarship on poetry and song often underscores how music and the singing voice tend to 'drown text' and make short shrift of carefully weighed poetic meters and stresses.[8] In some cases, it is the performer's breath and not the strict syllable count that forms the basis of oral metre (see Chapter 1 by Clarissa Vierke in this volume). But music also makes texts or textual fragments memorable and endurably part of one's body, whether one understands the language fully or only in part.[9] In fact, precisely when one does not understand the words, one can appreciate the power of the voice and the body of the performer on one's own somatic-physical bodily responses.

If singular oral performances can create lifelong memories, what is also important about oral genres, as they are experienced repeatedly over time, is how they become part of and shape our habitus, indeed some of our most visceral aesthetic tastes and responses. We only need to think of our favourite (or most hated) songs to know how deeply in our body their phrases, images, and sounds dwell. In the Indian context, the extraordinarily resilient popularity of Urdu poetry, particularly among non-Urdu speakers, rests on a familiarity with the basics acquired by listening to film songs and *ghazal* cassettes/recordings. Oral texts, in other words, are the first means through which poetic/aesthetic tastes come to dwell in our bodies. Well before reading our first book, each and every one of us spent years consuming (and sometimes producing)

2018), pp. 116–129 (p. 117).

8   See Jahan Ramazani's discussion in 'Poetry and Song' in *Poetry and its Others* (Chicago: University of Chicago Press, 2014), pp. 184–238 (pp. 185–186).

9   'In performance... music is experienced, not as something given to the body, but as something done through and with the body. Sound penetrates us, engaging us on a bodily level in fundamentally different ways than the visual'; Liora Bresler, 'What Musicianship Can Teach Educational Research', *Music Education Research*, 7.2 (2005), 169–183 (p. 177), https://doi.org/10.1080/1461380050016939. 'Besides, listening is mediated by previous information and expectations, and even 'vocal timbre is not an elementary sound of an essential body, but rather [...] both timbre and body are shaped by unconscious and conscious training that are cultural artifacts of attitudes towards gender, class, race, and sexuality'; Nina Sun Eidsheim, 'Voice as a Technology of Selfhood: Towards an Analysis of Racialized Timbre and Vocal Performance' (unpublished PhD thesis, University of California San Diego, 2008), p. 2.

literature orally and visually. This does not stop after we learn how to read: alongside the genres analysed by the contributors in this volume, many of us know a repertoire of prayers, anthems (national or otherwise), chants for political demonstrations ('no justice, no peace') or sports events, jokes, songs to accompany specific events ('happy birthday to you'), and we add to those repertoires on occasion.

We approached these reflections as scholars of world literature, who saw the almost exclusive focus of the discipline on written literature as a considerable limitation. For literary studies to be really 'worldly', we believe, they must account for the many oral literary worlds around us. Oral literary worlds help us put pressure on the definition of 'literature' in world literature, just as oral texts help put pressure on the definition of 'text' and broaden it beyond written texts to encompass not just visual and aural texts, but also other processes of 'entextualization' that are achieved, to quote Karin Barber, 'through the consolidation of discourse as object of exegesis and as quotation'.[10] It is this broader sense of 'text' that the essays in this book espouse. How does a focus on oral genres and traditions that are still alive and well today—and so do not belong to a pre-print past—help us to revisit and rethink the assumptions that underpin ideas of literature and world literature? What do oral genres have to say about what counts as a (literary) text, and about the power and functions of literature? What do they teach us about how we acquire literary tastes, even somatically, and live and practice them? What light do oral genres cast on some of the main aspects highlighted by world literature studies, namely circulation, location, and scale? Why, despite the interface between oral/written/digital platforms and so much ink spilt rejecting the reductive binary of orality/literacy, is literature in world literature only 'born printed'?

Each essay in this volume explores and develops these points from its located perspective, without seeking to be exhaustive or definitive. We do not aim for general definitions—such as the differences or relationship between poetry and song[11]—but we want to open avenues

---

10   Karin Barber, 'Text and Performance in Africa', *Bulletin of the School of Oriental and African Studies* 66.3 (2003), 324–333 (p. 332), https://doi.org/10.1017/S0041977X03000223. See also her *The Anthropology of Texts, Persons, and Publics* (Cambridge: Cambridge University Press, 2007).

11   See Ramazani, 'Poetry and Song'.

for exploration and conversation among scholars of folklore, heritage studies, music, literature, and world literature, and with colleagues belonging to different scholarly traditions (particularly in Ethiopia, India, and Morocco) that have so far been outside European and North American discussions of world literature.

Orature, Oral Literature, Oral Traditions

What's in a name? Scholars have suggested and used several terms to indicate unwritten verbal arts. Each term and definition stresses certain characteristics and sets up relationships (of difference, convergence, or specificity) with the other terms and with written literature.[12] Orature, the term coined in the 1970s by Ugandan linguist Pio Zirimu, defined as the use of utterance as an aesthetic means of expression, forcefully counters the tendency to view oral arts as inferior, less developed, or marginal compared to written literature, and pushes for a paradigm shift in which oral aesthetics do not need to define themselves against written literature to gain validity and value.[13] Instead of qualifying literature—the stable category—with the adjective 'oral', orature creates a hybrid term that destabilises, envelops, and swallows literature. The term orature has been championed by Ngũgĩ Wa Thiong'o, who argues that written and printed literature are but a small part of orature, which encompasses them.[14] Drawing on South African sculptor, poet, and storyteller Pitika Ntuli, Ngũgĩ suggests that orature is a 'fusion of all art forms', greater than the sum of its parts and deeply interconnected.

---

12   Literature itself has hardly remained a stable semantic category, of course, whether in the various European languages and cultural areas, or in the Arabic and Persian *adab*, Indian *kavya* and *sahitya*, Chinese *wénxué*, and so on.

13   Ngũgĩ Wa Thiong'o, 'Notes towards a Performance Theory of Orature', *Performance Research: A Journal of the Performing Arts*, 12.3 (2007), 4–7, https://doi. org/10.1080/13528160701771253

14   This is a view that some verbal and performance artists themselves have taken: transnational *Nautanki* artist Devendra Sharma, for example, writes: 'as I try more and more to bring "lok" [i.e. folk] into sahityik [literary]/cultural "mainstream" (or rather into an elitist narrow circle of legitimate sahitya having almost no audience these days—maybe I am generalizing here), I realize the politics of the powerful urban/mainstream writers and artists who are really determined to keep away the "crowd" (otherwise they will be very quickly overwhelmed by the powerful "lok" or "folk" which is so much closer to people's hearts—equally in cities and villages)'; email communication to Francesca Orsini, November 2019.

By contrast, Ngũgĩ opposes the term 'oral literature' on the grounds that it incorporates and subsumes the oral into the written, implying a dependent position and obscuring the autonomy of orality.[15] By contrast, in Chapter 9 of this volume, Sadhana Naithani uses 'orature' for oral performance genres that have a strong relationship with writing— whether harking back to a missing original text or drawing upon written textual sources to reconstruct and revive a style of storytelling.

Scholars like Ruth Finnegan prefer instead to retain the term oral literature.[16] Finnegan's key realisation was that oral forms must be celebrated for their spoken elements and audience presence, beyond their generic similarities with written forms. Oral performances are multi-sensory and dynamic, creating a 'multidimensional and embodied performance'. But—and this is an example of how centring oral forms casts a fresh light on literature as a whole—for Finnegan *all* literature, whether written or oral, has performative elements. Even silent reading is a performance, as the reader experiences the written word through their 'inner ear'. And writing's multimodal nature can be used to bring performance to the page. All literature, then, has a multiform plurality that must be celebrated. Therefore, Finnegan retains the term literature 'as an umbrella notion that can embrace all those displayed forms and events in which verbal artistry in some way plays a significant part'.[17] This expanded definition of 'literature' as verbal artistry can then be further qualified based on medium, with 'written' and 'oral' literatures as subsets. In her reasoning, therefore, 'literature' does not automatically mean 'written literature'. If the speaker is excluding unwritten literatures, then they must qualify 'literature' with 'written'.

While most of the contributions to this volume stress the continuing vitality, mutability, and adaptability of oral genres to contemporary individuals and societies across the world, a different emphasis can be

---

15   Ngũgĩ wa Thiong'o, *Penpoints, Gunpoints, and Dreams: Towards a Critical Theory of the Arts and the State in Africa* (Oxford: Clarendon Press, 2003), 111. Among those scholars who prefer 'orature', see Fiona Moolla, 'When Orature Becomes Literature: Somali Oral Poetry and Folktales in Somali Novels', *Comparative Literature Studies*, 49.3 (2012), 434–462, https://doi.org/10.5325/complitstudies.49.3.0434

16   Another scholar that prefers 'oral literature' is Isidore Okpewho, author of the foundational *African Oral Literature: Backgrounds, Character, and Continuity* (Bloomington and Indianapolis: Indiana University Press, 1992).

17   Ruth Finnegan, 'The How of Literature', *Oral Tradition*, 20.2 (2005), 164–187 (p. 180).

detected in those using the term 'oral traditions'. The term 'tradition' constructs a temporal continuity between the present and the past that feeds into processes of identity formation. 'Tradition' entails acts of sharing, preserving and transmitting, and is therefore premised on connecting a group of texts or performances with each other and attaching value to that connection. What counts as 'tradition' tends to be a terrain of socio-political struggle and contesting claims, for example between colonial, corporate, or state-sponsored projects on the one hand, and the communities who partake in those oral genres on the other. Vanessa Paloma Elbaz shows how twentieth-century Spanish philologists interpreted Sephardi oral literature in Morocco through the lens of sixteenth- and seventeenth-century Spanish *romanceros*, a move that enabled them to identify Sephardi oral literature as part of a long-lost Moroccan *hispanidad* in need of colonial restoration. The Sephardi repertoire, however, is far from frozen in time, and includes a much richer, more historically layered, more multilingual corpus than Spanish philologists presented. Contestations over 'tradition' could be between rival parties who each claim a 'tradition' as their own, or they could be a tussle over what counts or does not count as 'traditional', or whether a 'tradition' is worth preserving at all. 'Traditional' folk tales, for example, have recently been the object of heated discussions about whether the conservative ideologies they sometimes promote (think about the trope of the damsel in distress) impel us to stop honouring the canonical repertoire and create a new progressive one.[18] If 'orature' and 'oral literature' foreground questions of form and aesthetics, 'oral traditions' foregrounds attitudes towards history and historiography.

Oral Texts

The designation 'oral texts', in turn, helps us analyse the performance as a moment of 'entextualisation' that detaches and abstracts a given utterance from the flow of everyday discourse, thus 'constituting oral genres as something capable of repetition, evaluation and exegesis'.[19] It

---

18   See for example Kirsten Salyer, 'Are Disney Princesses Hurting Your Daughter's Self-Esteem?', *Time Magazine* (2016).

19   Barber, 'Text and Performance in Africa', p. 325; See also her *The Anthropology of Texts, Persons, and Publics*. See also Joel C. Kuipers, *Performance: The Creation of*

is precisely these strategies of formalisation and semiotic detachment that allow us to re-activate and re-embed a text in 'a new context of utterance, where it has an effectual engagement and dialogic force'.[20]

The particular form an oral text takes in a given performance is an 'instantiation' or concretisation of the oral text, which is the result of a set of choices, by an author or performer, for a given audience, in a given context, and at a given time—all aspects that matter and that the scholar must consider.[21] Depending on the specific genre conventions, the process of instantiation can entail different levels of improvisation, intervention, and recreation. The oral author is sometimes expected to perform a set text *verbatim*, such in the case of Somali *maanso* poetry,[22] or they can reassemble and readapt looser textual configurations belonging to the same narrative or thematic repertoire, such in the case of most oral epics, *malḥūn* concerts, and Sufi *qawwals*. In the case of the Somali *maanso*, the composer of the text and the reciter of the text are usually different figures, with creative agency attributed to the former and not the latter. The reciter, 'who was seldom a creative poet himself, was regarded merely as a channel of communication and a memory storage and was in no way a co-author or the version he recited'.[23] In other cases, the text is more fluid, and the performer has a broader range of creative possibilities in terms of words, tone, music, gestures, and movement. Sufi *qawwals* 'knot' together lines from different poetic texts as they sing,

---

Textual Authority in Weyewa Ritual Speech (Philadelphia: University of Pennsylvania Press, 1990), p. 7; and Michael Silverstein and Greg Urban, eds, *Natural Histories of Discourse* (Chicago: University of Chicago Press, 1996). Barber ('Text and Performance', p. 327) further notes that techniques of entextualisation often 'involve a certain reflexivity—a consciousness of text as something created in order to be expounded, recontextualized and reflected upon'.

20   Barber, 'Text and Performance', p. 326. As she puts it, using the example of praise poetry, 'it is the very consolidation of chunks of examinable, quotable, repeatable text which makes possible the dynamic processes of fluid incorporation, re-inflection and recycling' (Ibid.).

21   Barber, *The Anthropology*, p. 43.

22   Martin Orwin, 'On the Concept of 'Definitive Text' in Somali Poetry', *Bulletin of the School of Oriental and African Studies*, 66.3 (2003), 334–347, https://doi.org/10.1017/S0041977X03000235

23   B. W. Andrzejewski, 'The Poem as Message: Verbatim Memorization in Somali Poetry', *Journal of African Cultural Studies*, 23.1 (2011), 27–36 (p. 27), https://doi.org/10.1080/13696815.2011.581454

with the aim of providing a rich aesthetic as well as spiritual experience.[24] Regardless of the degree of improvisation required of the performers or the social perception of their role, instantiation always entails a degree of creative and intellectual agency: even in the case of the 'definitive text' of the Somali *maanso* memorized by heart, for example, 'the reciter added to the poetic texts explanations in prose which gave an account of the original circumstances [of composition]'.[25]

The authorship function, as we can see, is much more fluid and complex, and sometimes less salient, for oral texts than in the case of a printed name on a book cover. While nineteenth-century collections and studies of oral traditions tended to attribute authorship to the nameless collective of the people, twentieth-century collections and studies have dwelt on single storytellers and performers as literary agents with individual styles and artistic visions – one may think, for example, of Jeff Opland's extended documentation of Xhosa *imbongi* David Yali-Manisi's life and work.[26] Some performers, like Sundar Popo in Trinidad or Papa Wemba in Congo, turn out to have fans worldwide and successful careers to their name, but their oral texts often circulate widely without holding the memory of who the author was. Few listeners to the 'Phulauri bin chutney' song in the Hindi film *Dabanng 2* (2012) would know that Sundar Popo was its composer and original singer. Oral texts, in this sense, can help world literature to articulate more expansive definitions of authorship.

A main feature of oral texts is that their meaning is created in performance, through the live interaction between the performer, the audience, and the socio-physical space of performance. This also determines the shape and functioning of oral texts. In Chapter 9 of this volume, for example, Sadhana Naithani notes that textual content and form are more important at local levels and in smaller performance spaces, whereas at large-scale festivals the virtuoso performance skills

---

24 See Mikko Viitamäki, 'Poetry in Sufi Practice: Patrons, Poets and Performers in South Asian Sufism from Thirteenth Century to the Present' (unpublished PhD thesis, University of Helsinki, 2015).

25 Andrzejewski, 'The Poem', p. 27.

26 For example, Jeff Opland, *The Dassie and the Hunter: A South African Meeting* (Durban: University of Kwa Zulu-Natal Press, 2005); Jeff Opland, 'First Meeting with Manisi', *Research in African Literatures*, 35.3 (2004), 26–45; Jeff Opland, 'The Early Career of D. L. P. Yali-Manisi, Thembu Imbongi', *Research in African Literatures*, 33.1 (2002), 1–26.

and embodiment of performance become more important. Storytellers, oral poets, and performers can typically rely on their audiences' familiarity with tropes, stories, and characters, so that oral texts—particularly songs—can sometimes sound like shorthand. A single phrase, like *Jamunā ke tīr* ('the banks of the Yamuna'), immediately alerts listeners of a Sur song-poem that this is about milkmaids irresistibly attracted to Krishna. It evokes in a flash a whole aesthetic of the night in the forest and a structure of feeling centred on the milkmaid's mixture of fear and irresistible attraction. While listeners will have varying levels of competence, the music and the occasional explanations consolidate their poetic knowledge. In fact, an intriguing aspect of entextualisation in oral and performance contexts is how texts can be split or distributed across lyrics and explanation, modulated in different voices shifting between metre and prose, or apportioned to different people. 'The meaning of these texts, then', Karin Barber argues, 'is created not *by* individuals so much as *between* individuals, and a text exists only as part of a distributed field or network of texts'.[27]

Finally, we need to conceive of oral texts as dynamically spreading across genres, platforms, and languages. They require an expansive temporal and cultural-anthropological frame that goes beyond a single instantiation, genre, or even language. In Chapter 4 of this volume, Francesca Orsini borrows the idea of 'soft texts' from Ratnakar Tripathy to explain what happens to Bhojpuri fragments of cultural memory embedded in key terms within songs as the songs change language, and travel back and forth across the oceans of indenture migration and diaspora. Such song texts can appear more like shorthand. But they are still texts. Clarissa Vierke shows that the Fumo Liyongo tradition is 'fragmented [...] across multiple genres, thereby seriously calling textual boundaries into question [...]. Its fuzziness and amorphousness—where does the text start? Where does it end?— [...] urges us all the more to critically reconsider the (normative) notions of textual boundaries derived from the printed book' (Vierke, Chapter 1 in this volume, p. 51).

---

27   Barber, *The Anthropology*, p. 92.

Oral Texts in Anthropology, Folklore, and Literary Studies

Oral texts have been central to the development of comparative literature and of world literature—we only need to think of folk tales or epics—but in quite specific and limited (and limiting) ways. Throughout the nineteenth and twentieth centuries, Western scholarly interest in non-Western oral texts was driven for the most part by anthropological considerations.[28] Oral texts were mined for information about another people's culture, values, and worldview. The result of this anthropological orientation was 'the denial, for the oral text, of whatever aesthetic, intellectual, and, indeed, ideological criteria the model of written literature has been based upon'.[29] As ethnographic sources, oral texts were seen as stable, fixed repositories of collective signification. What Western anthropological scholarship valorised in non-Western oral texts was their alleged 'traditional' and 'pre-modern' character, in which cultural otherness could be located. At the same time, scholars sought to identify broad family resemblances, connections, and universal elements in folk materials from widely different and very distant contexts—an example being the structuralist theory of mythology proposed by Claude Lévi-Strauss.

Sadhana Naithani has pointed out the different impulses behind the collection of folklore in India and in other colonies compared to Europe: instead of the nationalist 'engagement of middle-class intellectuals, poets, and writers with the narratives and songs that were common among the majority of the populace' of [their society], in the colonies it was the colonial administrators (and their wives) and missionaries who undertook the first collections of 'folklore'—ostensibly to reveal the mind of the people, though they rarely elaborated on what this meant.[30] These

---

28   For the 1960s–1970s debates about the relationship between anthropology
     and the study of oral literature, see Ruth Finnegan, 'Attitudes to the Study
     of Oral Literature in British Social Anthropology', *Man*, 4.1 (1969), 59–69;
     Patrick Pender-Cudlip, 'Oral Traditions and Anthropological Analysis: Some
     Contemporary Myths', *Azania: Archaeological Research in Africa*, 7.1 (1972), 3–24,
     William P. Murphy, 'Oral Literature', *Annual Review of Anthropology*, 7.1 (1978),
     113–136. Heda Jason proposed a 'multidimensional approach' to oral literature
     able to combine anthropological and folklorist perspectives, 'A Multidimensional
     Approach to Oral Literature', *Current Anthropology*, 10.4 (1969), 413–426.
29   Jaco Alant, '"Did you say *oral literature?*" asked Walter Ong', *Literator*, 17.2 (1996),
     117–130.
30   Naithani, *The Story-Time*, p. 98.

figures of colonial administrators *cum* folklorists have been appraised in the scholarship through a dichotomy between condemnation of their politics and validation of their scholarship.[31] Naithani cautions against straitjacketing the impulse of folk collectors in a simple category of colonial power-knowledge: 'in the colonial context, there are many cycles of motivation—from macro to micro level, and from state to individual level'.[32] For Naithani, therefore, the field of folklore in the empire was a 'multimodal trail', 'beginning from a particular location and then going on to predictable and unpredictable terrains', producing 'loops of cultural definition' in the process. Colonial collectors worked individually, but were often in contact with colleagues elsewhere in the empire or with the Folk-Lore Society in London, 'where folklore from the whole Empire could be put on the same table and discussed'.[33]

And discussed it was along the same scholarly patterns. Both folklorists and ethnographers turned the 'expressive cultures of different peoples in many different local languages into English language texts' with scant regard for local informers, performers, and contexts.[34] *The Talking Thrush and Other Tales from India* (1922), 'collected by W. Crooke and retold by W.H.D. Rouse', embodies the transformation of Indian orature into English children's literature.[35] For the beautiful printed book, the re-teller anglicises and standardises the names of animal and human characters (the Phudki bird who goes to see a Behana in the first story becomes a Thrush who goes to see a Cotton-Carder); the endnotes carry details of the changes Rouse made to Crooke's stories and give the barest details of where the story was originally collected,

---

31　An example is the Italian orientalist and colonial administrator Enrico Cerulli, who rose to be the governor of two provinces of Italian East Africa under Benito Mussolini. Karla Mallette weighs Cerulli's scholarship and Fascist affiliations in *European Modernity and the Arab Mediterranean: Toward a New Philology and a Counter-Orientalism* (Philadelphia: University of Pennsylvania Press, 2011). James De Lorenzi is more damning towards Cerulli's track record and stance towards Ethiopian scholars; James De Lorenzi, 'The Orientalist on Trial: Enrico Cerulli and the United Nations War Crimes Commission', *Northeast African Studies*, 18.1–2 (2018), 165–200, https://doi.org/10.14321/nortafristud.18.1-2.0165

32　Naithani, *The Story-Time*, p. 18.

33　Ibid., p. 6.

34　Ibid., pp. 6, 7.

35　William Crooke and W.H.D. Rouse, *The Talking Thrush and Other Tales from India* (London: J. M. Dent & Sons, 1922).

and from whom.[36] A parallel process is visible in folk tales collections in Indian languages by Indian folklorists, who smoothed out dialectal/local linguistic features and stressed the cultural authenticity of the tales by invoking the figure of the grandmother, as in *Ṭhākurmār Jhūlī* or *Grandmother's Bag of Tales* (1907) by Dakshina Ranjan Mitra.[37] In revisiting the work of earlier folklorist Gerhard Lindblom, the Ugandan poet Okot p'Bitek notes how Lindblom's attempt not to interfere with the storyteller's performance changed the nature of the performance itself. Without a 'live, responsive, audience, taking up the chorus, laughing and enjoying the jokes', the storyteller 'sat facing a strange man who wrote down something, and not really seeing the fun'. The barrier that Lindblom erected between himself and the storyteller in the name of scientific objectivity emptied the performance and made it fake.[38]

The anthropological approach to oral texts as repositories of a people's 'culture' remained operative in the postcolonial period, when scholars from formerly colonised countries turned to oral texts as perceived sources of indigenous cultural authenticity, untainted by Western colonial modernity. In African philosophy, for example, this theoretical orientation came to be known as 'ethnophilosophy', and was later criticised for reproducing a view of African societies as static and internally homogeneous in their beliefs. Some of the philosophical paradigms in response to ethnophilosophy later replicated some of ethnophilosophy's assumptions. Henry Odera Oruka's 'sage philosophy', for example, opposed ethnophilosophy's collectivist, unanimist bias by valorising the individual thinking of singular 'sages'. Oruka wanted to push back against Eurocentric claims that philosophy is and can only be a 'written' enterprise, and therefore defined the 'sage' as somebody illiterate, operating outside of writing.[39] Such a philosophical programme, however, upheld the dichotomy between

---

36   Ibid., pp. 197, 1.

37   See Raahi Adhya, *The Fantastic World of the Bengali Roopkatha: Unpacking Gender, Generation and Genre* (unpublished PhD thesis, SOAS University of London, 2023).

38   Okot p'Bitek, *Hare and Hornbill* (London: Heinemann, 1978), p. xii.

39   For a critique of ethnophilosophy and sage philosophy, see Benedetta Lanfranchi, 'Rethinking World Philosophies from African Philosophy', *Journal of World Philosophy*, 7.2 (2022), 26–41, https://doi.org/10.2979/jourworlphil.7.2.03 and Benedetta Lanfranchi, '"Does this mean that there is philosophy in everything?": A Comparative Reading of Henry Odera Oruka's First and Second Order and Antonio Gramsci's First and Second Level Philosophy' in *Rethinking Sage*

orality as authentic and indigenous and writing as modern and global. Walter Ong further essentialised this distinction by describing orality and literacy as structuring two different ways of thinking or modes of consciousness. The 'literary mind' cannot work the way it does without writing: 'more than any other single invention, writing has transformed human consciousness', enabling analytical thinking, inventiveness, and innovation.[40] Just as the field of African philosophy has since developed a robust critique of ethnophilosophy and sage philosophy,[41] the technological determinism undergirding Ong's 'Great Divide' has been later criticised by many scholars, from Ruth Finnegan (in *Literacy and Orality*, 1988) to Karin Barber and Liz Gunner.

Finnegan's *Oral Literature in Africa*, now republished (2012) in the book series of which this volume is also part, made the influential claim that African oral forms should be considered 'literature', on the grounds that 'the assumptions that seem to set oral forms totally apart from written literature are in fact questionable or false', and all the various elements that feed into existing definitions of written literature 'are also recognizable in oral forms, often with exactly the same range of ambiguities'.[42] Both oral and written literatures are based on verbal expression geared towards aesthetic purposes, with accepted conventions of style, structure and genre with which individual authors can play. Both oral and written genres are named and patterned forms that are recognizable as such to speakers and audiences even as their patterns, themes, and boundaries are stretched, reshaped, and renewed. Overall, Finnegan makes a powerful argument against a dichotomous understanding of orality and literacy as two diametrically opposite forms of literature, stressing that 'if we do treat them as fundamentally of a different kind, we deny ourselves both a fruitful analytic approach and, furthermore, a wider perspective on the general subject of comparative

---

Philosophy Interdisciplinary Perspectives on and beyond H. Odera Oruka, ed. by K. Kresse and O. Nyarwath (London: Lexington Books, 2023), pp. 77–98.

40　Walter Ong, *Orality and Literacy* (New York: Routledge, 2002 [original 1982]), p. 76.

41　See Paulin J. Hountondji, *African Philosophy: Myth and Reality* (Bloomington: Indiana University Press, 1996) and, more recently, Kai Kresse and Oriare Nyarwath, eds, *Rethinking Sage Philosophy: Interdisciplinary Perspectives on and beyond H. Odera Oruka* (Lanham: Lexington Books, 2023).

42　Ruth Finnegan, *Oral Literature in Africa* (Cambridge: Open Book Publishers, 2012), p. 26, https://doi.org/10.11647/OBP.0025

literature'.[43] In general, the second half of the twentieth century has seen the emergence of a sophisticated body of scholarship on oral texts, their literariness, and their relationship with literature in other media.[44]

... and World Literature

Since its emergence in the early 2000s, however, the discipline of world literature has kept this scholarship at arm's length. John D. Niles finds it 'a point that scarcely needs to be argued' that 'all forms of narrative, even the most sophisticated genres of contemporary fiction, have their ultimate origin in [oral] storytelling'.[45] Whether in scholarly or common-sense understandings, however, world literature normally rests on an idea of literature as a constellation of *written* genres that are *read*, and on a historical-teleological shift from orality to writing and print.[46] As Caroline Levine has pointed out, opening statements and introductory sections of publications on world literature gesture towards oral literature before quickly sidelining it to concentrate on written genres, usually the novel.[47] For Venkat B. Mani, world literature involves bibliomigrancy, the circulation and reception of printed books. Gisèle Sapiro's studies of translation flows rest on data about translations of printed books.[48]

---

43 Finnegan, *Oral Literature in Africa*, p. 27.

44 This body of scholarship is vast, and it is impossible to do it justice here. See the important work by Paul Zumthor, *Oral Poetry: An Introduction* (Minneapolis: University of Minnesota Press, 1990); and two recent edited volumes: Charles Bernstein, ed., *Close Listening: Poetry and the Performed Word* (Oxford: Oxford University Press, 1998); Marjorie Perloff and Craig Dworkin, eds, *The Sound of Poetry / The Poetry of Sound* (Chicago: The University of Chicago Press, 2009).

45 John D. Niles, *Homo Narrans: The Poetics and Anthropology of Oral Literature* (Philadelphia: University of Pennsylvania Press, 1999), p. 2.

46 In this, we follow Caroline Levine, who argues that mass literacy projects and cheap Great Book series forged a strong connection between literacy, democracy, social progress, and upward mobility. 'The flip side of this politics is that it assumes literacy as itself the mark of progress and civilization and therefore implies that nonliterate societies are backward and primitive'; Caroline Levine 'The Great Unwritten: World Literature and the Effacement of Orality', *Modern Language Quarterly*, 74.2 (2013), 217–237 (p. 223), https://doi. org/10.1215/00267929-2072998

47 Levine, 'The Great Unwritten'.

48 See B. Venkat Mani, *Recoding World Literature: Libraries, Print Culture, and Germany's Pact with Books* (New York: Fordham University Press, 2016); Gisèle Sapiro, 'Translation and Symbolic Capital in the Era of Globalization: French Literature in the United States', *Cultural Sociology*, 9.3 (2015), 320–346, https://doi. org/10.1177/1749975515584080

For David Damrosch, world literary texts are those circulating beyond their culture of origin and 'read as literature'.[49] Christopher Prendergast acknowledges that 'both historically and geographically, the oral vastly exceeds the written' and that, even today, the oral 'remains the most fundamental mode of humankind's self-expression'[50] – but, despite this premise, he circumscribes the scope of world literature to written texts only: 'the idea of world literature cannot practically be taken to refer to all the verbal arts around the globe (among other things, it typically excludes cultures whose only or main form of self-expression is oral recitation unless and until they become transmissible through transcription)'.[51]

It seems to us, however, that the advantages to be gained by leaving orality out of world literature (a methodological simplification, a more stable definition of our object of study) do not offset what is lost. The exclusion from world literature of those 'cultures whose only or main form of self-expression is oral recitation', in Prendergast's words, might usefully narrow the scope of the discipline, but at the price of casting an implicit connotation of 'unwordly', perhaps even 'unliterary', onto a numerically sizeable portion of humankind. It is hard not to see reverberations of colonial hierarchies in this definitional move.[52] The West's 'scriptist bias' comes with its own fraught history, and a self-critical analysis of these colonial intellectual genealogies would only add strength and clarity to world literature.[53]

---

49   David Damrosch, *What is World Literature?* (Princeton: Princeton University Press, 2003), p. 6.

50   Christopher Prendergast, 'The World Republic of Letters' in *Debating World Literature*, ed. by C. Prendergast (London: Verso, 2004), pp. 1–25 (p. 4).

51   Ibid., p. 21.

52   The exclusion of oral expression from world literature also has a gendered dimension, as women were excluded from writing and publishing at various points of history. See Greg Buzwell, 'Women Writers, Anonymity and Pseudonyms', British Library Blog (2020). With regards to African literature, the argument has been made by Obioma Nnaemeka, 'From Orality to Writing: African Women Writers and the (Re)Inscription of Womanhood', *Research in African Literatures*, 25.4 (1994), 137–57, and Susan Arndt, *African Women's Literature: Orature and Intertextuality* (Bayreuth: Eckhard Breitinger, 1998). See also the special issue of *Research in African Literatures* 25.3 on 'Women as Oral Artists'.

53   In Roy Harris, *The Origin of Writing* (London: Duckworth, 1986), p. 46. Prendergast takes a position against the argument that a society only attains 'civilization' when it 'inscribes itself', pointing out that the association of 'civilization' with writing devalues oral expression and overlooks the fact that 'both historically and

Even within the current goals of the discipline, the exclusion of unwritten literatures limits our understanding of written literature itself. Many existing publications on world literature are still informed by a teleological view of orature as the chronological and aesthetic antecedent of written literature. The *Norton Anthology of World Literature*, for example, includes oral texts only in the initial sections dedicated to ancient literatures.[54] In African literary studies, oral genres are often treated as the raw materials out of which the African novel emerged, a framework that casts the novel as the end point of African literary histories. Of course, many written genres, including the novel, are in dialogue with oral genres—but, as Ayele Kebede Roba argues in Chapter 3, the presence of orality in the novel is not merely a decorative accessory or a flavourful interlude in the plot. The inclusion of transcribed oral texts in the novel is rather a conceptual intervention that changes the rules of the genre, whereby the plot is designed precisely to 'novelise orature', foregrounding a relationship of coevalness and simultaneity between orality and the novel, or what Russell West-Pavlov calls an 'aesthetics of proximity'.[55] The novel is turned into a written hub for the continuous circulation of oral texts. The transcriptions of oral texts are not just add-ons, but integral elements around which the text is built, and, in some cases, they are the real purpose of the narration. We cannot just talk about orature 'in' the novel; we are rather faced with a textual oralisation of the narrative that partly forces us to reconsider what the novel is, and how it works.[56]

---

geographically, the oral vastly exceeds the written; the former even today remains the most fundamental mode of humankind's self-expression', 'The World Republic of Letters', p. 4. Against this premise, as we have seen, he nevertheless excludes oral literature from the domain of world literature.

54   Martin Puchner et al., eds, *Norton Anthology of World Literature*, vols. 1–3 (New York: W. W. Norton, 2012-2018).

55   Russell West-Pavlov defines it as a 'proximate mode of meaning-making' that 'activates a mode of semiosis whose functioning is primarily somatic (that is, bodily, visceral, and material) rather than representational; it functions according to a dynamic or economy of "affect"; its condition of possibility is that of spatial contiguity; and that contiguity defines the modes of agency it makes possible', *Eastern African Literatures: Towards an Aesthetics of Proximity* (Oxford: Oxford University Press, 2018), p. 5.

56   See also Moolla, 'When Orature Becomes Literature'. In the case of Bhojpuri, to make another example, novels capitalise on the status and popularity of oral performers. See Pandey Kapil's novel *Phoolsunghi* (1977), loosely based on the life of singer-composer Mahendar Misar, whose English translation in 2020

In general, the written texts studied by world literature always exist and circulate as part of a complex range of intermedial channels, commutations, and translations. Written genres rub shoulders with oral genres in the same social spaces, with constant stylistic and technical cross-fertilizations. We can scarcely understand written literature in Somali, for example, without an awareness of the aesthetic and compositional primacy of oral poetry: what Somalis have done 'is to *add* literacy to their traditions of memorization and diffusion of orally composed poetry'.[57] In the case of Swahili poetry—in the *utendi* and *mashairi* forms— 'written and spoken forms flow into each other', and written pieces are understood to be only departure points for a new performer to transform them and reenact them.[58] In both the Somali and Swahili examples, we see literary genres transmitted through a mix of writing, memorization, tape or digital recordings, internet sharing and downloading. These genres have a written instantiation, but these written instantiations can only be understood through their multimedia connections and conversions. An exclusive focus on transmission 'through transcription', again going back to Prendergast, would not suffice. Thinking intermedially, instead, allows us to better understand what (written) world literature is and how it functions.

A whole range of written texts, to give another example, exist only in relation to oral traditions. After the great wave of studies into oral composition spearheaded by Andrew Lord's *Singer of Tales* (1960), which spurred a flurry of research into oral epics worldwide,[59] most scholars of contemporary orature point to the symbiotic combination of oral performance and some kind of writing 'at some point', either in the form of manuscript versions of songs and performance genres (see Clarissa Vierke, Chapter 1 of this volume); of handwritten copybooks and printed chapbooks acting as reminders to performers; of physical texts present as token presences during performance; or of memories

---

caused a sensation. Or Sanjeev's Hindi novel *Sutradhar* (2003) on the 'Bhojpuri Shakespeare' Bhikhari Thakur; see Orsini, Chapter 4 in this volume.

57   John William Johnson, 'Orality, Literacy, and Somali Oral Poetry', *Journal of African Cultural Studies*, 18.1 (2006), 119–136 (p. 134).

58   See Annachiara Raia, 'Texts, Voices and Tapes: Mediating Poetry on the Swahili Muslim Coast in the 21st century', *Matatu*, 51.1 (2020), 139–168.

59   See e.g. Stuart Blackburn et al., eds, *Oral Epics in India* (Berkeley: University of California Press, 1989), John D. Smith, *The Epic of Pabuji* (New Delhi: Katha, 2005); Lauri Honko, ed. *Textualization of Oral Epics* (Berlin: de Gruyter, 2011).

of a lost text from which a particular orature originated (see Sadhana Naithani, Chapter 9 of this volume).[60] Catherine Servan-Schreiber, for example, studied the publication and distribution of chapbooks of a large number Bhojpuri oral epics and songs by commercial publishers in northern India, peddled by itinerant colporteurs and singers along specific trade and migration routes into cities and villages Nepal and eastern India and the coolie diaspora.[61] These written texts cannot be studied outside of the oral, performative context that gives them currency and meaning.

Audiovisual and digital technologies have for the most part enabled and supported the reinvention of older genres and the emergence of new ones, offering new means for circulation that defy the dichotomy of written/unwritten.[62] Aldin K. Mutembei, for example, has studied WhatsApp narratives as an emerging genre in Swahilophone East Africa, showing how they mix verbal and non-verbal (photos, images, emojis) elements to creative stylistic effects. The recipient has an active role in sharing these messages and potentially in editing them to their liking, meaning that variants can branch out at any time and authorship is within

---

60   See also the chapters by Monika Horstmann, Christopher Novetzke, and Richard
     Widdess in *Tellings and Texts: Music, Storytelling and Performance in North India*,
     ed. by Francesca Orsini and Katherine Butler Schofield (Cambridge: Open Book
     Publishers, 2015), https://doi.org/10.11647/OBP.0062

61   See Catherine Servan-Schreiber, *Chanteurs itinérants en Inde du Nord: la tradition
     orale Bhojpuri* (Paris: L'Harmattan, 1999); and *Histoire d'une musique métisse à l'île
     Maurice: chutney indien et séga Bollywood* (Paris: Riveneuve éditions, 2010). From
     the point of view of world literature, the role of chapbooks for the transmission of
     orature importantly points to a whole other, more demotic domain of authorship,
     publishing, circulation, consumption, and recognition than that of 'proper' book
     publishers and bookshops. Apart from Servan Schreiber's seminal work, see also
     Francesca Orsini, 'Booklets and Sants: Religious Publics and Literary History'
     in *Imagining the Public in Modern South Asia*, ed. by Brannon Ingram, J. Barton Scott,
     and SherAli K. Tareen (London: Routledge, 2016), pp. 89–103; and 'Love Letters'
     in *Love in South Asia: A Cultural History*, ed. by Francesca Orsini (Cambridge:
     Cambridge University Press, 2006), pp. 228–258.

62   The argument that digital technologies have made it redundant to distinguish
     between 'oral' and 'written' literatures is powerfully made by Angelus Mnenuka,
     'Online Performance of Swahili Orature: The Need for a New Category?', *Eastern
     African Literary and Cultural Studies*, 5.3-4 (2019), 274–297, https://doi.org/10.1
     080/23277408.2019.1685752 In their introduction to the edited volume *Listening
     Up, Writing Down, and Looking Beyond: Interfaces of the Oral, Written, and Visual*
     (Waterloo: Wilfrid Laurier University Press, 2012, p. 1), Susan Gingell and Wendy
     Roy similarly ask their reader to 'open the door to transdisciplinary, multimodal
     communication'.

everybody's reach. The WhatsApp groups in which the narratives are shared provide a forum for the audience to comment on the narrative and discuss its meaning, in a way that approaches the live presence of the audience at a public recital (where the person who shared the story to the WhatsApp group plays the same role as the reciter). This is a genre that defies the distinction between oral and written, but whose circulation is as 'worldly' as that of some Anglophone novels.[63]

According to John Miles Foley, digital platforms have reproposed the same 'thought-technology' on which oral traditions are also based. Both the digital and the oral, he notes, are based on pathways and processes, not on static 'things'. The oral-digital can act as a starting point to deconstruct what we mean by 'book': from a unitary, fixed object to be consumed in a unilinear order, the book can be reimagined as a network of interconnected items that can be read in a variety of ways and directions.[64] Thinking intermedially, in this sense, can help us rethink the functioning of the material object of world literature *par excellence*.

This volume argues that contemporary and historical oratures raise questions that are directly relevant to world literature. Orature can fruitfully defamiliarize world literature's implicit reliance on written, indeed printed, texts when thinking about textuality, authorship, circulation, scale, translation, intermediality, recognition, the market, the meanings and functions of literature, and so on. The Nobel Prize for literature awarded to Bob Dylan in 2016, and arguably also that in 1997 to Dario Fo, who championed oral traditions in his work as a performer and playwright, signalled a recognition of the aesthetic value and importance of songs and orature-inflected playwriting, but have remained exceptions. What if, rather than considering song, storytelling, or performance as close kin to but nonetheless 'other' than poetry or literature,[65] they were simply part of literature? What if 'folk' artists were just artists?[66]

---

63 Aldin K. Mutembei, 'The Future of East African Kiswahili orature in the digital age: a case study of WhatsApp Narrative', *Studies of the Department of African Languages and Cultures*, 51 (2017), 33–52, https://salc.uw.edu.pl/index.php/SALC/article/view/21

64 John Miles Foley, *Oral Traditions and the Internet: Pathways of the Mind* (Urbana, Chicago and Springfield: University of Illinois Press, 2012).

65 As Bob Dylan himself put it in his 2016 Nobel Lecture.

66 Priyanka Basu, *The Poet's Song: 'Folk' and its Cultural Politics in South Asia* (London: Routledge, 2024).

Most of the chapters in this volume emphasise the longevity of oral texts and traditions even as they shift language, form, and location. Oral genres are everywhere, both old and new, constantly reinvented, resilient in time, and adaptable to varying socio-economic and technological conditions. The volume also pays attention, however, to the threats faced by some of these oral genres. In Chapter 6, Yenealem Aredo and Desta Desalegn Dinege analyse one such case study in Ethiopia, arguing that oral traditions in Na'o are in decline, paralleling the decline in the number of Na'o language speakers and the dispersion of the Na'o community away from their heartland. According to the Atlas of the World's Languages in Danger, published by UNESCO in 2009, a third of the 6,500 languages spoken around the globe today are in danger of disappearing forever. Oral genres can survive and readapt in different languages, but endangered languages frequently mean endangered oral traditions. In other cases, institutional neglect, or in the worst cases institutional repression and opposition, cast a shadow over certain traditions. The Moroccan *halqa*—the square often outside the historical boundaries of the city where storytellers, acrobats, magicians, snake charmers, singers, fortune tellers, medicinal plant sellers and other street performers ply their trades—is recognized by UNESCO as Intangible Cultural Heritage, but despite this international recognition, Fatima Zahra Salih explains in Chapter 5, it has experienced a period of neglect, and even attempts to completely erase it, by the officials in Moroccan cities. Even after its rehabilitation and even championing as national heritage by the state, it faces questions about its future, as in the case of other 'traditional' spaces. As the *Encyclopaedia of African Literature* reminds us, oral literature is 'something passed on through the spoken word, and because it is based on the spoken language, it comes to life only in a living community. Where community life fades away, orality loses its function and dies. It needs people in a living social setting: it needs life itself'.[67] An expansive definition of world literature to include oral traditions, then, would also interrogate the materiality of 'life itself' and the material processes that single out some forms of life for replacement and elimination.[68]

---

67 Simon Gikandi (ed.), *Encyclopaedia of African Literature* (London and New York: Routledge, 2003), p. 580.

68 For Hindi novelist Phanishwarnath Renu, only oral traditions have the potential to heal divided communities and put forward shared visions for the future;

Location

If location 'is not simply a geographical, historical, or cultural context but a standpoint, a position, an orientation, a necessarily partial and particular perspective, however complex, ample and multiversal it may be, from which [an author] represents and imagines a world', how does it play out in oral genres, and with what consequences for world literature?[69] Given the importance of embodiment and presence (spatial, for speakers and addressees), social relevance, and imaginative agility, oral genres are particularly rich sites for processes of worlding and active agents participating and intervening in these processes, to paraphrase Pheng Cheah.[70]

Oral genres come with their own politics of location, manifested for example in the space of performance and in the liminality of the performer.[71] In Chapter 5, Fatima Zahra Salih explores the marginality and bustling creativity of the space of the *halqa* (lit. circle) in Morocco. She notes that the 'familiarity and habit' that a storyteller like Omar Douâmi in the city of Beni Mellal in central Morocco was able to develop with his audience 'sealed a sort of contract between them, which translated in concrete terms into a spatially specific agora recognized by the city and its inhabitants. The magic of the spoken word is that it impacts both the public and the space that retains its memory' (p. 182).

Location may also mark the moment of composition. Oral authors creating new texts have ritual ways of connecting, both spiritually and intellectually, with the source of their inspiration. For composers of *qəne* poetry in Amharic and Ge'ez, for example, creative ideation is

---

Phanishwarnath Renu, *Parati Parikatha* (New Delhi: Rajkamal Prakashan, 1957); *Tale of a Wasteland*, translated by Madhusudan Thakur (New Delhi: Global Vision Press, 2012).

69 Francesca Orsini and Laetitia Zecchini, 'The Locations of (World) Literature: Perspectives from Africa and South Asia: Introduction', *Journal of World Literature*, 4.1 (2019), 1–12 (p. 2), https://doi.org/10.1163/24056480-00401003

70 Pheng Chea, *What is a World?* (Durham: Duke University Press, 2015), p. 2.

71 Traditional performers are holders of specialised knowledge and art within the performance space but often occupy low socio-economic positions; see Katherine B. Brown (now Schofield), 'Introduction: Liminality and the Social Location of Musicians', *Twentieth-Century Music*, 3.1 (2007), 5–12. Angelus Mnenuka warns against considering performer, audience and performance space as fixed and separate components of the performance, stressing instead their fluidity, 'Fluidity and Fixity of Performer, Audience and Performing Space', *UMMA: The Journal of Contemporary Literature and Creative Arts*, 8.1 (2021), 37–54.

marked by social self-seclusion and immersion into the natural world. Authors depart from their community for an isolated location, like a forest, and their poetic inspiration is the result of time spent in solitude and contemplation. They only reunite with other people once the *qəne* is fully formed in their mind and they are ready to recite it.[72] In this sense, literary creation follows a spiritually charged physical movement from a social space to a natural space and back. In other cases, the source of inspiration is even more literal. In Chapter 2, Assefa Tefera Dibaba and Adugna Barkessa Dinsa describe how Oromo singers (*shaayii*) derive their inspiration from a specific location: a mountaintop, an old tree. These are considered sacred places—the seats of gods, supernatural entities, and ancestors—and the process of artistic creation entails a reconnection with the spiritual world. The *shaayii* brings gifts and offerings to the gods and ancestors, and they will teach the *shaayii* new songs in turn. The physical embeddedness of these rituals of artistic creation shapes a politics of location, but also of dislocation. When those spaces of literary inspiration are destroyed, or people are forcibly separated from them, the connection between people and their environment breaks down, and so does the meaning-making enabled by that connection. The loss of space, is, in this case, also a loss of literature and history. But, as Assefa and Adugna's chapter shows, that brokenness can itself generate oral genres of disruption and displacement, who reorient the community towards new meanings. Creation can come from spatial connection, but spatial disconnection also generates its own poetics.

In this sense, oral texts not only derive meaning from the physical space in which they are composed and perform, but dynamically co-constitute and co-define those spaces in turn. They inscribe, story, and change locations as they migrate across geographies, genres, languages, platforms, and audiences. 'The cultural memory of Liyongo, like that of other epics, is tied to a specific geography', Clarissa Vierke writes (p. 58), namely to the Tana and Ozi deltas just opposite the Lamu archipelago on the northern Swahili coast. The Tana and Ozi deltas were an area of 'overlapping geographies', which become inscribed in the characterization of Liyongo as being of Persian (Shirazi) descent and in

---

72   A fictionalisation of this process of poetic creation is in the novel *Mine to Win* by Hiwot
     Teffera (Addis Ababa: Addis Ababa University Press, 2016), whose protagonist is a
     boy who goes through the school curriculum of the Orthodox Church.

the 'precious goods from afar: fruits, scents, and clothes' made available through Indian Ocean connections evoked in some of the early texts (Vierke, Chapter 1, p. 61). Mauritius becomes, in the songs of Bhojpuri indentured migrants working in the sugarcane plantations, *mirichiya*, a land of mirages and false promises, whose streets, they discovered, were not paved with gold after all. Later, as migrants became locals, *mirichiya* became *morisva dil mohela* (Mauritius charmed my heart).[73] In Sundar Popo's nonsense song, discussed by Francesca Orsini in Chapter 4, key Bhojpuri terms (*kudari, phulauri*) mix with local Trinidadian spaces (the cane field) and toponyms (Sangre Grande) and with 'exotic' English nursery rhymes to convey the specific location and orientation of Indians in Trinidad.

The disproportionate concern of world literature with global texts in print, global circulation, and global recognition, implicitly connotes the 'local' as inert and static, but even deeply private or localized forms of orature—like the Haketia songs of Sephardi women from Morocco, or the Oromo songs about ecological decay and dispossession—speak to world literary concerns through their potential comparative perspectives, whether on minor literatures and intimate repertoires, and how they transmit knowledge and affect that is considered too important to lose; or through a shared ecopoetic sensibility and response to ecological damage.

Transmission and Circulation

As Karin Barber has pointed out, 'texts survive because of the efforts that human beings go to, to mark them out, bind them up and project them across time and space'.[74] Oral texts that only exist embodied in the memory of human beings have to contend with death as a major moment of disconnection. The proverb 'when an old man dies, a library burns down' makes frequent appearance in scholarship on oral genres, often in relation to urgent appeals for the preservation of threatened traditions. The image conjures up an oral landscape where older people are the main repositories of literary and historical memories and the principal agents of its conservation and transmission. Yet, research on oral genres has identified many more agents and axes of oral

---

73   See Servan-Schreiber, *Histoire d'un musique metisse*, pp. 100, 167.
74   Barber, *Anthropology*, p. 28.

transmission. Older people teach younger people, of course, but older children also teach their younger siblings. Nor is transmission only monodirectional, from the older to the younger. As Tadesse Jaleta Jirata shows in Chapter 7, children are themselves creators and innovators and play an active role in literary transmission, and some genres are their exclusive preserve. Children's culture is not 'trivial and innocent' but 'artistic and complex', and it is able to shape adult interactions, too.[75] Such intergenerational creativity and cross-collaboration in the circulation and transmission of oral genres can be contrasted, at least partly, with the more distinct generational roles in written literature, where children are more passive—read to, or readers, but rarely legitimate creators. The intergenerational co-creation of oral texts, as we have seen, stretches beyond the living. Spirits, gods and ancestors speak from the afterlife, gift poets new songs, or manifest themselves when certain songs are sung. From this point of view, death is a form of disconnection that simultaneously generates new forms of connection. It is often the task of oral genres to enable the relationship between the living and the dead; between the material and the spiritual worlds. In these cases, the performance of a particular oral text is an illocutionary act: it brings back the ancestors and makes them speak.

Even when not outright illocutionary in their structure, many oral texts are tied to actions—they bring into being, demarcate some collective acts or activities, spur the audience to do something. This function is often globally portable. Political or protest songs often enjoy extraordinarily long lives over multiple locations and multiple generations, and can define an entire zeitgeist (see Karima Laachir, Chapter 10 of this volume). We only need to think of the global circulation of the song *Bella Ciao*, originally a rice-pickers' lament that became an anthem of the Italian partisans during World War II and has now been taken up by protesters in Kashmir and Iran, among other places. Later movements bring old songs back to life and charge them with new, urgent meanings with each reiteration. Virginia Pisano in Chapter 11 usefully declines different meanings of transmission with regards to the political songs of the Egyptian duo Ahmad Fu'ad Negm

---

75 This argument is made by Brian Sutton-Smith, Jay Mechling, Thomas W. Johnson, and Felicia McMahon, eds, *Children's Folklore: A SourceBook* (New York and Oxford: Routledge, 1995).

and Sheikh Imam in 1970s Cairo and their circulation through time and space, ending with important considerations about the pressures that international circulation can have on artists from political hotspots. The circulation of artists and singers between the south and the north of the Mediterranean is not politically neutral: protest singers are championed by European festivals and curators, but they feel the pressure to adhere to and project a particular stance and identity, with stifling consequences.

On a larger, transnational scale, then, although rhetorically institutions of world literature, including festivals, 'emphasise the systemic quality of circulation, in reality the networks that sustain it are more fragile, informal, and serendipitous'.[76] This holds true for written or printed literature—which, if not written in English, is often translated and circulates transnationally thanks to the efforts of small publishers. It also holds true for oral traditions and their performers, who face the challenge of addressing a contemporary audience that does not understand the long and rich textual tradition from which the texts they perform originated. In 1970s India, Sadhana Naithani writes, a new 'world of festivals—national festivals, folk festivals, regional arts, and crafts festivals' (and Festivals of India abroad)—provided:

> new venues for performance drawing new kinds of audience. A fissure between text and performance was inevitable, for text was limited by language, but the performance and music were not. So, performance of text remained more important in the local and traditional venues, but at new venues the universal language of the performer's style and music became the centre of attention (Naithani, Chapter 9, p. 269).

If oral performances offer a surfeit of sensory messages and experiences, then, language can become a barrier that needs to be circumvented with ingenuity. Naithani's chapter nonetheless stresses the dynamism and ingenuity of oral performers and genres, as people and performers come together to form new groups and communities, breaking down identitarian boundaries. A focus on orature, then, uncovers the vitality and the transnational, often transcontinental, expanse of subcultures and submarkets dedicated to oral forms, belying accounts of a single, though uneven, global market.

---

76 Orsini and Zecchini, 'Introduction', p. 6.

Transcription, Archiving, Translation

Folklorists, ethnographers, and literary historians today are revisiting the nationalist and/or colonial roots of early archiving and transcription projects.[77] Contemporary scholarship is more self-reflective about the protocols and politics of transcription.[78] John Niles, for example, highlights the difficulties inherent in 'scripting the voice' and the choices and biases involved in literate interventions imposed on an oral tradition. As print culture is 'saturated with connotations of literacy', documenting an oral text on the written page transforms its aesthetic integrity, producing a hybrid *tertium quid* (third entity). As a result, 'an oral-derived text is by its nature a hybrid form, something that is neither fully literary nor fully oral in nature'.[79] 'Textual refashioning' aimed at producing an ethno-poetic transcription may highlight the original performance elements and modalities on the written page to more fully bring the performance to life, but it still brings to the fore the question of whose performative voice do we hear—the original performer's, the ethnographer's, the editor's?[80] Moreover, since oral texts, as we have seen, have 'multiple centres of authority', Niles stresses the latent collaboration and negotiation integral to subsequent re-inscriptions that create an oral text. 'Oral textual scholarship', which Niles defines as 'using the medium of print to preserve traces of orality', requires a patient, responsible, responsive, attuned, and contextualised approach to oral texts. [81] The contributors to a volume like this, aimed at literary comparatists rather than linguistic anthropologists or folklorists, have tried to strike a balance between attention to performance and contextual elements and a focus on key oral textual elements/quotations while

---

77   See e.g. Sadhana Naithani, *The Story-Time of the British Empire: Colonial and Postcolonial Folkloristics* (Jackson: University Press of Mississippi, 2010); John Neubauer, 'Rhetorical Uses of Folk Poetry in Nineteenth-Century Central Europe' in *Studying Transcultural Literary History*, ed. by Gunilla Lindberg-Wada (Berlin: De Gruyter, 2006), pp. 88–97.

78   See for example Laura J. Murray and Keren Rice, eds, *Talking on the Page: Editing Aboriginal Oral Texts* (Toronto, Buffalo and London: University of Toronto Press, 1999).

79   John. D Niles, 'Orality' in *The Cambridge Companion to Textual Scholarship*, ed. by Neil Fraistat and Julia Flanders (Cambridge: Cambridge University Press, 2013), pp. 205–223 (p. 211).

80   Ibid., p. 219.

81   Ibid., p. 211.

providing readable translations, conscious that there is no 'right way' of doing so.

If transcribing an oral art form engenders a loss of the original performative voice, the digital archiving of performance can alleviate some of the 'problems of representation [...] endemic in print culture'. And indeed paratext-rich digital transcriptions as well as sound and audiovisual recordings of oral corpora have multiplied, from *Verba Africana* to the World Oral Literature project.[82] The edited volume *Oral Traditions in the Digital Age: Archiving Orality and Connecting with Communities*, published by the team of the World Oral Literature Project in the same book series as this volume, reflects on how digital technologies can be used in projects of knowledge and archive co-creation between researchers and communities. Consciously critical of the history of Western scholars' appropriation of other people's oral literature for economic profit and career advancement,[83] the World Oral Literature project made sure:

> that source communities retain full copyright and intellectual property over recordings of their traditions. [...] Returning digitised materials to performers and communities frequently helps to protect established living traditions, with materials used for language education as well as programmes that aim to revitalise cultural heritage practices.[84]

Archival recordings have been the springboard for the revival of oral traditions also in the case of Sephardi oral literature: 'Today, few older singers are alive,' Vanessa Paloma Elbaz writes in Chapter 8, 'though the repertoire is undergoing a revival through the professional performances of singers from the diaspora who often turn to archival recordings and scholarly transcriptions as sources' (p. 233). Janet Hayward finds digitally archived orature to be important in educational settings as well:

---

82   For the *Verba Africana* series, see Daniela Merolla, 'Verba Africana: African Languages and Oral literatures: DVD Documentation and Digital Materials' (2009).

83   See Lenore Keeshig-Tobias, 'Stop Stealing Native Stories' in *Borrowed Power: Essays on Cultural Appropriation*, ed. by B. Ziff and P. V. Rao (New Brunswick: Rutgers University Press, 1997), pp. 71–73.

84   Mark Turin, Claire Wheeler, and Eleanor Wilkinson, eds, 'Introduction' in *Oral Literature in the Digital Age: Archiving Orality and Connecting with Communities*, ed. by Mark Turin, Claire Wheeler and Eleanor Wilkinson (Cambridge: Open Book Publishers, 2013), pp. xiii–xxiii (p. xiv), https://doi.org/10.11647/OBP.0032. See also Sophie McCall, *First Person Plural: Aboriginal Storytelling and the Ethics of Collaborative Authorship* (Vancouver: University of British Columbia Press, 2011).

'oral traditions that have already been documented, and others yet to be accumulated, provide essential educational and scholarly resources in the development of decolonised curricula, and potentially serve as tools for the promotion of multilingualism and multiculturalism in the classroom and beyond'.[85] All these observations are pertinent to scholars of world literature in interrogating the politics of the (literary) archive, the pedagogy of the field in relation to language, and the legacies of the colonial relationship between Western scholars of literature and non-Western authors and audiences.

Some of these legacies have a bearing on translation as well. Translation is part and parcel of oral texts as they are retold, reframed, and repackaged each time for a new audience. But what about translation more narrowly defined as the crossing of linguistic boundaries to carry a text beyond its original language? This is an important issue that affects the circulation and recognition of oral genres within and as world literature. If, as we have seen, circulation on a larger scale tends to de-emphasise texts in relation to voice and music, or to modify and simplify them for the sake of broader circulation, this paradoxically means that oral texts like songs are less likely to be recognized as verbal art or poetry. This, in turn, can reinscribe the primacy of a small number of regional or 'global' languages. Is it a coincidence that the only singer-songwriter that ever won the Nobel Prize for literature composes and sings in English as his mother tongue?

Translations of oral texts can be roughly divided among academic-, performer/artist-, and fan-led, and each reveals a different, specific set of outcomes, strategies, challenges, and patterns of circulation. Academic translations may render the artistry and complexity of oral texts through skilful wording and paratexts, and thereby help establish their stature as world texts.[86] But the most successful case of translations of oral texts

---

85 Janet Hayward, 'Orality in the Digital Age' in *The Transformative Power of Language: From Postcolonial to Knowledge Societies in Africa*, eds. R. H. Kaschula and H. E. Wolff (Cambridge: Cambridge University Press, 2000), pp. 277–303 (p. 277).

86 E.g. J. P. Clark's translation and transcription of *The Ozidi Saga* from Izon into English (Ibadan: Ibadan University Press and Oxford University Press, 1977). For Isidore Okpewho, it did 'more than any other edition of African oral literature before it to give us a good picture of the oral performance in context,' especially in 'emphasizing as never before the relevance of, among other things, contextual circumstances (e.g. audience interjections) to the text of the oral narrative performance'; Isidore Okpewho, 'Towards a Faithful Record: On Transcribing and

that do not lose complexity or popularity is that of performer/artist-led translations. We may think of the massive translation and adaptation of the French songs of *chansonniers* like Georges Brassens and Jacques Brel into Italian by *cantautori* like Fabrizio De Andrè, Herbert Pagani, Gino Paoli, Giorgio Gaber, Fausto Amodei that helped renew the linguistic, thematic, and emotional landscape of Italian songs.[87] The translations and adaptations of French *chansons* gave lyrics primacy over music, and introduced a new realism defined by an anti-rhetorical language of everyday words from urban speech, sometimes even dialect.[88] Although Italian *cantautori* also drew on other sources and wrote their own songs, their adaptations of French *chansons* helped them to broaden the range of themes and affects sayable through song, including loneliness, incommunicability, existential angst, nostalgia, urban alienation, migration and industrialisation, marginalisation, power, violence, and sex as well as love.[89]

Finally, there is a vast archive on the internet of websites devoted to providing texts and translations of songs originally in Hindi, Arabic, and many other languages. If YouTube and other digital platforms have made a huge repertoire of songs in languages other than English widely available, many listeners and viewers are looking for translations of the song lyrics, and others are providing them. Translation of oral or performance texts more often than not takes place 'on the hoof', distributed across communities of fans or added as subtitles to videos.[90] The proliferation of websites offering transcriptions of song lyrics in multiple scripts and in translation highlights the need for and care towards translation, but also the different protocols of translation from

---

Translating the Oral Narrative Performance' in *The Oral Performance in Africa*, ed. by Isidore Okpewho (Ibadan: Spectrum, 1990), pp. 111–135 (p. 117).

87   See Enrico de Angelis, '*Le mal de Paris*: influenza della canzone francese su quella italiana', *Trasparenze*, 22 (1990), 41–50.

88   As in Nanni Svampa's translations of Brel into Milanese dialect.

89   de Angelis, '*Le mal de Paris*', p. 45. Fabien Coletti notes that Herbert Pagani's translations of Jacques Brel songs like *Le plat pays* (as *Lombardia*) and *Ces gens–là* (as *Che bella gente*) transpose not only Brel's Flemish landscape onto northern Italy, but also help Pagani outline processes of rapid socio-economic change accompanying the Italian postwar economic boom; Fabien Coletti, '«In Lombardia, che è casa mia»: traduzione, identità e stile negli adattamenti breliani di Herbert Pagani (1965–1969)', *Line@editoriale*, 8 (2016), n.p.

90   See Nikitta Adjirakor, 'African Language Literature and the Paradigm of World Literature', Mulosige webinar, 26 February 2011.

those of written texts.[91] These on-the-hoof, unofficial translations are a hugely important, if under-the-radar, tool in the transnational circulation of oral genres.

This Volume

This volume is inspired by scholarship questioning the oral-to-written teleology and the dichotomy between literate and non-literate cultures. The conference behind it, titled 'Oral Traditions in World Literature' and held in Addis Ababa in December 2019, included papers covering the Horn of Africa, the Maghreb, and South Asia—the three areas of the research project of which it was part ('Multilingual Locals, Significant Geographies' or MULOSIGE, 2016-2021, European Research Council Advanced Grant, based at SOAS University of London). Although the chapters in this volume focus on case studies from Africa, the Maghreb, and India, we hope that the range, importance, and vibrancy of the chapters will also alert readers to comparable examples in 'the West', where, we argue, orature is also strong and alive. Several events we ran as part of MULOSIGE aimed at giving visibility to oral literary production and oral performances in multilingual London, including multilingual storytelling and spoken-word poetry, and pushed for a greater scholarly recognition of oral genres in the West, where the criss-crossing of diasporas and mobilities opens new possibilities for oral reinvention. The three geographical and literary areas covered by this volume offer, of course, only a partial coverage of 'oral literary worlds' – and yet we decided not to regionally decline the title of this volume, as a provocation towards the habit of world literature to treat Anglophone literature as the default 'universal' and the non-Anglophone as an inevitably narrower deviation from this default universal.

It was important for us to hold a located discussion on 'Oral Traditions in World Literature' in Addis Ababa, where 'oral literature' has a programmatic salience that 'world literature' does not have. At the conference, some colleagues perceived an antagonistic relationship between the two, and saw the study of oral genres in local languages precisely as a reassertion of cultural difference against the assimilating

---

91   Examples include http://www.arabicmusictranslation.com/, 'Gitayan', https://www.giitaayan.com

and homogenizing motives of 'world literature'. For our colleagues based in Ethiopia, this was not just a theoretical discussion. Many of them study oral genres whose socio-historical trajectories were profoundly affected by Ethiopia's integration into the global capitalist system, for example as a result of development-induced displacement.[92] In this context, the study and collection of oral genres is not only a scholarly pursuit, but a form of resistance against ongoing violence. This tension is palpable in the different stances and varying levels of interest in world literature and transnational circulation that the chapters show. The effects of these tensions on knowledge production were tangible even for the conference participants that travelled to Addis Ababa for the first time: the conference, in the end, was held in a hotel over the university.

The discussions at the conference contributed to MULOSIGE's own positioning within the field of world literature. The members of the research project (July Blalack, Fatima Burney, Jack Clift, Itzea Goikolea-Amiano, Ayele Kebede Roba, Karima Laachir, Sara Marzagora, Francesca Orsini) share a general scepticism towards understandings of world literature aimed at fitting all global literary traditions onto a single map, or organising them according to universal 'laws of literary evolution'. Such goals, it seems to us, are inspired by a positivist, classificatory impulse that risks reproducing imperialist cartographies and eliding variability, fluidity, and contradictions to fit all-encompassing abstract models. Our response to these impulses is not to argue for the irreconcilability of difference or to celebrate local particularisms. We disavow the search for a 'solution' to the 'problem' of world literature, and advocate an open-ended methodology that, on the contrary, constantly generates new questions, even at the cost of leaving some unanswered. In fact, the unanswerability of certain questions is not a cost or a liability to us. Reckoning with the partiality of our understanding is not only a matter of scholarly ethics vis-à-vis the complexity of global literary histories and the multiplicity of their languages, but is also in itself an invitation to compare, for example by learning new languages and starting more conversations. World literature can then be recast as a process, not an object; and as a process, it derives more strength from the conceptual

---

92　For more information on development-induced displacement in Addis Ababa, see Marco Di Nunzio, 'Evictions for Development: Creative Destruction, Redistribution and the Politics of Unequal Entitlements in Inner-city Addis Ababa (Ethiopia), 2010–2018', *Political Geography*, 98 (2022), 1–9.

vocabulary of directions and routes than the conceptual vocabulary of maps, models, and roots.[93]

As we started considering oral genres, this reflection became even more pertinent. Oral genres are performed, and they are defined by performance. If we transcribe the lyrics of a praise poem in a book, or if we record the voice of the praise poet, or even if we film the whole performance, something of the original meaning of the text survives, but a lot more gets lost. Performance is meant to be transient, and its meaning resides in its impermanence, immediacy, and in the performer-audience dynamic. We can archive some of it, but we also should make peace with the meagreness of the archive over the experience. Again, this is not necessarily a limitation: transcriptions and recordings can acquire new meanings, start new processes of signification—or their inadequacy to capture the performance in full can also be an invitation to just experience that performance in its fleetingness.

We too had live performances at our 'Oral Traditions in World Literature' conference in Addis Ababa: Vanessa Paloma Duncan Elbaz performed songs belonging to the Moroccan Sephardi repertoire, and students from the university of Addis Ababa performed a range of Oromo songs. This volume does not capture those performances, just as elements of the conference presentations, as oral acts, are lost when they are transformed in book chapters. By putting together this volume, we too are, after all, turning an oral genre into a written one, but again this is not a unilinear teleology: just as the presentations were orally performed alongside PowerPoint slides with images, videos and hyperlinks, our book is also available to download from the internet as a digital product.

---

93   See James Clifford, *Routes: Travel and Translation in the Late Twentieth Century* (Cambridge MA: Harvard University Press, 1997).

Bibliography

Adhya, Raahi, *The Fantastic World of the Bengali Roopkatha: Unpacking Gender, Generation and Genre* (unpublished PhD thesis, SOAS University of London, 2023).

Adjirakor, Nikitta, 'African Language Literature and the Paradigm of World Literature', Mulosige webinar, 26 February 2011, http://mulosige.soas. ac.uk/african-language-literature-and-the-paradigm-of-world-literature/

Alant, Jaco, '"Did you say *oral literature*?" asked Walter Ong', *Literator*, 17.2 (1996), https://doi.org/10.4102/lit.v17i2.609

Andrzejewski, Boris W., 'The Poem as Message: Verbatim Memorization in Somali Poetry', *Journal of African Cultural Studies*, 23.1 (2011), https://doi. org/10.1080/13696815.2011.581454

Arndt, Susan, *African Women's Literature: Orature and Intertextuality* (Bayreuth: Eckhard Breitinger, 1998).

Barber, Karin, 'Text and Performance in Africa', *Bulletin of the School of Oriental and African Studies*, 66.3 (2003), https://doi.org/10.1017/ S0041977X03000223

——, *The Anthropology of Texts, Persons, and Publics* (Cambridge: Cambridge University Press, 2007).

Basu, Priyanka, *The Poet's Song: 'Folk' and its Cultural Politics in South Asia* (London: Routledge, 2024).

Bernstein, Charles, ed., *Close Listening: Poetry and the Performed Word* (Oxford: Oxford University Press, 1998).

Blackburn, Stuart et al., eds, *Oral Epics in India* (Berkeley: University of California Press, 1989).

Bresler, Liora, 'What musicianship can teach educational research', *Music Education Research*, 7.2 (2005), https://doi.org/10.1080/14613800500169399

Brown, Katherine B. (now Schofield), 'Introduction: Liminality and the Social Location of Musicians', *Twentieth-Century Music*, 3.1 (2007), https://doi. org/10.1017/S1478572207000308

Buzwell, Greg, 'Women Writers, Anonymity and Pseudonyms', British Library Blog (2020), https://www.bl.uk/womens-rights/articles/women-authors-and-anonymity#:~:text=In%20the%20late%2018th%20and,poems%20 anonymously%20was%20once%20commonplace

Clark, J. P., *The Ozidi Saga* (Ibadan: Ibadan University Press and Oxford University Press, 1977).

Coletti, Fabien, '"In Lombardia, che è casa mia": traduzione, identità e stile negli adattamenti breliani di Herbert Pagani (1965–1969)', *Line@editoriale*, 8 (2016).

Crooke, William and W. H. D. Rouse, *The Talking Thrush and Other Tales from India* (London: J. M. Dent & Sons, 1922).

Damrosch, David, *What is World Literature?* (Princeton: Princeton University Press, 2003).

de Angelis, Enrico, '*Le mal de Paris*: influenza della canzone francese su quella italiana', *Trasparenze*, 22 (1990), http://digital.casalini.it/4829346

De Lorenzi, James, 'The Orientalist on Trial: Enrico Cerulli and the United Nations War Crimes Commission', *Northeast African Studies* 18.1–2 (2018), https://doi.org/10.14321/nortafristud.18.1-2.0165

Di Nunzio, Marco, 'Evictions for Development: Creative Destruction, Redistribution and the Politics of Unequal Entitlements in Inner-city Addis Ababa (Ethiopia), 2010–2018', *Political Geography*, 98 (2022), https://doi.org/10.1016/j.polgeo.2022.102671

Dylan, Bob, '2016 Nobel Lecture in Literature', https://www.nobelprize.org/prizes/literature/2016/dylan/lecture/

Eidsheim, Nina Sun, 'Voice as a Technology of Selfhood: Towards an Analysis of Racialized Timbre and Vocal Performance' (unpublished PhD Thesis, University of California San Diego, 2008), http://escholarship.org/uc/item/0h8841kp

Finnegan, Ruth, 'Attitudes to the Study of Oral Literature in British Social Anthropology', *Man*, 4.1 (1969), 59–69, https://doi.org/10.2307/2799264

Finnegan, Ruth, *Oral Literature in Africa* (Cambridge: Open Book Publishers, 2012 [original 1970]), https://doi.org/10.11647/OBP.0025

Finnegan, Ruth. 'The How of Literature', *Oral Tradition*, 20.2 (2005), 164–187.

Foley, John Miles, *Oral Traditions and the Internet: Pathways of the Mind* (Urbana, Chicago and Springfield: University of Illinois Press, 2012).

Gikandi, Simon (ed.), *Encyclopaedia of African Literature* (London and New York: Routledge, 2003).

Gingell, Susan, Wendy Roy, eds, *Listening Up, Writing Down, and Looking Beyond: Interfaces of the Oral, Written, and Visual* (Waterloo: Wilfrid Laurier University Press, 2012).

Gunner, Liz, 'Ecologies of Orality' in *The Cambridge Companion to World Literature*, ed. by B. Etherington and J. Zimbler (Cambridge: Cambridge University Press, 2018), pp. 116–129.

Harris, Roy, *The Origin of Writing* (London: Duckworth, 1986).

Hiwot Teffera, *Mine to Win* (Addis Ababa: Addis Ababa University Press, 2016).

Honko, Lauri, ed. *Textualization of Oral Epics* (Berlin: de Gruyter, 2011).

Hountondji, Paulin J., *African Philosophy: Myth and Reality* (Bloomington: Indiana University Press, 1996).

Janet Hayward, 'Orality in the Digital Age' in *The Transformative Power of Language: From Postcolonial to Knowledge Societies in Africa*, ed. by R. H. Kaschula and H. E. Wolff (Cambridge: Cambridge University Press, 2000), pp. 277–303.

Jason, Heda, 'A Multidimensional Approach to Oral Literature', *Current Anthropology*, 10.4 (1969), 13–426.

Johnson, John William, 'Orality, Literacy, and Somali Oral Poetry', *Journal of African Cultural Studies*, 18.1 (2006), https://doi.org/10.1080/1369685060075035

Kapil, Pandey, *Phoolsunghi*, translated by Goutam Choubey (New Delhi: Penguin India, 2020).

Kresse, Kai and Oriare Nyarwath, eds, *Rethinking Sage Philosophy: Interdisciplinary Perspectives on and beyond H. Odera Oruka* (Lanham: Lexington Books, 2023).

Kuipers, Joel C., *Performance: The Creation of Textual Authority in Weyewa Ritual Speech* (Philadelphia: University of Pennsylvania Press, 1990).

Lanfranchi, Benedetta, 'Rethinking World Philosophies from African Philosophy', *Journal of World Philosophy*, 7.2 (2022), https://doi.org/10.2979/jourworlphil.7.2.03

——, '"Does this mean that there is philosophy in everything?": A Comparative Reading of Henry Odera Oruka's First and Second Order and Antonio Gramsci's First and Second Level Philosophy' in *Rethinking Sage Philosophy Interdisciplinary Perspectives On and Beyond H. Odera Oruka*, ed. by K. Kresse and O. Nyarwath (London: Lexington Books, 2023), pp. 77–98.

Lenore Keeshig–Tobias, 'Stop Stealing Native Stories' in *Borrowed Power: Essays on Cultural Appropriation*, ed. by B. Ziff and P. V. Rao (New Brunswick: Rutgers University Press, 1997), pp. 71–73.

Levine, Caroline, 'The Great Unwritten: World Literature and the Effacement of Orality', *Modern Language Quarterly*, 74.2 (2013), https://doi.org/10.1215/00267929-2072998

McCall, Sophie, *First Person Plural: Aboriginal Storytelling and the Ethics of Collaborative Authorship* (Vancouver: University of British Columbia Press, 2011).

Mallette, Karla, *European Modernity and the Arab Mediterranean: Toward a New Philology and a Counter-Orientalism* (Philadelphia: University of Pennsylvania Press, 2011).

Mani, B. Venkat, *Recoding World Literature: Libraries, Print Culture, and Germany's Pact with Books* (New York: Fordham University Press, 2016).

Merolla, Daniela, 'Verba Africana: African Languages and Oral Literatures: DVD Documentation and Digital Materials' (2009), https://www.africabib.org/rec.php?RID=34376265X

Molla, Rode, 'Children's Experiences Matter: An Interdisciplinary Approach', *Religious Education*, 118.2 (2023), https://doi.org/10.1080/00344087.2023.2184026

Moolla, Fiona, 'When Orature Becomes Literature: Somali Oral Poetry and Folktales in Somali Novels', *Comparative Literature Studies*, 49.3 (2012), https://doi.org/10.5325/complitstudies.49.3.0434

Mnenuka, Angelus, 'Online Performance of Swahili Orature: The Need for a New Category?', *Eastern African Literary and Cultural Studies*, 5.3–4 (2019), 274–297, https://doi.org/10.1080/23277408.2019.1685752

Mnenuka, Angelus, 'Fluidity and Fixity of Performer, Audience and Performing Space', *UMMA: The Journal of Contemporary Literature and Creative Arts*, 8.1 (2021), 37–54.

Murphy, William P., 'Oral Literature', *Annual Review of Anthropology*, 7.1 (1978), https://doi.org/10.1146/annurev.an.07.100178.000553

Murray, Laura J., Keren Rice (eds.), *Talking on the Page: Editing Aboriginal Oral Texts* (Toronto, Buffalo and London: University of Toronto Press, 1999).

Mutembei, Aldin K., 'The Future of East African Kiswahili Orature in the Digital Age: A Case Study of WhatsApp Narrative', *Studies of the Department of African Languages and Cultures*, 51 (2017), https://doi.org/10.32690/SALC52

Naithani, Sadhana, *The Story-Time of the British Empire: Colonial and Postcolonial Folkloristics* (Jackson: University Press of Mississippi, 2010).

Ngũgĩ Wa Thiong'o, 'Notes towards a Performance Theory of Orature', *Performance Research: A Journal of the Performing Arts*, 12.3 (2007), 4–7.

——, *Penpoints, Gunpoints, and Dreams: Towards a Critical Theory of the Arts and the State in Africa* (Oxford: Clarendon Press, 2003).

Niles, John D., *Homo Narrans: The Poetics and Anthropology of Oral Literature* (Philadelphia: University of Pennsylvania Press, 1999).

——, 'Orality' in *The Cambridge Companion to Textual Scholarship*, ed. by Neil Fraistat and Julia Flanders (Cambridge: Cambridge University Press, 2013), pp. 205–223.

Nnaemeka, Obioma, 'From Orality to Writing: African Women Writers and the (Re)Inscription of Womanhood', *Research in African Literatures*, 25.4 (1994), 137–157.

Neubauer, John, 'Rhetorical Uses of Folk Poetry in Nineteenth-Century Central Europe' in *Studying Transcultural Literary History,* ed. by Gunilla Lindberg-Wada (Berlin: De Gruyter, 2006), pp. 88–97.

Okpewho, Isidore, *African Oral Literature: Backgrounds, Character, and Continuity* (Bloomington and Indianapolis: Indiana University Press, 1992).

——, 'Towards a Faithful Record: On Transcribing and Translating the Oral Narrative Performance' in *The Oral Performance in Africa,* ed. by Isidore Okpewho (Ibadan: Spectrum, 1990), pp. 111–135.

Ong, Walter, *Orality and Literacy* (New York: Routledge, 2002 [original 1982]).

Opland, Jeff 'The Early Career of D. L. P. Yali-Manisi, Thembu Imbongi', *Research in African Literatures*, 33.1 (2002), 1–26.

Opland, Jeff, 'First Meeting with Manisi', *Research in African Literatures*, 35.3 (2004), 26–45.

Opland, Jeff, *The Dassie and the Hunter. A South African Meeting* (Durban: University of Kwa Zulu-Natal Press, 2005).

Orsini, Francesca, 'Booklets and Sants: Religious Publics and Literary History' in *Imagining the Public in Modern South Asia*, ed. by Brannon Ingram, J. Barton Scott, and Sher Ali K. Tareen (London: Routledge, 2016), pp. 89–103.

——, 'Love Letters' in *Love in South Asia: A Cultural History*, ed. by Francesca Orsini (Cambridge: Cambridge University Press, 2006), pp. 228–258.

Orsini, Francesca and Katherine B. Schofield, eds, *Tellings and Texts: Music, Storytelling and Performance in North India* (Cambridge: Open Book Publishers, 2015), https://doi.org/10.11647/OBP.0062

Orsini, Francesca and Laetitia Zecchini, 'The Locations of (World) Literature: Perspectives from Africa and South Asia: Introduction', *Journal of World Literature*, 4.1 (2019), https://doi.org/10.1163/24056480-00401003

Orwin, Martin, 'On the Concept of "Definitive Text" in Somali Poetry', *Bulletin of the School of Oriental and African Studies*, 66.3 (2003), https://doi.org/10.1017/S0041977X03000235

p'Bitek, Okot, *Hare and Hornbill* (London: Heinemann, 1978).

Paolini, Marco, 'Vajont: 9 ottobre 1963' (Rai Due and Moby Dick Teatri della Riviera, 1997), https://www.youtube.com/watch?v=q7CarpRflzs

——, *Il racconto del Vajont* (Milan: Garzanti, 2014).

Pender-Cudlip, Patrick, 'Oral Traditions and Anthropological Analysis: Some Contemporary Myths', *Azania: Archaeological Research in Africa*, 7.1 (1972), https://doi.org/10.1080/00672707209511556

Perloff, Marjorie and Craig Dworkin, eds, *The Sound of Poetry /The Poetry of Sound* (Chicago: The University of Chicago Press, 2009).

Prendergast, Christopher, 'The World Republic of Letters' in *Debating World Literature*, ed. by C. Prendergast (London: Verso, 2004), pp. 1–25.

Puchner, Martin, et al. (eds.), *Norton Anthology of World Literature*, vols. 1–3 (New York: W. W. Norton, 2012–2018).

Raia, Annachiara, 'Texts, Voices and Tapes: Mediating Poetry on the Swahili Muslim Coast in the 21st century', *Matatu*, 51.1 (2020), https://doi.org/10.1163/18757421-05101002

Ramanujan, A. K., 'Three Hundred *Rāmāyaṇas*: Five Examples and Three Thoughts on Translation' in *Many Rāmāyaṇas: The Diversity of a Narrative Tradition in South Asia*, ed. by Paula Richman (Berkeley: University of California Press, 1991), pp. 22–49.

Ramazani, Jahan, 'Poetry and Song', *Poetry and its Others* (Chicago: University of Chicago Press, 2014), pp. 184–238.

Renu, Phanishwarnath Renu, *Parati Parikatha* (New Delhi: Rajkamal Prakashan, 1957).

——, *Tale of a Wasteland*, trans. by Madhusudan Thakur (New Delhi: Global Vision Press, 2012).

Salih, Fatima Zahra, 'L'art de (ra)conter les films; entretien avec le conteur Moulay Omar Douâmi' (unpublished interview, 2008), https://www.academia.edu/10701385/Lart_de_ra_conter_les_films_entretien_avec_le_conteur_Moulay_Omar_Douâmi

Salyer, Kirsten, 'Are Disney Princesses Hurting Your Daughter's Self-Esteem?', *Time Magazine*, 22 June 2016, https://time.com/4378119/disney-princess-effect-on-girls/

Sapiro, Gisèle, 'Translation and Symbolic Capital in the Era of Globalization: French Literature in the United States', *Cultural Sociology*, 9.3 (2015), https://doi.org/10.1177/1749975515584080

Servan-Schreiber, Catherine, *Chanteurs itinérants en Inde du Nord: la tradition orale Bhojpuri* (Paris: L'Harmattan, 1999).

——, *Histoire d'une musique métisse à l'île Maurice: chutney indien et séga Bollywood* (Paris: Riveneuve éditions, 2010).

Shankar, Subrahmanyam, 'Literatures of the World: An Inquiry', *PMLA* 131.5 (2016), https://doi.org/10.1632/pmla.2016.131.5.1405

Silverstein, Michael and Greg Urban, eds, *Natural Histories of Discourse* (Chicago: University of Chicago Press, 1996).

Smith, John D., *The Epic of Pabuji* (New Delhi: Katha, 2005).

Sutton-Smith, Brian, Jay Mechling, Thomas W. Johnson, and Felicia McMahon, eds, *Children's Folklore: A Source Book* (New York and Oxford: Routledge, 1995).

Teffera, Hiwot, *Mine to Win* (Addis Ababa: Addis Ababa University Press, 2016).

Turin, Mark, Claire Wheeler, and Eleanor Wilkinson, eds, *Oral Literature in the Digital Age: Archiving Orality and Connecting with Communities* (Cambridge: Open Book Publishers, 2013), https://doi.org/10.11647/OBP.0032

Viitamäki, Mikko, 'Poetry in Sufi Practice: Patrons, Poets and Performers in South Asian Sufism from Thirteenth Century to the Present' (unpublished PhD thesis, University of Helsinki, 2015).

West-Pavlov, Russell, *Eastern African Literatures: Towards an Aesthetics of Proximity* (Oxford: Oxford University Press, 2018).

World Oral Literature Project, https://www.oralliterature.org

Zia Mohyuddin ke Saath Ek Shaam 2022 (An Evening with Zia Mohyuddin), YouTube, https://www.youtube.com/watch?v=GzYrqxHEaCE

Zumthor, Paul, *Oral Poetry: An Introduction* (Minneapolis: University of Minnesota Press, 1990).

1. A Hero's Many Worlds

The Swahili Liyongo Epic and World Literature

Clarissa Vierke

Introduction

The most reputed hero of the East African coast is Fumo Liyongo. Stories and songs attributed to this invincible warrior-poet are the most ancient Swahili texts for which we have evidence. But such stories and songs are not merely relics of the past. These oral traditions have been re-adapted over and over again, and have found their way into handwritten manuscripts, school- and children's books, stage performances, and YouTube videos. My aim in this chapter is to focus on the changing form of the ramified Liyongo tradition and the worlds it has generated. I will use this research to question the narrow notions of text and textual circulation that have hitherto dominated discussions of world literature.[1]

Oral Literature and the 'Narrow Church' of World Literature

More than the sum of all the literatures in the world, the term 'world literature'—as manifold as its definitions might have been—has

---

1   This article is partly the outcome of research conducted within the Africa Multiple Cluster of Excellence at the University of Bayreuth, funded by the Deutsche Forschungsgemeinschaft (DFG, German Research Foundation) under Germany's Excellence Strategy – EXC 2052/1 – 390713894.

    https://doi.org/10.11647/OBP.0405.01

consistently been used to evoke literature's existential gravitas. For Annette Werberger, world literature is a literature that belongs to all humankind, and endures over time because it deals with fundamental human questions of life and addresses all of humanity. Therefore, Werberger goes on to argue, all literature, including oral literature, aspires to be world literature.[2] Within the field of world literature, though, with its modernist bias and overwhelming focus on a more narrowly defined notion of written literature in a few Western languages, this has actually become an exceptional position. Since the 1960s, oral literature has increasingly been written out of academic literary studies.[3]

While the field of world literature seems all-embracing and open—as the term itself implies a purview of the whole world—there has been a growing call for the inclusion of languages from beyond the West and of genres other than the historically recent novel.[4] This entails exploring a multitude of dynamic historical and geographic worlds from the perspective of the longue durée, and also reopens discussions of what literature is. As Galin Tihanov underlines:

> There is today still an unresolved tension in the way we approach world
> literature in that our modern understanding of it has become too secular
> and too determined by attention exclusively to the written form they

---

2   Annette Werberger, 'Weltliteratur und Folklore' in *Vergleichende Weltliteraturen/Comparative World Literatures*, ed. by Dieter Lamping and Galin Tihanov (Stuttgart: Metzler, 2019), pp. 323–341.

3   See also Daniel Chamberlain, 'Histories of Literature and the Question of Comparative Oral Literary History' in *Or Words to That Effect: Orality and the Writing of Literary History*, ed. by Daniel Chamberlain and J. Edward Chamberlin (Amsterdam/Philadelphia: John Benjamins, 2016), pp. 33–46; Erhard Schüttpelz, 'World Literature from the Perspective of Longue Durée' in *Figuren des Globalen: Weltbezug und Welterzeugung in Literatur, Kunst und Medien*, ed. by Christian Moser and Linda Simonis (Göttingen: V&R Unipress, 2014), pp. 141–156 (p. 150). For Annette Werberger, but also Erhard Schüttpelz, the period between 1860 and 1960 is one of increasing global connections, in which the boundaries between oral and written literature are less categorical. Even if the study of oral texts of that time is not free of biases and misconceptions, both identify moments of comparison and productive exchange between written and oral cultures both in scholarship and writing before the 1960s. After 1960, in the postcolonial era and with an increasing emphasis on monolingual philologies, Werberger and Schüttpelz find oral literature increasingly denied its status as 'literature' in both the West and the former colonies.

4   Alexander Beecroft, *An Ecology of World Literature: From Antiquity to the Present Day* (New York: Verso, 2015); Caroline Levine, 'The Great Unwritten: World Literature and the Effacement of Orality', *Modern Language Quarterly*, 74.2 (2013), 218–237.

have assumed. This is wanting on two counts: first, it excludes huge verbal masses of the premodern epochs, and secondly, it impedes efforts to capture the pluralism of world literature beyond a Eurocentric vision.[5]

Arguing for productively exploring the 'broad church' of world literature, i.e. its full thematic and disciplinary breadth, Tihanov urges us to consider various *modi existendi* of world literature, drawing 'on the early impulses of engagement with orality [...] in collaboration with ethnology, folkloristics and performance studies, in order to situate world literature in a wider cultural-anthropological context and a veritable longue durée'.[6] Tihanov refers to Goethe's broad notion of world literature which goes beyond a categorization into oral and written forms and rather insists on 'verbal creativity' in total and 'as a process rather than artefact that is frozen in time through its commitment to script'.[7]

African literature, so famously rich in oral traditions—not merely of the past—has so far been explored very little in challenging this 'narrow church'.[8] The scholarly turn to the paradigm of globalization and the focus on transcultural identities have placed great emphasis on contemporary prose writing from the African diaspora. Works by the latest generation of the so-called Afropolitans, like Chimamanda Adichie's *Americanah* or Taye Selasi's *Ghana Must Go*, which have received global attention, have also partly fed into the discussion of world literature.[9] Highlighting Africanness and drawing on Black consciousness rhetoric with a cosmopolitan attitude, both the authors' biographies and their narratives suggest an emancipation from the essentializing narrative of Africa as disconnected from the rest of the

---

5   Galin Tihanov, 'Introduction' in *Vergleichende Weltliteraturen/Comparative World Literatures*, ed. by Dieter Lamping and Galin Tihanov (Stuttgart: Metzler, 2019), pp. 283–287 (p. 285).

6   Tihanov, 'Introduction', p. 286.

7   Ibid., p. 285.

8   For criticism, see Sara Marzagora, 'African-language Literatures and the "Transnational Turn" in Euro-American Humanities', *Journal of African Cultural Studies*, 27.1 (2015), 40–55; Clarissa Vierke, 'Other Worlds: The 'Prophet's Ascension' as World Literature and Its Adaptation in Swahili-speaking East Africa' in *Vergleichende Weltliteraturen/Comparative World Literatures*, ed. by Dieter Lamping and Galin Tihanov (Stuttgart: Metzler, 2019), pp. 215–229.

9   Dieter Lamping, 'Was ist Weltliteratur? Ein Begriff und seine Bedeutungen' in *Perspektiven der Interkulturalität: Forschungsfelder eines umstrittenen Begriffs*, ed. by Anton Escher and Heike Spickermann (Heidelberg: Winter, 2018), pp. 127–141 (p. 137).

world. Nonetheless, Western literary institutions, Western readership, and the book industry and its preferred genre (the novel)—typically in English, sometimes in French or Portuguese—have remained the point of reference for measuring global reach. The more 'worldly' African literature becomes, the more scholars relegate African languages and their variety of literary *modi existendi* to the background.[10]

In the 1990s, along similar lines, Karin Barber criticized the postcolonial focus on 'writing back', a focus that paradoxically reproduces the colonial fixation on a Western centre as well as relegating African-language literatures to a primordial past. This temporal divide creates a dichotomy between modern literature 'writing back' in the former colonial languages, on the one hand, and unchanging 'traditional literature', fundamentally oral, on the other hand.[11] This postcolonial echo of the great divide between oral and written not only fatally associated writing with literary value, but also prevented a serious exploration of oral literature, which was downplayed as the 'precursor and background, out of which modern anglophone written literature somehow emerged or grew'.[12] Equally fatally, the oral became an unquestioned, but also celebrated sign of 'African cultural authenticity' in the novel itself, beyond critical scrutiny and encompassing a wide range of stylistic phenomena, from the use of dialogue to idiomatic speech and proverbs, as well as the recourse to oral tales.

In this chapter, I concentrate on the circulation and, consequently, adaptation across media of the most renowned heroic epic tradition on the Swahili coast, namely the tales and songs of Fumo Liyongo. I find inspiration in perspectives that cut across normative dichotomies of orality and written-ness, popular and highbrow literature. Liz Gunner, for example, has framed the journey of the West African Sunjata epic through Alexander Beecroft's notion of literary ecologies with a similar double optic of circulation and media adaptation.[13] For Beecroft, ecology, unlike the economics-derived metaphors of the field of world literature,

---

10   See also Levine, 'The Great Unwritten', p. 225.

11   Karin Barber, 'African-language Literature and Postcolonial Criticism', *Research in African Literatures*, 26.4 (1995), 3–28.

12   Barber, 'African-language Literature', p. 7.

13   Liz Gunner, 'Ecologies of Orality' in *The Cambridge Companion to World Literature*, ed. by Ben Etherington and Jarad Zimbler (Cambridge University Press, 2018), pp. 116–132.

offers a paradigm that can encompass more complex interactions between the distinct and various influences (including religion, politics, media, etc.) on the niches in which literatures survive. Since one of Beecroft's major concerns is to go beyond tight notions of European modernity as the measure of literature, he opts for a practice-oriented definition of literature, which emerges in practices of reception and is closely tied to notions of language and political identity.[14] As a result, his approach also invites oral literature and manuscript cultures into the debates of world literature.

Already in the twentieth century, scholarship on epic traditions, which both Liz Gunner and I focus on, played an important role in rehabilitating orality at the core of the Western canon, starting from the fundamentally oral nature of Homer's epics. These debates questioned the dichotomy of orality and writing and highlight the oral culture of the West. Although they have hardly featured in recent debates about world literature, they did foster great comparative scholarship on the orality of the African epic, particularly in the 1980s (against Ruth Finnegan's claim that there was no epic in Africa, an assertion based largely on criteria derived from writing cultures).[15]

So far, the Fumo Liyongo tradition—fragmented as it is across multiple genres, thereby seriously calling textual boundaries into question—has not been taken much into consideration in the debate on the epic in Africa. Its fuzziness and amorphousness—where does the text start? Where does it end?—is one of the reasons why I find it such an interesting case study, since it urges us all the more to critically reconsider the (normative) notions of textual boundaries derived from the printed book.

In seeking to identify recurrent motifs in discussions of world literature, Dieter Lamping speaks of the intertextual 'dialogues' that eminent texts create, since their motifs and references recur in other texts, so that world literature can be considered as a continuous network.[16] One can take Lamping's formulation, extending its remit (which largely embraces the novel) in order to shift the emphasis to literary resonances

---

14 Beecroft, *Ecologies*, pp. 16, 17–21.

15 Ruth Finnegan, *Oral Literature in Africa* (London: Clarendon, 1970); Mugyabuso M. Mulokozi, *The African Epic Controversy* (Berlin: Fabula, 2002).

16 Dieter Lamping, 'Weltliteratur?', p. 135.

across the lines that usually demarcate genres, media and regions, as this essay does, decentering Europe in the process. One can also use it for a layered and multiple literary history that takes into account not only bouts of forgetting, but also the capacity of a text to live on in various forms.

Such recurrence is also emphasized in the inspiring nineteenth-century Russian school of historical poetics, pioneered by the Russian literary scholar Alexander Veselovsky, recently promoted by Boris Maslov in his inclusive, non-canonical study of 'world poetry'.[17] Historical poetics implies an ethnographic view of the longue durée that also involves a consideration of popular culture or folklore, and a literary history that is not teleological but involves constellations of 'non-synchronous elements' yet also allows for the sudden resurfacing of seemingly forgotten images and forms. As I will show, the literary history of Liyongo is not unilinear. Firstly, writing did not simply replace orality. Secondly, the Liyongo story is not one unified text and did not follow one singular path of monodirectional change. For instance, while episodes of his adventures were increasingly streamlined into a multitude of separate narratives, poetic songs found their way into manuscripts in Arabic script, before being largely forgotten. Only much later, in the twenty-first century, did they reappear in new forms as part of staged storytelling and digital renderings. Before turning to his verbal art, in the following, I will briefly introduce the protagonist, Fumo Liyongo.

The Fumo Liyongo Saga

Fumo Liyongo is the classical superhero from the East African coast: he makes the impossible come true and proves himself in many daunting adventures that are the core of a number of oral traditions on the East Africa coast. Having been deprived of the throne of the sultanate of Pate—the most important city-state in northern Kenya until the eighteenth century—by his half-brother Daudi Mringwari, he escapes all attacks ventured against him. For instance, when his half-brother Mringwari hatches a plot to shoot him dead by inviting him to climb

---

17   Boris Maslow, 'Lyric Universality' in *The Cambridge Companion to World Literature*, ed. by Etherington and Zimbler, pp. 133–148 (p. 135).

a palm tree to collect the best coconuts for a feast, Fumo Liyongo sees through the trap, takes his bow and arrow, and shoots the coconuts down instead of climbing on the tree. In another episode, he escapes a dungeon by using a file his mother had baked into a bread loaf and smuggled into prison.

Like a typical epic hero, Fumo Liyongo is believed to be a historical character. However, the dating of his life has frequently been a point of intense discussion among folklorists and historians. While a few scholars, relying on oral sources and local Swahili and Arabic chronicles, have dated Liyongo's life to a period before the thirteenth century, several historians situate him in the sixteenth and seventeenth centuries.[18] Given these diverse suggestions, the only safe claim is that the world emerging from the ancient Liyongo narrative is one that predates the eighteenth century. For the historian Randall Pouwels, the Liyongo narrative and songs reflect a fundamental transition of power in the region: power moved from clans in the Tana delta, like Liyongo's Bauri clan, to new elites on the islands of Pate, and later Lamu. While the former—perfectly embodied by Fumo Liyongo—adhered to cultural practices influenced by Indian Ocean connections but mostly from the African mainland, like beliefs in spirits, cognatic patterns of inheritance, shifting agriculture, and oral poetry traditions, the latter—embodied by Liyongo's half-brother Mringwari—introduced more 'literate Shari'a based rules favouring patrilineage'.[19] The Liyongo texts echo the beginning of what becomes a wave of 'Arabization' reaching the coast from across the Indian Ocean, changing older rituals, legal practices, and literary preferences as Islamic hagiographic poetry in Swahili became more important.

The Liyongo tradition is not one fixed and definable text but refers to a variety of texts. There are oral Liyongo *tumbuizo* songs, which are the oldest Swahili poems of which we have evidence, predating the

---

18 Randall Pouwels, 'Eastern Africa and the Indian Ocean to 1800: Reviewing Relations in Historical Perspective', *The International Journal of African Historical Studies*, 35.2–3 (2002), 285–425 (p. 407), DOI:10.2307/3097619; Reinhard Klein-Arendt, 'Liongo Fumo: Eine ostafrikanische Sagengestalt aus der Sicht der Swahili und Pokomo', *Afrikanistische Arbeitspapiere*, 8 (1986), 57–86; Ibrahim Noor Shariff, 'The Liyongo Conundrum: Re-Examining, the Historicity of Swahili's National Poet-Hero', *Research in African Literatures*, 22 (1991), 153–167.

19 Pouwels, 'Eastern Africa', p. 407.

eighteenth century. Rather than conveying a plot-driven narrative, this dance poetry is polyphonic and seems to be only loosely connected to the overall Liyongo narrative. The songs were most probably interspersed between prose adventure episodes like the ones just mentioned, and probably formed part of dance rituals and poetic competitions on the northern Swahili coast. While the songs survived merely in writing from the nineteenth century onwards, since Islamic poetry partly obliterated older song traditions, the narrative episodes have been preserved orally: Lamu elders still narrate Liyongo stories. These were streamlined into more coherent, written narrative poems or prose tales as early as the twentieth century; more recently, they have found a new life of secondary orality on the internet. In the following, we will navigate the shifting dynamics of the Liyongo epic and its making of changing worlds.

World-making in Fumo Liyongo's Ancient *Tumbuizo*

Pijiyani p'embe, vigomamle na t'owazi
T'eze na Mbwasho na K'undazi
Pija muwiwa k'umbuke mwana wa shangazi
Yu wapi simba ezi li kana mtembezi
Fumo wa Shanga, sikiya, shamba, mitaa pwani
Fumo wa Shanga, chambiya Watwa fungiyani?
Fumo achamba mfungeni
Kikaze miyo nguo nawapa za kitwani

Strike for me the horns, the long drums, and the cymbals,
so that I may dance with Mbwasho and K'undazi.
Strike, you who owe a debt (of Kikowa), so that I may remember
    (my) cousin.
Where is the mighty lion? He is like an inveterate wanderer!
Fumo of Shanga, reckon well, (roams) the land and the coastal areas.
Fumo of Shanga asked the Watwa people: 'Why are you putting me
    in fetters?'
Fumo (Mringwari) ordered: 'Tie him up!'[20]

These are the first lines of the *Utumbuizo wa Kikowa* ('The *Utumbuizo* of the *Kikowa* Meal'). The *kikowa* feast refers to the cultural practice of an opulent banquet whose guests take turns providing the food. In this instance,

---

20   In Gudrun Miehe et al., eds, *Liyongo Songs: Poems Attributed to Fumo Liyongo* (Cologne: Köppe, 2004), p. 36.

Liyongo shoots coconuts down from a palm tree to avoid his murder.[21] Rather than reporting the incident, the poem or song (both terms can be used interchangeably to refer to *utumbuizo*) stages several exclamatory voices, relying on bipartite or tripartite verses. These voices include a dancing narrator (possibly Liyongo?); Liyongo's rival, Mringwari; and a third-person account of Liyongo by the Fumo of Shanga, who roams the land and accuses the Watwa, a subgroup of the Oromo, of imprisoning him on Mringwari's behalf. An impression of opacity and 'strangeness' is created, as often found in other in oral traditions, which literary history, puzzled by the phenomenon, has tended to downplay or neglect, as Chamberlin notes.[22] The *Utumbuizo wa Kikowa*, like the other Liyongo poems of this period, is hardly remembered in the Lamu archipelago of northern Kenya where the poems once flourished. This oblivion is not a recent phenomenon, however. Already by the end of the nineteenth century, they seem to have become less frequent, since important local scholars, like the erudite Rashid bin Abdallah, who scribed the poem below (see Figure 1.1), felt the need to preserve them. As a result, the oral songs have survived only in written form in Arabic script manuscripts.

The specific genre with which the Fumo Liyongo poems are associated, the *utumbuizo*, is not in use anymore either. Our idea of its rhythm and how it was performed is vague, which is a pity, since in contrast to later written poetic genres the *utumbuizo* was primarily an oral poem, meant to be performed. Unlike the later genre of the *utenzi*, whose audible elements, like rhythm, metre, and rhyme, were written down in carefully arranged script, the representation of *utumbuizo* verse is mostly erratic. In 'The Utumbuizo of the Kikowa Meal', for instance, the poetic lines do not correspond to manuscript lines (Fig. 1.1)—the first manuscript line ends with *kumbuka* 'remember' in the middle of the verse—and the caesuras (the three inverted hearts) are but a random

---

21 The tradition of the *kikowa*—or *chikowa* in Pokomo—was not only a Swahili cultural practice, but widespread throughout the whole Tana region; see Thomas Geider, *Die Figur des Oger in der traditionellen Literatur und Lebenswelt der Pokomo in Ost-Kenya* (Cologne: Köppe, 1990), p. 145.

22 On 'strangeness' in oral traditions, see J. Edward Chamberlin, 'Preliminaries' in *Or Words to That Effect: Orality and the Writing of Literary History*, ed. by Daniel Chamberlain and J. Edward Chamberlin (Amsterdam/Philadelphia: John Benjamins, 2016), pp. 3–32 (p. 16). On the complicated editorial history of the Liyongo songs, see Miehe et al., ed., *Liyongo Songs*, pp. 1–15.

decoration, inserted even in the middle of metrical units, rather than a rhythmic guideline. *Tumbuizo* depended largely on embodied practices of performance and memorized knowledge and was not committed to paper: its metre was not founded on a strict syllable count (represented by letters in the *utenzi*), but on the performer's breath. The polyphonic nature of its lines has made scholars wonder how to arrange them on the page.

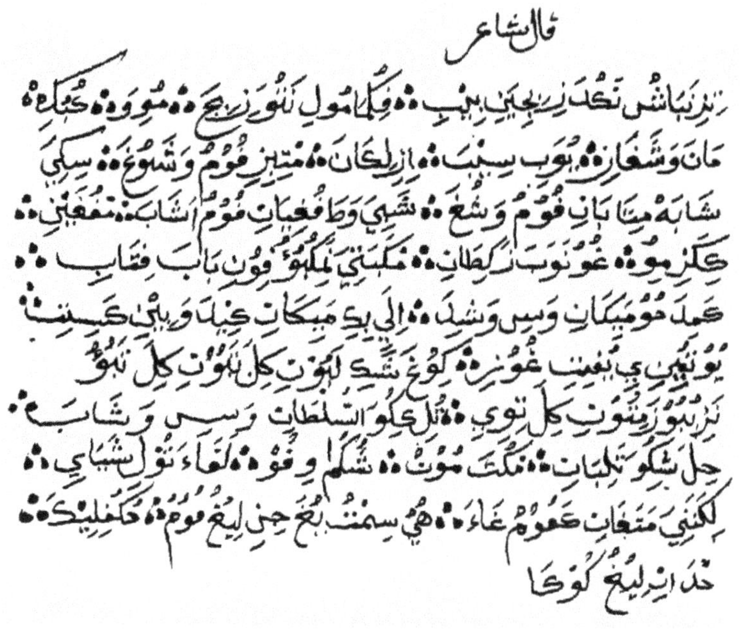

Fig. 1.1 The *Utumbuizo wa Kikowa* in the handwriting of Rashid bin Abdallah (MS 47754, Taylor Collection, SOAS). The first verses of the poem are reprinted above.

We know little about the performance, either. In some sources, *tumbuizo* are associated with a dance genre, the *gungu*, which used to be widespread all along the coast, from what is now northern Kenya to northern Mozambique. The *tumbuizo* might have existed in a different form in each city-state, and it seems to have fallen out of fashion towards the end of the nineteenth century. While in Mombasa it was associated with the New Year's celebration according to the Persian calendar,[23]

---

23   Charles Sacleux, *Dictionnaire swahili-français* (Paris: Institut d'Ethnologie, 1939), s.v.

Steere observed a *gungu* of a different form in Zanzibar in the mid-nineteenth century: 'It is the custom to meet at about ten or eleven at night and dance until day-break. The men and slave women dance, the ladies sit a little retired and look on. [...] The first figure is danced by a single couple, the second by two couples'.[24] The French missionary Charles Sacleux describes the *tumbuizo* as serene and festive, performed 'on solemn occasions' such as weddings, to which some of the songs attributed to Liyongo also make reference.[25] Poems themselves also often evoke a context of dance and music. The *Utumbuizo wa Kikowa*, for example, does not begin with the formulaic imperative to bring writing utensils, so conventionally evoked in later *tenzi*, but to beat cymbals (*t'owazi*) and drums (*vigomamle*) to set the rhythm for the dance.

The language quoted in Figure 1.1 is boastful and provocative. Liyongo is referred to as a mighty lion, reminiscent of African praise poetry traditions. In the Swahili context, this kind of language is typically found in verbal duels, *kujibizana*, which have lived on in many forms—from socialist *ngonjera* poetry to contemporary hip-hop battles—and are also connected to the *gungu* tradition of the northern parts of the coast. According to one fragmentary historical source, one of the few Swahili descriptions mentioning poetic practice prior to the twentieth century, the *gungu* (perhaps derived from Persian *gong*), referred to a night-long ritualized poetic competition, possibly also involving dance. At the beginning, the *shaha*, the master poet, 'ties up an animal'. In other words, he composes an enigmatic poem, which the poets must 'untie' in order to solve the riddle. The one who 'unties it' is the winner, and is formally recognized as *shaha*, a highly prestigious social title.[26] It seems likely that Liyongo *tumbuizo* also formed part of such *gungu* performances, since they not only make reference to *gungu* but also share its highly metaphorical language—calling on the poetic rivals to decode its meaning—as well as an often-boastful tone of self-praise.

These observations already question both the boundaries of the literary text—since it formed part of a larger ritualized performance

---

24   Edward Steere, *Swahili Tales as Told by Natives of Zanzibar* (London: Society for Promoting Christian Knowledge, 1870), p. xi.

25   Sacleux, *Dictionnaire*, s.v.

26   The fragment is stored in the collection of William Taylor at SOAS and reproduced in Lyndon Harries, *Swahili Poetry* (Oxford: Clarendon, 1962), pp. 172–173.

with musical accompaniment—as well as the notion of writing. Even writing as such did not turn the Liyongo poems, which still depended on oral performance, into written literature. As I explore in the following sections, the worlds emerging from the Liyongo songs are also not easily classifiable, either.

The Shifting Worlds of Fumo Liyongo Texts

The cultural memory of Liyongo, like that of other epics, is tied to a specific geography. The world of the ancient Fumo Liyongo *tumbuizo* is that of the northern Swahili coast: the Tana and Ozi deltas just opposite the Lamu archipelago with the ancient Swahili city-state of Pate. The pre-eighteenth-century northern East African coast has a double orientation, towards both the sea and the mainland, which is also reflected in the *tumbuizo*. Involved in Indian Ocean trade through commercial hubs like Kilwa and Pate since the first millennium CE, the Swahili islands also depended economically on Swahili clans living closely together with neighbouring ethnic groups on the mainland. These Swahili clans engaged in shifting cultivation as well as exchange with hunters and, above all, Cushitic pastoralists, who complemented the maritime economy of fishing and long-distance trade in goods. According to the pioneering scholar of Swahili folklore Alice Werner, local traditions regularly described Fumo Liyongo as being of Persian descent, from a lineage belonging to the early Swahili culture of far-reaching Indian Ocean trade originating mostly in Shiraz (Persia). At the same time, his story and songs also characterize Fumo Liyongo as being uniquely part of the ethnic and cultural contact zone of the African coast.[27]

The Tana delta is an area of 'overlapping cultures', as Alice Werner describes it. She travelled to the area at the beginning of the twentieth century and was taken to Liyongo's grave in Kipini in 1913.[28] Liyongo, she was told, came from the town of Shaka (sometimes also spelled 'Shagga' or 'Shanga'), probably etymologically related to Shungwaya,

---

27   Alice Werner, 'A Traditional Poem Attributed to Liongo Fumo' in *Festschrift Meinhof* (Hamburg: Friederichsen & Co., 1927), pp. 45–54 (p. 46); Pouwels, 'Eastern Africa', pp. 400–408.

28   Alice Werner, 'Some Notes on East African Folklore', *Folklore*, 25.4 (1914), 457–475 (p. 457).

another name for the region and the mythical homeland of the Swahili, as well as other culturally and linguistically related Bantu-speaking ethnic groups, like the Pokomo. The Pokomo intermarried with and adopted cultural practices such as hunting from their Cushitic-speaking neighbours, for example the Dahalo, as well as Oromo-speaking groups, like the Watwa (mentioned above in the *Utumbuizo wa Kikowa*).[29] Not only are there Pokomo and Dahalo oral traditions about Liyongo (see below)—in which Liyongo is portrayed as a slave-raiding tyrant ruling over the region of the Tana delta—but we also find recurrent references to other ethnic groups in the Swahili *tumbuizo*. In the *Gungu la Mnara Mp'ambe* (*Gungu* of the Dignified Lady), the Oromo, who in the seventeenth century came from what is now Ethiopia, are portrayed as invading warriors: 'The Galla came with weapons, with weapons determined to start a fight' (*Kuyiye mgala na mata/na mata uyiye kutaka kuteta*).[30] In the *Utumbuizo wa Kumwongoa Mtoto* (Lullaby), Liyongo is depicted as 'dancing with the Watwa' (*akateza Liyongo na Watwa*).[31]

The world emerging from many of these poems is that of the cultural and natural environment of the northeast African coast, commonly referred to as the *nyika* 'bush' or 'wilderness', constructed over time as being inhabited by evil spirits and in opposition to the distinctive Swahili urban culture portrayed in later poetry. The powerful Fumo Liyongo is usually not described as an urban dweller residing in the typical Swahili stone house.[32] Liyongo is instead portrayed as a warrior, 'an inveterate wanderer' in the bush, as the *Utumbuizo wa Kikowa* calls him. This characterization is impossible to imagine from a later vantage point that associates Swahili culture almost exclusively with an urban environment of cultural refinement, in opposition to the *ushenzi* 'primitivism' of the *nyika*.

---

29 Klein-Arendt, 'Liongo Fumo', pp. 57–86; Alice Werner, 'The Swahili Saga of Liongo Fumo', *Bulletin of the School of Oriental Studies*, 4 (1926/28), 247–255.

30 Miehe et al., *Liyongo Songs*, pp. 54, 55 (stanza 8). The term 'Galla' in reference to Oromo groups is nowadays mostly considered derogatory.

31 Ibid., pp. 44, 45.

32 On the house as symbolic marker of Swahili Islamic cultural distinction, in opposition to the dwellings of commoners and slaves, as well as the unordered wilderness which was associated with the wild spirits threatening to encroach on urban spaces, see Mark Horton and John Middleton, *The Swahili: The Social Landscape of a Mercantile Society* (Oxford: Blackwell, 2000), pp. 115ff.

In the *Utumbuizo wa Kumwawia Liyongo* (The Shining of the Moon on Liyongo), Liyongo is 'the mighty leopard', or a hunter praising his bow and arrow in the *Utumbuizo wa Uta* (Bow Song): 'Let me praise my bow, made from the supple twig of the ebony tree'.[33] The bow is 'his father and mother who parented him' in the *Utumbuizo wa Ukumbusho* (Remembering Past Deeds).[34] Liyongo hunts an 'elephant, whose ear is like an *uteyo* basket', and 'a deer and swift antelopes'.[35] In the *Utumbuizo wa Kumwongoa Mtoto* (Lullaby), he is depicted evading every attack, riding 'on a leopard', eating wild nuts and fruits in the bush as well as drinking palm wine.[36] This was a common Pokomo practice, considered haram by later Islamic scholars, whose voices becomes more dominant in the whole area from the eighteenth century onwards.

While the Liyongo *tumbuizo* are much more oriented towards the African interior than all later Swahili poetry, they do not merely conjure up a world of overlapping cultural influences in the East African mainland. References to the wider Indian Ocean and its far-reaching networks already figure in some of the Liyongo *tumbuizo*. In the following poem, *Utumbuizo wa Liyongo Harusini* (The Poem of Liyongo at a Wedding)— according to Jan Knappert, 'the oldest known dance song in Swahili and perhaps any Bantu language'—the guests at Liyongo's sister's wedding are asked to adorn themselves with fine attire and scents.[37]

> *Mujipake na twibu hiyari* ◆ *yalotuwa kwa zema ziungo*
> *Choshi ni maambari na udi* ◆ *fukizani nguo ziso ongo*
> *Fukizani nguo za hariri* ◆ *na zisutu zisizo zitango*
> *Pachori na zafarani* ◆ *na zabadi twahara ya fungo*
> *Na zito za karafuu* ◆ *tuliyani musitiwe tʼungo*
> *Na itiri na kafuri haya* ◆ *ndiyo mwiso wa changu kiungo*

Put on choice scents made of the best ingredients;
treat your spotless clothes with **incense** of **ambergris** and **aloewood**;
treat your **silken garments** and finely made *zisutu* **clothes**
with **patchouli** and **saffron** and pure **civet musk**,
and grind them (all together) with **clove buds**, lest people criticize you;
and (finally) add **perfume** and **fine camphor** to complete the ingredients.

---

33   Miehe et al., eds, *Liyongo Songs*, pp. 46, 47.
34   Ibid., pp. 72, 73.
35   Ibid., p. 47.
36   Ibid., pp. 44, 45.
37   Jan Knappert, 'Liongo's Wedding in the Gungu Meter', *Annales Aequatoria*, 12 (1991), 213–226 (p. 214). The verses below (stanza 10–15) are taken from Miehe et al., eds, *Liyongo Songs*, p. 40 (emphasis mine).

In this poem, Indian Ocean connections are evoked through precious goods from afar: fruits, scents, and clothes (set in bold). The guests are asked to put on elegant clothes, silken garments, and *zisutu* (cotton fabric with a red- and blue-checked pattern imported from India). Fragrances were not only important in rituals, but, like clothes, a sign of patrician status. Exquisite perfumes of patchouli, saffron, and expensive civet musk, as well as cloves, were widely traded substances in the Indian Ocean world. While civet musk became an important export good from the Swahili Coast,[38] cloves (like cinnamon, nutmeg, and pepper), originally imported from Asia, became much sought-after spices in the Indian Ocean economy. As a result, these spices were also increasingly grown on huge (slave) labour-intensive plantations on Zanzibar and Pemba from the eighteenth century onwards. The scents, textiles, and spices traded were part of what the historian Thomas Vernet characterizes as the 'premodern phase' of the Swahili Indian Ocean trade.[39] As he shows, relying mostly on Portuguese, French, and British sources from the fifteenth to eighteenth centuries, Swahili captains and sailors from Pate island travelled to Madagascar and the Comoros. They not only received goods like cottons and silks, glass, spices, porcelain, and bronze ware from Arab and Indian traders, but also sent their own boats, full of ivory, tortoiseshell, and dried fish, to southern Arabia and western India.

The Liyongo songs animate this early, widely connected world of the Swahili coast, facing both the land and the sea. This would disappear completely from the newly created Islamic poetry of the eighteenth and nineteenth centuries, authored by scholars adhering to Sufi orders with a new religious zeal, who mostly composed their poetry about the prophets, the hadith, and legendary battles of Islamic history. Rather than East African contexts of hunts or weddings, it was the Arabian Peninsula in the time of the Prophet that provided the setting for the newly created, written *tenzi*, which supplanted the older, oral *tumbuizo*. These shifting worlds of poetry reflect what the historian Randall Pouwels describes as a wave of Arabization, which changed a number of cultural as well as literary practices. For Pouwels, the conflict

---

38   Horton and Middleton, *Swahili*, p. 13.

39   Thomas Vernet, 'East African Travelers and Traders in the Indian Ocean: Swahili Ships, Swahili Mobilities ca. 1500–1800' in *Trade, Circulation, and Flow in the Indian Ocean World*, ed. by Michael Pearson (New York: Palgrave Macmillan, 2015), pp. 167–202. See also Horton and Middleton, *Swahili*, pp. 13ff.

characterizing the Liyongo story echoes a fundamental transition in the region: that of power moving from the Swahili clans in the Tana delta—like Liyongo's Bauri clan, living in close interaction with their hunting and farming neighbours—to new, proudly Islamic clans of the islands of Pate, and later Lamu, who played active roles in the Sufi brotherhoods.[40]

Thus, the *tumbuizo* portray, in a unique form, an early world at the crossroads of multiple cultural affiliations across the ocean, as well as with the mainland. The rhythmically driven *tumbuizo*, not bound to a linear plot, are different from later poetry, but all follow Liyongo narratives. While most of the *tumbuizo* do not make direct reference to the Liyongo narratives, they rather create poetic miniatures of dances and hunting scenes in which fruits, trees, and objects play a more crucial role than the acting characters. They work as a succinct poetic commentary that make East African scenes and voices emerge in a poetic and sensorially palpable way.

Overlapping Dynamics: Colonial Collections and Manuscripts in Arabic Script

The oral genre of the *utumbuizo*, in particular its metrics and sung recitation, largely fell out of use in the nineteenth century, as did much of the ritual of verbal duelling between master poets associated with the *gungu*.[41] Two primary dynamics bore an influence on Swahili literary production, and on the Liyongo story in particular, in the nineteenth century.

First, German and British colonial administration and education, in conjunction with foreign missionary engagement, prompted an emphasis on writing and reading and the fostering of new genres, like the essay, the travelogue, the short story, and the novel.[42] New Swahili literary texts were produced, such as translations from the world literary canon, like Schiller's *Wilhelm Tell*, which appeared in the Swahili

---

40   Pouwels, *Eastern Africa*, p. 407.

41   Verbal duelling outside the *gungu* did not disappear, however, but continued in a variety of different forms.

42   See Thomas Geider, 'Weltliteratur in der Perspektive einer Longue Durée II: Die Ökumene des swahilisprachigen Ostafrika' in *Wider den Kulturenzwang: Migration, Kulturalisierung und Weltliteratur*, ed. by Özkan Ezli, Dorothee Kimmich, and Annette Werberger (Bielefeld: transcript, 2009), pp. 361–401.

newspaper *Kiongozi*, published from the 1890s onward. The introduction of modern Western literature, closely linked with print technology, was just one side of the coin, however. As Schüttpelz notes with respect to the gradual dominance of the narrow Western notion of modern literature in Europe from the eighteenth century onward, the categorical separation of oral and written literature, which denied oral literature any literary value, also yielded a counter effect, namely a heightened interest in documenting popular as well as oral literature.[43] In a similar way, German and British missionaries, scholars, and layman philologists arrived in East Africa with new narratives and genres, on the one hand, but they also valued and began documenting Swahili oral literature, on the other.[44] In an effort to preserve the Swahili literary tradition and to introduce it to both a European academic audience as well as a broader public, a whole series of books and articles on Swahili oral literature as well as the manuscript culture of its poetry was created in the shadow of imperialism between roughly 1850 and 1950. After independence, this production also fed into the East African nation-states' creation of 'culturally authentic' national literature.

Secondly, as mentioned previously, the period between the eighteenth century and 1950 is also when Swahili manuscript culture flourished: a whole new kind of Swahili written poetry emerged, composed and copied in Arabic script. As in many other contexts of vernacularisation worldwide, this poetry was authored by a small elite of highly learned, mobile (Hadhrami) scholars, versed in both Arabic and Swahili and mostly affiliated with the Sufi ʿAlawiyya brotherhood, who were part of the far-reaching Muslim networks across the Indian Ocean.[45] Though they had settled in East Africa earlier on, from the eighteenth century

---

43 Schüttpelz, 'World Literature', p. 148; also Erhard Schüttpelz, 'Weltliteratur in der Perspektive einer Longue Durée I: Die fünf Zeitschichten der Globalisierung' in *Wider den Kulturenzwang*, ed. by Özkan Ezli, Dorothee Kimmich, and Annette Werberger (Bielefeld: transcript, 2009), pp. 339–360 (p. 351).

44 Schüttpelz, 'Weltliteratur', pp. 375–382. See also Gudrun Miehe, 'Preserving Classical Swahili Poetic Traditions: A Concise History of Research up to the First Half of the 20th Century' in *Muhamadi Kijuma: Texts From the Dammann Papers and Other Collections*, ed. by Gudrun Miehe and Clarissa Vierke (Cologne: Köppe, 2010), pp. 18–39.

45 See Clarissa Vierke, 'Poetic Links across the Ocean: On Poetic "Translation" as Mimetic Practice at the Swahili Coast', *Comparative Studies of South Asia, Africa and the Middle East*, 37.2 (2017), 321–335, https://doi.org/10.1215/1089201x-4132941

onward they promoted education and learning in Arabic (resulting in what I earlier called 'a wave of Arabisation'), but increasingly also in Swahili. They began systematically translating Arabic Sufi poetry into Swahili, including the *Umm al-Qurā*, a thirteenth-century Arabic ode to the Prophet, called the *Hamziyya* in Swahili; the *Miraji*, a poem about the Prophet's ascension to the seven heavens; and the *Utenzi wa Uhud*, depicting a legendary battle that took place during the Prophet's lifetime.[46] For these scholars, Swahili poetry in metrical forms, newly adapted from long, southern Arabian forms, served to address the broader, non-Arabic-speaking parts of the population, and acted as a counterreaction to Christian missionary activities.

These two nineteenth-century dynamics—Western incursions and the Hadhrami promotion of vernacular Swahili written literature—were unequal, as writing did not mean the same thing in both contexts. The former represented a collection of verbal traditions in the context of a print culture inclined towards private reading by a Western audience. The latter infused a pre-existing manuscript culture almost exclusively reserved for religious texts in Arabic with new practices of writing and oral recitation in poetic Swahili. Yet the two dynamics did not contradict each other, but rather added to each other in various ways. The manuscripts of Swahili poetry also fascinated European philologists, who began to collect, edit, and publish them.[47]

Print did not replace manuscript writing, either, but rather fostered it. Swahili intellectuals furnished Europeans with manuscripts and explanations, but also began to research their own culture and literature more systematically, committing vanishing traditions, like the Liyongo *tumbuizo*, to writing or adapting them to written poetic genres. Most of the Liyongo *tumbuizo* have survived chiefly in manuscripts written in the nineteenth century—a time when the first printed versions of the Liyongo poetry and narratives, previously transmitted in a strictly oral

---

46 On the *Hamziyya*, see Lyndon Harries, 'A Swahili Takhmis from the
     Swahili Arabic Text', *African Studies*, 11.2 (1952), 59–67, https://doi.
     org/10.1080/00020185208706867 For an overview of the *Miraji*, see Vierke,
     'Worlds', pp. 215–229. On the *Utenzi wa Uhud*, see Haji Chum, *Utenzi wa Vita vya
     Uhud*, ed. by H. E. Lambert (Nairobi: East African Literature Bureau, 1962).
47 For an overview, see Miehe, 'Preserving', pp. 18–39.

fashion, also came into being.[48] The *tumbuizo* were primarily written down by two scribes, Mwalimu Sikujua and the aforementioned Rashid Abdallah, by commission of and in cooperation with William Taylor, the Anglican Bishop of Mombasa. Later, Muhamadi Kijuma (1855–1945), who copied most of the Swahili manuscripts currently kept in London and Hamburg, played an important role in furnishing scholars with poems and explanations—including the German Africanist Ernst Dammann; the philologist Alice Werner; and the editor William Hichens, who planned a whole exquisite anthology of Liyongo poetry.[49] Muhamadi Kijuma is also credited with adapting the Liyongo tradition to the dominant poetic narrative form of the time, the *utenzi*.[50] Thus, both Western and East African scholars documented the oral narratives of Fumo Liyongo. The newly produced manuscripts laid the foundations for Swahili manuscript archives not only in East Africa, but also in Europe.[51] More importantly, they consecrated Swahili as a literary idiom, with an Islamic written literary tradition comparable to Turkish or Persian.

In the middle of the nineteenth century, Edward Steere, Anglican Bishop of Zanzibar, published a volume of Swahili oral tales, many of which, like Swahili versions of the *One Thousand and One Nights*, had travelled across the Indian Ocean.[52] Even Liyongo had reached Zanzibar: Steere documented a narrative account of the story, as told by

---

48   There is one earlier, unique example: the reputed Sufi scholar and poet Sayyid Abdullahi bin Nasiri (c. 1720–1820 CE), renowned for his *Al-Inkishafi*, *the* Swahili poetic masterpiece of mystical reflection, wrote—in a five-line *takhmisi* form derived from southern Arabian verse prosody—the so-called *Takhmisi*, the earliest written Liyongo poem, also called the *Wajiwaji*. This is another example of the synergies between Sufi manuscript culture and the adaptation of oral poetry. Steere (*Tales*, pp. 453ff.) reproduced part of the *Takhmisi*. Later, Carl Meinhof published a critical text edition based on several manuscript versions; Meinhof, 'Das Lied des Liongo', *Zeitschrift für Eingeborenen-Sprachen*, 15 (1924–25), 241–265.

49   In the 1930s, Hichens started a series called Azanian Classics, in which two poems, the *Utenzi wa Mwana Kupona* and the *Mikidadi na Mayasa*, were published. Hichens had planned for more Swahili poetry to be published, but the editions of the Liyongo poems and others were never produced. Manuscripts of these poems can be found in the SOAS Swahili Manuscripts Collections.

50   See *Muhamadi Kijuma*, ed. by Miehe and Vierke.

51   Swahili philology became a recognized academic discipline first at the Seminar of Oriental Studies in Berlin, then at SOAS in London, and, gradually, also in Dar es Salaam— writing working again as a proof of literary value.

52   Geider, 'Weltliteratur'.

Sheikh Mohammed bin Ali, with a few abridged lines of the *tumbuizo* interspersed in the narrative. Steere recognized the formal importance of those lines and considered them the formulaic core and 'skeleton' of the story.[53]

According to Steere, the narrative was a prose abridgement of an earlier narrative poem, probably similar to the *Utenzi wa Liyongo*, which Muhamadi Kijuma would later write down for Alice Werner in 1913, but which was only published much later, after independence in East Africa.[54] Born as a hagiographic genre that gained prominence in the context of the Sufi movement described above, the *utenzi* was soon used as a template to document not only contemporary history—first the German colonial raids, and later World War II—but also local oral traditions like the Fumo Liyongo epic.

Unlike the polyphonic cycle of the *tumbuizo*, a coherent narrative plot characterizes the *utenzi*. Similar to the prose account documented by Steele, the 232 stanzas of the *Utenzi wa Liyongo* create sequences of cause and consequence between episodes, from the *kikowa* meal to the escape from the dungeon, to Liyongo's ultimate death, which does not figure in the *tumbuizo*. In both the *Utenzi wa Liyongo* and Steere's prose account, Liyongo, a huge giant, is invulnerable. Only a copper needle thrust into his navel can kill him, as his son, who is the one who commits the murder, finds out. Mortally wounded, Liyongo forces himself down a well, where he dies standing upright, weapons in hand, so that people are at first afraid to approach him.

Elements such as the *kikowa* meal, the imprisonment, and particularly the later details of the plan to kill Liyongo feature not only in the Swahili prose account and its offshoots (including the digital adaptations, on which more below), but also form part of the Bantu Pokomo and Cushitic Dahalo oral narrative traditions of the Tana delta, attesting to their overlapping narrative cultures.[55] Unlike later Swahili narrative adaptations, both Steere's prose account and Kijuma's *Utenzi wa Liyongo*

---

53   Steere, *Tales*, p. vii.

54   Like many other poems that Muhamadi Kijuma wrote down, it is not clear if he created the *utenzi* version himself or relied on a pre-existing *utenzi* composed by someone else.

55   See Klein-Arendt, 'Liongo Fumo', pp. 13ff.; Geider, *Oger*, p. 144; Mauro Tosco, *A Grammatical Sketch of Dahalo Including Texts and a Glossary* (Hamburg: Buske, 1991), pp. 117–119.

portray Liyongo as interacting with neighboring Bantu and Cushitic groups, including through forms of mutual support, but also through oppression and violence.[56] These aspects completely disappear in later versions, but bear a resemblance to, or are present in the Pokomo and Dahalo renditions. Contrary to the heroic depictions of Liyongo in the Swahili *tumbuizo* (and dominant in later written and digital adaptations), Liyongo is a tyrant not only in the Pokomo and Dahalo versions, but also in the Swahili prose account recorded by Steere, according to which he 'oppressed the people exceedingly' (*akaauthi mno watu*).[57] In the Pokomo tradition documented by Gustav Fischer in 1880, for instance, Liyongo is much feared, since he enslaves many—symbolically re-narrating a long history of oppression by Swahili rulers. All later narratives instead characterize these clashes as an internal Swahili conflict over the right to rule, while the *Utenzi wa Liyongo* and the prose account recorded by Steere contain both aspects.[58]

In the *Utenzi wa Liyongo*, it is *fitina* 'intrigues' that annoy the sultan of Pate and supply the cause for conflict, hinting at a (later?) Swahili narrative re-layering of the story. References to (ambivalent) relations with the mainland still figure in both the prose account and the *Utenzi wa Liyongo*, however, where even the Oromo 'masters of the bush' fear Liyongo's strength, and tactically marry one of their women to him.[59] Therefore, in the Swahili versions as well as in the Pokomo tradition documented by Fischer, the decision is made to kill him during the *kikowa* feast, after which the copper needle ultimately does the job.[60] Markedly different from the opaque *Utumbuizo wa Kikowa*, the *Utenzi wa*

56　See also Muhammad Kijuma, *Utenzi wa Fumo Liyongo*, ed. by Abdilatif Abdalla (Dar es Salaam: Chuo cha Uchunguzi wa Lugha ya Kiswahili, Chuo Kikuu cha Dar es Salaam, 1973), p. i.

57　Steere, *Tales*, pp. 438–439; Geider, *Oger*, pp. 144ff.

58　Gustav Fischer, 'Das Wapokomo-Land und seine Bewohner', *Mitteilungen der Geographischen Gesellschaft in Hamburg*, 1878–79 (1880), 1–57. See also Ferdinand Würtz, 'Die Liongo-Sage der Ost-Afrikaner. Kleine Mittheilungen', *Zeitschrift für Afrikanische und Ozeanische Sprachen*, 2 (1896), 88–89.

59　Kijuma, *Utenzi*, p. 4 (stanza 45).

60　Fischer, 'Wapokomo', pp. 1–57. See also Würtz, 'Liongo-Sage', pp. 88–89. In the Dahalo tradition, documented by Mauro Tosco, 'Fumo Aliongwe' is also pricked in the navel by his only child, who was sent by 'the Swahili people' who 'did not love Fumo Aliongwe' (Tosco, *Dahalo*, p. 117).

Liyongo, whose style is prescribed to be *wazi* 'clear', carefully explains the strategy to kill Liyongo.[61]

Likisa shauri lao	This was their plan—
Wakenenda kwa kikao	To go to the feast
Mkoma waupatao	On reaching a doum palm,
Hupanda mtu mmoya	[They would ask] one person to climb it.
Na wao maana yao	And they meant that
Siku Liyongo apandao	When Liyongo climbed it,
Wamfume wute hao	They would shoot him,
Zembe kwa wao umoya	All together, with their arrows.

The different sequence of the episodes in the prose account and Kijuma's *utenzi* reflects the variability of the oral tradition; but it also reflects an effort at streamlining the narrative, linking episodes that were once only loosely aligned and weeding out the incoherent and incomprehensible parts of the oral tradition.[62] Unlike the Liyongo *tumbuizo*—even the written versions of which depend so heavily on the audience's background knowledge, drawing on a shared world by means of frequent allusions—both the prose account and the written *utenzi* are self-contained texts. They do not depend on a knowledgeable audience and are not necessarily part of a performance or recitation in which a reciter may mimic certain actions, perform with props, or change his voice based on which character is speaking, and who can also explain allusions or refences.

Moreover, in Steere's prose account only a few lines of the Liyongo songs are added—exactly the opposite of the *tumbuizo* manuscripts, where only the songs are recorded, since the episodes were certainly well known and only poetry was deemed important enough to be written down. The Liyongo prose account is cast as a third-person narrative, echoing Western readerly expectations and inclination towards prose.[63] The prose account is far removed from the oral rendition and is no

---

61   Kijuma, *Utenzi*, p. 5. The two stanzas, 58 and 59, are taken from the same publication. The translation is mine.

62   See Gunner's (*Ecologies*, pp. 116–132) comparison of the thoroughly documented oral versions of the Sunjata epic with narrative translations freed of all variations and obscurity, targeting a Western audience interested in the world's literature.

63   By contrast, Steere (*Tales*, p. v) defines the learner of Swahili as the target reader.

longer even meant for recitation. Bound/confined in/to a book, it travels beyond East Africa; not unlike many other documented oral traditions, it would become part of a print library of the world's folklore.[64]

Fumo Liyongo in Nationalist and Pan-Africanist Worlds

The *Utenzi wa Liyongo* increasingly took on a printed form in the twentieth century. In independent East Africa, Kijuma's poem was first printed, in 1964, in the journal of the East African Swahili Committee, a former colonial body created to standardize the Swahili language and continued by the newly independent socialist national state of Tanzania, eager to craft its own national literary canon.[65] Fumo Liyongo became a national hero, a role model fighting for the 'rights of [people] when they are oppressed' (*akiwatetea haki zao muda wanapodhulumiwa*), as the blurb of the 1973 re-edition styled him in the Marxist rhetoric of liberation—doing away with all ambivalent and diverse perspectives.[66] While Mringwari, Liyongo's rival, became the prototypical villain, residing in the palace, Liyongo turned into a revolutionary siding with the downtrodden and fighting for freedom. Liyongo's world became a national and socialist one.

Neither Schüttpelz nor Werberger, when reflecting on when oral literature was taken out of formal definitions of 'literature' and survived merely as a subcategory (oral literature or folklore), consider the period of European imperial expansion or the rise of the modern notion of literature from the eighteenth century onward a decisive point in time; instead they cite the 1960s, when notions of the 'world' and 'literature' drastically shrank in the West.[67] In the early twentieth century, more literary genres and media, including oral ones, were part of people's lived experience, allowing for a broader perspective on verbal arts in the world. According to Schüttpelz and Werberger, this increased awareness found echo in many more studies of oral literatures, as well as their scholarly discussion.

---

64 On the interrelationship between notions of world literature and the world's literatures and their corresponding book series, see Levine, 'Unwritten'.

65 *Utenzi wa Fumo Liongo—The Epic of King Liongo*, ed. by Jan Knappert (Dar es Salaam: East African Swahili Committee, 1964).

66 Kijuma, *Utenzi*.

67 Schüttpelz, 'World Literature', p. 150; Werberger, 'Folklore', p. 323.

In independent East Africa, too, the nation's search for a modern literature institutionalized by universities and schools reduced the scope of literature's *modi existendi*, while various forms of verbal art continued to flourish just outside the institutions' doors. In the modern context—first of the colonial state and later of the nation—school, print, and prose became an inseparable triad. School education relied predominantly on written/printed literature, reinforcing the dominance of the novel and modern poetry, and conceptually separated this literature from oral traditions of communal dance, poetic exchange, and recited poetry, as well as the rhetorical education of the Qurʾanic schools and *chama cha ngoma* (dance societies). Literature became an academic subject in its own right, separate from historiography, religion, or philosophy, which were (and continue to be) largely the domain of recited discourse embedded in communal practices unrecognized by state institutions. In Dar es Salaam, the Swahili term *fasihi* 'literature' was coined—on the analogy of 'English literature'—at the university in the 1960s, in the context of independence and the search for a new literature that would lend its imagination to the modern state's discourse of progress. The creation of the notion of modern Swahili literature, with reference to Marxist notions of realism such as *kioo cha jamii* (mirror of society), entailed the emergence of another category, namely *fasihi simulizi* or *fasihi ya asili*, oral literature or traditional literature. A line was drawn between the two, and oral literature (*fasihi simulizi*) began to exist merely as a subcategory. The nation's fundamental modern myth of a new beginning ascribed large parts of the oral tradition to the nation's past on the basis of a unilineal account of literary history.

As part of the construction of a Swahili national literary canon in both Kenya and Tanzania, the *Utenzi wa Liyongo* was reprinted in the 1970s, and East African scholars like Joseph Mbele, Ibrahim Noor Shariff, and Mugyabuso Mulokozi increasingly researched various Liyongo narrative traditions in the 1980s and 1990s—also in response to the broader interest in orality, now a subject in its own right.[68] Again, the

---

68   See, for instance, Joseph Mbele, 'The Identity of the Hero in the Liongo Epic',
      Research in African Literatures, 17 (1986), 464–472; Mugyabuso Mulokozi, *Tenzi Tatu
      Za Kale* (Dar Es Salaam: Taasisi Ya Uchunguzi Wa Kiswahili, 1999); and Ibrahim
      Noor Shariff, 'The Liyongo Conundrum: Re-Examining the Historicity of Swahili's
      National Poet-Hero', *Research in African Literatures*, 22 (1991), 153–167.

academic focus was on the *utenzi* and narrative traditions, rather than the older poetic songs of the *tumbuizo*. On the creative side, adaptations of the Liyongo story as a children's book appeared, and the story was staged time and again in school classrooms.[69] The latter phenomenon hints at the fact that oral recitation did not disappear, but morphed into new forms. The consecration of the Liyongo story in the sacred halls of national literature is not the endpoint of its literary history: oral literature is robust, not in the sense that it remains unaltered, but in the sense that, due to its remarkable adaptability, it does not simply die out.[70] The Liyongo story has proven chameleonic, and its persistence is grounded in its disrespect for any boundary-drawing: 'The popular is opportunistic, hybrid or syncretic in its unashamed, "unlearned" borrowings from the past and present, as it shows its lack of reverence or respect for any demarcation between oral and written, tradition and modernity, or Africa and the West'.[71]

Nowadays, Fumo Liyongo is far more present on stage and in YouTube videos than in written print adaptations. The Liyongo story has been staged in the context of literary and cultural festivals, which increasingly intersect with the digital realm of the internet. For instance, in the context of the Somali Heritage Week at the Awjama Omar Cultural Research and Reading Centre in Nairobi in 2017, the Liyongo tale was sung in English and Swahili in a newly created, hybridized oral style of storytelling, with a male and a female narrator singing and drumming, a recording of which circulated more widely on YouTube.[72] The 'African' bilingual performance, involving drumming (previously not part of the Liyongo narratives), targeted both an urban Nairobi audience as well as a global public with a preference for storytelling, also reinvigorating the link between 'Africanness' and orality. In these new forms, digital and performative iterations of African oral traditions have been achieving a global reach, partly even overshadowing the novel. Storytelling has become an auratic term, and not only for 'Afropolitan' audiences. It reemphasizes performance and orality, which

---

69 An example of the children's book is Bitugi Matundura, *Mkasa wa Shujaa Liyongo* (Nairobi: Phoenix, 2001).

70 See also Michael Chapman, '"Oral" in Literary History: The Case of Southern African Literatures' in *Or Words to That Effect*, pp. 149–161.

71 Chapman, p. 151.

72 See e.g. *'Fumo Liyongo'* (Awjama cultural center, 2018).

blend into digital representation. The same is true of the global and East African phenomenon of spoken word events, which have gained much prominence in imagining African worlds in the past two decades.

The digital medium adds to the changing ecology of the Liyongo story, which has become part of an all-African literary heritage, particularly for an African diaspora increasingly in search of its African roots. The animated YouTube film 'Prince Liongo: Tragedy of an Illegitimate Son' in the *Home Team History* series—which aims to teach African history to the African diaspora with the slogan 'Know thyself, remember your ancestors'—renders the Liyongo narrative part of an African archive, countering its absence from Western-dominated historiography. Here, Liyongo figures in a series meant to create a grand narrative of African history, from the Mali Empire and the Fulfulde jihad in West Africa to Shaka the Zulu in South Africa. The video starts with an 'African' soundtrack of warrior dances before the storyteller, speaking in sonorous American English, narrates the animated sequence, complete with sound effects. Though the story lacks the *kikowa* episode and Liyongo's imprisonment, the major conflict of the Swahili narrative— that of Liyongo and his half-brother Mringwari, with Liyongo ultimately murdered with a copper needle—is largely preserved.[73]

Fig. 1.2 The dead Fumo Liyongo leaning against the well, so that the women are afraid to fetch water. Video still from 'Prince Liongo: Tragedy of an Illegitimate Son'.

---

73 'Prince Liongo: Tragedy of an Illegitimate Son', *Home Team History*.

In an even more complex interplay of writtenness, staged orality, and newly created visuals, the Dutch project 'Ubuntopia' produced a Dutch-language children's graphic novel (also available in English) under the title *Fumo Liyongo en de Dans van de Drums*, written by Leontine van Hooft and richly illustrated by the Rwandan illustrator Jean-Clauda Ngumire; this was also presented in the form of live storytelling sessions and recorded for YouTube.[74] 'Written for children with a connection to Africa' (*geschreven voor kinderen met een connectie met Africa*), the graphic novel aims at 'preserving very old [oral] legends and tales to prevent African wisdoms from disappearing' (*om échte oude [orale] legends en verhalen te conserveren, om te voorkomen dat de Afrikaanse wijsheden*).

Fig. 1.3 Liyongo arriving at the palace in Pate after walking a distance that would normally take four days in only one day. Page from Leontine van Hooft and Jean-Claude Ngumire, *Fumo Liyongo en de Dans van de Drums verdwijnen*.[75]

---

74   The Liyongo story is part of Leontine van Hooft and Jean-Claude Ngumire, *Balla and the Forest of Legends: The Chronicles of Ubuntopia, Part 1* (GreenDreamWorks, 2019).

75   Quoted from the website https://ubuntopia.world. My translation.

Ubuntopia invents an entire 'African' world: the frame narrative of the comic portrays the Liyongo story—as well as the South African adaptation *Queen Numbi and the White Lions*, which is also part of the book—as an orally transmitted tale, narrated by the griot Balla to Aimée, a young girl of colour. The mystical Balla, summoned by the 'Sages of the World' to retell the stories, is the keeper of the African heritage. While the Liyongo story is explicitly situated in East Africa, the frame narrative creates a syncretic world, with dialogues using Swahili greetings as well as *'funga alafia'* (a welcome phrase loosely attributed to West Africa that has circulated widely in world music), Ghanaian Anansi stories, and Balla playing the Mande kora, a figure borrowed from West African griot iconographies. The graphic novel translates the Liyongo narrative, largely in line with the prose account, into a sequence of panels, through which the author Leontine van Hooft guides her audience, also by showing these visuals in the live storytelling sessions. 'African' orality, evoked both in the narrative and through its mediatized performances, blends Belgian comic traditions and middle-class Dutch practices of *voorlezen* (reading out loud)—in the video, Leontine van Hooft is sitting in an armchair, telling the story—in speaking of and to the transcultural audience.

Fig. 1.4 Leontine von Hooft reading from *Fumo Liyongo en de Dans van de Drums* during Children's Book Week in 2020. Video still from https://www.youtube. com/watch?v=7rdrOmDpXVc&t=8s

Interestingly, what resurfaces in each of these examples is not just orality, but the Liyongo figure and tale, which is not simply replaced by a modern, written canon of literature but rather continues to thrive. This brings us back to the notion of non-teleological poetic history that I referred to at the beginning of this chapter. As Alexander Veselovsky found in his lecture 'From the Introduction to Historical Poetics' (1894), 'old images, echoes of images, suddenly appear when a popular-poetic demand has arisen, in response to an urgent call of the times. In this way popular legends recur; in this way, in literature, we explain the renewal of some plots, whereas others are apparently forgotten'.[76] Adapting his psychological view of literary history to the Liyongo tale, we find the discovery of 'old images', figures, and plots particularly in African diasporic contexts in Europe and the USA that, implicated as they are in the logic of the market, are in urgent 'popular-poetic' need of alternative tales about their own identities. The digital mode creates synergies with this process, since it offers the possibility to circumvent the restrictive regime of publishing houses and written canons and to address wider audiences, and it fosters newly mediatised oralities, proudly marking Africanness.

The reappearance of Liyongo in newly adapted forms of orality, then, speaks to Maslov's emphatic argument, drawing on Veselovsky, that literary history is characterized more by transmutation than by sheer continuity.[77] It is a perspective that also emphasises multiple timelines and the diversity of literary history: there is not one single line of development and progress, contrary to the teleological idea that oral literature gives way to the novel. While Maslov's perspective allows for ruptures and forms of forgetting, it also underlines the persistence of literary form, which can be re-explored even after years, decades, or centuries of silence or oblivion. On the one hand, there is the psychological and 'poetic' impetus underlined by Veselovsky, i.e. a universal human need for images and narratives ('legends'); and, on

---

76 Quoted in Ilya Kliger and Boris Maslov, 'Introducing Historical Poetics: History, Experience, Form' in *Persistent Forms: Explorations in Historical Poetics*, ed. by Ilya Kliger and Boris Maslov (New York: Fordham University Press, 2016), pp. 1–36 (p. 5).

77 Maslov, 'Universality', pp. 133-148.

the other hand, changing 'calls of the time' nourish the need to find new imaginaries or to re-explore older ones.

If, in the contemporary contexts of the African diaspora, the search for identity has resulted in the rediscovery and adaptation of many oral traditions, it is the aesthetic nature of images, figures, and plots, I wish to add, which plays a decisive role in fostering the imagination and allowing reinterpretation. Here I refer to aesthetics in its etymological sense of 'sensual perception': because Liyongo is a concrete figure placed so powerfully before our eyes, he has survived in people's memory and nourished their imagination. As his manifold reinterpretations, from tyrant to freedom fighter, show, the captivating figure of Liyongo cannot be reduced to one meaning, nor can his palpable figure be reduced to a single logical argument or idea. Instead, Liyongo has recurrently emerged as a novel 'revelation', as Veselovsky puts it, with the power not only to comment on our current world, but also to imagine new worlds:[78] the 'utopia' in Ubuntopia refers precisely to this.

Conclusions

My account questions the teleological view of Western literary and written influence as an all-pervasive force that rendered hitherto inert forms of oral literature increasingly obsolete. There was no fundamental, earthquake-like shift brought about by Western modernity, which did away with anything pre-existing. Rather, fundamental shifts happen all the time, as my focus on mediatized orality, i.e. orality adapted to new media, from writing to the digital realm, suggests. Even writing does not simply replace orality, since on the Swahili coast writing has coexisted with orality for a long time, as the cases of the Liyongo *tumbuizo* and the *utenzi* also show: both were recited but also written in Arabic script long before they made their way into Roman script and into new renditions. Thus, it is rather the relationship *between* writing (in different scripts) *and* orality and their institutions which changes over time. Western endeavours to collect and print Swahili oral traditions for a global library interacted dialectically with the manuscript production of the widely connected Muslim brotherhoods. Both print and manuscript

---

78   In Kliger and Maslov, 'Historical Poetics', p. 5.

poetry threatened some oral genres (like the *tumbuizo*) and played a decisive role in preserving them. While the Liyongo tale is still part of local oral traditions in northern Kenya, it has also transcended written and printed representation and found new forms in the digital sphere. This process hints at the fundamental dynamism of literary forms, the fuzziness and amorphousness of texts and genres, and further questions (constructed) dichotomies of orality and literacy. The so-called Liyongo epic is not one, neatly defined text: Liyongo stories and songs have always been shaped by multiple and often interplaying influences from different directions.

Even the worlds of which the Liyongo narrative is part and which it constructs are fuzzy and dynamic. The world of Liyongo does not simply grow bigger or more complex over time, from a locally confined dance tradition to the digital sphere. The Liyongo *tumbuizo* evoke far-reaching Indian Ocean connections as well as the overlapping, multi-ethnic context of the Tana delta, where Liyongo stories have been shared across linguistic and cultural boundaries. Some aspects of this multi-ethnic space, with its multiple perspectives, partly recur in the *utenzi* and prose accounts as well as in contemporary versions told by elders on Lamu; but these elements are increasingly lost in later print and digital adaptations, which streamline the various literary *modi existendi* into a single, coherent, written narrative. The nineteenth-century coexistence of manuscript poetry, printed collections, and dance and narrative traditions in several languages, located and circulating in different worlds, is in fact more (or at least as) diverse in terms of literary form and circulation than the present-day spectrum that ranges from printed texts to comic books, digitized performances, and animated films. All of this reminds us of the complexity of literary configurations, a complexity that is not particular to African contexts but to all verbal art, once we move away from the 'narrow church' of defining a literary work by its author and by the printed pages between book covers, or from defining literary history as moving in only one direction, as has too often been done in the context of world literature.

Bibliography

Barber, Karin, 'African-language Literature and Postcolonial Criticism', *Research in African Literatures*, 26.4 (1995), 3–28.

Beecroft, Alexander, *An Ecology of World Literature: From Antiquity to the Present Day* (New York: Verso, 2015).

Chamberlain, Daniel, 'Histories of Literature and the Question of Comparative Oral Literary History' in *Or Words to That Effect: Orality and the Writing of Literary History*, ed. by Daniel Chamberlain and J. Edward Chamberlin (Amsterdam/Philadelphia: John Benjamins, 2016), pp. 33–46.

Chamberlin, J. Edward, 'Preliminaries' in *Or Words to That Effect: Orality and the Writing of Literary History*, ed. by Daniel Chamberlain and J. Edward Chamberlin (Amsterdam/Philadelphia: John Benjamins, 2016), pp. 3–32.

Chapman, Michael, '"Oral" in Literary History: The Case of Southern African Literatures' in *Or Words to That Effect: Orality and the Writing of Literary History*, ed. by Daniel Chamberlain and J. Edward Chamberlin (Amsterdam/Philadelphia: John Benjamins, 2016), pp. 149–161.

Chum, Haji, *Utenzi wa Vita vya Uhud*, ed. by H. E. Lambert (Nairobi: East African Literature Bureau, 1962).

Finnegan, Ruth, *Oral Literature in Africa* (London: Clarendon, 1970).

'*Fumo Liyongo*', Awjama cultural center (2018), https://www.youtube.com/watch?v=2anOMFLs4-M&t=231s

Fischer, Gustav, 'Das Wapokomo-Land und seine Bewohner', *Mitteilungen der Geographischen Gesellschaft in Hamburg*, 1878/79 (1880), 1–57.

Geider, Thomas, *Die Figur des Oger in der traditionellen Literatur und Lebenswelt der Pokomo in Ost-Kenya* (Cologne: Köppe, 1990).

——, 'Weltliteratur in der Perspektive einer Longue Durée II: Die Ökumene des swahilisprachigen Ostafrika' in *Wider den Kulturenzwang: Migration, Kulturalisierung und Weltliteratur*, ed. by Özkan Ezli, Dorothee Kimmich, and Annette Werberger (Bielefeld: transcript, 2009), pp. 361–401.

Gunner, Liz, 'Ecologies of Orality' in *The Cambridge Companion to World Literature*, ed. by Ben Etherington and Jarad Zimbler (Cambridge: Cambridge University Press, 2018), pp. 116–132.

Harries, Lyndon, 'A Swahili Takhmis from the Swahili Arabic Text', *African Studies*, 11.2 (1952), 59–67.

——, *Swahili Poetry* (Oxford: Clarendon, 1962).

Horton, Mark and John Middleton, *The Swahili: The Social Landscape of a Mercantile Society* (Oxford: Blackwell, 2000).

Kijuma, Muhammad, *Utenzi wa Fumo Liyongo*, ed. by Abdilatif Abdalla (Dar es Salaam: Chuo cha Uchunguzi wa Lugha ya Kiswahili, Chuo Kikuu cha Dar es Salaam, 1973).

Klein-Arendt, Reinhard, 'Liongo Fumo: Eine ostafrikanische Sagengestalt aus der Sicht der Swahili und Pokomo', *Afrikanistische Arbeitspapiere*, 8 (1986), 57–86.

Kliger, Ilya and Boris Maslov, 'Introducing Historical Poetics: History, Experience, Form' in *Persistent Forms: Explorations in Historical Poetics*, ed. by Ilya Kliger and Boris Maslov (New York: Fordham University Press, 2016), pp. 1–36.

Knappert, Jan, ed., *Utenzi wa Fumo Liongo – The Epic of King Liongo* (Dar es Salaam: East African Swahili Committee, 1964).

——, 'Liongo's Wedding in the Gungu Meter', *Annales Aequatoria*, 12 (1991), 213–226.

Lamping, Dieter, 'Was ist Weltliteratur? Ein Begriff und seine Bedeutungen' in *Perspektiven der Interkulturalität: Forschungsfelder eines umstrittenen Begriffs*, ed. by Anton Escher and Heike Spickermann (Heidelberg: Winter, 2018), pp. 127–141.

Levine, Caroline, 'The Great Unwritten: World Literature and the Effacement of Orality', *Modern Language Quarterly*, 74.2 (2013), 218–237.

Maslow, Boris, 'Lyric Universality' in *The Cambridge Companion to World Literature*, ed. by Ben Etherington and Jarad Zimbler (Cambridge: Cambridge University Press, 2018), pp. 133–148.

Mbele, Joseph, 'The Identity of the Hero in the Liongo Epic', *Research in African Literatures*, 17 (1986), 464–472.

Meinhof, Carl, 'Das Lied des Liongo', *Zeitschrift für Eingeborenen-Sprachen*, 15 (1924–25), 241–265.

Miehe, Gudrun, 'Preserving Classical Swahili Poetic Traditions: A Concise History of Research up to the First Half of the 20th Century' in *Muhamadi Kijuma: Texts From the Dammann Papers and Other Collections*, ed. Gudrun Miehe and Clarissa Vierke (Cologne: Köppe, 2010), pp. 18–39.

Miehe, Gudrun and Clarissa Vierke, eds, *Muhamadi Kijuma: Texts from the Dammann Papers and Other Collections* (Cologne: Köppe, 2010).

Miehe, Gudrun et al., eds, *Liyongo Songs: Poems Attributed to Fumo Liyongo* (Cologne: Köppe, 2004).

Mulokozi, Mugyabuso, *Tenzi Tatu Za Kale* (Dar Es Salaam: Taasisi Ya Uchunguzi Wa Kiswahili, 1999).

Pouwels, Randall, 'Eastern Africa and the Indian Ocean to 1800: Reviewing Relations in Historical Perspective', *The International Journal of African Historical Studies*, 35.2–3 (2002), 385–425.

'Prince Liongo: Tragedy of an Illegitimate Son', *Home Team History*, https://
www.youtube.com/watch?v=q3ll-IofyEU&t=33s

Sacleux, Charles, *Dictionnaire swahili-français* (Paris: Institut d'Ethnologie,
1939).

Schüttpelz, Erhard, 'Weltliteratur in der Perspektive einer Longue Durée I:
Die fünf Zeitschichten der Globalisierung' in *Wider den Kulturenzwang:
Migration, Kulturalisierung und Weltliteratur*, ed. by Özkan Ezli, Dorothee
Kimmich, and Annette Werberger (Bielefeld: transcript, 2009), pp. 339–360.

——, 'World Literature from the Perspective of Longue Durée' in *Figuren des
Globalen: Weltbezug und Welterzeugung in Literatur, Kunst und Medien*, ed. by
Christian Moser and Linda Simonis (Göttingen: V&R unipress, 2014), pp.
141–156.

Shariff, Ibrahim Noor, 'The Liyongo Conundrum: Re-Examining the Historicity
of Swahili's National Poet-Hero', *Research in African Literatures*, 22 (1991),
153–167.

Steere, Edward, *Swahili Tales as Told by Natives of Zanzibar* (London: Society for
Promoting Christian Knowledge, 1870).

Tihanov, Galin, 'Introduction' in *Vergleichende Weltliteraturen/Comparative World
Literatures*, ed. by Dieter Lamping and Galin Tihanov (Stuttgart: Metzler,
2019), pp. 283–287.

Tosco, Mauro, *A Grammatical Sketch of Dahalo: Including Texts and a Glossary*
(Hamburg: Buske, 1991).

van Hooft, Leontine, and Jean-Claude Ngumire, *Balla and the Forest of Legends:
The Chronicles of Ubuntopia, Part 1* (GreenDreamWorks, 2019), https://
www.youtube.com/watch?v=7rdrOmDpXVc&t=8s

Vernet, Thomas, 'East African Travelers and Traders in the Indian Ocean:
Swahili Ships, Swahili Mobilities ca. 1500–1800' in *Trade, Circulation, and
Flow in the Indian Ocean World*, ed. by Michael Pearson (New York: Palgrave
Macmillan, 2015), pp. 167–202.

Vierke, Clarissa, 'Other Worlds: The "Prophet's Ascension" as World Literature
and Its Adaptation in Swahili-speaking East Africa' in *Vergleichende
Weltliteraturen/Comparative World Literatures*, ed. by Dieter Lamping and
Galin Tihanov (Stuttgart: Metzler, 2019), pp. 215–229.

——, 'Poetic Links across the Ocean: On Poetic "Translation" as Mimetic Practice
at the Swahili Coast', *Comparative Studies of South Asia, Africa and the Middle
East*, 37.2 (2017), 321–335.

Werberger, Annette, 'Weltliteratur und Folklore' in *Vergleichende Weltliteraturen/
Comparative World Literatures*, ed. by Dieter Lamping and Galin Tihanov
(Stuttgart: Metzler, 2019), pp. 323–341.

Werner, Alice, 'A Traditional Poem Attributed to Liongo Fumo' in *Festschrift
Meinhof* (Hamburg: Friederichsen & Co, 1927), pp. 45–54.

——, 'Some Notes on East African Folklore', *Folklore*, 25.4 (1914), 457–475.

——, 'The Swahili Saga of Liongo Fumo', *Bulletin of the School of Oriental Studies*, 4 (1926/28), 247–255.

Würtz, Ferdinand, 'Die Liongo-Sage der Ost-Afrikaner. Kleine Mittheilungen', *Zeitschrift für Afrikanische und Ozeanische Sprachen*, 2 (1896), 88–89.

2. Ecopoetic and Ecolinguistic Approaches to 'Broken Places'

Orature of Displacement Around the Ethiopian Capital

Assefa Tefera Dibaba and Adugna Barkessa Dinsa

Introduction

This chapter explores the relationship between Oromo oral literature and the environment through the lens of the emerging disciplines of ecopoetics and ecolinguistics, problematizing those cases in which the relationship becomes 'broken' due to forced displacement. We want to approach Oromo oral traditions through historically and geographically sensitive categories, focusing on what is important for the poets themselves, as opposed to forcing Western literary categories onto the Oromo literary tradition.[1] The discipline of world literature has often assumed the universal applicability of Eurocentric critical categories to non-Western literary traditions. Here, we want to argue against this top-down perspective and propose a bottom-up framework that foregrounds the geographies, themes, and conceptions of literature that

---

1   Assefa Dibaba, 'Oromo Orature: An Ecopoetic Approach, Theory and Practice' (Oromia/Ethiopia, Northeast Africa), *Humanities* (2020), 9–28 (p. 27), https://doi.org/10.3390/h9020028

        https://doi.org/10.11647/OBP.0405.02

are significant for local Oromo poets. This does not imply a disavowal of the discipline of world literature, but a different perspective on it.

As we are writing this chapter in 2020, Development-Induced Displacement (hereafter DID) is intensifying in Ethiopia, profoundly impacting people's lives and the environment in which they live. It has disrupted the people's ecology, including their literary ecology, separating them from the places they call 'home' and eroding their sense of attachment to their local environments. Everywhere around the world, the trend appears to be the same: indigenous people are being evicted from their land in the name of industrialisation, urbanisation, and 'development'. We are interested in oral traditions as a way in which people make sense of the environment around them, and how this meaning-making changes when the link between people and their 'significant geographies' is broken. Thus, one goal of the present study is to contribute to the ongoing environmentalist discourse about the exploitation and destruction of natural landscapes, which is of global concern. Indeed, our analysis of the oral traditions that emerged as a result of forced displacement has a comparative resonance, as it connects Oromo verbal creativity to the verbal creativity of other indigenous people facing evictions and land loss.

Throughout the twentieth century and up to the present, literary studies in Ethiopia have tended to privilege the analysis of written literature in Amharic and, less prominently, Tigrinya. Oral traditions, particularly those of the many other Ethiopian languages, have been severely neglected and themselves 'displaced' and 'evicted' from academic discourse and cultural institutions. In our research areas, Koyyee Faccee and Boolee Arraabsaa, located around the Ethiopian capital, the victims of DID have been forced to live in 'broken places', where their voices and their 'broken narratives' have been, for the most part, marginalised and left unheard. The people we interviewed during our fieldwork have suffered an immensurable human and environmental catastrophe over the years. The chapter centres their songs, narratives and the verbal creativity with which they have made sense of their displacement and resisted state hegemony.

Development-Induced Displacement in Ethiopia

As reported by the Internal Displacement Monitoring Center (IDMC), internal displacement can be caused by, among other factors, natural disasters (droughts, floods, earthquakes, landslides, wildfires), military conflicts, and other forms of violence. Whether caused by natural or man-made disasters, the scale and pace of displacements is increasing over time. According to a United Nation High Commissioner for Refugees (UNHCR) 2015 report, the number of displaced people in 2007 all over the world was 42.7 million. In 2016, almost a decade later, this figure increased to 65.6 million. After only a year, in 2017, the number of displaced people in the word reached 68.5 million. Countries highly affected by internal displacement include Syria (4.9 million), Afghanistan (2.7 million), South Sudan (2.4 million), Myanmar (1.2 million), and Somalia (1.1 million).[2]

A major cause of DID is land eviction ordered by state authorities or local institutions in the name of urbanisation, industrialisation, and resource exploitation. One case in point is the Ogoni people, evicted from the River State in Nigeria and still not benefiting from oil revenues 20 years after the Ogoni environmental campaigner Ken Saro-Wiwa was executed for his political activism.[3] Until early 2018, Ethiopia was mentioned as one of the countries *hosting* displaced people. For example, in 2017 Ethiopia was hosting 14,000 Somali refugees.[4] This is only half of the story, however. In the last few years, Ethiopian state authorities have been directly responsible for the displacement of Ethiopia's own citizens, not only in the name of development, but also as a punitive measure against the protest movements against the government that erupted in the country from 2014.[5] Of the many forms of DID

---

2 UNHCR, 'Global Trends on Forced Displacement' (2018), UNHCR Global Trends - Forced Displacement in 2017.

3 Ken Saro-Wiwa fought the Shell Oil Company and the state for turning what was once a thriving ecosystem into a desolate black moonscape with gas flares, air and water pollution, and oil spills; see Joya Uraizee, 'Combating Ecological Terror: Ken Saro-Wiwa's "Genocide in Nigeria"', *JMMLA*, 44.2 (2011), 75–91.

4 UNHCR, 'Global Trends on Forced Displacement'.

5 In the first half of 2010, for example, the number of people forced to flee their homes in Ethiopia due to systemic violence reached 1.4 million, recorded as the highest in the world; see 'Internal Displacement: Global Overview of Trends and Developments in 2010' (2011). According to Tesfa, 'DID affects the overall living condition of the displaced households, particularly the low-income and vulnerable

happening in Ethiopia at the moment, this chapter focuses specifically on the displacement caused by urban expansion or urban restructuring projects. According to Stanley, more than half of the internally displaced people in the world in 2004 suffered from urban redevelopment projects.[6] Over the past decade, dwellers residing around, or at the edge of, Ethiopian cities have been profoundly affected by DID, resulting in the loss of houses, lack of access to roads and electricity, and lack of job opportunities for the displaced population.[7]

The Oromo people attach a special significance to Addis Ababa, traditionally known as Finfinne, meaning 'fountain', 'sacred well', or 'hot spring' in Oromo due to the presence of thermal waters. Finfinne was renamed 'Addis Ababa' ('new flower' in Amharic) in 1887 during the reign of emperor Menelik II, who chose it as his new capital precisely because his wife Taytu and his entourage liked taking mineral baths in the hot springs. Our two research areas, Koyyee Faccee and Boolee Arraabsaa, are to the immediate south of the Ethiopian capital. The people living here still retain a memory of the old Finfinne that predated Menelik's settlement in the area. According to the local tradition and historical records, before 1887 Finfinne was mostly inhabited by the Oromo clans of Gullalle, Ekka, Galan, and Abbichu. It was partitioned into twelve districts, each administered by a local clan chief.[8] Under the rule of Ras Tafari (1916-1930), later crowned emperor Haile Selassie (1930-1974), Oromo names for towns, cities, mountains, and features of the natural environment were replaced by Amharic names as part of an imperial project of 'nation building' under 'one language,' 'one culture,' and 'one religion'. This process of renaming obscured the earlier history

---

groups in Ethiopia'; Tesfa Teferi GebreEgziabher, 'The Effects of Development-Induced Displacement on Relocated Households: The Case of Addis Ababa' (MA Thesis, The Hague, International Institute of Social Studies, 2014), p. ix.

6   Jason Stanley, 'Development-induced Displacement and Resettlement', *Forced Migration Online Research Guide*, Refugee Studies Centre, University of Oxford (2004)

7   Tesfa ('The Effects of Development-Induced Displacement') and Ambaye Getu and Assefa Abeliene ('Development-Induced Displacement and Its Impacts on the Livelihoods of Poor Urban Households in Bahir Dar, North Western Ethiopia', *AHMR*, 1.3 (2017), 310–313) have studied in particular the DID around the city of Bahir Dar.

8   See Svein Ege, *Class, State, and Power in Africa: A Case Study of the Kingdom of Shawa (Ethiopia) about 1840* (Wiesbaden: Harrassowitz Verlag, 1996).

of local people, alienating them at a linguistic level from the places that informed their past and their sense of identity.

When it comes to the Ethiopian capital, the older loss of Finfinne to Addis Ababa has recently been compounded by new forms of displacement. The Ethiopian government is undertaking a large-scale policy of evictions around the city, ostensibly to pursue construction projects in response to the increasing rates of urbanisation. This policy, under the name of 'Addis Ababa Integrated Master Plan', was designed and imposed from above, without involving local residents in the decision-making process. In Koyyee Faccee and Boolee Arraabsaa, most of the local residents targeted by the evictions identify as part of the Tulama branch of the Oromo people. Their main sources of livelihood have traditionally been agricultural produce and livestock. Their cattle and pack-animals like horses, mules, and donkeys benefited from vast grazing lands in the area. The land is fertile and well-suited for agriculture, and local people grew wheat, barley, *teff* (a cereal indigenous to the Ethiopian highlands), and vegetables like tomatoes and onions. Not only have the people traditionally living in Koyee Faccee and Boolee Arraabsaa been forced to leave their land and former homes, but the two districts have also seen an influx of refugees from the inner city of Addis Ababa, who were themselves forcefully relocated to condominiums built on the land evicted from farmers. As a result, not only were the old inhabitants of these areas forced to leave their lands, but the new inhabitants are also refugees who had themselves been evicted from their former inner-city neighbourhoods.[9]

According to available data, the Oromo constitute the most numerous ethnic group in Northeast Africa. They speak a Cushitic language called Afaan Oromoo (rendered in English as 'Afan Oromo' or simply as 'Oromo'), which is the fourth most widely spoken language in Africa after Arabic, Swahili, and Hausa.[10] During most of the twentieth century, the Oromo were split across different administrative zones; but following the post-1991 restructuring of the Ethiopian state along

---

9 Tesfa, 'The Effects of Development-Induced Displacement'; and Zwedie Berhanu, 'Impact of Urban Redevelopment on the Livelihoods of Displaced People in Addis Ababa: The case of Casanchis Local Development Plan' (MA thesis, Addis Ababa University, 2006).

10 Abdulaziz Lodhi, 'The Language Situation in Africa Today', *Nordic Journal of African Studies*, 2.1 (1993), 79–86 (pp. 79, 84).

ethno-federalist lines, a new regional state called Oromia was carved in the south of the country, and although there are still Oromo living in other administrative regions, with the creation of Oromia the Oromo have gained a more representative political home. Although figures are contested, some sources (albeit dated) suggest that the Oromo population makes up nearly half of the total population of Ethiopia, while other sources claim that Oromia is the largest Ethiopian region by population and area.[11]

Literary Ecologies in the Context of Development-Induced Displacement

The current wave of displacement has both reactivated the memories of the old nineteenth-century dispossession, as well as generating a new oral literature of sorrow and resistance.[12] The clash between farmers and central governments has always been accompanied by a clash of narratives. The government narrative of development promised to integrate the city with the surrounding areas, offering new homes and making clean water, electricity, health, and educational institutions more accessible to the inhabitants. The local narratives (one may call them 'survival narratives') blame the Master Plan for its top-down nature and for the lack of a proper consultation process, for the destruction of farming and of the natural environment in the area, and for violently severing people's link with the place they call home.

Oral literature is central to the deconstruction and reconstruction of identities, and shape people's attachment to the natural and built environments. Ecopoetics and ecolinguistics use the term 'literary ecology' to describe how people's sense of environment, or the sense of place, is conveyed through verbal creativity. Literary ecologies have both a mental and a social component. The mental component refers

---

11   Paul Baxter, 'Boran Age-Sets and Generation-Sets: Gada, a puzzle or a maze?' in
      Age, Generation and Time: Some features of East African Age Organisations, ed. by Paul
      T.W. Baxter and Uri Almagor (London: C. Hurst, 1978), pp. 151–182.

12   Assefa Tefera Dibaba, 'Oromo Social Resentment: Re-envisioning Resentment
      Theory, an African Perspective', *Journal of Pan-African Studies*, 11.7 (2018), 96–122
      (p. 96); Aberra Degefa, 'Addis Ababa Master Development Plan: A Program for
      Development or for Ethnic Cleansing?', *RUDN Journal of Sociology*, 19.1 (2019),
      31–39; and Alemayehu Kumsa, 'The Oromo National Memories', *RUDN Journal of
      Sociology*, 19.3 (2019), 503–516.

to beliefs, values, and worldviews, whereas the social components refer to everyday verbal and non-verbal actions and interactions. How people behave towards each other as humans and how they treat their environment depend on the systems of meanings in which they partake. Ecolinguistics brings both linguistic and ecological perspectives to bear on the analysis of these literary ecologies.[13] Much of its enquiry traces how literary ecologies arise and how they change and are changed by language.

Changes in landscapes trigger changes in the people's ecological identity through a process of renegotiating new spatial symbols and meanings. This means that environmental change forces people to modify the stories by which they live. As Stibbe puts it, 'stories about socio-economic situations, ecological progress, environmental degradation, urbanization, etc. have profound impact on how people treat each other and their environments that life depends on'.[14] At the same time, people often use narratives to challenge and resist the stories that have been externally ascribed to them.[15]

In the case of the Addis Ababa Master Plan, the displacement and evictions can be understood through the clashing of narrative ecologies of displaced people on the one side and of the displacing agents on the other. The narrative agency of the local people in shaping the narrative around the Master Plan is a fundamental point, as it shows that local people are not only passive victims of the evictions, but active agents in contesting them, including through literature. The implementation of the Master Plan was in fact one of the elements that triggered a wave of protests throughout the Oromia region beginning in 2014, and this chapter shows how the protests mobilised older oral literary traditions and created new ones. This heated political moment, in other words, coincided with the deployment of a formidable oral literary apparatus, through which people were mobilised and collective grievances expressed. In this sense, top-down development narratives and bottom-up local narratives have created for the same location contested ecological identities—another key notion in both ecopoetics and ecolinguistics.

---

13   Arran Stibbe, *Ecolinguistics: Language, Ecology and the Stories We Live by* (London: Rutledge, 2021); and Ruby Rong Wei, 'Ecolinguistics: Language, Ecology and the Stories We Live', *Southern African Linguistics and Applied Language Studies*, 36.2 (2018), 161–163.

14   Stibbe, *Ecolinguistics*, p. 2.

15   Wei, 'Ecolinguistics'.

Ecological Identities: People, Place, and Meaning-making

Ecological identity consists of 'the feelings, experience, and the knowledge that people have developed over years about their physical and social environments'.[16] The feelings we develop on the basis of our local values, beliefs, experiences and expectations determine who we are in relation to where we live.[17] Ecological identities map the ways in which people identify with their surrounding environment and the way in which that environment impacts processes of in-group socialisation, people's social networks, and their relationship with their neighbours.[18]

The environment, then, is not merely an inert backdrop to human life, or a passive object of human activities. Rather, it shapes personal and collective belonging, and it is an active component of people's understanding of themselves and their place in the world.[19] In other words, the landscape is part and parcel of people's meaning-making process, and it shapes their thought, ideas, and sense of personal and collective self. In *Wisdom Sits in Place*, Keith Basso argues that 'the meaning of landscapes and acts of speech are personalized manifestations of a shared perspective on the human condition'.[20] How people understand their position vis-à-vis the geography surrounding them also shapes how they cognitively and epistemologically process new events, foreign places, and 'other' people. Basso argues that members of a local community 'involve themselves with their geographical landscape in at least three ways': firstly by simply observing the physical aspects of the landscape, secondly by using the landscape and engaging in different physical activities that modify the landscape, and thirdly by communicating about the landscape and 'formulating descriptions and other representations of it that they share in the course of social

---

16 Andrew J. Weigert, *Self, Interaction, and Natural Environment: Refocusing Our Eyesight* (Albany: SUNY Press, 2018), p. 250.

17 Anna Duszak, 'Us and Others: An Introduction' in *Us and Others: Social identities across language, discourses and cultures*, ed. by Anna Duszak (Amsterdam & Philadelphia: John Benjamins, 2002), pp. 1–28.

18 Manuel Castells, 'The Greening of the Self: The Environmental Movement' in *The Power of Identity*, Vol. II (Blackwell, 2010), pp.168–191.

19 Ülo Valk and Daniel Sävborg, *Storied and Supernatural Places: Studies in spatial and social dimensions of folklore and sagas* (Finnish Literature Society/SKS, 2018).

20 Keith Basso, *Wisdom Sits in Places* (Albuquerque: University of New Mexico Press, 1996), p. 73.

gatherings'.[21] In other words, the socialization and networking systems of a community are part and parcel of the environmental identities constructed through the community's ecological values.

Place is therefore far more than geographical location. Physical landscapes are always linked to, and filtered through, mental and cultural landscapes. Place is the site of memories that attract and inspire people, and attachment to those memories is also attachment to that specific place. Place therefore mediates a people's sense of history. If memories of events are also memories of the places where those events happened, the landscape becomes a historical text, that local people are able to read by learning how certain events are attached to certain locations. Historical memory, in this sense, is geographically constructed, both at a collective and at a personal level. Our biographical experiences are inseparable from the places where we dwelled, and our own sense of self is shaped by the places where our ancestors lived and died. As a consequence, the impossibility of accessing those places also means the impossibility of accessing first-hand the memories attached to those places, generating a sense of historical loss and alienation. This may result in a profound sense of disempowerment.[22] When people lose their environmental knowledge, they may also lose their sense of community, and their ability to collectively come together, cooperate, and mobilise. Detaching individuals and groups from the physical environments to which they have a historical and psychological attachment triggers pain and anger. As Basso puts it, 'when these attachments to places are threatened, we may feel threatened as well. Places, we realise, are as much part of us as we are part of them'.[23]

Once individuals and groups are forcibly separated from their natural and built environments, they are disconnected from their social networks, from their tangible and intangible cultural heritage, from their sources of income and livelihood, and from their religious landscape of holy places.[24] The undermining or loss of ecological identities may also lead to the loss of political and religious systems. Several indigenous

---

21 Ibid.
22 See Rick Altman, *The Theory of Narratives* (New York: Colombia University Press, 2008).
23 Basso, *Wisdom*, pp. xiii–xiv.
24 A. M. McCright and T. Nichols Clark, *Community and Ecology: Dynamics of Place, Sustainability, and Politics* (Bingley: Emerald Group Publishing Ltd, 2006).

customs and institutions depend on a specific geography. The council of elders may need to gather around a holy tree; midwives and diviners may need to use local herbs and fruits; artisans and craftspeople may need to work with local materials; religious leaders may need to perform rituals at local shrines by sacred rivers or mountaintops, and so on. In some cases, especially when the ecological severance has been violently caused by an identifiable process, institution, or group (as opposed for example to a natural disaster), political grievances are likely to arise and new forms of resistance can emerge.

Ecopoetic Theory and Practice: Oral Poetry and Environmental Embeddedness

Ecopoetics can help us take the analysis one step further in the direction of verbal creativity and literary production. If ecolinguistics tends to map the use of specific words, syntaxes, registers, and dialects in the context of literary ecologies, ecopoetics traces the specific aesthetic forms through which literary ecologies are textually expressed. Jan Vansina's fieldwork observation of a Rwandese performer highlights the link between oral literature, poetics and nature—and exemplifies a typical ecopoetic instance of composition of a folk song close to nature. As he put it: 'I have seen a poet on a hilltop in Rwanda mulling over his composition for hours, presumably day after day, until he felt it was perfect'.[25] In this poetic practice, creative inspiration is tied to a particular location (the hilltop) and a particular practice of social isolation, in which the poet withdraws from the community and immerses himself in nature, in order to channel his verbal and imaginative skills.

We witness something very similar for the Tulama Oromo, for whom poetic inspiration is also linked to a specific natural location, which the poet visits in order to reconnect with their source of creative inspiration. During fieldwork in Selale in 2010, for example, one of the authors asked his informants (Mr Gurmu Badhaadha, Mr Taddasa Galate, and Mr Haile Tufo)[26] where their folk songs come from. Their answers pointed to specific locations: Odaa Jilaa in Mogor Valley, Haroo Calanqoo in the

---

25   Jan Vansina, *Oral Tradition as History* (Madison, WI: University of Wisconsin Press, 1985), p. 12.
26   All informants have consented to being named in this publication.

Jama gorges, and Tullu Qaawa near the Ilu and Qacama mountains in Yayya Gullalle. These are sacred places where people go for meditation, to seek divine advice on tragedies such as disease and crop failure, or to ask the ancestral spirits (*faloo*) for protection and good fortune. The informants were clear that the songs 'belonged' to those specific places, and were constitutive sonic parts of those spiritual landscapes. Mr Taddasa Galate (who lives in Sole, Daalatti in Yaayya) said that traditionally songs were composed on the mountain of Tulluu Qaawa, where the spirit of an old lady is heard singing songs nonstop throughout the night between the last day of the old year and the first day of the new one. This old deity or muse is called Jaartii Qaawa or Jaartii Xoomi, and people visit the mountaintop to bring her gifts and offerings and learn new songs in exchange. Deities, or spirits of muses, often appear to the singer (*shaayii*) camouflaging as birds or other wild animals, and inhabit specific locations. People point at specific locations as 'home' to a particular musical deity. Mr Mabre Goofe and Mr Gurmu Badhaadha reported that at Holqa Calanqo in Hidhabu Aboote, another deity or muse called Abbaa Toochii guides and tutors the singer who seeks refuge in the muse's cave. A third deity was mentioned by Mr Gurmu Badhaadha, according to whom every New Year's Day and during the new harvest season, the *shaayii* travels to the Mogor River, climbs the Odaa Jila, a sacred tree, carefully ties themselves up with a rope to avoid accidentally falling asleep and slipping down and, covered by foliage and in confinement for days and nights, meditates on Ateete, the Oromo goddess of fecundity. After this creative 'rite of passage', the *shaayii* comes home with new songs that he shares in the secular place of the community, initiating continuous group rehearsals.

We can call this form of verbal creation ecopoetic *practice*, as opposed to the academic discipline. An ecopoetic practice is an ecocreative human communication with the nonhuman, a meditative human connectedness to nature. This meditative communication involves saying prayers; composing and singing songs, or telling stories in certain locations; naming totems, idolizing deities and offering tree coronations; summoning and glorifying God at hilltops; making sacrifices at river banks; carrying out farming and harvesting rites; offering libations to shrines; visiting graveyards and tabooing sacred groves; and communicating with nature. Much of this ecopoetic practice finds full expression in the biannual Oromo *Irreecha* festival, when people pray for rain on a hilltop in March and for thanksgiving at a lakeside in September.[27] Through such folkloric and ecopoetic practices of mediation and meditation, humans learn to find and reclaim the place they call 'home'.[28] Against the backdrop of this worldview, ecopoetics is a theory and praxis of the human-nature nexus, a deliberate life-form close to nature within the locale, contrary to, or complementary with, the dominant culture.

The Song of Displacement

The displacement that followed the top-down implementation of the Addis Ababa Master Plan, as we mentioned, also triggered older memories of displacement about the time Finfinne was occupied by Menelik II's army and imperial court in the 1880s. This has led both scholars and ordinary people to revisit the 'brokenness' of their historical links with Finfinne. During his fieldwork in the region of Shewa in 1970–1971, Tamene Bitima collected various Oromo historical poems, including what we may call Finfinne's 'Song of Displacement', thought to have been sung by an unidentified Salale folk singer and of uncertain dating.[29] The song is still performed by the Tulama Oromo living in the area, and serves today as a model and inspiration for new folk songs as the struggle for Finfinne/Addis Ababa has reignited.

In the lyrics, the singer grieves the loss of Finfinne, described as a sacred site with lush nature—a description that resonates with the historical record. At the very beginning of the twentieth century, for example, French traveller Martial de Salviac described the area as a 'luxuriant' and 'opulent' 'oasis'. De Salviac marvelled at the 'greenery' and 'shade' that 'delight the eyes all over', making the landscape look like 'a garden without boundary'.[30] He also mentioned the temperate,

---

27   See Admasu Shunkuri, 'Erracha Oromo Tradition in Thanksgiving: Its Assimilation in Ethiopia', *Ethiopian Review*, September 5, 1998.

28   J. Edward Chamberlin, *If This is Your Land, Where are Your Stories? Finding a Common Ground* (Toronto: Knopf Canada, 2003).

29   Recently republished in *Oromo Oral Poetry Seen from Within*, ed. by Catherine Griefenow-Mewis and Tamene Bitima (Köln: Rüdiger Köppe, 2004), pp. 42–43.

30   Martial de Salviac, *An Ancient People in the state of Menelik: the Oromo, Great African Nation* [French original 1901, translated by Ayalew Kanno] (East Lansing, Michigan: Ayalew Kanno, 2005), p. 21.

salubrious climate, the fertility of the soil, the solidity of the houses, and even 'the beauty of the inhabitants'.[31] All of this, the song repeats, is 'no more'. Freedom has been lost and the whole landscape has also been lost. The feeling of rupture in the song is total, and the loss is framed as irretrievable. The song mentions both the loss of the physical environment (the meadow, the wild grass, the mineral springs), but also of the associated social environment (assemblies and elders' councils). Yet, the song also contains an element of resistance, and it proudly calls all the lost places by their original Oromo names. These places may be lost, but they are unapologetically claimed as 'ours'.

Inxooxxoo irra bahanii	No more standing on the Entoto hilltop,
Caffee ilaauun hafee	to watch the meadow and wild grass below, no more.
Finfinne loon geessanii	No more taking cattle to Finfinne,
Hora obaasuun hafee	to water at the mineral spring, no more.
Oddoo Daalattiirratti	No more gathering on Oddo Daalattii,
Yaa'iin Gullallee hafee	where the Gullalle assembly used to meet, no more.
kooraa Dhakaa Araaraa	No more elders' council
jaarsummaa taahuun hafee	at Dhakaa Araaraa, no more.
Hurufa Boombiirratti	No more taking calves
Jabbilee yaasuun hafee	to the meadow at Hurufa Boombii, no more.
Gafarsatti darbanii	No more going to Gafarsa
Qoraan cabsachuun hafee	to collect firewood, our maiden, no more.
Bara jarri dhjufanii	The year the enemy came,
loon keenyas in dhumanii	our cattle perished.
Eega Mashashaan dhufee	Since [Menelik's general] Mashasha came,
Birmadummaan in hafe	freedom has vanished.

---

31 Ibid.

Place names carry historical significance in constructing the ecopoetics of a given place. The Tulama Oromo singer recounts the toponyms, eponyms, and ethnonyms of the memory sites around Finfinne. Mount Inxooxxoo (usually rendered in English as 'Entoto') was the first location where Menelik's court settled, though it later relocated to the area below the mountain, since the mountaintop lacked firewood and water. Hurufa Boombii was an area apparently used as commons, whose resources were shared among the people. Later renamed Jan Meda, it ironically remained an open public space and continued to be used for religious festivals, public celebrations, military reviews, and sport events. Dhakaa Araaraa, according to the song, was a rocky hilltop where the Oromo used to assemble to deliberate political and religious matters of public concern. It was later chosen by the Ethiopian emperor as the site of the imperial palace, but the memory of its ancient past was not lost, at least judging from the presence in the area, until recently, of a restaurant and bar called Dhakaa Araaraa. The song also mentions the famous hot springs—used for bathing and medicinal purposes—that attracted Emperor Menelik's wife Taytu to the area. The poem grieves the loss of Finfinne, but at the same time brings it back to life, with its old toponyms, its landscape, and vivid pictures of the local people's old ecological identity. The song is about historical loss, but invoking the old placenames also carries a sense of possibility: it may be impossible for those old ecological identities to be restored, but the utopia of the past can become the utopia of the future.

Narrative Discourses of Displacement

The 'Song of Displacement' was first collected nearly fifty years ago. In this section, by contrast, we analyse the oral texts we gathered first-hand during fieldwork in Boolee Arraabsaa and Koyyee Faccee in the late 2010s. This section includes oral texts collected by informants in the two areas, interviewed either individually or in groups. When informants relayed these oral compositions to the researcher, they performed them in a normal voice, stressing the lyrics and avoiding the loud, declamatory style that is common in performance. In this sense, when the setting is academic and not an organic performance context, the texts tend to be recited as poems and not sung. Our focus will be mainly on the linguistic devices, lexical units and narrative strategies employed by the victims of displacement to express their perspective. Linguistic devices are some of the most powerful realisations of the socially constructed representations of self and other.[32] They have the power to legitimise or delegitimise the practices and strategies involved in the constructions of identity. Through them, speakers encode a specific relationship to their environment and a particular political perspective on their experience of displacement.

Structurally, lexical units (such as wording, antonyms, toponyms, glottonyms, and ethnonyms) build larger units such as phrases and clauses in sentence constructions. Functionally, they impact the realisation of the discursive practices and strategies used in identity construction.[33] The texts of displacement collected from the informants contain different lexical units that overtly show where the dwellers place the blame for the destruction of their environment and the violent detachment from their ancestral homes.

Wording a concept in one way or another can profoundly change the intended meaning. The wording of the following composition contains important semantic connotations:

Fayyuu dide madaan keenya	Our wound refused to be cured
Akkuma madaa qubaa nu guba	It burns just like a finger's wound
Madaa mogolee nutti ta'e	It became the wound on someone's knee
Madaan keenya qoricha hinarganne	Our wound did not get medicine
Nuyi qoricha fayyisu hinarganne	We did not get the healing medicine
Baroota darban keessas madoofne	We have been wounded in the past era
Bara kana kessa madaan itii caale	It became serious in this era
Kaleessis har'is nu madeesse	Both yesterday and today made us wounded

---

32   See Ekaterina Povova, *Self and Other: Representations in Contemporary Russian Discourse on Migration* (unpublished PhD thesis, University of Edinburgh, 2012).

33   See Winston Kwon, Ian Clark, and Ruth Wodak, 'Micro-Level Discursive Strategies for Constructing Shared Views around Strategic Issues in Team Meetings', *Journal of Management Studies*, 51.2 (2014), 265–290; M. A. K. Halliday, *An Introduction to Functional Grammar* (London: Edward Arnold, 1994).

<table>
<tr><td>Garuu bakka handhuurri keenya
   itti awwaalamerraa nu
   kutuun itticaale</td><td>However, detaching from the place
   where our umbilical cord is
   buried seriously continued</td></tr>
<tr><td>Buqqasi lafa abbaarraan ittuma
   fufe</td><td>Displacement from our fathers' home
   is continued</td></tr>
<tr><td>Ilmaan keenya kan boru mataa
   nuu ta'antu qubata dhabe</td><td>Our children who will lead us
   tomorrow, were denied land to
   settle</td></tr>
</table>

Key words include *madaa* 'wound' (with its forms, *madoofne* 'we were wounded', and *madeesse* 'made us wounded'), *qoricha* 'medicine', *handhuura* 'umbilical cord', *buqqaasa* 'displacement', *mataa* 'head', *abbaa* 'father', and *qubata* 'land/residence'. The words *madaa, handhuura, mataa, qoricha, abbaa, buqqaasa* and *qubata* are simple nouns, while *madoofnee* and *madeesee* are complex passive and active forms of verbs. All are concrete words, but with added textual and contextual meanings. Semantically, *madaa* refers to an injury that hurts, *madoofnee* indicates the receivers ('we') being wounded, whereas *madeesee* indicates the agents of the wounding ('they'). *Handhuura* and *mataa* are parts of the body, both essential to keep the body alive. The word *buqqaasa* denotes pulling up what has been fixed or stable, and *qoricha* refers to a substance or plant that can heal a disease or a wound. The poem draws a clear line between the displacement of the past and the displacement of the present. The pain of displacement is described as a long-standing illness, the physical pain of an open wound for which there is no available medicine. The loss of the environment is framed as a loss of blood or the loss of a limb—something that severely undermines the victim's survival and human integrity.

Antonyms are 'words or expressions that are opposite with respect to some components of their meanings'.[34] They feature prominently in this other composition below:

<table>
<tr><td>Isa du'aa gadi jirra</td><td>We are below the dead</td></tr>
<tr><td>Nu warra jiraatu du'aadha</td><td>We who seem alive are dead</td></tr>
</table>

---

34   William D. O'Grady and Michael Dobrovolsky, *Contemporary Linguistics Analysis: An Introduction* (Toronto: Copp Clark Pitman, 1996), p. 234.

Har'a asirraa, bor achirraa nu kaasu	They displace us today from this [place], tomorrow from that place
Bishaan qulqulluu jedhan	They promised to provide us with clean water
Garuu xuraa'aa nu obaasan	They made us drink unclean water
Nuun iyyoomsanii soosoman	They became rich making us poor
Nuun beelessanii ofii quufan	They are satisfied by starving us

Binary oppositions include *du'aa / jiraa* ('dead/alive'), *qulqulluu / xuraa'aa* ('clean/unclean'), *iyymmaa / sooruma* ('poverty/prosperity'), *beelessuu / quufsuu* ('starvation/satisfying'), *har'a / kaleessa* ('today/ yesterday'), and *asii / achii* ('here/there'). These contrasting (we/ us vs they/them) expressions are used to reflect the exclusion of the displaced people from decision-making about matters that deeply affect their life and the environment in which they live. The agency is firmly in the hands of the displacing group, which benefits economically from the displacement and gains a relatively better life for themselves (*prosperity, alive, satisfying*, etc). The displaced instead have no agency to determine their fate, and following the displacement they are forced to live dislocated lives in 'broken places'.

Rhetorical devices offer important semantic information on the circumstances of language users. The focus of rhetorical devices includes objects, persons, and situations that participants choose in order to explicitly or implicitly compare them to other familiar elements. Rhetorical devices serve as linguistic means to realize experiential and relational values.[35] The rhetorical devices repeatedly used in these poems include *metaphor, personification*, and *antithesis*.

In everyday language practices, people choose *metaphor* to explain themselves, reflect their attitudes and values to others, and react to others' attitudes towards them in an implicit manner.[36] A recurrent metaphor in the oral compositions collected during fieldwork describes

---

35   See Ruth Wodak and Martin Reisigl, *Discourse and Discrimination: Rhetoric of Races and Anti-Semitism* (London: Routledge, 2001).

36   See Shirin Zubair, 'Silent Birds: Metaphorical Constructions of Literacy and Gender Identity in Women's Talk', *Discourse Studies*, 9.6 (2007), 766–783; and J. Stern, 'Metaphor, Semantic and Context' in *The Handbook of Metaphor and Thought*, ed. by Raymond W. Gibbs, Jr. (Cambridge: Cambridge University Press, 2008), pp. 262–279.

the land as 'mother', 'father', 'kin', 'food', 'cloth', 'bone', and the closing verse sums it up by saying that land is 'life':

Lafti haadha	Land is mother
Lafti abbaadha	Land is father
Lafti lammiidha	Land is kin
Lafti nyaata	Land is food
Lafti kafana	Land is cloth
Lafti lafeedha	Land is bone
Lafti jireenya	Land is life

In this oral poem, land is implicitly compared with relatives (mother, father, kin), food, clothing, and life. The land nurtures and takes care of people, just like parents nurture and take care of their children. The metaphor inscribes the land into the family ('land is kin') as a member that is nourishing and reliable; the family metaphor also indicates that people were born (or, even more strongly, the land gave birth to them) and grew up on the land. The metaphor collapses the boundary between physical and social geographies. The informants at Boolee Arraabsaa and Koyyee Faccee stressed that because they have been displaced from their land, they consider that their life has been drastically disrupted. The loss of land is akin to the loss of close family members, and therefore being displaced is akin to being an orphan. The poem also associates displacement to nakedness, hence bodily vulnerability, and to starvation. The recurring metaphors repeatedly compare loss of land to the loss of bodily integrity. The land was so integral to the identity of the individual that displacement is experienced as an attack on an individual's body, almost like an amputation.

Personification attributes human qualities and faculties to an inanimate entity:

Finfinneen kun maaliif nu affanaaqqalti?	Why has Finfinne displaced us?
Magaalaan kun Oromia nyaachaa har'a geesse	This city became the way it is today by eating Oromia
Finfinneen Oromoo nyaattee gabbatte	Finfinne became fat by eating the Oromo
Har'allee lachanuu nyaachaa jirti	Even today, it is eating both

<table>
<tr><td>Magaalattiin lafa, muka,
laga nyaachaa jirti</td><td>The city is eating our land, our trees,
and our rivers</td></tr>
<tr><td>Laaftoon, Ekkaan, Labuun,
Qaallittiin haadubbatan</td><td>Let Lafto, Eka, Labu and Kaliti speak</td></tr>
</table>

Finfinne is framed as an agent with human qualities, namely a person who is hungry and eats. The city is considered responsible for displacing the Oromo and 'eating them up'. This personification indicates that the Oromo contributed, to their detriment, essential resources to the expansion of the city. They gave their lives for the city, and yet Finfinne remains greedy and ravenous and cannot be satisfied. In its eating spree, the city is also accused of having desecrated the ecology of the Oromo, including mountains, rivers, memory sites, sacred places, and trees. Placenames like Laaftoo, Ekkaa, Labuu, Qaallittii are 'broken places' swallowed and 'silenced' by the ever-expanding Finfinne. Much like the 'song of displacement', the list evokes a disappearing (or already disappeared) geography around Ethiopia's capital city. All these natural places have been lost to a wave of uncontrolled and self-interested urbanisation. Such personification seems to allow the singers to avoid naming specific individuals to avoid retaliation in an already politically tense environment.

Similarly, *antithesis* is the rhetorical device the informants used in the poems to address the narrative clashes between the people and the government. Ruzibaeva defines antithesis as 'a stylistic device of contrast in art or oratory, consisting in a sharp contrast of concepts, positions, and images, conditions, interconnected by a common construction or internal meaning'.[37] This next oral poem is entirely built on antonyms, creating a structure of antithesis in which official promises are contrasted with the miserable reality on the ground:

<table>
<tr><td>Saamichi hinjiru jechaa saamu</td><td>Telling us, no more raiding, they raid
us</td></tr>
<tr><td>Duutii hinjiru jechaa ajjeesu</td><td>Telling us, no more killing, they are
killing us</td></tr>
</table>

---

37   Nigora Ruzibaeva, 'Peculiarities of the Antithesis in the Literary Text', *European Journal of Research and Reflection in Educational Sciences*, 7.11 (2019), 149–152 (p. 150).

Affanaaqqaluun dhaabate jechaa kaasu	Telling us, no more displacing people, they are displacing us
Bishaan qulqulluu jecha xurii nu obaasan	Promising clean water, they made us drink dirty water
Barumsa nuun jechaa nu wallaalchisan	Promising to educate us, they made us illiterate

Each line starts with verbs that denote a verbal act ('telling', 'promising') followed by the official state propaganda. The second part of each line contrasts the official propaganda with a statement that the exact opposite is happening. The official narrative promised people that the government would protect them against the danger of being raided, killed, displaced, and would improve their quality of life. These were insincere promises, though. Not only did the government not protect the people, but it was itself responsible for plundering, murdering and displacing them. Not only did the government not provide clean water and schools, it forced people to drink dirty water and made them illiterate. The poet sees through the lies of the government, and holds it accountable for attempting to deceive the people with false promises and appease their anger with empty words.

Code-switching is another ecolinguistically important element used in these oral poems. Most Tulama Oromo living in the research site know Amharic (the official government language) as well as Oromo, and can code switch between the two languages. The code-switching can be bent to generate specific meanings:

*Finfinneen kun maaliif nu **affanaaqqalti?***	Why has Finfinne displaced us?
***Akkabaabii** kana faalan*	They polluted this environment
***Shittaa** qilleensa keenyaa faalan*	They polluted the odour of our air
***Maasaa** keenya onsan*	They deserted our farm yard
*abbaafi ijoollee **allayaayya'an***	They separated family members
indeganaa battanan	They misplaced them again
akkanaan of nu dadhabsiisan	In this way they made us weak

All the lines of this extract contain Amharic words which the speakers have incorporated in the Oromo composition. The words have been 'Oromised', i.e. pronounced according to Afaan Oromo phonology and adapted to the Oromo grammar. The Amharic words (*affanaaqqalti, akkabaabii, shittaa, maasaa, allayaayya'an,* and *battanan*) relate to displacement and its impacts. The first two show the act of displacing (*affanaaqqalti*) the inhabitants from the area (*akkabaabii*) where they had lived for a long time. The use of Amharic words draws the audience's attention to the ecologically destructive impact of displacement by the Amharic-language government, such as polluting the environment, cutting people off their land, and breaking families apart.

Other oral poems further emphasise the contrast between past and present. This contrast was implicit in the 'song of displacement', which kept repeating that the past is 'no more'. Some of the themes recur: the loss of land, wealth, resources, and food. Once again, a past of relative abundance is contrasted with a present of poverty and starvation:

Dur qabeenya qabna	In the past we had wealth
Waan nyaannuu waan uffannu qabna	We had food and cloth
Waan qonnu qabna	We had land
Waan ittiin qonnu qabna	We had oxen to till our land
Waan dhalu qabna	We had cows
Waan elmamu qabna	We had cows to drink milk [from]
Har'a marti hinjiru	Today we have nothing
Midhaan nyaataa hinjiru	We have no crop to eat
Dhugaatiin duraanii hinjiru	We have nothing to drink
Lafti qonnaa hinjiru	We have no land
Sa'i elmatu hinjirtu	We have no cow
Qotiyyoon hinjiru	We have no ox
Martuu waan buqqaaneefi	Because all of us were displaced

In this poem, displacement is once again presented as a radical fracture in people's lives, marking a drastic lowering of their living standards and forcing them into conditions of extreme economic precarity, in which their basic needs for food and drink are not being met. If some of the poems we just saw emphasise the contrast between a happy past and a painful present, some insist on tracing a direct line of continuity between the discriminatory practices of successive Ethiopian regimes. There is no happy past conjured up by this composition, for example:

Kanuma duraatu har'as ta'aa jira.	What was in the past is happening in the present
Hayilesillaaseen akaakayyuu buqqise	Haile Selassie displaced our grandfather
Dargiin abbaa keenya buqqis	The Derg displaced our father
Kun ammoo ilma buqqisaa jira.	This one [government] is displacing the son

Rather than building a contrast between past and present, the composer here indicates that the present displacement is just more of the same. The displacement faced by people in the present, the lyrics stress, is but the latest manifestation of a long history of violence and exploitation by the Ethiopian state. The imperial regime of Emperor Haile Selassie (1930–1974) displaced the generation of today's grandfathers; the military regime of the Derg (1974–1991) displaced the generation of today's fathers; and the current EPRDF government (1991–present) displaced today's children. Every Oromo family and every generation has been scarred, and—to go back to the metaphor of the open wound of an earlier poem—carries the wounds of earlier displacements.

All in all, these oral compositions tend to present a positive view of the natural environment, with which the people are described to have a relationship of intimate and bodily interdependence. In the interviews, recurring expressions were *keenya jireenyi lafarratti* ('our life is based on the land'), *keenya jireenyi mukarratti* ('our life is dependent on trees'), *jireenyi loon keenyaa margarratti* ('our cattle's life is dependent on grass'), *lafti keenya lafee keenya, lafa dhebnaan homaa hinqabnu, kunuunsuu qabna* ('our land is our bone; having no land means having nothing, and so we have to preserve it'). These sentences highlight how the speakers see themselves as part and parcel of an ecosystem in which they depend on the land for their livelihood, but they see the land as far more than a mere object of exploitation. Rather, the land is perceived as something to be loved, respected, thanked and, more crucially, preserved. Stressing how people's lives depend on the land acknowledges the power of nature to keep people alive, and the duty of people to protect their environment. The land is a subject in its own right: a family member that takes care of people and that should be taken care of in return.

Recorded Songs

In this last section, we analyse the lyrics of two songs that became famous among those protesting the Addis Ababa Master Plan. Here we enter the domain of the music industry: these songs were recorded by famous artists with accompanying videos, and they have millions of hits on YouTube. These songs share many themes and tropes with the oral poems gathered on the field and handed down orally, thus showing the synergies between the oral tradition and the music industry. Recording artists draw from the oral repertoire, and the songs analysed in this section feed back into the world of oral traditions, creating a rich audio-visual interconnection. Tracing a continuity between oral traditions and the digital audio-visual world of recording technologies and the internet also allows us to point at the dynamism and adaptability of oral traditions. Far from disappearing with the advent of new technologies, oral traditions have capitalised on the possibilities that new technologies offered to address a larger audience, complement sound with image, and promote the verbal creativity of gifted artists.

The first song is 'Maalin Jira!' (2015), meaning 'Distracted!', by the late Oromo artist, Hacaaluu Hundeessaa, who was shot to death outside of his house in the Ethiopian capital in June 2020, in his early thirties. The assassination sent shockwaves throughout Ethiopia, igniting a new wave of Oromo protests against the government. The song has gone viral and has currently over fifteen million views on YouTube, veritably becoming one of the anthems of the Oromo opposition.[38] The themes are directly in line with those we have analysed in the oral poems: alienation, deprivation, and resentment. The song tells the story of an individual who has been harassed and forcibly removed from his ancestral home, and now feels confused and broken by strong feelings of homesickness, melancholy, and nostalgia. His mind is troubled by the grief of historical loss and by a woeful love. Hacaaluu mentions various sub-groups of the Tulama Oromo (Gulalle, Abbichu, Galaan), stressing their former unity and the social harmony that used to exist between them. The subsequent displacement is framed against this idyllic backdrop, contrasting once again the prosperous past of 'love' with the decline (the 'fall') of the present.

---

38 Haacaaluu Hundeessaa, 'Maalan Jira'; for a version with English subtitles, see Hachalu Hundessa, 'Maalan Jira! With ENGLISH Subtitle'.

Gullalleen kan Tufaa	Gullalle of Tufaa
Gaara Abbichuu turee	and Abbichu's mountainous land
Galaan Finfinnee marsee	and Galaan surrounds Finfinne
Silaa akka jaalalaa	so, love contains all
Walirraa hin fagaannuu	we never chose to grow apart
Jara t' nu fageessee!	but they pushed us to fall!

Compared to the oral poems, this song is more optimistic about the possibility of resistance: all is not lost if the people come together: the video shows scenes of communal dancing and smiling youth. Indeed, the theme of unity is central in the lyrics. The 'mountain' keeps the singer separated from his beloved, a metaphor for the divisions ('divisions we never chose') among the Oromo engineered by the government to politically disempower them. The mountain is then a metaphor for the oppressive system, which must be 'levelled' for the people to be able to come together. The protest movement is compared to a bulldozer that will flatten the mountain and rekindle the lost unity.

Diiganii, gaara sana	Level that mountain
gaara diigamuu hin malle	not easy to bulldoze
nu baasan addaan baane	they set us apart
nu addaan bahuu hin malle	division we never chose

The second song is by Galaanaa Gaaromsaa and is titled 'Amala Kee' (2016), meaning 'Your Vibe'. It is a well-known and popular song, and the video has around five million views on YouTube.[39] The song denounces the evictions, contrasting the 'home' people lost with the anonymous buildings built on it.

Salgan Haroo Abbaa Makoo	The nine pools of Abba Makoo,
iddoo gabaa hin qotani	it is taboo to plow a marketplace.
dur manni keenya asoo	Oh, our home used to be here.
gamoo itti ijaarattanii	They evicted us to erect these buildings.

---

39   Galaanaa Gaaromsaa, 'Amala Kee (Official Video)'

In the song, natural places like the nine pools of Abba Makoo are ecological references to the ongoing land grabs, evictions, rural-urban migration, urbanisation and industrialisation. The coverage of the Oromo protests has mostly focused on political and economic grievances, but the poems and songs we have analysed show that the mobilisation against the government was also motivated by environmental grievances. The Oromo movement for equal political and economic rights, in this sense, was also, importantly, a movement for environmental justice.

Conclusions

In this chapter, we have shown the importance of ecopoetic and ecolinguistic approaches to past and contemporary oral literature. We have drawn on a variety of sources: oral poems collected by other scholars and published; poems collected directly on the field; interviews on the field; and songs circulating on television and the internet. These sources show the vitality of oral traditions, and the way in which print, recording technologies and the internet can help preserve oral texts and spread them to even larger audiences.

Ecopoetics and ecolinguistics allowed us to identify the conception of nature underpinning the oral poems of the Tulama Oromo living in the Koyyee Faccee and Boolee Arraabsaa areas, and the effects of Development-Induced Displacement on their ecological identities. The poems pit the people's narrative ecology, in which people and land are linked not only in economic, but also spiritual terms, against the government's narrative ecology, in which the land is just to be exploited to make way for urbanisation. In the chapter, we wanted to foreground local people's perspectives and their voices, to counteract their exclusion from the decision-making process about the future of their land and their homes. This approach privileges bottom-up approaches to literary production over the top-down analytical models that have generally been typical of disciplines such as world literature. The people we have interviewed—refugees who live in poor conditions—are far from the glittery world of literary prizes, boardroom meetings with the CEOs of international publishing houses, and fashionable literary festivals in which authors sign their freshly printed books. We wanted to present the dispossessed—those who are the victims of modernity, not the winners of the game—as literary subjects as aesthetically sophisticated and as aesthetically powerful as the famous cosmopolitan novelists on whom world literature departments in Western academia have almost exclusively concentrated.

Ecopoetics and ecolinguistics also allow us to map in what ways certain geographies are 'significant' for the people who live in them, and the meanings people attach to their environment, not only in terms of identity but also in terms of poetic inspiration. Hegemonic political narratives around the world privilege 'development' over the preservation of ecosystems, whereas the oral poems of the Tulama Oromo show an acute awareness of the need for a greater environmental consciousness. We can find in these poems a lucid environmentalist critique of pollution and uncontrolled urbanisation. Even more profoundly, we can find in these poems a philosophy of nature as something to be taken care of, as opposed to the hegemonic developmentalist view of nature as an inert source of resources to be extracted, or a physical space to be occupied. Such oral traditions powerfully capture the human and environmental costs of developmentalist practices.

More broadly, far from disappearing in the face of 'modernity', as some teleological narratives of literary evolution argue, oral traditions have instead been able to see through the contradictions of modernity, in some cases much more incisively than written literature. New oral poems have been created in Ethiopia to denounce crony capitalism and Development-Induced Displacement, demonstrating the ability of oral traditions not only to be in dialogue with modernity but also to point at alternative anti-capitalist modernities. The nostalgia for a lost past that we find in many oral poems also indicates possible ways to a different future. Indeed, these oral traditions not only lament how old ecological and ecopoetic identities have been irretrievably 'broken', but also articulate new, powerful forms of resistance, bringing people together and inciting political mobilisation against political, economic and environmental injustice. If displacement has disempowered the people, these oral poems re-empower them.

Bibliography

Degefa, Aberra, 'Addis Ababa Master Development Plan: A Program for Development or for Ethnic Cleansing?', *RUDN Journal of Sociology*, 19.1 (2019), https://doi.org/10.22363/2313-2272-2019-19-1-31-39

Altman, Rick, *The Theory of Narratives* (New York: Colombia University Press, 2008).

Dibaba, Assefa Tefera, 'Oromo Social Resentment: Re-envisioning Resentment Theory, an African Perspective', *Journal of Pan-African Studies*, 11.7 (2018).

Dibaba, Assefa Tefera, 'Oromo Orature: An Ecopoetic Approach', *Theory and Practice* (Oromia/Ethiopia, Northeast Africa), *Humanities*, 9.2.28 (2020), https://doi.org/10.3390/h9020028

Basso, Keith, *Wisdom Sits in Places* (Albuquerque: University of New Mexico Press, 1996).

Berhanu, Zewdie, 'Impact of Urban Redevelopment on the Livelihoods of Displaced People in Addis Ababa: The case of Casanchis Local Development Plan' (MA thesis, Addis Ababa University, 2006).

Berkes, Fikret, *Sacred Ecology* (Philadelphia: Taylor & Francis, 1999).

Baxter, Paul T. W., 'Boran Age-Sets and Generation-Sets: Gada, a puzzle or a maze?' in *Age, Generation and Time: Some features of East African Age Organisations*, ed. by Paul T.W. Baxter and Uri Almagor (London: C. Hurst, 1978), pp. 151–182.

Castells, Manuel, 'The Greening of the Self: The Environmental Movement' in *The Power of Identity*, Vol. II (Blackwell, 2010), pp. 168–191, https://onlinelibrary.wiley.com/doi/epdf/10.1002/9781444318234.fmatter

Chamberlin, J. Edward, *If This is Your Land, Where are Your Stories? Finding Common Ground* (Toronto: Knopf Canada, 2003).

de Salviac, Martial, *An Ancient People in the State of Menelik: the Oromo, Great African Nation* [French original 1901, translated by Ayalew Kanno] (East Lansing, Michigan: Ayalew Kanno, 2005).

Duszak, Anna, 'Us and Others: An Introduction' in *Us and Others: Social identities across language, discourses and cultures*, ed. by Anna Duszak (Amsterdam & Philadelphia: John Benjamins, 2002), pp. 1–28.

Ege, Svein, *Class, State, and Power in Africa: A Case Study of the Kingdom of Shawa (Ethiopia) about 1840* (Wiesbaden: HarrassowitzVerlag, 1996).

Gaaromsaa, Galaanaa, 'Amala Kee (Official Video)', YouTube, 2017, https://www.youtube.com/watch?v=isaZSb7E5zY

Ambaye, Getu and Abeliene, Assefa, 'Development-Induced Displacement and Its Impacts on the Livelihoods of Poor Urban Households in Bahir Dar,

North Western Ethiopia', *AHMR*, 1.3 (2017), 310–313, https://www.scielo.
org.za/scielo.php?pid=S2410-79722015000300004&script=sci_arttext

Griefenow-Mewis, Catherine and Bitima, Tamene, eds, *Oromo Oral Poetry Seen
from Within*, with an introduction by Wilhelm J.G. Möhlig (Köln: Rüdiger
Köppe, 2004).

Hundeessaa, Haacaaluu, 'Maalan Jira: New Afan Oromo Official Music Video
2015', YouTube, https://www.youtube.com/watch?v=gliv_skuGL8

Hundessa, Hachalu, 'Maalan Jira! With ENGLISH Subtitles', by Ermias Tasfaye,
YouTube, 2021, https://www.youtube.com/watch?v=Ri7bf7nGN1Y

Halliday, M. A. K., *An Introduction to Functional Grammar* (London: Edward
Arnold,1994).

IDMC, 'Internal Displacement: Global Overview of Trends and Developments
in 2010' (2011), https://api.internal-displacement.org/sites/default/files/
publications/documents/2011-global-overview-2010-global-en.pdf

Kumsa, Alemayehu, 'The Oromo National Memories',
RUDN Journal of Sociology, 19.3 (2019), https://doi.
org/10.22363/2313-2272-2019-19-3-503-516

Kwon, Winston, Clark, Ian and Wodak Ruth, 'Micro-Level Discursive Strategies
for Constructing Shared Views around Strategic Issues in Team Meetings',
Journal of Management Studies, 51.2 (2014), https://doi.org/10.1111/
joms.12036

Lodhi, Abdulaziz Y. 'The Language Situation in Africa Today', *Nordic
Journal of African Studies*, 2.1 (1993), https://web.archive.org/
web/20180422114052id_/http://www.njas.helsinki.fi/pdf-files/vol2num1/
lodhi.pdf

McCright, A. M. and Clark, T. Nichols, *Community and Ecology: Dynamics of
Place, Sustainability, and Politics* (Bingley: Emerald Group Publishing Ltd,
2006).

Nezami, Syed Raihan Ahmed, 'The Use of Figures of Speech as a Literary
Device: A Specific Mode of Expression in English Literature', *Language in
India*, 12.2 (2012), 659–676.

O'Grady, William D. and Dobrovolsky, Michael, *Contemporary Linguistics
Analysis: an Introduction* (Toronto: Copp Clark Pitman, 1996).

Povova, Ekaterina, *Self and Other: Representations in Contemporary Russian
Discourse on* Migration (unpublished PhD thesis, University of Edinburgh,
2012), https://era.ed.ac.uk/handle/1842/7901

Ruzibaeva, Nigora, 'Peculiarities of the Antithesis in the Literary Text',
European Journal of Research and Reflection in Educational Sciences, 7.11 (2019),
http://www.idpublications.org/wp-content/uploads/2019/09/Full-Paper-
PECULIARITIES-OF-THE-ANTITHESIS-IN-THE-LITERARY-TEXT.pdf

Shunkuri, Admasu, 'Erracha Oromo Tradition in Thanksgiving: Its Assimilation in Ethiopia', *Ethiopian Review*, September 5, 1998, https://www.ethiopianreview.com/index/1443

Stanley, Jason, 'Development-induced Displacement and Resettlement', *Forced Migration Online Research Guide*, Refugee Studies Centre, University of Oxford (2004), https://citeseerx.ist.psu.edu/document?repid=rep1&type=pdf&doi=b082f24dd24bf7640420c0f33ed2da8bfdb6a19b

Stern, Josef. 'Metaphor, Semantic and Context' in *The Handbook of Metaphor and Thought*, ed. by Raymond W. Gibbs, Jr. (Cambridge: Cambridge University Press, 2008), pp. 262–279.

Stibbe, Arran, *Ecolinguistics: Language, Ecology and the Stories We Live by* (London: Rutledge, 2021).

Tesfa, Teferi GebreEgziabher, 'The Effects of Development-Induced Displacement on Relocated Households: The Case of Addis Ababa' (MA Thesis, The Hague, International Institute of Social Studies, 2014).

UNHCR, 'Global Trends on Forced Displacement' (2018), UNHCR Global Trends - Forced Displacement in 2017.

Uraizee, Joya, 'Combating Ecological Terror: Ken Saro-Wiwa's "Genocide in Nigeria"', *JMMLA*, 44.2 (2011), https://www.jstor.org/stable/23622093

Valk, Ülo and Sävborg, Daniel, *Storied and Supernatural Places: Studies in spatial and social dimensions of folklore and sagas* (Finnish Literature Society/SKS, 2018), https://doi.org/10.21435/sff.23

Vansina, Jan, *Oral Tradition as History* (Madison, WI: University of Wisconsin Press, 1985).

Wei, Ruby Rong, 'Ecolinguistics: Language, Ecology and the Stories We Live', *Southern African Linguistics and Applied Language Studies*, 36.2 (2018), https://doi.org/10.2989/16073614.2018.1547983

Weigert, Andrew J., *Self, Interaction, and Natural Environment: Refocusing Our Eyesight* (Albany: SUNY Press, 2018).

Wodak, Ruth and Reisigl, Martin, *Discourse and Discrimination: Rhetoric of Races and Anti-Semitism* (London: Routledge, 2001).

Zubair, Shirin, 'Silent Birds: Metaphorical Constructions of Literacy and Gender Identity in Women's Talk', *Discourse Studies*, 9.6 (2007), https://doi.org/10.1177/146144560708127

3. The Novelization of Orature in Ethiopian Village Novels

Ayele Kebede Roba

Introduction

> We recognise in oral literature a fundamental and indeed 'organic'
> aspect of the African imagination. For all their undoubted diversity,
> the manifestations of the imagination in our traditional societies have
> one common denominator—they rely primarily on an oral mode of
> realisation.
>
> —Abiola Irele[1]

Unlike elsewhere in Africa, in Ethiopia the study of the mutual influence
between literature and orature has so far not received significant attention.
Just as in many other parts of Africa, written literary production has
not been as popular as orature in Ethiopia, despite the long history of
writing in Geez (since the first century CE).[2] Notwithstanding this fact,
Ethiopian literary studies tend to only celebrate the written traditions in
Geez and Amharic and to present oral traditions as inferior, especially
if they are in Ethiopian languages other than Amharic. The syllabi of
Ethiopian university literature courses devote a disproportionate amount

---

1   Abiola Irele, 'The African Imagination', *Research in African Literatures*, 21.1 (1990),
    49–67 (p. 54).
2   See Albert Gerard, *Four African Literatures: Xhosa, Sotho, Zulu, Amharic* (Berkeley:
    University of California Press, 1971). Donald Crummey shows that even in
    literate Christian communities, writing did not replace orality for administrative
    functions; see 'Literacy in an Oral Society: The Case of Ethiopian Land Records',
    Journal of African Cultural Studies, 18.1 (2006), 9–22.

    https://doi.org/10.11647/OBP.0405.03

of time to the Amharic literary tradition. This creates a bias against literatures in Ethiopian languages without a long history of writing. For advanced degrees orature and literature are studied separately, in different departments, units or programmes. Orature is largely confined to folklore departments, while written literature is studied in literature departments. Many of the theses dealing with orature in Ethiopia have focused on the anthropological and sociological aspects of orature rather than its literary and formal elements.[3] This disciplinary divide perpetuates the notion that 'Amharas and Tigrayans have a *history*, whereas other [Ethiopian] peoples have only an anthropology'.[4]

Against this divide, this chapter deals with two Ethiopian novels that engage directly with orature and in which orature in fact plays a dominant role. Through their novelization of oral texts, the novels show the relationship between orature and literature as part of a continuum. The fact that these are village novels is not coincidental, for the village novel is a mediatory genre that reflects the interplay or mutual co-existence of oral and written literature. The practice of writing village novels, particularly about villages inhabited by marginalised peoples, is a recent literary phenomenon in both the Amharic and Afan Oromo literary traditions. It dates to the 1990s, after the restructuring of the Ethiopian state along ethno-federalist lines. This political change opened an institutional space for writers to explore Ethiopia's multi-ethnic make-up in their works. Fiqremarqos Desta and Dhaba Wayessa have pioneered the genre in Amharic and Afan Oromo, respectively, writing about characters who speak languages that are not the authors's own. Both Fiqremarqos Desta's Amharic novel *Evangadi* (1998) and Dhaba Wayessa Afan Oromo novel *Gurraacha Abbayaa* (*The Black Man from Abbaya*) (1996) incorporate a variety of oral forms in order to depict the worldviews of Ethiopian peoples who have had no culture of writing

---

3   See Tolessa Addisu, 'The Historical Transformation of a Folklore Genre: The Geerarsa as a National Literature of the Oromo in the Context of Amhara Colonization in Ethiopia' (unpublished doctoral thesis, Indiana University, 1990); Asafa, Tafarra, 'Towards a Political Sociology of Oromo Literature: Jaarsoo Waaqoo's Poetry' (unpublished doctoral thesis, Addis Ababa University, 2003); Assefa, Tefera, 'Ethnography of Resistance Poetics: Power and Authority in Salale Oromo Folklore and Resistance Culture, Ethiopia, Northeast Africa' (unpublished doctoral thesis, Indiana University, 2015).

4   Christopher Clapham, 'Rewriting Ethiopian History', *Annales d'Éthiopie*, 18.1 (2002), 37–54 (p. 40).

until recent times. Arguably, the direct quotation of oral texts in the original Gumuz language in *Gurraacha Abbayaa* is more impactful than the paraphrasing or translating of oral texts into Amharic in *Evangadi*, a strategy that reflects the linguistic and literary homogenization of mainstream Amharic literature. Before I analyse and compare the novelization of orature in the two novels, the next sections explain my key concepts and approach and introduce the novels.

Approaches and Terminology

The preference for writing/literature over orality/orature in Ethiopian history and literary studies is an example of the evolutionist approach of scholars such as Jack Goody and Walter Ong.[5] This evolutionist approach traces a 'linear progression' from orality to writing, with the implication that as a society progresses the latter supersedes the former. Writing is considered a marker of modernity and, by extension, literature is treated as more advanced and sophisticated than orature.

This privileging of literature over orature was rejected by a group of scholars who are commonly identified as 'integrationists', notably Ruth Finnegan and Robert Horton, who argued that literature and orature are inseparable and mutually non-exclusive.[6] For them, 'oral genres continued to be created in literate societies, and [...] structures of oral literature survived in written literature'.[7] The integrationists aimed to shift 'the focus from dichotomies to a cognitive continuum where orality and literacy share several qualities'.[8] For Finnegan, though there may be differences owing to factors like the modern technologies used by literate communities, orature equals literature in artistic complexity.[9] For Russell H. Kaschula, 'Oral and written literature are literature in their own right, interacting at some point, remaining autonomous in many ways, backed by the same culture and society, and performing

5   See Jack Goody, *The Interface Between the Written and the Oral* (Cambridge: Cambridge University Press, 1987); Walter Ong, *Orality and Literacy* (London: Routledge, 2002).

6   See Richard Horton and Ruth H. Finnegan, eds, *Modes of Thought, Essays on Thinking in Western and Non-Western Societies* (London: Faber and Faber, 1973).

7   Daniella Merolla, 'Introduction: Orality and Technauriture of African Literatures', *Tydskrif Vir Letterkunde*, 51.1 (2014), 80–88 (p. 81).

8   Ibid., p. 82.

9   See Ruth H. Finnegan, 'The How of Literature', *Oral Tradition*, 20.2 (2005), 164–187.

the same function of commenting on that society and the world in general'.[10] There is little difference between them 'in terms of the aims and functions of literature, [...] and they are both fuelled and moulded by the culture that underlines them'.[11]

Scholars of African literature have put forward strong arguments for the central role of oral traditions in African literary development. According to Abiola Irele, for example, 'the African imagination is represented by the body of literature produced by, within, and for the traditional societies and indigenous cultures of Africa. This literature forms an essential part of what is generally considered the oral tradition in Africa'.[12] In other words, people who did not develop a writing system, vehicle their imagination, culture, aspirations, frustrations, history and memory through oral expressions. At the same time, we can trace a network of mutual influence and exchanges between written and oral literary genres.

In order to resolve the unproductive binary between orature and literature, some scholars have tried to redefine and reconceptualise 'literature' itself. Ong spoke about the difficulty in finding a generic term that '[includes] both purely oral art and literature'.[13] Finnegan too wrestled with the problems related to the definition of literature: 'I suggest that we should envisage it not as definable by reference to Western written genres, but as an umbrella notion that can embrace all those displayed forms and events in which verbal artistry in some way plays a significant part'.[14] Others have gone even further and argued that the name 'oral literature' is inhibiting and does not effectively capture the true characteristics of oral imaginative thinking. Ugandan linguist Pio Zirimu was the first to introduce the alternative concept of 'orature' in order to stress the literary aspect of orally-produced imaginative expressions, though he used this word interchangeably with 'oral literature'.[15] Ngũgĩ Wa Thiong'o follows Pitika Ntuli's in defining

---

10   Russell H. Kaschula, 'Exploring the Oral-Written Interface with Particular
      Reference to Xhosa Oral Poetry', *Research in African Literatures*, 28.1 (1997), 173–191
      (p. 174).
11   Ibid., p. 186.
12   Irele, 'The African Imagination', p. 53.
13   Ong, *Orality and Literacy*, p. 13.
14   Finnegan, 'The How of Literature', p. 180.
15   See Ngũgĩ wa Thiong'o, 'Notes towards a Performance Theory of Orature',
      Performance Research, 12.3 (2007), 4–7.

orature as 'more than the fusion of all art forms. It is the conception and reality of a total view of life. It is the capsule of feeling, thinking, imagination, taste, and hearing. It is the flow of a creative spirit'.[16] For Ngũgĩ, orature is characterised by genre 'fluidity' and 'performance'. In this chapter I use 'orature' to refer to forms of orally performed and enacted imaginative expressions, mostly marked by the actual or imagined presence of an audience (in both novels elements of orature are accompanied by short descriptions of their performance). These forms range from short witty expressions like proverbs to longer genres such as oral narratives (tales), oral poetry and folk song. Conversely, I use 'literature' to refer to written forms of imaginative expression.

The Novel and Orature

The capacity of the novel to accommodate assorted genres of orature and literature makes the novel a ground where oral and written traditions can productively interact. For Mikhail Bakhtin, the novel inherently resists the homogenisation and monologisation of experiences, stories, trajectories, voices, and languages.[17] His dialogic perspective allows the interplay between multiple genres to be envisaged. For Eileen Julien, Fiona Moolla, and Olankunke George, orature in the African novel does not play only an ornamental role but is an analytical category.[18] In her study of Nuruddin Farah's novels, for example, Fiona Moolla finds 'a strong oral element in the novel in its reliance on alliteration, imagery, and symbols common to oral verse as well as in its use of folk tales'.[19] Boris W. Andrzejewski shows that poetic inserts in one Somali novel do the work of 'foregrounding, that is, enhancing the relevance

---

16 Ibid., p. 5.
17 See Mikhail Bakhtin, *The Dialogic Imagination: Four Essays by M. M. Bakhtin*, ed. by Michael Holquist, translated by Carlyin Emerson and Michael Holquist (Austin: University of Texas Press, 1981); and *Problems of Dostoevsky's Poetics*, ed. and trans. by Caryl Emerson (Manchester: Manchester University Press, 1984).
18 Eileen Julien, *African Novels and the Question of Orality* (Place: Indiana University Press, 1992); and 'African Literature' in *Africa*, ed. by Phyllis M. Martin and Patrick O'Meara (Bloomington: Indiana University Press, 1995), pp. 295–312; Fiona Moolla, 'When Orature Becomes Literature: Somali Oral Poetry and Folktales in Somali Novels', *Comparative Literature Studies*, 49.3 (2012), 434–462; and George, Olankunke 'The Oral–Literate Interface' in Irele, *The Cambridge Companion to the African Novel*, pp. 15–30.
19 Moolla, 'When Orature Becomes Literature', p. 455.

of and attracting attention to particular aspects or themes'.[20] Emanuel Obiechina argues that the folk tales in Chinua Achebe's *Things Fall Apart* (1958) serve 'diverse formal, thematic and aesthetic purposes', and offer 'insight to clarify the action, to sharpen characterization, to elaborate themes and enrich the setting and environment of action'.[21]

In Ethiopia, the novel, considered the most 'advanced' literary genre, is highly dependent upon orature. This undermines the idea of a 'linear progression' from orature to literature. The village novels discussed in this chapter, *Evangadi* and *Gurraacha Abbayaa*, present oral worlds in which orature plays a significant role.[22] Therefore, I argue, this genre provides productive cases for the study of the relationship and interconnection between literature and orature. Orature is present in these novels in the form of work songs, cattle songs, hunting songs, love songs, music, folk tales, and proverbs. Through a close reading of the novels, this chapter shows how the novels incorporate different types of orature and represent their oral qualities and performative aspects. Though they differ in their effects, these elements of orature help elaborate on key conflicts and cultural events, sharpen characters, enrich plots and themes. My approach is one of close and contextual reading. I look at specific and concrete examples as well as indirect references to oral texts and analyse their narrative relevance.

The novels typically use description to foreground the performance that accompanies elements of orature, thereby showing the interdependence between orature and literature. The elements of orature we find in these novels are trimmed to be in accord with the narrative purpose and therefore not the same as the 'original' oratures/performance. In order to capture these strategies and the repurposed elements of orature, I use the term 'novelized orature', adapted from Emmanuel Obiechina's notion of 'narrative proverbs', to designate stories embedded in novels that 'perform organic and structural functions of proverbs in oral

---

20   Boris W. Andrzejewski, 'Modern and Traditional Aspects of Somali Drama', *Journal of African Cultural Studies*, 23.1 (2011), 85–95 (p. 98).

21   Emmanuel Obiechina, 'Narrative Proverbs in the African Novel', *Oral Tradition* 7.2 (1992), 197–230 (p. 204).

22   Fiqremarqos Desta, *Evangadi* (Addis Ababa: NA, 1998); Wayessa Dhaba, *Gurraacha Abbayaa* (A Black Man from Abbaya) (Washington DC: Fettan Printers, 1996).

speech and in creative literature'.[23] For Obiechina, 'narrative proverbs are autonomous stories that appear in different genres and narrative registers within different structural linguistic plans and are embedded inside larger, more inclusive narratives. *They function as images, metaphors, and symbols and advance the meanings and formal qualities of the narratives in which they occur*' (emphasis added).[24] Obiechina uses the term 'proverb' functionally, to underline the function that elements of orature play in the novel. I prefer 'novelized orature', which can be both functional and denotative. 'Novelized orature' refers to poetic inserts such as folk songs and poems, which are a regular presence in African novels, and designates different forms of orature, tales/ stories, songs, and poetry, that are included in the novels as part of their narrative. Novelized orature is different from orature proper in that it is reworked, appropriated, or dialogized, to use Bakhtin's term, to serve a variety of narrative purposes in the novel.

Novelized orature in the novels can be analysed at two levels, the textual and the extra-textual. For Isidore Okpewho, written texts may represent the oral characteristics of orature in 'the ways in which the words are organized and the resources within the words that ensure the effectiveness of the oral performance'. If the stylistic qualities of orature include 'repetition', 'parallelism', 'piling and association', 'tonality', 'ideophones', 'digression', 'imagery', 'allusion' and 'symbolism', written texts can draw attention to 'the style and techniques of presentation', and to 'all those aspects that make oral literature as an art form somewhat distinct from written literature'.[25] In the novels under discussion, we find strategies of repetition, digression, and symbolism, among others. My analysis considers these elements when focusing on the embedded texts (songs, poems or stories). But authors can also help readers be aware of 'the conditions or circumstances in which the words of oral literature are delivered and the effect of these circumstances on the text that is produced'.[26] In order to explain this aspect of novelized orature, I consider the extra-textual information provided in the novels in the

---

23   Obiechina, 'Narrative Proverbs in the African Novel', p. 199.

24   Ibid., p. 200, emphasis added.

25   Isidore Okpewho, *African Oral Literature: Backgrounds, Character, and Continuity* (Bloomington: Indiana University Press, 1992), p. 70.

26   Ibid.

form of what I call 'commentary'. These are the comments, descriptions and explanations about oral poetry, folk songs and folk tales given by the narrator and characters. It is through this commentary that some of the crucial aspects of novelized orature are represented.

I understand the village novel as a mediatory genre, for it foregrounds oral genres, performances, and local varieties of language. Novelization creates an interface or interplay between written and oral texts for a unified narrative effect. Orature is novelized by putting it to the service of narrative purposes such as enriching characterization, contextualizing themes, and explaining events.

Orature, I argue, can be used to 'localise' the novel to a specific region and multilingual context. In this regard, my analysis conforms to Franco Moretti's idea of the novel as an imported form that relies significantly on local resources (both local materials and local forms, in my view).[27]

To this end, this chapter first examines the narrative and textual strategies employed by the authors to novelize orature and to foreground 'an ongoing relationship of coevalness and simultaneity' between the novel and orature.[28] Second, the chapter explores how orature shapes the overall narrative structure of the novels, but also how the novels contribute to the preservation and transformation of orature. Lastly, the chapter explores how the authors contest the alleged 'linear progression' from oral to written and unsettle the hierarchical relationship between literature and orature. First, though, let me briefly present the two novels and their authors.

Evangadi and *Gurraacha Abbayaa*

Despite being written in different Ethiopian languages and presenting the experiences of different peoples, Fiqremarqos' Amharic novel *Evangadi* and Dhaba's Afan Oromo novel *Gurraacha Abbayaa* share important features. Both novels present the quotidian life of people who live in remote villages. *Evangadi* is set among the Hamar people living in south-western Ethiopia, and *Gurraacha Abbayaa* among the Gumuz people in western Ethiopia. The Hamar and the Gumuz reside

---

27   Franco Moretti, 'Conjectures on World Literature', *New left review*, 2.1 (2000), 54–68.
28   Olankunle, 'The Oral–Literate Interface', p. 17.

in geographically peripheral areas in Ethiopia, which place them on the margins of the state in terms of political, educational, and economic benefits.[29] By choosing to write about these communities, Fiqremarqos and Dhaba explicitly counter the marginalisation of peripheral peoples in Ethiopian literary studies. The novels effectively introduce these peoples to mainstream Ethiopian cultural institutions, national media, and academics. Furthermore, Fiqremarqos and Dhaba use Amharic and Afan Oromo, respectively, to give voice to people who do not speak those languages as their mother tongue, thereby deterritorialising these two major Ethiopian languages and challenging the nationalist ideology whereby one ethnicity is defined by just one language, and a language belongs to that ethnicity alone. In so doing, these novels resist ethnic labels that promote linguistic nationalism. The two novels are similar in giving so much space to orature *and to oral worlds that are not the authors' own*. This is unusual in the context of Amhara and Oromo nationalisms. The purpose of appropriating oral texts by each novel reflects stark difference, as we shall see. It also differs from the general argument about orature and the novel in Africa, where what is also at stake is a choice between African languages and English/French. Before I discuss how the two novels novelize orature, let me briefly introduce them.

Evangadi

Fiqremarqos Desta, the author of *Evangadi*, was born in Bahir Dar, the capital of the Amhara regional state. A native Amharic speaker, he was a chemistry teacher before he shifted to creative writing.[30] Fiqremarqos has written six novels, and *Evangadi* is the second in his trilogy on the Hamar people. It presents the village life of the Hamar people and their south-western Ethiopian neighbours such as the Kuyegu, the Mursi, and the Erbore peoples. The south-western part of Ethiopia is economically, infrastructurally, and politically marginalized—and Fiqremarqos is among the few individuals to have visited the area out of their own

---

29 See John Markakis, *Ethiopia: The Last Two Frontiers* (Woodbridge: James Currey, 2011).

30 As he explains in an interview for *Maleda TV* (2018).

academic or artistic curiosity.[31] He lived among the Hamar for several years, and claims to have become a Hamar man.

By setting his novels among peripheral communities, Fiqremarqos radically departs from the Amharic literary canon, which only describes the experiences of Amharic-speaking people and tends to present non-Amharic speaking people pejoratively.[32] To my knowledge, Fiqremarqos is the first Amhara author to write about non-Amhara people without appearing to negatively portray them. His innovation is not only in terms of theme and setting, but also in terms of his engagement with Hamar linguistic and oral imaginative expressions. For example, the novel is named after a popular Hamar oral genre, the *evangadi*, a night-time dance accompanied by oral songs.

Evangadi presents Ethiopia as a home of many peoples with a variety of cultures. It challenges the view of Ethiopia 'as an outpost of Semitic civilization', presenting it instead 'as an ethnographic museum'.[33] An ethnographic novel that fictionalises anthropological research (through the figure of the foreign researcher, Karlet), *Evangadi* also thematizes the search for lost facets of one's identity and culture (through the figure of Konchit) as well as other peoples' cultures. It includes few direct examples and quotations of orature, and always in Amharic translation, thereby undermining its own pluralizing efforts by homogenizing linguistic and literary diversity, arguably a reflection of mainstream Amharic literature. Though it is still open to the non-Amharic oral world, the effects of the voices presented through novelized orature are less impactful when compared to *Gurraacha Abbayaa*.

The novel includes two main plot lines and two sets of characters, either interested in other cultures or with mixed identities and keen to retrieve layers of their own plural identity, who intersect in Hamar territory after travelling out of and back to Ethiopia, or across different regions within the country, thereby encountering other speakers and cultures that are not their own. One plot follows Sora Galcha, an Ethiopian man who

---

31   Clapham, 'Rewriting Ethiopian History'.

32   See Jeylan Hussein, 'A Critical Review of the Political and Stereotypical Portrayals of the Oromo in the Ethiopian Historiography', *Nordic Journal of African Studies* 15.3 (2006), 256–276.

33   Donald Donald, *Greater Ethiopia: The Evolution of a Multiethnic Society* (Chicago: University of Chicago Press, 1974), p. 17.

has relocated to Spain. Sora is from the Erbore people in south-western Ethiopia and was educated in the Ethiopian capital, Addis Ababa, but he soon grows dissatisfied with his life in the capital and decides to emigrate to Spain. There, he meets Konchit Peso Beni, an Ethio-Spanish woman, whose family is from the Kuyegu community in south-western Ethiopia. The two decide to travel from Spain back to Kuchiru, in the Kuyegu land, in search of the relatives of Konchit's grandfather, Edward Lokaye, who was abducted by slave raiders when he was only a small boy. This is therefore a search for identity. After a dreary and dangerous journey along the lower part of the Omo River, Konchit and Sora meet Delti, a Hamar man who has moved to Kuchiru. Since Sora knows the Hamar language, Delti can communicate with them and he helps them find Konchit's relatives.

The second plot follows British anthropologist Karlet Alfred, who first appeared in Fiqremarqos' first novel, *Behind the Buska* (1995), as a researcher travelling to the Hamar land for fieldwork. In *Evangadi*, Karlet travels back to the Hamar, after presenting her research in the UK, to meet her friend Delti, with whom she fell in love during her fieldwork. Her relationship and re-union with Delti and deep connection with the Hamar symbolize a successful interplay or connection between oral and written worlds. Before she arrives in the territory of the Hamar, Karlet travels to various places in central and northern Ethiopia, and in her interactions with other people she expresses her appreciation for the cultural diversity of Ethiopia. In these conversations, she challenges other characters who hold negative views of Ethiopia, including a British diplomat who speaks of Ethiopia as a poor and backward country. After visiting old churches and monasteries in northern Ethiopia, Karlet travels back to the Hamar region. This movement enables the novel to connect the northern region of Ethiopia—which is usually presented in the mainstream literature and history as the centre of Ethiopian civilization—with the often-marginalized southern region. When Karlet arrives in the Hamar region, though, she discovers that Delti has left without telling anyone about his whereabouts. Karlet joins his friends and family in searching for him. According to a divination ritual performed by Hamar elders, Delti is near Kuchiru village. When the team arrives at Kuchiru, they find Delti with Sora and Konchit. The three have finally found information about Lokaye, and are celebrating.

Karlet is happy to be reunited with Konchit, whom she had already befriended in Spain. At the end, Karlet, Konchit, Sora and several other people from the Hamar leave for Geneva in Switzerland to participate in a festival organized by Karlet to promote Ethiopian multiculturalism. The representatives of different ethnic groups in Ethiopia showcase their songs, cultural dances, and dressing styles.

The novel fictionalises the anthropological research carried out among the peoples in the southern and south-western Ethiopia.[34] Karlet Alfred is a fictional representation of the foreign anthropologist, but she is also committed to celebrating the rich cultural heritage of Ethiopia. She argues, for example, that Ethiopia is a multi-ethnic and multicultural country, and that it is inappropriate to generalise a problem one observes in a certain locality or community as representative of 'Ethiopian' culture. The novel narrates a sequence of peaceful encounters between people with different cultural and linguistic backgrounds, including the Hamar, their neighbours, and Europeans. Throughout the novel, the presence of orature is recognizable at the levels of form and content through direct or indirect references made by the characters, narrators, and author.

Gurraacha Abbayaa

Dhaba Wayessa has been described by senior Oromo writers like Isayas Hordofa and Gaddisa Birru as a pioneer of Oromo literature, a role model, and a source of inspiration for many young Oromo writers.[35] Dhaba's novels and short stories are canonical texts in Oromo literary studies and are used as textbooks for students of Oromo literature in Ethiopian high schools, colleges, and universities. They have received significant literary attention and favourable literary criticism.

Dhaba was born in an Afan Oromo speaking family in Wallaga in western Ethiopia, which allowed him to learn the culture of non-Oromo groups in this part of the country. He later moved to the USA, where he currently resides. *Gurraacha Abbayaa* (1996) is his second novel, and

---

34　See, for example, Ivo Strecker, *The Hamar of Southern Ethiopia: III: Conversation in Dambaita.* (Berlin: Klaus Renner, 1970).

35　Isayas Hordofa and Gaddis Birru shared with their views about Dhaba Wayessa in 2018 when I interviewed them for my PhD research.

it was reprinted three times—a notable success for an Oromo novel. While the back cover testimonials praise Dhaba for his close attention to *Oromo* culture and history,[36] *Gurraacha Abbayaa* shows that Dhaba has as attentive ears for the imaginative expressions and culture of the Gumuz as for the Oromo. In fact, the novel is accompanied by 6 pages of glosses of Afan Oromo and Gumuz words and 2 pages of glosses of literary terms in Afan Oromo and English.

Unlike other Oromo novels, *Gurraacha Abbayyaa* focuses entirely on non-Oromo ethnic groups. It thematises cultural norms (and their transgression) and inter-group conflict and it includes several songs, interestingly attributing to the Gumuz some forms that are popular among the Oromo, like the *geerarsa* and *dhaaduu* (heroic war poems). This may be a way for Dhaba to imply cross-cultural influence or shared literary practices between these two neighbouring communities. Just as *Evangadi* subverts and innovates the Amharic literary canon, *Gurraacha Abbayaa* moves thematically and geographically beyond the Oromo-centred narratives of the Oromo literary canon, thereby expanding the spatial imagination and thematic horizon of the Oromo novelistic tradition. The novel resists the monolingual use of the Oromo language by inflecting it with many traces of the Gumuz language.

Gurraacha Abbayaa is set in the village of Mattin in Gumuz land in western Ethiopia. The plot revolves around the conflict between an Amhara man, Gebru Teferra (who speaks Oromo and Gumuz), and a Gumuz man, Bacangire Bakalo, and the consequence of the conflict for both their families, with a particular emphasis on Bacangire's children. The first half of the novel presents the conflict between Bacangire and Gebru and the series of vengeful attacks involving relatives on both sides. The conflict began when Gebru started an adulterous relationship with a married Gumuz woman called Yalunge, an affair which is presented as offensive for the Gumuz community. Arrogant Gebru escalates the conflict by disclosing his affair with Yalunge and killing her husband, who is Bacangire's brother. Bacangire retaliates. The retaliation between

---

36   The testimonial by the Ethiopian Amharic-language poet Tsegaye Gebre-Medhin, for example, says: 'Dhaba shows that he is a dedicated student of Oromo mythology with love and respect for the culture. [...] He has an ear for the music of Oromo language, he uses his talent to translate the dance, music, costume, and proverbs of the people. He brings the people on the stage, not cultural caricatures'; Dhaba, *Gurraacha Abbayaa*, back cover.

the two families escalates until both Gebru and Bacangire are killed, and the feud ends with Gebru's family destroying Bacangire's village, exterminating all the people and animals in that village, and leaving only two survivors, Bacangire's teenage children Teto and Doca. Most events in the first half of the novel are accompanied by songs like *geerarsa* and *dhaaduu*, which characters like Gebru use to mark their achievements.

The second half of the novel is devoted to Teto's violations of Gumuz cultural norms. Unlike the other Gumuz youngsters who are extrovert and playful, Teto is a taciturn boy, who has been in a state of psychological distress since early childhood following the death of his mother, a pain worsened by his father's murder. After the destruction of Mattin, Doca and Teto relocate to another Gumuz village, Luquma, where Teto starts a romantic affair with a Gumuz girl, Yenchen Banzi, during which he contravenes several cultural norms. For example, he shakes Yenche's hand while she is in menstrual isolation, he has sexual intercourse with her before marriage, and he ends up killing her brother in order to be able to marry her without having to offer his sister Doca to Yenche's brother in exchange. Teto's lack of respect for the norms of Gumuz culture proves to be not only his own undoing, but also his sister's. When Teto attempts to force her to marry Yenche's brother in an exchange marriage, Doca kills herself. Teto himself is killed by another Gumuz man who is married to Yenche. In this part, the novel incorporates a few oral texts that are part of cultural events and rituals, like marriage blessing.

The title of the novel, meaning 'The Black Man from Abbaya', invokes the Abbaya, the main river flowing through Gumuz territory, and also refers to the skin colour of the Gumuz people. 'The Black Man' refers specifically to Teto (*gurraacha* is masculine in Afan Oromo). The title is taken directly from the words of a minor character, Ayalnesh, who hosts Teto at her home when he runs away from Luquma after his cultural infractions. It is Ayalnesh who addresses Teto as 'Gurraacha Abbayaa', literally 'the black man from the land around the river Abbaya'. Though specifically used to address Teto in this context, the expression extends to all the Gumuz as 'the black people living on the land around this river'. While the Gumuz racially characterise the Ethiopian highlanders, particularly the Amhara, as *diimaa*, or 'the red people', the Amhara highlanders, on their part, called the Gumuz *sanqalla* or *shanqilla*, an Amharic term with pejorative connotations meaning 'black people'.

Evangadi and *Gurraacha Abbayaa* follow different approaches in representing the 'multilingual local' oral worlds of the Hamar and the Gumuz, as already mentioned.[37] Francesca Orsini's notion of 'multilingual local' urges us to pay attention to the range of existing language practices in a particular locale, and to the ways in which texts and archives typically privilege some and thereby exclude other languages, voices, and stories. The 'multilingual local' therefore asks to consider the linguistic positionality of texts and authors. Within Ethiopian literary politics, where the monolingual Amhara literary paradigm has tended to suppress the languages of peripheral and politically marginalized groups, and of those who rely on orality as a means of literary expression, this question acquires particular significance.

Fiqremarqos filters the Hamar oral world through literate characters who travel through Hamar territory. Unlike Fiqremarqos, Dhaba presents the interactions and encounters between non-literate characters without giving any evidence of written practices among Gumuz communities. Linguistically, Dhaba gives more space to the Gumuz language than Fiqremarqos does to the Hamar language. We read many Gumuz words, sentences, and even a couple of poems in *Gurraacha Abbayaa*. Fiqremarqos instead includes only a few untranslatable words in the Hamar language such as *evangadi,* a dance that has no equivalent in Amharic. However, in both novels, though to varying degrees, we encounter the voices, worldviews, and experiences of indigenous peoples. One way in which their voices, experiences, and worldviews are represented is through different forms of orature: folk tales, folk songs, and proverbs. The novels differ in this regard, too, as the next section shows. Whereas *Gurraacha Abbayaa* directly quotes fragments of orature in Gurmuz to make its presence more palpable, *Evangadi* mostly mentions, translates and/or paraphrases Hamar orature, weakening the effect. As a result, despite its ethnographic and pluralising intentions, the novel appears less committed to making space for orature.

37　Francesca Orsini, 'The Multilingual Local in World Literature', *Comparative Literature*, 67.4 (2015), 345–374.

Novelized Orature in *Evangadi* and *Gurraacha Abbayaa*

> The continuity with the oral tradition is evident in the novels written
> in the African languages, in which the derivation of content and mode
> is direct and immediate. But the oral–literate interface, in its various
> manifestations, can also be felt as a quality of the fictional works of many
> an African writer, reflecting either a conscious design or, as is often
> the case, the effect of a cultural retention determined by the African
> background (Abiola Irele).[38]

In his Introduction to *The Cambridge Companion to the African Novel*,
Abiola Irele argues that the oral-written interface common to many
African novels makes oral texts not only resources for local colour in
these novels but rather a structural element. At the same time, the use
of oral texts for local colour cannot be ignored, as it plays a crucial role
in the process of localization of the novel. Both *Evangadi* and *Gurraacha
Abbayaa* embed oral texts/orature within the main narration. *Evangadi*
includes a folk tale and songs from the oral tradition; *Gurraacha Abbayaa*
folk songs, proverbs, and oral poetry like blessing. This section presents
the strategies used by the novels to novelize orature and their interplay
between orature and literature. It also examines how the novels retain
the performative aspect of orature by indicating the presence of the
audience and describing the performance when presenting oral texts.
As a genre that constitutively mediates between different genres, the
novel, I argue, actively blurs the binary between literature and orature.

The two novels employ direct quotation, characterisation and the
character system, and narrative commentary to incorporate oral texts
into their narratives, though they differ in the effects they create. As
already mentioned, the inclusion of orature in each novel is prompted
by the description of cultural ceremonies, social events, and conflicts
between characters.

In *Gurraacha Abbayaa*, the narrator uses the third person to describe
the use of folk songs in the characters' daily lives. For example, when
Gebru comes home after killing Badija, the narrator describes him
performing a heroic *geraarsa* song (see below, and also Tadesse Jirata,
Chapter 7 in this volume) to celebrate his heroism:

---

38   Abiola Irele, ed., *The Cambridge Companion to the African Novel* (Cambridge & New
     York: Cambridge University Press, 2009), p. 1.

> When Gebru chants the *geerarsa*, his voice falls and rises like a tree hit by a whirlwind. It dips and then rises. He boasts as he recites the *geerarsa*, he boasts. The elders and women jump back and forward. When Gebru feels exhausted because of his repeated boastings, they run towards him. They hug him and kiss him. He jumps and dances, and they jump and sing with him.[39]

For the most part, though, orature is incorporated in both novels through direct speech, with the narrator including a direct quotation from an oral text, whether a tale or song, performed by the characters. In *Evangadi*, one folk tale is cited in order to contextualise a cultural practice. When Karlet comes back to Hamar land and finds her Hamar friends preparing to search for Delti and the Hamar elders conducting a divination ritual to gather more information on Delti's whereabouts and safety, she is struck by the absence of women from the ritual and asks an old man, Galtambe, about it. Galtambe relies on his memory to answer the question. He thinks for a while before recalling a Hamar folk tale that explains the exclusion of women from community affairs.

> Once Borjo's[40] legs got stuck in the mud, he saw Hamar women passing near him as he was trying to get out of the mud. Borjo asked the women for help. But the women showed him no pity, they were busy with their tasks and engaged in their own conversation. Thinking that he was joking, they told him that they were too busy to help. Borjo was disappointed and cursed them: 'May you never be up to any serious business. May you always be busy with insignificant tasks. May you be forever petulant'.
>
> After a while, Borjo noticed a group of Hamar men coming along, who were going to collect honey from the nearby forest. The men carried fire to keep the bees away and needed to walk quickly as their fire was about to die. Borjo asked them for help, too. The men responded at once and put all their belongings aside and helped him. He blessed them: 'May you be responsible for the important business of your community. May you be able to solve the problems facing your people. May you be wise and calm'.
>
> Since then, only men have been destined to bear all the responsibilities. The rights of thinking, discussing and deciding on the causes and the concerns of the Hamar community have been granted only to men.[41]

---

39   Dhaba, *Gurraacha Abbayaa* p. 17.
40   Borjo is the name of a Hamar deity.
41   Fiqremarqos, *Evangadi*, pp. 212–213.

This is an etiological tale that gives a mythical explanation for the gender-based inequality practised in the Hamar community. The author tries to retain the oral characteristics of this story, both through narrative commentary (he tells us that the story has descended orally from the Hamar ancestors) and through the structure of the tale itself. Galtambe must rely on his memory, and this is indicated by the pause he takes before launching into the story, and he uses the expression 'once', typical of oral storytelling, to indicate the undefined past in which the story is set. Lastly, his short and simple sentence structures reflect the style of oral narratives. Though the novel on the whole largely uses short sentences, those in Galtambe's story sound as if they are narrated orally to a listener.

Evangadi also cites folk songs to convey the relationship between humans and nature among the Hamar. These songs are presented, translated into Amharic, in the first chapter of the novel, in the context of the romantic relationship between two Hamar youths, Delti and Dara. Dara loves Delti, though she knows he has a fiancée, and decides to tell him about her feelings. While mulling over how to approach him, she finds out that Delti occasionally spends the night on Buska Mountain, the tallest mountain in Hamar land. One evening, she follows him to the top of the mountain and spends the night with him. During their time together, Delti leaves Dara alone for a while. Dara meditates on the happy moments they have enjoyed together during the night and starts singing a song to express her feelings to the moon and the stars. The narrator tells us that while singing she dances and plays a traditional musical instrument called *turumba*.[42]

> *...though you are alone, moon,*
> *please witness my wish of being with my hero.*
> *You, stars, you seem disappointed and keep silent,*
> *you hate to share my happiness.*

The stars blinked. She saw them telling her, 'Keep it up!'.

> *If so, if so,*
> *Hey! Sing for us love songs,*
> *Please dance and let us dance together, let us feel happy.*
> *Whenever my hero moves around like a heifer...*

---

42   The songs appear in italics in the novel, and the ellipses are in the original.

When Delti comes back and finds Dara dancing and singing alone, he is impressed by her dance and starts singing along.

> *Speak out, sky, speak out, oh earth, on what happened,*
> *let the mountain speak out,*
> *let the forest witness where I have stayed the whole day.*
> *Baldambe, Lalombe, Galtambe...*[43]
> *all my friends, please speak out.*
> *Is Bankimoro'slaw repudiated?*[44]
> *Or his words invalidated?!*
> *I have not thrown down my enemy,*
> *I have not killed a lion or a giraffe... with my gun.*
> *Please speak out Zergiya, a gift from my father,*[45]
> *Have you seen me when I feel tired or strong?*
> *Please speak out, birds, on what you have seen yesterday.*
> *Are the principles of my father or his words needed no more...?*[46]

The song is important from the perspective of narrative content, because of the role it plays in the narrative, and because of the formal quality it brings to the novel. It features as part of the Hamar protagonist Delti's childhood recollections and enhances his sweet memory of love. The song signifies the connection between Dara, Delti, and their environment, and how the Hamar people enjoy a life without deprivation in their natural habitat. The language and structure of this and other novelized songs reflect the characteristics of orature: lexical parallelism, repetition (line 5), the use of figurative language (mainly personification), and the commentary (between lines 4 and 5, and lines 8 and 9) giving information about the performative aspects of the songs are the elements that foreground the song's oral qualities.[47] The main literary device used in these songs is personification, and its narrative function is to foreground the relationship between humans and nature,

---

43   These are names of Delti's friends.
44   A Hamar deity.
45   Zergiya is the name of a cultural gift among the Hamar people.
46   Ibid., pp. 39–40.
47   The personification of the inanimate is popular in orature, Ngũgĩ reminds us:
     'Humans are definitely part of nature. In that sense they are not different from
     animals and plants that all depend on the same environment of earth, air, water,
     and sun. They are products of the same mother-environment. Orature takes that
     for granted. Hence in the narratives of orature, humans, birds, animals, and plants
     interact freely, they often assume each others' forms, including language. Humans
     in distress talk to birds and give them messages' ('Notes', p. 5).

blurring the differences between them and establishing an effect of intimacy.

Other than this, the narrator in *Evangadi* tells us that when the Hamar celebrate *evangadi*, they dance, jump and sing. Similarly, in the last section of the novel, when we read about the multicultural festival in Geneva organised by Karlet as part of her research, the narrator tells us that the representatives of various Ethiopian communities perform several dances and sing folk songs—though without describing or quoting any song in particular or any concrete example of orature.

Gurraacha Abbaayaa includes a total of seven folk songs, a proverb and blessing. As with the oral tale in *Evangadi*, the songs are introduced in the context of discussions among the characters on socio-cultural issues such as farming, conflict, cultural festivities, and marriage, in line with the novelization of the oral world of the Gumuz people. In fact, the novel mostly discusses cultural issues through oral texts. To represent Gumuz views, the text uses Gumuz characters with their indigenous names, and sometimes has them speak directly in their own language.

The first example of folk song occurs right in Chapter One, which presents the Gumuz culture of communal farming and situates Teto, the main protagonist, in this context. One day, Teto is walking alone in the bush and hears the voices of a large number of people harvesting and singing work songs. One song is quoted in the Gumuz language and paraphrased in Afan Oromo, the language of the novel. At a first hearing, Teto does not understand what the song is really about. As he approaches the group of people, he hears the following words:

> *Maatiyaa dumaatisiyaa qomisaa*
> *Eesaalskee maanjaa lumbaa*
> *Hoo-ho-hoo-ho-hoo-ho-hoo*
> *Hoo-ho-hoo-ho-hoo-ho-hoo.*[48]

The narrator tells us the meaning of the song in a short phrase, '*Obbolessi kee jabaataadha- akka ibidaa*' (Your brother is as strong as fire), and confirms that the song is a group work song (*weedduu daboo* in Afan Oromo).[49] The song is not really about farming, though, but rather about the conflict between Bacangire and Gebru, and this is how the

___

48   Dhaba, *Gurraacha Abbayaa*, p. 12.
49   Ibid.

novel relates orature to its plot. Bacangire is likened to iron, for he is expected to avenge his brother Badija, killed by Gebru. The song, as a result, directly relates to the main plot of the novel (in the first two lines), while lines 3-4 consists of ideophones (the 'hoo-hoo' sound). In this context, the ideophones are used sound to get all the singers to join together and motivate one another during agricultural work (see Desta and Yenaleam, Chapter 6 in this volume). Ideophones are a distinctive feature of songs in this novel.

Songs, in other words, mark and punctuate important events in the culture of the Gumuz. While Teto is alone in the bush, speculating about the meaning of the song, two Gumuz girls come up to him. One teases him by saying, 'You seem a lone hunter', while the other girl says, 'We wish that you could make a kill and make us sing and celebrate', once again an allusion to to conflict between Bacangire and Gebru.[50] In fact, interestingly *Gurraacha Abbayaa* also includes two genres of heroic war poems, *dhaaduu* and *geerarsa*, that are famous among the traditional Oromo people and are performed in situation of serious conflict such as wars, battles, raids, or other military endeavours. The novel presents the *dhaaduu* and *geerarsa* as if they are Gumuz genres. In *Gurraacha Abbayaa*, the poems are performed in the context of the feud between Bacangire's and Gebru's families. They are narrative representation of the strong relationship and shared cultural practices between the Oromo and the Gumuz.

When Gebru returns home with the genitals and limbs of Bacangire's brother, Badija, as evidence of the killing, his relatives and friends celebrate his achievement for several weeks. The celebration is marked by different types of boastful song (*dhaaduu*) sung by Gebru himself and his friends, and the description lingers on the loud and multifarious singing in a remarkable representation of performance: 'Those unable to attend the celebration due to old age or other reasons listen to them from their homes. Women's songs, their ululation, young boys' songs, the killer's bragging... all together they rouse the hearts of men and women'.[51]

Dhaaduu 'constitutes a man's personal history, upon which his reputation is built, for it is through his prowess that he is remembered

---

50　Dhaba, *Gurraacha Abbayaa*, p. 14.
51　Ibid., p. 1.

during his own life-time and through which he will leave his mark on the future', writes Aneesa Kassam. 'They are recited at a very rapid pace, thus conveying the young man's agitation and anger. In them he usually exaggerates his bravery, and there is a subtle play on words'.[52] Gebru's *dhaaduu* and *geerarsa* songs convey some of the same characteristics:

> *Abbaa Gabruu Tafarraa…*[53]
> I have gone through the river valley
> and dried the throat
> of the black man from Mattin,
> whose fame was far reaching.
> I went through the village of Mattin
> and ruined his jaw.
> I went through the village of Mattin
> and got rid of my grudge.
> *Abbaa Gabruu Tafarraa…*
> my *facha*[54] is unique
> for the hairs around the genitals are curled up,
> his teeth are sharp they can cut raw meat.
> He can carry *gaya*[55] in his left hand
> and hold *saya*[56] in his right hand.
> I made him jump over a tree log
> and made him to stand on his knees,
> and made him throw away his gun
> and made him eat sand…[57]

The boastings in the song celebrate and exaggerate Gebru's achievements. The narrator describes the audience's reactions as validating Gebru: 'admiration from his sisters-in-law… the songs of the young girls… and the *geerarsa*, along with the songs, seem to have swollen Gabru's heart'.[58] This commentary alerts the reader to the power of the performance—a power that the written text struggles to convey. When it comes to the

---

52   Aneesa Kassam, 'The Fertile Past: The Gabra Concept of Oral Tradition', *Africa*, 56.2 (1986), 193–209 (pp. 199–200).

53   *Abbaa Gabruu Tafarraa*: 'Teferra, Father of Gebru', a proud appellative.

54   *Facha* is a piece of the human body, either limbs or genitals, usually kept by killers as proof that they have killed their enemies.

55   *Gaya* is a traditional tobacco smoked by the Gumuz.

56   *Saya* is a cow.

57   Dhaba, *Gurraacha Abbayaa*, pp. 16–17.

58   Ibid., p. 17.

other *geerarsa* by Gebru, quoted below, Gebru is said to be influenced by the audience and to reflect it back.

> *... Abbaa Gabruu Tafarraa*
> I am relieved of the scorn of the *sanqalla*'s women
> And I am done with my revenge on the *sanqalla* of Abbaya...[59]

The fact Gebru is an Amhara who speaks both Oromo and Gumuz and sings a *geerarsa* can be read as a strategy to emphasise the strong presence of the Oromo language among the Gumuz.

Novelized songs can also be used to voice criticism and express popular reaction. After Gebru ends his celebration, he wants to visit the nearby market village in order to hold another celebration there, but Bacangire kills him first. The narrator tells us that 'a few days after Gebru murdered Badija, the cattle keepers *also* produced a song about Gebru's defeat' (*'Otuu oolee hin bulin tikeen* illee *weedduu itti mogaaste'*). The word *'illee'* (also) indicates that the cattle keepers are not the first group to produce a song about Gebru's death and that other social groups in Gumuz land have already condemned Gebru's action. The cattle keepers sing:

> Gebru, a hero of Axaballa,
> but the *sanqalla* is his lord...
> Did he think that the blood of the *sanqalla* of Adare[60]
> was a dog's blood or a cat's blood...?
> Whenever Gebru hunts,
> why does he not think twice?
> For it is inevitable that one may be measured
> by the very measure he uses to measure others...[61]

Though this is a cattle herders' song sung while herding the cattle, this song is not a work song but rather responds to the most important event they have witnessed in their community, the conflict between the main characters. As such the song provides crucial commentary on the novel's plot. As in the previous examples, the song employs symbolism, metaphor ('dog's blood' and 'cat's blood' in lines 3-4 conveying how the Gumuz are looked down upon by Gebru and equated with animals),

---

59 Ibid.
60 *Adare* is a term for village in the Gumuz language.
61 Ibid., p. 38.

and questioning (lines 3-6) to demonstrate Gebru's wrong-headed perception of the Gumuz's weakness. The song presents an effective use of figurative language, and the fact that the poem is a rejoinder to Gebru's boasting puts the two songs in conversation, creating a network of oral texts through which communities make sense of events, reflect upon their relationship with other communities, and memorialise the past. By using this network of songs for poetic and thematic purpose, the novel creates an orature-novel interface.

So far, I have discussed songs, mostly *geerarsa,* recited after an event. *Gurraacha Abbayaa* presents another *dhaaduu* recited in anticipation of an event. This time the reciter is Teto, the main protagonist, who remembers having heard it from his father. When his sister, Doca, refuses to marry Yenche's brother in exchange for Teto marrying Yenche and kills herself by drowning into the Abbaya River, he decides to kill his would-be brother-in-law so that he can marry Yenche without an exchange of brides between the two families. Before he sets out to commit this murder, Teto remembers some lines of a *dhaaduu* that he used to hear from his father. The poem hints at the murder he is about to undertake.

> A waylayer who hunts overnight!
> A waylayer who has no shadow!
> Who walks warily!
> Who never misses when he aims![62]

Before he commits the murder, Teto repeats some of the lines of the poem ('A waylayer who has no shadow/ who never misses his aim!')[63]. The repetition focuses on the action that the singer is going to undertake and highlights his own strength. The fact that Teto remembers this song from his late father reflects the novel's recognition of the generational oral transmission of such oral texts.

Unlike *Evangadi,* in *Gurraacha Abbayaa* most orature is generated by a specific event and is described to be performed in a lively context. The narratives in the novel and the elements of orature are meaningfully weaved together, creating an effective interaction. In most cases *Gurraacha Abbayaa* directly quotes oral texts. This creates a strong interface between the novel and orature and reflects the effect of oral

---

62   Ibid., p. 129.
63   Ibid., p. 133.

texts on the narrative development of the novel. As mentioned earlier, direct quoting is a more effective way of 'localizing' or locating the novel in a particular socio-cultural and political context than the paraphrasing or indirect referencing of *Evangadi.*

The novelization of orature is also represented through characterization and the character system. *Evangadi* features characters from both literate and oral communities, and we learn about the oral world of the Hamar and their imaginative culture through non-literate characters like Delti, Dara, and Galtambe. These characters share their experiences with one another and support each other in understanding their respective communities. The novel presents their oral knowledge as part of the narrative, honouring and valorising it. This trait is present also in *Gurraacha Abbayaa*, with major characters like Gebru (who is not a Gumuz) and Teto (who is) and minor characters like Yenche's father.

Conclusion

Orature is inducted primarily to eschew scriptocentric representation systems —Anjali Gera Roy[64]

This chapter has explored the relationship between orature and literature at formal and content levels and conceptualized their relationship through the term 'novelization'. Novelization involves a set of techniques and choices to represent oral texts and create an interface or effective co-existence of oral and written texts in a novel for narrative and aesthetic purposes. The Ethiopian village novels analysed in this chapter employ devices such as personification, repetition, symbolism, and metaphor; direct and indirect quotation of orature, whether in the original language spoken by the characters or through paraphrase and translation into the language of the novel; and narratorial commentary to novelize orature and foreground 'an ongoing relationship of coevalness and simultaneity' between the novel and orature.[65] These elements not only reflect the presence of orature in the societies depicted, but also inform and shape the development of the story and the narrative

---

64   Anjali Gera Roy, 'The Folktale in Achebe's Fictions' in *Oral Tradition in African Literature,* ed. by Chin Ce and Charles Smith (Nigeria: Handel Books 2015), pp. 30–50 (p. 41).

65   George, 'The Oral–Literate Interface', p. 17.

structure of the novels, for example by enriching and explaining events, conflicts, cultural themes, or views about cultural practices. In *Evangadi*, novelized orature explains the gendered views of the Hamar community, while in *Gurraacha Abbayaa* it conveys a worldview about socio-cultural life, and particularly about conflict and marriage. Orature, as Obiechina argues, has the flexibility to be incorporated into novelistic narratives because of the openness of the novel as a genre. However, not all novels are equal to this task. Village novels, this chapter has argued, are particularly suited because they engage extensively with oral worlds and cultural practices of rural, sometimes remote communities.

At the same time, Obiechina argues, narrative proverbs or novelized orature 'function as images, metaphors, and symbols and advance the meanings and formal qualities of the narratives in which they occur'.[66] The two novels present concrete examples of orature and their oral/performance qualities while modifing them for narrative purposes. For example, in *Evangadi* novelized orature is used to represent the views of the Hamar community on gender-based divisions of labour, while characterization is used to present a Western oppositional view to such division, as the dialogue between the white female anthropologist, Karlet, and the Hamar characters Goiti and Galtambe shows. Besides, in the words of Anjali Gera Roy, 'far from contributing to their novels' anthropological flavour or acting as symbolic devices, folk materials juxtapos[e] an alternative idiom–of African orature–with its own unique manner of structuring reality'.[67] In *Evangadi*, Karlet embodies the Western encounter with the alternative worldview of the Hamar people, which she comes to respect. Novelized orature not only opens the novel to specific multilingual locals, then, but presents an 'alternative idiom' and carries an 'organic aspect of African imagination' even when appropriated by the novel. As such, novelized orature is a useful analytical category that, this chapter has showed, plays a similar role in African novels in postcolonial languages (as in the case of Obiechina writing on Achebe) and in African languages. This chapter thus participates in the scholarship on orality and the African novel, but with the important twist that the comparison is not between the novels' colonial/postcolonial language vs. orature in African languages, but

---

66   Obiechina, 'Narrative Proverbs', p. 200.
67   Roy, 'The Folktale in Achebe's Fictions', p. 31.

rather of novelized orature within Afrophone texts. While the novels do not participate in the colonial language debate, they do participate in the debate within Ethiopian literature, which has a domestically colonial character. Therefore, my chapter adds to the African language debate by highlighting a situation in which the role of the colonial language is occupied by an African national language, Amharic. But while issues of unequal resources and exclusion are germane to the Ethiopian situation just as for Europhone African literature, Amharic—unlike English, French, or Portuguese—does not give Ethiopian writers a wider audience or connect them to writers elsewhere in Africa. The novel here does not imply an Afropolitan move or audience, though it still relates to African literary studies, from which Ethiopian literature has largely kept separate.

The novelization of orature can also be read as a form of literary resistance against the oppositional division between orature and literature as well as against the dominant voices in the novels. It is also a means through which the novels make oral texts travel or be more visible beyond their original linguistic context, by transforming oral texts into written texts. For the evolutionists, the transformation from oral to writing is a 'linear progression' leading to the replacement of orature with literature, which is considered more advanced and sophisticated. As this chapter shows, this is not true, as orature can be distinctively present in the novels with some of its major inherent qualities foregrounded. In short, the novelization of orature makes it possible to disseminate orature to reading audiences. In other words, novelization is the narrative technique through which orature and literature interact and support each other in presenting the multiple experiences and stories of a certain group of people.

Lastly, what implications does such a reading have for the study of Ethiopian literature, African literature, and world literature? While *Evangadi* uses Amharic to present the experiences of marginalized people and can be said to linguistically belong to mainstream Ethiopian literature, the novel's attempt to reconcile or at least mitigate the antagonistic relationship between literatures in Amharic and other Ethiopian languages is a novel and positive gesture within the Amharic literary tradition. In presenting Amhara immigrants as arrogant and disruptive presences that bring doom to Gumuz villages, *Gurraacha*

Abbayaa can be said to implicitly oppose the cultural and linguistic domination of the Amhara. But since this Afan Oromo novel focuses entirely on Gumuz and Amhara characters and uses Oromo infused with Gumuz and Amharic terms, it also distances itself from Amharic- and Oromo-centred narratives. We can read the two novels as oppositional within the mainstream Amharic-focused paradigm of Ethiopian literature, which pits an Amhara literary 'centre' against the Oromo and other further 'peripheries'. *Gurraacha Abbayaa* mediates between two peripheries, while *Evangadi* mediates between the West, the Amharic 'centre', and a further, oral, 'periphery'.

At the same time, while both novels exemplify Moretti's idea that the novel outside Europe is a hybrid of imported form and local colour, they challenge Casanova's proposition that literatures in marginalized or minor languages strive to achieve recognition from the centre.[68] Both novels are in fact outside the circuit of world literature and of the (Anglophone) novel as a globally circulating form. At the same time, novelized orature in the two novels can help counter the exclusionary definition of literature in world literature studies, which excludes orature from the definition of (world) literature. While novelized orature in these Afrophone novels does not show any influence of the dominant world languages, it highlights the workings of multilingual realities and of the oral worlds both inside and outside the novels, thereby implicitly denouncing how monolingual literary paradigms suppress the languages of peripheral and politically marginalized groups and of those who rely on orality as a means of literary expression. In short, the novelized orature in these novels proves the continued importance of orality and of oral imaginative and artistic expressions for both individuals and groups and stresses the need to acknowledge orature as a living part of literature, including of world literature.

---

68   Pascale Casanova, *The World Republic of Letters* (London: Verso, 2004).

Bibliography

Tolessa, Addisu, 'The Historical Transformation of a Folklore Genre: The Geerarsa as a National Literature of the Oromo in the Context of Amhara Colonization in Ethiopia' (unpublished doctoral thesis, Indiana University, 1990).

__________, *Geerarsa folksong as the Oromo national literature: a study of ethnography, folklore, and folklife in the context of the Ethiopian colonization of Oromia* (Lewiston: Mellen Press, 1999).

Ahmed, Ali Jimale and Adera, Taddesse, eds, *The Road Less Traveled: Reflections on the literatures of the Horn of Africa* (Trenton: Red Sea Press, 2008).

Andrzejewski, Boris W., 'Modern and Traditional Aspects of Somali Drama', *Journal of African Cultural Studies*, 23.1 (2011), https://doi.org/10.1080/1369 6815.2011.581461

Tafarra, Asafa, 'Towards a Political Sociology of Oromo Literature: Jaarsoo Waaqoo's Poetry' (unpublished doctoral thesis, Addis Ababa University, 2003).

Dibaba, Assefa Tefera, 'Ethnography of Resistance Poetics: Power and Authority in Salale Oromo Folklore and Resistance Culture, Ethiopia, Northeast Africa' (unpublished doctoral thesis, Indiana University, 2015), https://www.proquest.com/openview/60ec72177f5e63bc5178f28ff7b877c7/1?pq-origsite=gscholar&cbl=18750

Bakhtin, Mikhail, *The Dialogic Imagination: Four Essays by M. M. Bakhtin*, ed. by Michael Holquist, translated by Carlyin Emerson and Michael Holquist (Austin: University of Texas Press, 1981).

Bakhtin, Mikhail, *Problems of Dostoevsky's Poetics*, ed. and trans. by Caryl Emerson (Manchester: Manchester University Press, 1984).

Casanova, Pascale, *The World Republic of Letters* (London: Verso, 2004).

Clapham, Christopher, 'Rewriting Ethiopian History', *Annales d'Éthiopie*, 18.1 (2002), https://doi.org/10.3406/ethio.2002.1013

Crummey, Donald, 'Literacy in an Oral Society: The Case of Ethiopian Land Records', *Journal of African Cultural Studies*, 18.1 (2006), https://doi.org/10.1080/13696850600750251

Damrosch, David, *What Is World Literature?* (Princeton: Princeton University Press, 2003).

Wayessa, Dhaba, *Gurraacha Abbayaa* (A Black Man from Abbaya) (Washington DC: Fettan Printers, 1996).

Finnegan, Ruth. H., 'The How of Literature', *Oral Tradition*, 20.2 (2005), 164–187, https://doi.org/10.1353/ort.2006.0004

Desta, Fiqremarqos, *Evangadi* (Addis Ababa: NA, 1998).

George, Olankunke, 'The Oral–Literate Interface' in *The Cambridge Companion to the African Novel*, ed. by Abiola Irele (Cambridge: Cambridge University Press, 2009), pp. 15–30.

Gerard, Albert, *Four African Literatures: Xhosa, Sotho, Zulu, Amharic* (Berkeley: University of California Press, 1971).

Goody, Jack, *The Interface Between the Written and the Oral* (Cambridge: Cambridge University Press, 1987).

Horton, Richard and Finnegan, Ruth, eds, *Modes of Thought, Essays on Thinking in Western and Non-Western Societies* (London: Faber and Faber, 1973).

Hussein, Jeylan, 'A Critical Review of the Political and Stereotypical Portrayals of the Oromo in the Ethiopian Historiography', *Nordic Journal of African Studies*, 15.3 (2006), https://doi.org/10.53228/njas.v15i3.27

Irele, Abiola, 'The African Imagination', *Research in African Literatures*, 21.1 (1990), 49–67.

———, ed., *The Cambridge companion to the African novel* (Cambridge: Cambridge University Press, 2009).

Julien, Eileen, *African Novels and the Question of Orality* (Place: Indiana University Press, 1992).

———, 'African Literature' in *Africa*, ed. by Phyllis M. Martin and Patrick O'Meara (Bloomington: Indiana University Press, 1995), pp. 295–312.

Kaschula, Russell H., 'Exploring the Oral-Written Interface with Particular Reference to Xhosa Oral Poetry', *Research in African Literatures*, 28.1 (1997), https://www.jstor.org/stable/3820777

Kassam, Aneesa, 'The Fertile Past: The Gabra Concept of Oral Tradition', *Africa*, 56.2 (1986), 193–209, https://doi.org/10.2307/1160632

Levine, Donald, *Greater Ethiopia: The Evolution of a Multiethnic Society* (Chicago: University of Chicago Press, 1974).

Markakis, John, *Ethiopia: The Last Two Frontiers* (Woodbridge: James Currey, 2011).

Merolla, Daniella, 'Introduction: Orality and technauriture of African literatures', *Tydskrif Vir Letterkunde*, 51.1 (2014), 80–88, https://doi.org/10.4314/tvl.v51i1.8

Moolla, Fiona, 'When Orature Becomes Literature: Somali Oral Poetry and Folktales in Somali Novels', *Comparative Literature Studies*, 49.3 (2012), 434–462.

Moretti, Franco, 'Conjectures on World Literature', *New Left Review*, 2.1 (2000), 54–68.

Obiechina, Emmanuel, 'Narrative Proverbs in the African Novel', *Oral Tradition*, 7.2 (1992), https://journal.oraltradition.org/wp-content/uploads/files/articles/7ii/7_2_complete.pdf

Okpewho, Isidore, *African Oral Literature: Backgrounds, Character, and Continuity* (Bloomington: Indiana University Press, 1992).

Ong, Walter, *Orality and Literacy* (London: Routledge, 2002).

Orsini, Francesca, 'The Multilingual Local in World Literature', *Comparative Literature*, 67.4 (2015), 345–374.

Roy, Anjali Gera, 'The Folktale in Achebe's Fictions' in *Oral Tradition in African Literature*, ed. by Chin Ce and Charles Smith (Nigeria: Handel Books 2015), pp. 30–50.

Strecker, Ivo, *The Hamar of Southern Ethiopia, III: Conversation in Dambaita* (Berlin: Klaus Renner, 1970).

Thiong'o, Ngũgĩ Wa, 'Notes towards a Performance Theory of Orature', *Performance Research*, 12.3 (2007), https://doi.org/10.1080/13528160701771253

4. Fluid Texts

Bhojpuri Songs and World Literature

Francesca Orsini

Introduction

In late 2020, the English translation of the 1977 Bhojpuri novel *Phoolsunghi* created a stir in the Indian press.[1] The rural Bhojpur region, straddling the states of Bihar and Uttar Pradesh in northern India and the southern part of Nepal known as the Terai, is known for its wonderfully rich, old, and still vibrant tradition of orature. *Phoolsunghi*, written by veteran Bhojpuri literary activist Pandey Kapil and translated by Delhi academic Gautam Choubey, himself the grandson of a major Bhojpuri novelist, revolves around the famous Bhojpuri poet and songwriter Mahendar Missir (1866-1946), the singer-courtesan Dhelabai (d. 1931), and their patron, in the late colonial period.[2] Reviewers praised the elegant translation for 'open[ing] up the local culture and tradition to a larger audience', and noted that although 'Bhojpuri culture has generated

---

1   I humbly dedicate this chapter to the late scholar Catherine Servan-Schreiber, who dedicated her life to the study of Bhojpuri orature and who sadly passed away prematurely in November 2021. This chapter would not have been possible without her brilliant and extensive scholarship, particularly her two books: *Chanteurs itinérants en Inde du Nord: la tradition orale Bhojpuri* (Paris: L'Harmattan, 1999) and *Histoire d'une musique métisse à l'île Maurice: chutney indien et séga Bollywood* (Paris: Riveneuve éditions, 2010).

2   Kapil Pandey edited the Bhojpuri magazine *Bhojpuri Sammelan Patrika* and established the first All India Association of Bhojpuri Writers, the Akhil Bharatiya Bhojpuri Sahitya Sammelan.

      https://doi.org/10.11647/OBP.0405.04

sociological and scholarly interest, its literary merit hasn't travelled as deeply into the Anglophone world'.[3]

In colonial times, the Bhojpur region, which had long been a centre of saltpetre and other trade, became a centre of opium and sugarcane cultivation as well as of large scale labour migration.[4] Bhojpuri traders and labourers travelled not just to the Calcutta jute mills and the tea plantations in Assam, but also across the Black Water, or *Kala Pani*, as indentured labourers or *girmitiya* to colonial plantations in Mauritius, British Guyana, Trinidad, Natal in South Africa, Fiji, Malay and so on. Indeed, a decade before the English translation of *Phoolsunghi*, two lines from a Bhojpuri women's folk song in Amitav Ghosh's novel *Sea of Poppies* (2009) accompany Diti on the boat trip that will eventually take her to Mauritius—the first tranche of the opium trilogy that successfully shows the entanglements of global trade, the British empire, and oceanic geographies, between the Bhojpur region, Bengal and Bombay in India, China, and the plantation islands/coolie colonies.[5]

But does Bhojpuri orature really need to enter a novel in English in order to become visible and part of world literature? Or can we use the world of Bhojpuri orature itself, a world encompassing epics, songs, theatre, live performances and printed chapbooks, and more recently cinema, TV channels, and digital music videos and circulating, thanks to the Bhojpuri diaspora, across a vast part of the world, to prise open the restrictive definition of literature in world literature as that which is *'read as literature'*, in David Damrosch's formulation?[6]

At one end, Bhojpuri orature is part of world literature through its rich tradition of oral epics (*gathas*), living repositories of cultural memory narrated by specialists but also printed in chapbook and book form

---

3   Aarushi Agrawal, 'The World of Pandey Kapil's *Phoolsunghi*: Gautam Choubey
      on Translating the Novel, Bhojpuri Literary Culture', *Firstpost*, 23 December 2020;
      Somak Ghoushal, '*Phoolsunghi*: a Bhojpuri Classic Revived in English', *mintlounge*,
      20 November 2020. The Jaipur Literature Festival dedicated an (online) panel to
      the translation; see 'Phoolsunghi: The Scent of a Text| Jaipur Literature Festival
      2021'.
4   The bibliography is vast; see e.g. Badri Narayan, *Culture and Emotional Economy of
      Migration* (New Delhi: Routledge India, 2016).
5   Amitav Ghosh, *Sea of Poppies* (New York: Picador, 2009).
6   David Damrosch, *What is World Literature* (Princeton: Princeton University Press,
      2003), p. 6.

from the early twentieth century.[7] These are among the many regional and caste oral epics attested throughout South Asia, themselves part of a tapestry of oral epics that have already been accepted into world literature, though usually oral epics are studied by anthropologists or students of folklore rather than of literature.[8] Song, as artistic and expressive forms, both are and are not acknowledged as literature.[9] On the one hand, songs are poems set to music that draw upon the same pool of referents, images, tropes, and characters as poetry. On the other hand, text is only one element in a song alongside melody, rhythm, and voice. Indeed, many songs seem to work with the briefest textual hints: instead of whole texts, we have resonant phrases, words (*dulhin* or bride, *roti* or bread, *chulha* or hearth, *kudari* or spade, etc.), instruments and melodies. Wendy Doniger made a distinction between 'fluid texts', which are texts that can be and are changed in transmission, and 'fixed texts' that cannot.[10] Ratnakar Tripathy, who has studied contemporary musical culture in Bihar, speaks of 'soft texts' and even looser evocations of text in song lyrics:

> The idea of the text I feel remains as indispensable as ever through its oral, printed and digital incarnations. By 'text' I mean here an original frame of meaning as a point of reference even if it's imaginary/imagined/posited. With various degrees of fluidity, portability and replicability, it is possible to place and indeed classify literary outputs in a continuum, and fixed labels are perhaps avoidable to retain a greater loyalty to the empirical and the existential. I feel the phrases 'hard text' and 'soft text' should do for the interim with several in-betweens of course.

> The text remains important and melody/rhythm alone are never enough even for the grossest songs. The vulgarest songs are often the richest in

---

7   See Servan-Schreiber, *Chanteurs Itinerants*.

8   See Martin Puchner, Suzanne Conklin Akbari, Wiebke Denecke, Barbara Fuchs, Caroline Levine, Pericles Lewis, and Emily R. Wilson, eds, *The Norton anthology of world literature* (London and New York: WW Norton, 2018). Exceptions in South Asia include David Shulman, V. Narayana Rao and Rich Freeman; see *Oral Epics in India*, ed. by Stuart H. Blackburn (Berkeley: University of California Press, 1989).

9   For a recent discussion, based largely on English texts, see Jahan Ramazani, 'Poetry and Song', *Poetry and Its Others* (Chicago: University of Chicago Press, 2014), pp. 184–238.

10 Wendy Doniger, 'Fluid and Fixed Texts in India' in *Boundaries of the Text: Epic Performances in South and Southeast Asia*, ed. by J. Burkhalter Flueckiger and L. J. Sears (The University of Michigan: Center for South and Southeast Asian Studies, 1991), pp. 31–42.

> metaphors – an irony not unlike the 'filthiest abuses'. But my ethnographic
> work in 2010 startled me for the great anxiety the lowliest singers
> expressed over the quality of their lyrics, many of them dreaming of a
> muse-lyricist who would write songs for them. They were surprisingly
> aware of the low quality of their words and their heavy dependence on
> melody, timbre and rhythmic extravagance. [...] Incantatory lyrics sung
> loudly and danced with cut both ways – they drown the words but also
> highlight selected text.[11]

Such a formulation of text is very far from our usual literary
understanding of a literary text as something that you cannot say in
any other way.[12] But, as this chapter argues, resonant phrases and words
characterize the worldly circulation of Bhojpuri songs across space
and time, their resilience and adaptation as well as their compressed
historicity. For this reason, this chapter does not focus on *Phoolsunghi*
and its English translation, or on *A Sea of Poppies*, but rather on Bhojpuri
songs, and takes Trinidadian singer Sundar Popo's 1970s mixed-
language hit 'Phulourie Bina Chutney Kaise Bani' (How can you have
phulouri without chutney?), recently revived in the Hindi blockbuster
film *Dabanng 2* (Fearless 2, 2012, dir. Arbaz Khan), as an unlikely, and
consciously provocative, example.

Bhojpuri Orature

As already mentioned, Bhojpuri is spoken across two states in colonial
and independent India (eastern Uttar Pradesh and western Bihar) and
southern Nepal, as well as among the Bhojpuri diaspora. Despite its
very rich oral literature including oral epics (*gathas*) and songs (*git*),
and its large number of speakers (50 million declared it as their mother
tongue in the 2011 Indian Census, with many more second language
speakers and a further two million speakers across the world), Bhojpuri
has struggled for recognition.[13] Despite movements agitating for its
recognition in the 1960s and 1970s, it is yet to be recognized as an official

---

11   Ratnakar Tripathy, Personal communication, November 2019.
12   Karin Barber at 'Roundtable on Contemporary African Oral Traditions', SOAS, 20
      November 2019.
13   See 'List of languages by number of native speakers
      in India', *Wikipedia*, https://en.wikipedia.org/wiki/
      List_of_languages_by_number_of_native_speakers_in_India.

language by the Indian Constitution. It has largely remained an oral and unofficial language, regionally and culturally important but giving way to Hindi in formal contexts. In fact, whether in India or in the former plantation colonies in the Indian Ocean and the Caribbean, linguistically Bhojpuri has always co-existed with other languages, whether Hindi, Creole, and French or English.

Further, in the case of Bhojpuri even literature revolves around orature. While there are Bhojpuri book publishers and literary institutions that bring out bulletins and magazines, they often celebrate orature and commemorate its vastly more popular creators, like the humbly born playwright and impresario Bhikhari Thakur (1887–1971), known as the 'Bhojpuri Shakespeare', or Mahendar Missir, as in the novel *Phoolsunghi* already mentioned.[14]

Bhojpuri society is mainly constituted of martial/warrior, mercantile, and pastoral castes; it is divided by inter-caste conflict between landowners, cattle herders, and agriculturalists, and is strongly patriarchal. Bhojpuri oral epics typically revolve around forbidden inter-caste or inter-clan romances, or around migrant heroes. They are associated with particular castes (like Ahir pastoralists, or Musahar labourers) and are typically recited and/or sung by men with the accompaniment of a drum (*dholak*) and string-instrument (*sarang*). Songs, by contrast, are typically sung by women as part of everyday work or on ritual and festive occasions and cover a wide range of genres—there are grinding songs, wedding songs, spring, monsoon, and festival songs (*kajri*), and so on. As in other regions of South Asia, while music and singing are considered auspicious, indeed necessary for auspicious events like weddings and births, professional singers, particularly itinerant ones, are considered impure and are often low-caste: celebrated during the performance for their artistry, they are nonetheless socially 'liminal'.[15] Singing, and especially dancing, was and to some extent still is considered a profession for women of ill repute.[16]

---

14   Bhikhari Thakur is the hero of the recent Hindi novel *Sutradhar* by Sanjeev (New Delhi: Rajkamal Prakashan, 2016).

15   See Servan-Schreiber, *Chanteurs itinerants*; also *Histoire*, p. 41; see also Katherine Butler Brown (Schofield), 'The Social Liminality of Musicians: Case Studies from Mughal India and Beyond', *twentieth-century music*, 3.1 (2007), 13–49.

16   See Anna Morcom, *Illicit Worlds of Indian Dance: Cultures of Exclusion* (London: Hurst & Co., 2013) for the stigma associated with women from traditional

There was already a widespread culture of internal and external (often seasonal) migration from Bhojpur to Nepal, Assam, Calcutta, Burma, and Bombay as an avenue to upward mobility, even before indenture brought men and (a smaller but still a substantial number of) women from the region to the sugarcane colonies of Mauritius (since 1830), Trinidad and Guyana (1845), Natal in South Africa (1860), and Fiji (1879) after the abolition of slavery in 1833.[17] The historiography of coolie migration has emphasized the deep trauma of oceanic migration and the quasi-slavery conditions of labourers, who left pushed by extreme poverty.[18] Servan-Schreiber has partly questioned this narrative and argued instead that pull factors and habits of migration (which shifted 'from river to sea') should be taken more into account.[19] Sugarcane was already established by the British in the Bhojpur region, and a number of castes traded saltpetre and other local products along networks that were both mercantile and religious.[20] The mattock or curved spade for digging (*kudari*) features in several indenture songs, as we shall see.[21]

Even before indenture there was a strong tradition of Bhojpuri songs about exile and separation, with the wife singing about her suffering (*biraha*) while her husband is away (*bides*), fighting or working.[22] (As Camille Buat has noted, women in Bhojpuri orature are always imagined as sedentary and confined while men are mobile, whereas from the beginning one third of Bhojpuri migrants in Calcutta were women.)[23] Sitting on the rooftop, the woman 'looks at the road' (i.e. waits) and suffers because of loneliness, unfulfilled sexual desire, humiliation

---

communities of performers, including the Bhojpur region.

17   Hugh Tinker, *A New System of Slavery: The Export of Indian Labour Overseas, 1830–1920* (London: Oxford University Press, 1974).

18   E.g. Ibid.

19   Servan-Schreiber, *Histoire,* Ch. 3.

20   Shahid Amin, *Sugarcane and Sugar in Gorakhpur* (Delhi: Oxford University Press, 1984), Servan-Schreiber, *Histoire,* pp. 32–35.

21   See G. A. Grierson, *Bihar Peasant Life* (Calcutta: Bengal Secretariat, 1885), pp. 5–6.

22   Usually in Hindi one distinguishes between *videsh* (*videś*, abroad), and *pardes* (*pardeś*, in a different region but within the same country), but the Bhojpuri songs do not distinguish between the two, and the husband who leaves for Calcutta, or Burma, or Assam can be called *Pardesi* or *Bidesi*. The *batohi* (traveller) also travels abroad for work, but in the songs and in the *Bidesia* plays he acts as the messenger carrying the wife's letter and admonishing the errant husband.

23   Camille Buat, presentation for 'Orature, Literature and History: Exploring Northern Indian Popular Culture (19c-20c)', SOAS, University of London, 29–31 May 2018.

at the hands of her mother- and sisters-in-law, because without her husband she cannot fully participate in the pleasures of the seasons and in seasonal festivities, and because she is jealous and worries that he has been enticed by a rival wife (*sautin, pardesiya*) abroad. These topoi and 'structure of feeling' recur across a range of song genres (*purbi, kajli, barahmasa, biraha*), and single words like *biraha, sautin, bides* are enough to evoke the whole structure. Songs direct attention to the aching youthful body of the woman to express sexual tension, others point to fruit, vegetables, food items and birds to voice desire and signal the pleasures that the wife cannot have:

> *Pardesiya balam se yari lagal pardesiya*
> *jano jevenli puri kachauri*
> *jano ke jevena men barphi bhari pardesiya*
> *jano piyeli bhar bhar ke madhuva*

> My husband has fallen for a woman abroad (*pardesiya*),
> his lover scoffs *puris* and *kachauris*,
> his lover eats her full of *barfis*,
> his lover drinks her full of honey,
> she keeps a bottle (*ged'ua*) full of perfume, that foreign/stranger woman.
> He makes her sleep on the top floor,
> on a bed with a fringed bedspread.
> She can roam the city and the bazaar
> my husband has fallen for a woman abroad.[24]

In the early twentieth century, folk playwright Bhikhari Thakur dramatized this dynamic and created a new form of musical theatre, which he called *Bidesia* (Foreigner), around the historical and socio-emotional experience of migration. His most famous play, also called *Bidesiya*, features a restless husband (Bidesi) who is itching to leave the village and his newly-wedded bride, the bride (Pyari Sundari) who tries in vain to stop him, and an elderly traveller (Batohi) who agrees to take her message to Bidesi, who is enjoying himself in Calcutta with his mistress (Randi, lit. prostitute). Prose dialogue includes several comedic exchanges, but the bulk of the text consists of songs, Batohi's songs which call upon the errant husband to leave his mistress and return home, and Pyari Sundari's songs of waiting and longing. Interestingly,

---

24   Krishna Dev Upadhyay, *Bhojpuri lokgit*, 2 vols. (Allahabad: Hindi Sahitya Sammelan, 1954 and 1956), quoted in Servan-Schreiber, *Histoire*, p. 51.

the songs do not advance the play's narrative but repeat and elaborate, using different styles, the characters' main message. Thakur achieved enormous renown in the Bhojpur area and among the Bhojpuri diaspora in India and Burma.[25]

Another song genre that achieved considerable creativity, success, and circulation in performance (with competing 'parties') is the *birha* (< *biraha*), a composition associated with cattle-herders and milk producers or Ahirs, who perform it with powerful voice projection (*uthan*). Some *birhas* deal with topical events or current activities, and there have been political and nationalist *birhas* in both India and in Mauritius, or *birhas* about famous dacoits. Songs of migration spoke of the oceanic crossing as deception.[26] For example, a *birha* that became very popular in Mauritius in the 1920s laments the hard labour and 'mirage' that Mauritius had proved to be for labourers (*marich* means mirage in Hindi):

idhar udhar kan planté	Here, there we planted cane
bich men makai	and corn in the middle.
ek dari golmal to kiya	You mess up a single row
to mila chamkai	you get a good shining!
desh chhore bhaiya	We left the country, brother,
ai ai Mirichiya	and came to Marichiya
mar kudari, nich pachhari	dig the spade, turn it round,
chal agari	move ahead
yebi Mirichya ke rit	these are the ways of Marichiya[27]

Note the (slight) use of Creole (*kan planté*) and the mention of the curved spade as the labourer's tool, which we will find again in the 'Phulouri' song.

Beginning in the 1880s, Bhojpuri music genres also 'generated a veritable market economy' of printed booklets, which circulated widely at least until the end of the twentieth century thanks to a vast network of itinerant peddlers.[28] This is significant, because it points to the importance of chapbooks as textual aids, supporting the consumption

---

25   See Badri Narayan, *Bidesia: Migration, Change, and Fold Culture* (Allahabad: North Central Cultural Centre, 2005).

26   E.g. 'Sunike nam ham Marich ke dipva ho' in *Lal Pasina*, quoted in Servan-Schreiber, *Histoire*, p. 101.

27   Servan-Schreiber, *Histoire*, p. 100.

28   Servan-Schreiber, *Chanteurs itinerants*; also *Histoire*, p. 55.

and circulation of orature, and also as a parallel circuit to that of books, usually the only circuit considered in world literature studies.[29] Instead, like the *literatura de cordel* in Brazil, Bhojpuri chapbooks illuminate a system of reproduction of oral texts and of production of new texts along similar lines for an eager, often semiliterate reading public.[30]

Though this is only a brief introduction, it shows how Bhojpuri songs have existed and circulated on a growing number of platforms (see also Vierke, Chapter 1 in this volume): in intimate or community settings, sung by women or by itinerant male singers; in print as chapbooks; as part of Bidesia and other folk theatrical performances, or as competitions between 'singing parties'. More recently, Bhojpuri songs have been part of an economy of live performances ('concerts') and audio cassettes in 1980s, and of VCDs since the 2000s, with professional singers performing and recording devotional and/or ribald songs.[31] The large Bhojpuri diaspora also arguably sustained the development of a Bhojpuri film industry in Bombay, which seems to have peaked in the 1990s, and a vibrant subculture of Bhojpuri YouTube music channels— what Ratnakar Tripathy has called a 'Music Mania'.[32]

Otherwise, Bhojpuri songs regularly appear as part of Hindi films, where they tend to signify a subaltern sexual energy, often played on a stage by a professional dancer or 'item number', or else homely tradition. The song 'Phulouri Bina Chutney' in *Dabanng 2* exemplifies the former, as we shall see, while 'Pag pag mohe liye jaun tori balaiya' ('My prayers

---

29   For texts as aids to oral performance, see Christian L., Novetzke, 'Note to Self: What Marathi Kirtankars' Notebooks Suggest about Literacy, Performance, and the Travelling Performer in Pre-Colonial Maharashtra' in *Tellings and Texts*, ed. by F. Orsini and K. Butler Schofield (Cambridge: Open Book Publishers, 2015), pp. 169–184, https://doi.org/10.11647/OBP.0062

30   See Marco Haurélio, *Literatura de cordel: do sertão à sala de aula* (Pia Sociedade de São Paulo-Editora Paulus, 2014). In one of her lectures at SOAS in May 2018, Catherine Servan-Schreiber outlined a possible comparative approach to chapbook literature through the theme of revenge.

31   See Peter Manuel, *Cassette Culture: Popular music and technology in North India* (Chicago: University of Chicago Press, 1993); Ratnakar Tripathy, 'Music Mania in Small-town Bihar: Emergence of Vernacular Identities', *Economic and Political Weekly*, 47.22 (2 June 2012), pp. 58–66; Akshaya Kumar, 'The Insurrectionary Lateral-ness of Bhojpuri Media' in *Hinglish Live: Language Mixing Across Media*, ed. by F. Orsini and Ravikant (Hyderabad: Orient BlackSwan, 2021), pp. 223–258.

32   Tripathy, 'Music Mania'. See Avjit Ghosh, *Cinema Bhojpuri* (New Delhi: Penguin India, 2010), and Akshaya Kumar, *Bhojpuri Cinema in the Comparative Media Crucible* (New Delhi: Oxford University Press, 2021).

will protect you at every step'), in the late 1980s superhit film *Mainne Pyar Kiya* (I've Loved, dir. Sooraj Barjatiya, 1989), signifies tradition. Sung in a deep, 'rustic' voice—a far cry from the usual shrill voice of female playback singers from Lata Mageshkar onwards—by celebrated middle-class 'folk singer' Sharda Sinha, who Ratnakar Tripathy calls 'exaggeratedly respectable middle-class housewife-like', the song is accompanied by 'traditional' drumming and the auspicious sound of the Indian oboe or *shehnai,* associated with weddings. The bashful heroine sings of her love and devotion to her boyfriend while performing quasi-marital gestures: she prepares *chai* and knits a sweater for him, appears shyly before him surrounded by her friends, massages his tired legs and rests her head on his feet while he sleeps, and fasts as married women do. Text, voice, instruments, rhythm—all scream 'tradition' here.[33]

Bhojpuri Songs in the Diaspora

'there is no Bhojpuri music without songs'

(Catherine Servan-Schreiber)

'la seule façon de garder notre lingue vivante, c'est par la musique'

(Ravin Sowamber, told to C. Servan-Schreiber)

'you must have a tune and a story'

(Sundar Popo)

---

33   'Let me tell you, my beloved,
       at every step my prayers will protect you. REFRAIN
       I'll fall like the rain,
       gather monsoon clouds.
       My heart longs
       to take you in my arms but
       my wretched shyness
       stops my feet. REFRAIN
       I know not the ways of the world,
       to me you are vermillion
       in my hair's parting
       you the bangles
       on my wrists. REFRAIN
       I love all your colours,
       the sad and happy moments.
       I'll stay with my beloved,
       we'll share our troubles
       and spend our life together';
       Sharda Sinha, Padmashri, 'Kahe tose sajna', lyrics by Asad Bhopali.

As in other plantation colonies, already in the 1860s indentured workers in Mauritius founded villages and started buying up plots of land after their contracts expired. By 1920, 45% of the cultivated land belonged to Indian families.[34] Bhojpuri became a lingua franca in the countryside (as opposed to the coastal areas and towns), so widely spoken that even Chinese traders learnt it. The *baithaka* or 'sitting' was an important social and cultural institution in Mauritian villages where much music was played and songs were sung, while women sang wedding songs at women-only *soirées* called *gamat* or *git gawai*.[35]

Paradoxically, in Mauritius Bhojpuri has enjoyed more official recognition than in India, though its fortunes have waxed and waned over time and with the passing of generations. Bhojpuri found some early support as a language of primary education—with Sir Arthur Phayre in 1878 and Basdeo Bissoondayal's Jan Andolan or People's Movement in 1930–1946. In the 1980s it replaced Hindi as one of the languages of TV news. As Servan-Schreiber puts it: 'The parallel between the status of Bhojpuri in India itself and in Mauritius is astonishing. Its role as ancestral language in Mauritius is weakened by the fact that it is looked down upon in India, where despite the efforts of local leaders it is still to be recognized as a scheduled language in the Constitution'.[36]

In the 1930s, though, Creole gained ground while Bhojpuri was devalued as a rural dialect. In fact, Bhojpuri lost ground to Creole in everyday speech, and to standard Hindi in education and religion.[37] Writers like Abhimanyu Unnuth (1937–2018), the most renowned Mauritian Indian writer, chose Hindi for their poems, plays, and fiction, and all his works were published in India. His historical novel *Lal Pasina* (Red Sweat, 1980), which claims to present the 'authentic history' of indentured labourers, the 'little men', in opposition to the official history

---

34   Servan-Schreiber, *Histoire*, p. 71.

35   Ibid., pp. 96–97, carefully parses which genres of Bhojpuri remained current in Mauritius: she notes that the professionally specialised repertoire became a collective heritage, that oral epics like *Alha* were parcellised into songs, and that some of the women's seasonal songs lost their natural referents in the new climate.

36   Ibid., p. 78.

37   A Hindi Pracharini Sabha or Society for the Propagation of Hindi was established in 1924, and in the 1950s it was Hindi, alongside Urdu and Gujarati, that was taught in school as an 'Oriental language', whereas Bhojpuri remained only a spoken language (Ibid., p. 81). Hindi, however, remains only a literary, written language.

of the island, is dotted with Bhojpuri songs, which work as authentifiers.[38] In fact, partly because of the needs of democratic politics on the road to independence (in 1968), partly thanks to the organization Sewa Shivir (Service Camp) that revived Bhojpuri songs as 'heritage' and campaigned for the preservation of popular culture, and partly because of the revaluation of ties with India after independence, Bhojpuri in Mauritius regained value.[39] In the 1980s, Chutney music acted as a catalyser for the revival of Bhojpuri. As Servan-Schreiber puts it, 'The history of Mauritian Chutney music is linked to a great extent to the evolution of the status of the language [Bhojpuri]. The relationship then reversed itself, and the status of the language came to depend in turn upon the success of the music'.[40]

By comparison, Trinidad was further away from India, migration was more diversified, and there was greater language loss to Creole and English: 'by the end of the 1960s, [even] Hindi was no longer a strong marker of difference, because most Indians communicated with each other in English'.[41] Only songs and religious practices (like recitations of Tulsidas's *Ramcharitmanas*, the sixteenth-century version of the Ramayana written in an idiom close to Bhojpuri) preserved the language. Moreover, in Trinidad Indians came to the foreground in national consciousness only in the 1990s with Basdeo Panday's successful campaign for Prime Minister. In fact, ethnomusicologist Peter Manuel views the emergence of Chutney and Chutney Soca music in Trinidad as both 'a concerted revival and assertion of Indian identity' *and* a 'new spirit of creolization and syncreticism'.[42]

---

38   A point made by Alena Rettová with regard to Swahili novels at the Roundtable on Contemporary African Oral Traditions held at SOAS, 20 November 2019. In the novel *Lal Pasina*, the first leader of the labourers, Kisan Singh, himself writes songs and a kind of play in Bhojpuri.

39   As Servan-Schreiber (*Histoire*, p. 165) notes, this included also the many booklets of new songs written from the 1960s by Roodraduth Pokhun, the 'Tenor with the golden voice' who also founded a music school; several of these songs were on new themes like 'progress' (*pragati*), 'family planning', Hindi, and Mauritius ('*morisva dil mohela*', 'Mauritious enchanted our hearts', see below); see Roodraduth Pokhun, *Bhojpuri git* (Port Louis: Nalanda Press, 1972).

40   Servan-Schreiber, *Histoire*, p, 78.

41   Aisha Mohamed, 'Love and Anxiety: Gender Negotiations in Chutney-Soca Lyrics in Trinidad', *Caribbean Review of Gender Studies*, 1 (April 2007), 1–42 (p. 4).

42   Peter Manuel, *East Indian Music in the West Indies: Tān-singing, Chutney, and the Making of Indo-Caribbean Culture* (Philadelphia: Temple University Press, 2000), p. 168; also Mohamed, 'Love and Anxiety', p. 3.

The resilience and circulation of Bhojpuri songs in both Mauritius and Trinidad was closely linked to this process of adaptation. In both cases, scholars have spoken of a movement from the 'wedding tent' to the performance stage of the fête or the local talent competition. In the process, music was creolised through local encounters with Soca in Trinidad and Séga in Mauritius—both closer to African styles—in order to create danceable music, spawning various sub-styles, from Chutney-Soca to Séga-Bollywood. In the repertoire of female songs sung in the context of women-only wedding soirées, songs were often very ribald and full of sexual innuendoes; these were now reinvented as dance music, with more instruments, professional male and a few female singers, and a 'new body language' of dance in gender-mixed environments, giving rise to occasional tensions.[43]

In terms of the song texts, Bhojpuri lines and topoi were combined with either Creole in Mauritius, or English in Trinidad. New topics were added to the older 'structures of feeling' linked to love, marriage, family, and migration; these involved tensions between city and rural life, jobs and unemployment, and a more localized and shared identity as Mauritians, signalled by local toponyms.

So Anilsingh Ramessur sang of a wife who now looked for her husband not in Calcutta but in Rose-Hill and Curepipe.[44] Migration, Roodraduth Pokhun suggests, was over: the *Pardesi* had arrived and had no desire to return:

> *Morisva dil mohela*
> *hind maha sagar ke, tara morisva,*
> *sab ke, dil mohela, hã hã dil mohela.* [...]
> *man ke rijhaveola, **pamplemus** bagiya.*
> *acharaj **samarel** ke, sat rangi matiya.*
> *hĩya ake pardeshi laute na khojela.*
> *morisva sabke dil mohela.*[45]

---

43   See Mohamed, 'Love and Axiety' and Servan-Schreiber, *Histoire.*

44   '*Rozil me kojli*
      Curepip me kojli
      Kone kone khojab Saiyan tohar suratiya
      Suna suna lagela dilwa'. Servan-Schreiber, *Histoire*, p. 217.
      I searched Rose-Hill,
      I searched Curepipe,
      I looked for your dear face in every corner,
      My heart feels so so empty

45   Pokhun, 'Morisva dil mohela', *Bhojpuri git*, p. 8.

> *Mauritius enchants the heart*
> Mauritius, the star of the Indian Ocean,
> enchants every heart, yes, yes. [...]
> The garden of *Pamplemousses* delights the heart,
> the seven-colour earth of *Chamarel* astounds.
> Once here the *Pardesi* seeks no return,
> Mauritius enchants every heart.

Another band, the Bhojpuri Boys, instead sang of travels (*'Dadi gail Angleterre, Angleterre ghume, la France ghume'*, Grandma went to England, toured England, toured France) and new migrations (*'Naya sirey'*, Once Again, 2003).[46] We find the *bazariya* again, this time not as the site of the heroine's rival but of the dressed up (*'saj dhaj ke'*) heroine herself:

> *Lutayi gayo bhauji bich bazariya*
> *bich bazariyam bich bazariya*
> *Khube saj dhaj ke ham gaili bazariya*
> *koi khinch choli aur khinch lahanga*
> *Lutayo gayo bhauji.*[47]

> *Bhauji* (sister-in-law), I was harassed
> right in the middle of the bazaar.
> I went all dressed up, to the bazaar,
> One pulled my blouse, one pinched my skirt,
> I was harassed, *Bhauji*.

If in some songs the *bazariya* is still a dangerous place where one gets molested (one's virtue is 'looted'), elsewhere the city and its modern conveyances, or the Fancy-Fair, become sites of excitement and romance:

> *Bus ke soferwa*
> *Bus ke soferwa paink painkoo karela*
> *Ham lapareille hath mein leke karat katila*
> *Kahan jaiba? Kahan ootarba? Sabse poochila*
> *Ham lapareille hath mein leke karat Katila*
> *Pari niyar chokri ghanta bhajawela*
> *Ham chhatake hali se kanwati kholila*
> *Bus ke soferwa...*[48]

> The bus driver [*soferwa*, chauffer] hoots, hoots,

46　See Servan-Schreiber, *Histoire*, pp. 224–225.
47　Anerood Boyjonauth, 'Bhauji'; Ibid., p. 209.
48　'Master' Vinod Sewduth, 'Bus ke soferwa'; Ibid., p. 196.

I grab the instrument and punch the tickets.
Where are you going? Where do you get off? I ask everyone,
I grab the instrument and punch the tickets.
A girl pretty like a fairy rings the bell,
I whizz past her to open the door,
the bus driver.

Fantifair
Fantifair mein gaili mama, dholl-puri bechatani
Ego chokri hamko dekhlan, dholl-puri bechal hogal
Mama bole mama – Hamro shaadi karadge na…[49]
Fancy-Fair

I went to the Fancy-Fair, mama, to sell *dholl-puri,*
A girl looked at me, and all my snacks were sold.
I told mama – Do set my marriage up…

'Music is the only way we can keep our language alive', Catherine Servan-Schreiber was told in Mauritius.[50] And indeed, whereas formal literary *writing* by Mauritian and Fijian Indians has largely been in Hindi, songs have been in Bhojpuri, Creole, or a mixture of the two. Keeping Bhojpuri alive, even as a marker of tradition, has involved, unsurprisingly, processes of adaptation to new media platforms and new subjects, and of musical and linguistic creolisation, as Catherine Servan-Schreiber has shown. As a result, Bhojpuri texts have become 'softer' and 'looser', evoking familiar elements while registering historical, cultural, and linguistic change.

How Can you Have Phulouri without Chutney?

It is in this context of adaptation and creolisation that we need to read Trinidadian singer-songwriter Sundar Popo's 1970s 'How can you have phulouri [a falafel-like fried snack made with pulse flour] without chutney?' (*Phulouri Bina Chutney Kaise Bani?*), one of the first hit Chutney songs.

As already mentioned, in Trinidad in the late 1960s Bhojpuri music 'spilled over from the wedding tent onto the stage of the chutney fete' and the carnival. With Chutney music, English became the primary

---

49   Roodranuth Pokhun, 'Fantifair'; Ibid., p. 171.
50   Servan-Schreiber, *Histoire*, p. 225.

language, and the music added *soca* rhythms and instruments.[51] Professional male singers like Sundar Popo (1943–2000) and female singers like Drupati Ramgunai became famous, and not just locally. As Tina Ramnarine recounts, 'after a deal between Rohit Records in US and Moean Mohammed of Windsor Records in Trinidad, Sundar Popo became a household name in countries such as Holland, Africa, Australia, New Zealand, Fiji, Mauritius and India'.[52]

The refrain of the song is in Bhojpuri and probably 'traditional'. But it is only a fragment anchoring a song that positively delights in mixing references and languages. 'At that time', writes Aisha Mohammed, 'it was not conceivable how Indian music, and the Indian community, could retain "Indianness" without an Indian language. Songs like Popo's "Nana and Nani" or "Phulourie bin chutney", offered a solution, though it was not recognized at the time. The use of familiar folk melodies, and Indian-style enunciation [...] gave the songs an "Indian" sound while widening their appeal to non-Hindi speakers'.[53]

> Kaise bani
> Phulourie bina chutney kaise bani
>
> I went Sangre Grande to meet Lal Beharry
> I pull out meh kudari and shave off te darhi[54]
> Phulourie bina chutney kaise bani
>
> Me and meh darling was flying in a plane
> The plane catch a fire and we fall inside the cane
> Kaise bani, kaise bani
> Phulourie bina chutney kaise bani

---

51   'A number of changes occurred as chutney spilled over from the wedding tent onto the stage of the chutney fete [in Trinidad]. English became the primary language, artistes began incorporating soca beats and other elements, and male artistes came to dominate the scene. In the private space of the Hindu wedding, chutney enabled women to express their ideas on a range of topics from sexuality, to husbands, to marriage. In the public sphere of chutney, the participation of men made it an important area in which Indian men and women could renegotiate gendered identities. As chutney evolved into chutney-soca, this process of negotiation was influenced by Black and North American sex/gender belief systems'; Mohamed, 'Love and Anxiety', p. 39.

52   Tina Ramnarine, *Creating Their Own Space: The Development of an Indian-Caribbean Musical Tradition* (Kingston, Jamaica: University of the West Indies Press Jamaica). See also Mohamed, 'Love and Anxiety'.

53   Mohamed, 'Love and Anxiety', p. 5.

I beating meh drum and ah singing meh song
The only thing ah missing is meh bottle ah rum
Kaise bani...

Jack and Jill went up ah hill
to fetch ah pale of water
Jack fell down and broke 'is thumb
and Jill came tumbling after
Little Jack Horner sit in a corner
Eating his Christmas pie
He put his thumb and pull out a plum
And said what a good boy am I
Kaise bani...

When asked about the text ('In your song, "Phoulourie Bina Chutney", you have these nursery rhymes, "Jack and Jill went up the hill" and "Little Jack Horner sat in a corner", and then something about the cane fields. What's the meaning of that song?'), Sundar Popo downplayed it as nonsense:

Well, it's just a chutney song. It don't carry great meaning. It's rhyme: 'Me and my darling was flying in a plane, the plane catch a fire and we fall inside the cane.' It brings many meanings and it's how you will interpret it.[55]

Yet, as indeed others have already noted, the nonsensical text is not that random at all: it contains familiar references to food (*phulouri* and chutney), which in Bhojpuri songs often carry sexual innuendoes; another reference to plantation labour through the sugarcane field and the labourer's tool, the spade (*kudari*); a local toponym (Sangre

---

54   As sung by Sundar Popo ('Kaise Bani'), this line is a little unclear; this is what
       I made of it after listening several times (meaning, 'I went [to] Sangre Grande
       to meet Lal Bihari, I took out my spade and shaved off his beard'); as covered in
       the Bhojpuri film 'Bhaiya Dooj' (1985, dir. Qamar Narvi) by a female playback
       singer (I could not confirm the name) and played on stage by a duo of perfomers
       with sexually suggestive thrusting and grinding gestures, at this point the female
       performer clearly threatens the man with an imaginary weapon ('Kaise Bani').
       In the version sung by Kanchan available on YouTube, she changes it to 'and
       say about Shridhari'; the author is also disingenuously elided by declaring it an
       'Indian Folk Song' (Kanchan Babla, 'Kaise Bani'). Another song lyrics website
       gives it as 'I pull out meh coudharry and take out te dharry' ('Kaise Bani (1980s)
       Lyrics, YouTube link no longer available).
55   In Ramnarine, *Creating their own Space*, p. 169.

Grande); some images of migration/mobility (the plane); a stereotype of Trinidadian songs (meh bottle ah rhum); and nursery rhymes that speak of a basic, oral contact with formal English. In other words, in its combination of evocative textual fragments, the song expresses—in a compressed and imaginative way—the historical experience of Indian migrant labourers, in a musical language that is both familiar but also understandable beyond the community.

Sundar Popo sang the song simply, to a traditional rhythm and accompanied by a shehnai-sounding clarinet and *dholak* and *tabla* drums (his father was an accomplished drummer in *tassa* ensembles). But when the Indian early pop husband-and-wife duo Babla and Kanchan—who pioneered disco accompaniment to other traditional forms like 'disco dandiya' and toured performing for the Indian diaspora in the 1980s— took up the song, they made it more upbeat and danceable. They added a synthesiser, and Kanchan sang it in the high-pitched voice of Indian playback singers. Interestingly, following the treads of comments on the YouTube versions it becomes clear that these once novelty songs have themselves become 'collective memory' and evoke in many listeners memories of family parties, festivities, and old records.

The song became a hit once more in the Bollywood blockbuster *Dabanng 2*, in which Salman Khan (the once tender hero of *Maine Pyar Kiya*) is a small-town police officer of unorthodox means. When he finds himself surrounded by notables who are really criminals at a wedding celebration, he suddenly hears the song and starts twisting to the beat, and the next thing we know he is dancing and singing on stage alongside the sexy female performer.[56] In *Dabanng 2* the song text is drastically curtailed and partly changed—the local Trinidadian toponym of Sangre Grande or the spade, *kudari*, of the plantation labourer are no longer there. Nor even sugarcane. Instead, the couple falls from the airplane on fire onto a... train, a more familiar reference in India?[57] Performed in an Indian context, the Bhojpuri text becomes even more of an anchor, while

---

56   The singers are Mamta Sharma and Wajid ('Kaise Bani Kaise Bani—The Chatni Song, *Dabanng 2*')

57   'Me and my darling were travelling on a plane, The plane catch fire and we fall inside a train' ('Kaise Bani Kaise Bani—The Chatni song, *Dabanng 2*').

the English lines fall within the category of funny code-mixing familiar from many Bhojpuri songs.[58]

Let me end here with a provocation. How can this song, however important it may be as a cultural memory, and however wide its circulation within and outside the regime of copyright, be 'read as world literature'?! Surely the older Bhojpuri folk songs are more easily included as part of world folklore, maybe even the political *birhas* as expressions of a postcolonial consciousness, but this contemporary dance number?

Here is where the arguments offered by Liz Gunner and Ratnakar Tripathy are instructive. Instead of whole texts, we have resonant phrases, even single words (*phulouri, kudari*), instruments and melodies, what with Tripathy we may call 'soft texts' or even looser evocations of texts. We also have elements recomposed to suit new circumstances: in India and in the diaspora, Bhojpuri songs are *both* folklore and heritage (manifested in community singing and printed song collections) *and* mixed-language songs-and-dance numbers, performed at concerts, inserted into films, and now available on YouTube. Again, Tripathy's observations on how new song texts are created through reiteration and familiarity are useful here: 'The text, whether inherited, partly borrowed, re-assembled or based on templates of text/melody/rhythm, *appeals to familiarity*. [...] I wish to emphasize the reiterative/referential part, whether textual, melodic, or more rarely perhaps as rhythm'. Enterprising artists mine 'more and more from the traditional stocks' 'for new stuff'. He concludes, 'Yes, some forms do get left behind though it's difficult to claim that they will always remain so due to their inherent limitations (as music can easily break away from its traditional context a bit like griot)'.[59]

The usual criteria for inclusion in world literature are circulation, recognition/consecration, and artistry. But if we want to acknowledge orature, with its resilience and circulation, as part of world literature, other criteria are needed. 'How then do we begin to rethink orality, in order to bring about a model of world literature which is truer to

---

58   Examples include 'Banal ba *mood* dehiya bhail ba *powerful*' ('I'm in the mood, my
      body has become powerful'), or 'Hamra marad chahi *horn* dabawe wala ho' ('I
      need a man who will press my horn'); Kumar, 'The Lateralness', p. 134.
59   Tripathy, personal communication, November 2019.

the broad spectrum of verbal arts?', Liz Gunner asks. She frames the obstacles clearly:

> Orality is often seen as existing outside the confines of world literature, excluded largely because the heavy weight of print pushes it aside: words spoken, sung, or performed as aesthetic events are considered to be external to the domain of print, and thus to the modes of circulation conventionally associated with the term 'world literature'. Even if we keep to the term 'oral literature' we confine orality to a zone so peripheral that its points of connectivity, its potential links to 'world literature', are virtually erased.[60]

Instead, Gunner suggests that we consider the different modes of production and circulation (ritual, live performance, radio, booklet, YouTube, etc.) among audiences 'within different spheres or ecologies of literary practice' as '*co-existing* rather than *successive*' (see also Vierke, Chapter 1 in this volume).[61] Following Gunner, I have argued that the Bhojpuri song 'exists through multiple practices, each of which sustains its presence in the modern world'.[62] Instead of the (almost exclusive) centrality of print and the written text, I have pointed to the relay of multiple platforms and institutions—*baithkas, matikoor, git gawai* and *gamat* wedding sessions, carnivals, fêtes, competitions, radio, YouTube, record and film companies, lyricists, musicians, studios, etc.—needed in order to make song texts like these circulate 'worldwide'. This is not a unified system, but rather a relay of institutions and agents catering to different publics, in which print may, or may not, be involved. In the process, texts necessarily change and adapt, sometimes dramatically. They get chopped up and partly replaced but, as Ratnakar Tripathy argues, the text, or its evocation, is still there—a soft text. But even these soft texts matter, and mean, a lot to their audiences, and even a nonsense song like 'Kaise Bani' can be 'read as world literature' in terms of a testament to the resilience and transformation that orature must undergo in order to survive and thrive, finding new audiences and

---

60 Liz Gunner, 'Ecologies of Orality' in *The Cambridge Companion to World Literature,* ed. by B. Etherington and J. Zimbler (Cambridge: Cambridge University Press), pp. 116–129.

61 Ibid., pp. 122, 126.

62 Ibid., p. 122. Or, as Catherine Servan-Schreiber puts it, 'the variety/pop song (*chanson de variété*) is as relevant to the artistic and anthropological debate as the traditional styles it traverses' (*Histoire*, p. 27).

new platforms over time. 'Kaise Bani' by itself may not be recognizable as world literature but, as I have tried to argue, read in the context of Bhojpuri orature, its history and transformations both in India, in the diaspora, and in the 'significant geography' formed by the enduring connections between the two, even the 'soft text' of this song and its music reveal traces of this history and the many actors involved.

For a resilient orature like that of Bhojpuri, a language that displays what Ratnakar Tripathy calls 'persistent orality' and seems to resist print, it may be futile/self-defeating to look for literary consecration through printed literature and its system of translation and distribution, whatever the success of the English translation of *Phoolsunghi* may be. Rather, the textual and technological dynamics around songs like 'Kaise Bani' point us towards how we can recognize Bhojpuri orature as world literature without it necessarily having to go through the 'stage' of print.

Bibliography

Agrawal, Aarushi, 'The World of Pandey Kapil's *Phoolsunghi*: Gautam Choubey on Translating the Novel, Bhojpuri Literary Culture', *Firstpost* (2020) https://www.firstpost.com/art-and-culture/the-world-of-pandey-kapils-phoolsunghi-gautam-choubey-on-translating-the-novel-bhojpuri-literary-culture-9113031.html.

Amin, Shahid, *Sugarcane and Sugar in Gorakhpur* (Delhi: Oxford University Press, 1984).

Badri Narayan, *Bidesia: Migration, Change, and Folk Culture* (Allahabad: North Central Cultural Centre, 2005).

——, *Culture and Emotional Economy of Migration* (New Delhi: Routledge India, 2016).

Bhopali, Asad, 'Kahe tose sajna', https://www.hinditracks.in/kahe-tose-sajna-lyrics

Brown (Schofield), Katherine Butler, 'The Social Liminality of Musicians: Case Studies from Mughal India and Beyond', *Twentieth-Century Music*, 3.1 (2007).

Damrosch, David, *What is World Literature* (Princeton: Princeton University Press, 2003).

Doniger, Wendy, 'Fluid and Fixed Texts in India' in *Boundaries of the Text: Epic Performances in South and Southeast Asia*, ed. by J. Burkhalter Flueckiger and L. J. Sears (The University of Michigan: Center for South and Southeast Asian Studies, 1991), pp. 31–42.

Ghosh, Amitav, *Sea of Poppies* (New York: Picador, 2009).

Ghosh, Avjit, *Cinema Bhojpuri* (New Delhi: Penguin India, 2010).

Ghoushal, Somak, '*Phoolsunghi:* a Bhojpuri Classic Revived in English', *mintlounge* (2020), https://lifestyle.livemint.com/how-to-lounge/books/-phoolsunghi-a-bhojpuri-classic-revived-in-english-111605847235303.html

Grierson, George A., *Bihār Peasant Life: Being a Discursive Catalogue of the Surroundings of the People of that Province, with Many Illustrations from Photographs Taken by the Author* (Calcutta: Bengal Secretariat Press, 1885), https://archive.org/details/cu31924072688025

Gunner, Liz, 'Ecologies of Orality' in *The Cambridge Companion to World Literature*, ed. by B. Etherington and J. Zimbler (Cambridge: Cambridge University Press, 2018), pp. 116–132.

Haurélio, Marco, *Literatura de cordel: do sertão à sala de aula* (São Paulo: Pia Sociedade de São Paulo-Editora Paulus, 2014).

'Kaise Bani', from the film *Bhaiya Dooj*, https://www.youtube.com/watch?v=1xWMRfis5hQ

'Kaise Bani Kaise Bani – The Chatni song *Dabanng 2*', https://www.youtube.com/watch?v=iTPVQtNT10w

'Kaise Bani lyrics', https://genius.com/Kanchan-kaise-bani-lyrics

Kanchan and Babla, 'Kaise Bani', https://www.youtube.com/watch?v=JDduRClBAGU

Kumar, Akshaya, *Bhojpuri Cinema in the Comparative Media Crucible* (New Delhi: Oxford University Press, 2021).

Kumar, Akshaya, 'The Insurrectionary Lateral-ness of Bhojpuri Media' in *Hinglish Live: Language Mixing Across Media*, ed. by F. Orsini and Ravikant (Hyderabad: Orient BlackSwan, 2021), pp. 223–258.

'List of languages by number of native speakers in India', https://en.wikipedia.org/wiki/List_of_languages_by_number_of_native_speakers_in_India

Mani, Venkat B., 'Multilingual Code-Stitching in Ultraminor World Literatures: Reading Abhimanyu Unnuth's *Lāla Pasīnā* (1977) with Amitav Ghosh's *Sea of Poppies* (2008), *Journal of World Literature*, 3.3 (2018), https://doi.org/10.1163/24056480-00303009

Manuel, Peter L., *Cassette Culture: Popular Music and Technology in North India* (Chicago: University of Chicago Press, 1993).

——, *East Indian Music in the West Indies: Tān-singing, Chutney, and the Making of Indo-Caribbean Culture* (Philadelphia: Temple University Press, 2000).

Mohammed, Aisha, 'Love and Anxiety: Gender Negotiations in Chutney-Soca Lyrics in Trinidad', *Caribbean Review of Gender Studies*, 1 (April 2007), https://sta.uwi.edu/crgs/april2007/journals/aisha_mohammed.pdf

Morcom, Anna, *Illicit Worlds of Indian Dance: Cultures of Exclusion* (London: Hurst & Co., 2013).

Novetzke, Christian L., 'Note to Self: What Marathi Kirtankars' Notebooks Suggest about Literacy, Performance, and the Travelling Performer in Pre-Colonial Maharashtra' in *Tellings and Texts*, ed. by F. Orsini and K. Butler Schofield (Cambridge: Open Book Publishers, 2015), pp. 169–184, https://doi.org/10.11647/OBP.0062

'Phoolsunghi: The Scent of a Text| Jaipur Literature Festival 2021', https://www.youtube.com/watch?v=neT0WUm045Y

Ramnarine, Tina K., *Creating Their Own Space: The Development of an Indian-Caribbean Musical Tradition* (Kingston, Jamaica: University of the West Indies Press, 2001).

'Roundtable on Contemporary African Oral Traditions', SOAS, University of London, 20 November 2019, http://mulosige.soas.ac.uk/contemporary-african-oral-traditions-recording/

Servan-Schreiber, Catherine, *Chanteurs itinérants en Inde du Nord: la tradition orale Bhojpuri* (Paris: L'Harmattan, 1999).

——, *Histoire d'une musique métisse à l'île Maurice: chutney indien et séga Bollywood* (Paris: Riveneuve éditions, 2010).

Sundar Popo, 'Kaise Bani', https://www.youtube.com/watch?v=GnMSmWgoupc

Tinker, Hugh, *A New System of Slavery: The Export of Indian Labour Overseas, 1830–1920* (Oxford: Oxford University Press, 1974).

Tripathy, Ratnakar, 'Music Mania in Small-town Bihar: Emergence of Vernacular Identities', *Economic and Political Weekly*, 47.22, 2 June 2012.

Unnuth, Abhimanyu, *Lal Pasina* (New Delhi: Rajakamal Prakashan, 2010).

Upadhyay, Krishna Dev, *Bhojpuri lokgit*, 2 vols. (Allahabad: Hindi Sahitya Sammelan, 1954 and 1956).

5. Erasure and Rehabilitation of the *Halqa* in Morocco

The Vicissitudes of an Intangible Cultural Heritage

Fatima Zahra Salih

Introduction

Jamaâ El Fna Square in Marrakesh is a public square characterized by a double definition, in terms of both toponym and heritage. In 2001 it was included in the UNESCO list of Intangible Cultural Heritage for representing 'a unique concentration of popular Moroccan cultural traditions performed through musical, religious and artistic expressions'.[1] It can unequivocally be described as a 'site of memory' or *'lieu de mémoire'*, in the definition given by Paul Ricoeur in *Memory, History, Forgetting*:[2]

> The transition from corporeal memory to the memory of places [*lieux de mémoire*] is assured by acts as important as orienting oneself, moving from place to place, and above all inhabiting. It is on the surface of the habitable earth that we remember having traveled and visited memorable sites. In this way, the 'things' remembered are intrinsically associated with places.

---

1   'Cultural Space of Jemaa el-Fna Square', UNESCO.
2   Paul Ricoeur, *Memory, History, Forgetting* (Chicago: University of Chicago Press, 2004), p. 41. (Original edition: *La Mémoire, l'Histoire, l'oubli*, Paris: éd. Seuil, 2000, p. 49.)

  https://doi.org/10.11647/OBP.0405.05

Contrary to what one might think, Jamaâ El Fna Square is not unique. In Moroccan cities it is common to find a public square dedicated to popular street shows: acrobats, magicians, snake charmers, singers, fortune tellers, storytellers, sellers of medicinal plants and other gris-gris or talismans—in short, a sample of popular traditions accumulated over centuries. This can be witnessed in cities such as Fez (Boujloud Square), Meknes (Lahdim Square), Oujda (Sidi Abdelwahab Square), Taroudant, Safi, Essaouira, and so on. These cities are all known for their squares, commonly referred to by Moroccans as *halqa*.

First of all, we must pay particular attention to the name *halqa*, which comes from Arabic. Literally, *halqa* means a circle or a ring, hence it is applied to anything that has a circular or semi-circular shape. In the Arab world, teaching (*dars*) held in schools and madrasas historically took place in circles, with the students sitting in a semicircle around their teacher. This kind of instruction was called '*halaqat* [pl. of *halqa*] *dars*'. The circle is also present in various manifestations of Arabo-Muslim culture and seems to be at the basis of its imagination, whether in architecture (the patio in the middle of the house, the mosque or the madrasa) or in the popular dances of certain regions such as Hallil de Gourara in Algeria, for example.

This circularity, moving between the sacred and the profane, entered Moroccan popular culture and its transmission and gave legitimacy to the intangible cultural heritage of the *halqa*. I believe that the relationship between the *halqa* and the tradition of the circle is beyond doubt: the word here denotes both the container space and the content, the form and the popular art that is practiced there.

A Place, a Memory

According to Pierre Nora, the concept of *lieu de mémoire* applies to a toponymic space that is transformed into a place imbued with collective memory.[3] This makes it a place that combines topographical and other immaterial dimensions. This is confirmed by Paul Ricoeur when he explains that:

> These memory places [*lieux de mémoire*] function for the most part in the manner of reminders, offering in turn a support for failing memory, a struggle in the war against forgetting, even the silent plea of dead memory.[4]

---

3   Pierre Nora, 'Between Memory and History: Les Lieux de Mémoire', *Representations* 26 (1989), 7-24.

Certainly, Paul Ricoeur's definition, like Pierre Nora's, concerns the historical aspect of space and place. However, these definitions can also apply to the *halqa,* since it is an integral part of collective memory. Moreover, the combination of three meanings within the same word *halqa*—a place or square; a popular entertainment practice; and a memory—is not fortuitous but indicates that these dimensions are inseparable, and that any alteration in one seriously impacts the others. The strength of the link underlying the three dimensions is revealed, therefore, to be double-edged: any failure of one implies the disappearance, erasure, and therefore oblivion of the others. This mark of fragility emerges in all its strength when we understand the *halqa* as a *lieu de mémoire* whose sustainability is currently threatened. This is why the urban redevelopments that have affected the various *halqa* squares in Morocco have played a major part in the total or partial disappearance of the art of the *halqa* and disrupted its intergenerational transmission.

Fig. 5.1 The storyteller Omar Douâmi in the square of Souk Barra, Beni-Mellal, Morocco. Photograph by l'Atelier du conte, 2011.

---

4   Ibid.

Threats and Perils of Intangible Heritage

As a public space, the *halqa* has experienced several upheavals in
the second half of the twentieth century, because the first leaders of
Moroccan cities in the post-independence period lacked knowledge
about its cultural significance. Indeed, since modernisation was
understood as economic and scientific development, the erasure of the
space of the *halqa* seemed to be important in order to eradicate what was
then considered to be the remnants of a popular culture without value,
folklore in the negative sense of the term, even charlatanism.

Fig. 5.2 Halqa at the Souk Barra, Beni-Mellal, Morocco. Photograph by l'Atelier
du conte, 2011.

This lack of knowledge about the heritage value of the *halqa* and the
intrinsic relationship between space and practice was compounded by
intense contempt. Hence the redevelopment plans carried out in almost
all the cities of Morocco (less so in Marrakech) precipitated the outright
erasure of these public squares. Between the 1970s and the 2000s, in
Oujda, Fez, and Meknes the *halqa* square was converted into a bus stop,

a road, or a parking lot. Given the deep and strong connection between these places and collective memory, *halqa* practitioners and their public were destabilized in their traditional relationship. The disappearance or semi-disappearance of these heritage spaces caused a rupture in the chain of intergenerational transmission and social bonding that had been woven for centuries.

The exceptional place that is the *halqa* poses distinct questions because of its topographical location. In fact, if we observe its urban positioning, we notice that the *halqa* is usually outside the city walls. It abuts the medina without really inserting itself within it. This is the case in Marrakesh, Oujda, Fez, Meknes and probably elsewhere as well. In Beni-Mellal, where a single storyteller has occupied the square for forty years, the square is called Souk Barra, or 'the outer souk'.

One wonders about the reasons for choosing this location and its possible meanings.

- Is there a conscious or unconscious relationship between the choice of the location of the *halqa* as contiguous but outside the city and the *halqa* itself as a popular practice outside social norms and conventions?

- Does this location index the marginalization that the *halqa* has always suffered as a tolerated but unrecognized practice?

- What has been the relationship between the scholarly culture officially practiced inside Moroccan cities and the popular culture represented by the *halqa* in the public square outside the medina?

These are questions whose answers may reveal the deep reasons that have precipitated the erasure of many *halqa* squares over several decades, and the denial of which the *halqa* and its practitioners have fallen victim.

The Moroccan *Halqa* as a Space of Marginality?

When we observe the popular practices taking place in the *halqas* in Morocco, we find a number of peculiarities that make them hard to classify, and that render them objects of an admixture of admiration and rejection by their public and by society at large. In a *halqa* we find musicians, acrobats, snake charmers, and storytellers, and not only them: we also meet nail- or glass-eaters, female and male fortune tellers, healers, drinkers of boiling water and other extravagant individuals with paranormal powers, *majdubins* or *haddauis* (as they are nicknamed), people possessed by mysterious forces.

Among the types of performance that occur in the *halqa* we find theatre, music and dance, three kinds of popular art in which notions of gender are more fluid than in traditional society. In the travelling troupe of *Ouled Hmar*, for example, female characters are played by men.[5] The dancers are men dressed as women, often openly queer-presenting. Conversely, a woman wishing to practice music in the *halqa* square disguises herself as a man, cuts her hair, and camouflages her body in order to gain access to it.[6] In this sense, the *halqa* is a subversive place par excellence, which tolerates what the laws and customs of a traditional society prohibit and punish. In the past, the *halqa* played the role of collective stress relief for male audiences, and made it possible to approach, through laughter and fiction, political, sexual or other taboo subjects sanctioned by society.

Within everyday life, the *halqa* thus stands as a place of all possibilities, where the collective imagination is concretised and where several symbolic boundaries imposed by society are defied. Deborah Kapchan, an American researcher who has resided in Morocco and devoted several publications to Moroccan cultural heritage, defines the *halqa* as follows:

> The suq is constructed as socially 'low', the locus of popular performance and chicanery. Performance in the suq takes the form of public oratory [...]. The halqa is the public arena for social license, a site where almost anything can be said with impunity. Because of the expressive liberties taken in the halqa, it is a marginal site; a man of honour would be embarrassed to be found there.[7]

Such marginality, which applies to the performance of the *halqa*, applies equally to the *hlayqis* and to the space hosting them.[8] This involves a triple marginality, of place, genre and practictioner, controlled

---

5   *Ouled Hmar* is a well-known travelling theatre company in the Haouz region
    encompassing Marrakech and surrounding Safi.
6   See 'Chleuh, Dancing Boys, Jemaa al Fnaa Square, Marrakech'.
7   Deborah Kapchan, *Gender on the Market: Moroccan Women and the Reviving of
    Tradition* (Philadelphia: University of Pennsylvania Press,1996), p. 38.
8   A person who practices the *halqa* is called *hlayqi* in Moroccan Arabic or Darija.

and tolerated by traditional Moroccan society, which I think reveals a degree of societal wisdom. This wisdom was completely rejected, however, when Morocco first came into contact with modernity in the twentieth century. This resulted in a near-total misunderstanding of the *halqa* and of its social, spatial, and heritage dimensions, which resulted in repeated calls for its erasure.

Jamaâ El Fna Square, or the Exception among Moroccan *Halqas*

Between 1956—the date of Morocco's independence—and the 2000s, Jamaâ El Fna Square in Marrakesh underwent several urban redevelopment projects that almost precipitated its demise, and it was only saved by the will, commitment, and shouts of alarm from a number of intellectuals. It was transformed into a place of resistance by the latter, against urbanization movements that I would describe as ignorant. The word El Fna, just like *halqa*, comes from the Arabic *al-fanaa*. It refers either to the patio, the central space of a house, a mosque, or another building, or to the open space attached to them. This name can be explained by the location of this square in relation to the city and its El Kutubia Mosque. The intervention, in 2003, of the Moroccan Ministry of Culture and Morocco's ratification of the UNESCO Convention for Intangible Cultural Heritage were the lifelines that saved the famous square and protected it from threats of erasure.

The consequences of this ratification extended to other cities and other categories of Moroccan intangible heritage: the engagement fair or *Moussem des fiançailles* of Imilchil, the fair or Moussem of Tan Tan, the cherries' fair or *Moussem des cerises* in Sefrou, the dance of Tiskiwin in Imintanout, and many other fairs or forms of popular practices. One can argue that since 2003, Morocco has become aware of the cultural as well as the economic value of its intangible heritage and has begun to treat many reputed popular practices as heritage. In the same spirit, other cities like Fez, Oujda, and Meknes have undertaken urban redevelopment in order to recover their *halqa* squares, which they had long ago tried to erase and destroy. However, despite this clear transformation of Morocco's official position vis-à-vis its intangible cultural heritage, the following questions arise. What impact have the years of destruction of the *halqa* had, on collective memory on the one hand, and on its transmission on the other? Is it as easy to recover this memory as it is to recover the space associated with it?

The Storyteller as Keeper of Popular Memory

What would become of the *halqa* without the storyteller? What is the future of the popular tale without the person who ensures its oral transmission and, consequently, its viability? The answer is obvious and requires no explanation: the death of the storyteller—in the literal and figurative sense—represents a threat to the survival of the popular tale, a form which lives only through the one who tells it and transmits it via the act of storytelling. Hence we have an interest in the storyteller in any attempt to collect or safeguard the oral tale.

This role played by the storyteller is amplified by the other dimensions relating to his mission: 1) An undeniable artistic or artisanal dimension, given that the live show the storyteller presents to his audience is a performance; 2) A social dimension, due to the storyteller's role as a weaver of links in society; 3) An anthropological dimension, given the social codes that the storyteller illustrates.

I have been working on oral heritage since 2002 by setting up a workshop for the benefit of students and an annual festival to which researchers and storytellers are invited. By doing so, I have been able, within my university, to establish a stable link between academic research and the storytellers' practice, two dimensions that do not traditionally come together, since they are part of two supposedly contradictory paradigms, namely high culture and popular culture. This experience, which lasted ten years, allowed us to break down the epistemological boundaries between these two cultural spheres and to create bridges of dialogue, in particular with four popular Moroccan storytellers: Omar Douâmi in Beni-Mellal; Mohamed Bariz and Abderrahim El Maqori (nicknamed Al-Azaliya) in Marrakesh, and Mohamed Mokhlis in Fez.

Let me take the example of Omar Douâmi, a master storyteller of the *halqa* in Morocco who practiced the *halqa* for more than forty years in the square called Souk Barra and who, unfortunately, died in August 2018. The square of Souk Barra, as its name suggests, lies outside the walls of the ancient city of Beni-Mellal. This topographical location places it at the margins, and at the same time it authorizes a degree of freedom of speech. My collaboration with Douâmi gave rise to a variety of outputs, including interviews, monographs, a film, academic articles, and so on.[9] With regards to Douâmi, our enquiry must first of all attend to his particular corpus, which drew from popular Arabic literature (the *Thousand and One Nights*, the epic of Dahir Bibars, Saïf Bnou Douyazan, the epic of Antar Bnou Chaddad, and so on); from popular memory; but also, quite unusually, from films, which Douâmi adapted to oral storytelling and to the taste of the public. As he put it:

> When I go to the cinema to see a film, I only remember what forms the main plot and the adventures. Once at the *halqa*, and it's almost always the next day, I tell almost the same plot as the film but with variations accessible to my audience. I change the names of the characters, the names of the cities. It is never a known country, it is always a distant or nameless country, an imaginary country.[10]

Apart from the popular tales Douâmi had listened to during his childhood and youth, a wide variety of other sources constitute the repertoire of the storyteller, who carries out research and sorts, cuts, and adapts his material before meeting his audience. By observing the storyteller's library and his performance in front of the public, we were able to observe two important facts. First, the books of popular Arabic literature placed on the desk are detached from their binding and meticulously classified in blocks of sheets (see Figs. 5.3 and 5.4).

Second, when Douâmi told his story in public orally and in Moroccan Arabic or Darija (see Fig. 5.5), he held in one hand the pages of a book, which represented a selection made by the storyteller himself from the chosen story. The sheets held in his hand helped him find his bearings from time to time.

---

9   See Fernando de Azevedo, 'Le derneir des Hajjiahs'; and Jacques Combe and Fatima Zahra Salih, 'Bollywood sur souk'.

10   Fatima Zahra Salih, 'L'art de raconter des films: Entretien avec Omar Douâmi', p. 1.

Fig. 5.3 Omar Douâmi in his office, surrounded by his books. Author's photograph.

Fig. 5.4 Omar Douâmi's books without their bindings. Author's photograph.

Fig. 5.5 Omar Douâmi giving his *halqa* with a book page in his hand. Photograph by l'Atelier du conte, 2011.

As he put it:

> At the beginning, I spent the nights thinking, composing intrigues, adding adventures, and the next day I would tell stories in the square of the souk... [laughter followed by silence]. That's how I was doing it... [Laughs]. And the story or the tale of the film can be modeled according to my desires... my moods. I can rework it as I please, tell it in half an hour, an hour, or a month. An adventure... a knot... a beginning and an end and that's it... that's how... that's the way I did and I still do from time to time in recent years... Sometimes, any adventure, I turn it into a tale.[11]

Far from systematically repeating the repertoires common to storytellers in Morocco, or even in the Arab-Amazigh world, Omar Douâmi demonstrated originality and a great ability to innovate, to reformulate in local speech, and to revisit both bookish and cinematic sources. In his own words:

11　Ibid., p. 2.

> When I first told stories, I would only tell the *Arabian Nights*. I realized that my colleagues were telling almost the same stories. In addition, the public, by dint of listening to almost the same tales, ended up learning them by heart... I would cite as examples: 'The fisherman and the djinn', 'The porter and the three little girls', 'Badia Al Zaman Al-Hamadani', 'Shahrayar and Shahraman'. I thought a lot about how I could stand out and have something special. And as I was a lover of cinema and especially of Bollywood films, I had the idea of telling films. The advantage with these films is that they are all based on excellent stories which gather together all the ingredients of a tale: sorcery, adventure, courage, evil and good... And each adventure that seemed appropriate to the main plot of the film, I integrated into my story.[12]

Another characteristic of the storyteller's performance is that it is interactive and relies on the involvement of the public to continue. This adds a social value to the role of the storyteller, who knows how to symbiotically gather around himself audience members from multiple social strata.

The opening of the story is in the form of an invitation to collectively recite the prayer to the Prophet Muhammad ('Pray on the Prophet!', he said, and the audience chanted unanimously: '*Allahoma salli wa sallam âla sayidina Mhhammad*'). Like a magic formula, the prayer unites the audience with the storyteller and opens up the world of the imagination. This repetition bestows on the performance a ritual character.

Moreover, the public storyteller most often takes a seated position. Omar Douâmi affirmed that this is necessary when it comes to telling the Sirat and other stories known for their length.

> When I tell stories, I am always on my feet. I was going back and forth in the Halqa so that people could see me... and I was turning so that people could see me. See my facial expressions, my gestures and hear my voice. [Silence] When I recite the Sira, I am seated. But, sometimes, while telling and without wanting to, I stand up ... I also change my voice and the tone of my flow according to the moods of the characters to mark the difference between the situations.[13]

Douâmi himself had a chair on which he sat while his audience sat on the ground around him (see Fig. 5.5). Holder of the word, the storyteller

---

12 Ibid., pp. 2–3.
13 Ibid., p. 4.

is respected and listened to throughout the time of a story. He is the focus of everyone's undivided attention, as befits a good orator. The loyalty of the public is a frequently observed phenomenon, one we associate with the implicit contract tying the public to the storyteller, whose talent alone can explain this secret bond. This so-called 'talent' is illustrated by several techniques, among which suspense is a major one. Suspense is used during the performance when the storyteller, after reaching a climax in the plot, suspends the narration and hands around his *tarboush* to collect money from the audience. Suspense is also produced in a calculated fashion to ensure the return of the public the next day and afterwards. According to one of the anecdotes told by Omar Douâmi, late one evening a man accompanied by his elderly father came knocking on his door to ask him to finish telling the story to his father, who could not sleep because he was so worried about what was to come.

Conclusions

The investment in heritage as an incentive for the development of cultural tourism has long been a slogan brandished by different professionals from the various sectors concerned—hence the resurgence in interest towards the 'heritagization' of certain cultural traditions in different regions of Morocco. Jamaâ El Fna Square in Marrakech is no exception and has suffered the evils of an excess of folklorization at the expense of the real work needed to safeguard its heritage. While *halqa* shows are held daily in the square and the number of (Moroccan and foreign) audience members is high, it is no exaggeration to say that there are almost no storytellers left, and that the famous square has now more restaurants than *hlayqis*. The heritagization of Jamaâ El Fna Square has saved it from fatal erasure but has not protected it from profound changes that could alter its authenticity and its real cultural value.

Today, after the rehabilitation of the *halqa* in Morocco, questions still arise about its place in modern culture as well as about its future. Is it enough to physically restore *lieux de mémoires* destroyed for decades to ensure the continuity of cultural practices related to them? As for storytellers and other practitioners whose chain of transmission has been fractured, can they rise from the ashes and can transmission remain sustainable?

Douâmi's long experience and regular presence in the town square allowed him to demarcate an exclusive topographical space and an audience that nothing and no one could alter, at least until his death. The familiarity and habit that he was able to develop with his audience sealed a sort of contract between them, which translated in concrete terms into a spatially specific agora recognized by the city and its inhabitants. The magic of the spoken word is that it impacts both the public and the space that retains its memory.

Paradoxically, though, the storyteller, so present and respected in the public square, loses his public fame and the strength of his word in so-called conventional society. The social denigration from which this profession has suffered has had a negative effect on its transmission as intangible heritage to younger people. The activities carried out by the Storytelling Workshop at our university have allowed young people to encounter various styles and traditions and to become aware of the possibilities of recreating the art of storytelling and of breathing new life into this ancestral heritage shunned by our modern societies. Our efforts to remedy this situation have included diversifying the sessions by inviting storytellers from several countries who have similar experiences (France, Belgium, Quebec, Palestine, Egypt, Algeria, Tunisia, Senegal, and others) and who have learnt how to innovate and bring about a revival of the art of storytelling, as is the case of the Maison du Conte in Brussels in Belgium, the Maison du Conte in Chevilly-Larue in France, and many other initiatives. In Jordan, Palestine and Egypt, an independent and free school called 'Mujawara' brings together (mainly young) apprentice storytellers and master storytellers. This experimental method is considered to emanate organically from the local culture, which believes in this intergenerational pedagogical relationship between master and apprentice.[14] Indeed, since the art of storytelling is learned through practice and transmission, it would be impossible to confine it to a strict and predetermined methodology.

---

14   In Arabic, Mujawara means being around someone in a kind of neighborhood. Here, the word designates a neighborhood of learning. It is a concept coined by Dr Munir Fasheh which has been adopted by Al Multaqa Al Arabi and its partners in various Arab countries; see Mounir Fasheh, 'Experiments in Radical Pedagogy in Palestine', 'Mujawara ma' Munir al-Fasheh'.

This is why it is worthwhile to look at the innovative styles of today's young storytellers, who live in an ultra-connected world, where the digital plays an extremely important role (as Sadhana Naithani does in Chapter 9 in this volume). Linked to the daily practices of the members of a community, the art of storytelling evolves and changes according to the transformations the community experiences. Are we witnessing the birth of a new generation of storytellers, who manage to be more compatible with our changed cultural environment? Does the digital represent a new *halqa* for young storytellers?

Bibliography

Azevedo, Fernando de, 'Le derneir des Hajjiahs', https://youtu.be/ZbheUMxQ-p8

Ben, Belga, 'Kafash khadimat ma' al-mafya al-italiya', https://www.youtube.com/watch?fbclid=IwAR0Emqir9lSykZ_i-pjURlrwrA4noZaEm4cujF4l6pNxnjr9IYWwRqzDw_Y&v=ojAjo7ORS1c&feature=youtu.be

Canetti, Elias, *The Voices of Marrakesh: A Record of a Visit* (London: Penguin UK, 2012).

'Chleuh, Dancing Boys, Jemaa al Fnaa Square, Marrakech', https://youtu.be/M1dPLRtJkJc

Collective, *From The Immateriality of Cultural Heritage,* under the direction of Ahmed Skounti and Ouidad Tebbaa, UNESCO (Marrakech: Walili Printing, 2011).

Combe, Jacques and Fatima Zahra Salih, 'Bollywood sur souk', https://www.academia.edu/23657191/Bollywood_sur_souk

'Cultural space of Jemaa el-Fna Square', https://ich.unesco.org/en/RL/cultural-space-of-jemaa-el-fna-square-00014

Fasheh, Mounir, 'Experiments in Radical Pedagogy in Palestine' in conversation with Mayssoun Soukarieh, Institute of Education, UCL, London, 17 October 2019, https://www.youtube.com/watch?v=djbj-kts_04

Kapchan, Deborah, *Gender on the Market: Moroccan Women and the Revoicing of Tradition* (Philadelphia: University of Pennsylvania Press, 1996).

'Mujawara with munir fasheh', الخلطة في السر :فاشة منير مع مجاورة, https://www.youtube.com/watch?v=63cXp8GsFMk (2014)

Nora, Pierre, 'Between Memory and History: Les Lieux de Mémoire', *Representations* 26 (1989), 7-24.

Ricoeur, Paul, *Memory, History, Forgetting,* tr. by Kathleen Blamey and David Pellauer (Chicago: University of Chicago Press, 2004). Original edition, *La Mémoire, l'Histoire, l'oubli* (Paris: Seuil, 2000).

Salih, Fatima Zahra, 'L'art de raconter des films: Entretien avec Omar Douâmi', https://flshbm.academia.edu/FatimaZahraSalih

6. A Contextual and Functional Analysis of Na'o Folk Songs

Desta Desalegn Dinege and Yenealem Aredo

Introduction

This study was conducted in the Decha district or *woreda* of the Kaffa Zone, in the Southern Nations Nationalities and People's Region (SNNPR) of Ethiopia. The region is inhabited by three main ethnic groups: Kaffa, Chara, and the Na'o, who are the concern of this study. The Na'o community, whose language is called Naayi, live in most parts of Decha district. Naayi is categorized under the Omotic language family spoken in the southwestern parts of Ethiopia.[1]

According to oral traditions, the Na'o used to have a small independent kingdom. The different districts were governed by chiefs, who operated under the authority of the king, or *kyas*. In the seventeenth century, the Na'o kingdom was conquered by the neighbouring kingdom of Kaffa, and the Na'o king became a vassal and tributary of the Kaffa king. Further disruptions happened in the 1970s, when a series of conflicts between Kaffa feudal leaders, the military government, and the Na'o resulted in a wave of displacement.[2] As a result, the Na'o people are

---

1   Azeb Amha, 'The Omotic Language Family' in *The Cambridge Handbook of Linguistic Typology*, ed. by Alexandra Y. Aikhenvald and R. M. W. Dixon (Cambridge: Cambridge University Press: 2017), pp. 815–853 (p. 815).

2   'The reason that the Naayì people came to the Dulkuma, Aybera, Kosa, and Jamdos villages was due to the war between the feudal lords of Decha Awraja and the military government in the time from 1976 to 1977'; Yilma Aklilu, 'Some Notes on the Nayi Grammar' in *Ethiopia in Broader Perspective: Papers of the XIIIth International Conference of Ethiopian Studies (Kyoto 12–17 December 1997)*, ed. by

    https://doi.org/10.11647/OBP.0405.06

now scattered in three main territorial pockets. The bulk of the Na'o people live in the Decha district of the Kaffa administrative zone, near the town of Bonga. Smaller communities live in Dulkuma village in the Shoa-Bench district of the Bench-Maji zone, 150 kilometres away from Bonga, and in the villages of Aybera, Kosa and Jomodos of the Sheko district of the Bench-Maji and Shekicho zones. As a result of the scattered settlements of the community in different areas, where other languages are spoken or dominant, the Naayi language and Na'o culture are currently endangered.

The causes of language endangerment include, 'the decrease in the number of speakers, cultural dominance, overt repression, natural catastrophes, marginalization of the community's languages and cultures, economic factors, political dominance, educational policies, global influences and influence of other communities'.[3] According to Dessalegn, there are five levels of language endangerment: 1) A language is potentially endangered if the children start preferring the dominant language and learn the obsolescing language imperfectly; 2) A language is endangered if the speakers are young adults and there are very few or no child speakers; 3) A language is seriously endangered if the speakers are middle-aged or past middle age; 4) A language is terminally endangered or moribund if there are only a few elderly speakers left; 5) A language is dead when there are no speakers left at all.[4] The Naayì language falls in the second of these five levels in that its youngest speakers are young adults and there are very few or no child speakers. For this reason, the Naayì is classified as status 7B, that is, it is threatened with extinction.

Samson Seid defines the Na'o as a 'completely oral culture', in which knowledge and social values are transmitted exclusively orally or ritually, without a written component.[5] According to the 2007 Census, the total Na'o population is between 3,000 and 7,190 people, of whom only 3,600 speak Naayi as their mother tongue. The community of

---

Katsuyoshi Fukui, Eisei Kurimoto, and Masayoshi Shigeta (Kyoto: Shokado Book Sellers, 1997), pp. 601–618 (p. 601).

3   Dessalegn Gebeyehu, 'On the Verge of Dying: Languages in Ethiopia', *OGMIOS Newsletter, Foundation for Endangered Languages*, 52 (2013), 3–13 (p. 5).

4   Ibid., p. 4.

5   Samson Seid, 'Ethnic Language Shift of Nao', *Endangered Languages Project* (2012), 1–23 (p. 3).

Naayi speakers is very small compared with that of Kafinoono, the language of the neighbouring Kaffa people, whose number is estimated at 870,213.[6] Many Na'o have adopted Kafinoono as their main language, as they depend on it in their interactions with their neighbours. A large proportion of Na'o people who speak Naayi as their mother tongue master at least another language, and only 1,137 are reported to be monolingual. Fluency in Naayi is also geographically determined, and tends to survive only in the Decha district, the area where the biggest portion of the Na'o population lives. The small size of Na'o communities has pushed them to adopt the host language and culture, even more so in the Shoa-Bench and Sheko districts, where Na'o ethnic clusters are small and isolated. Living at such close proximity to much more numerous and politically influential communities has therefore strongly influenced the trajectory of Na'o culture and their language.

The ability to speak Naayi carries strong generational connotations. As Samson writes, 'in Decha, the older generation speaks the Na'o language. On the other hand, children and adolescents do not speak the language of their parents'.[7] Our fieldwork confirmed this statement. Older people speak Naayi very well, while the adult generation often resort to Kafinoono terms when speaking Naayi. Youths, especially those in high school, communicate with each other predominantly in Kafinoono, and only use Naayi from time to time when they are communicating with their family. Schooling plays a big role in this generational shift, and the educational approach in the region compounds the vulnerability of Naayi.

Schools are one of the main agents of language spread, and Naayi is struggling without any institutional recognition in the education sector, a situation compounded by the lack of an official orthography.[8] Because the Kaffa is the biggest ethnic group in the area, schools tend to employ Kafinoono as their main language. No schools in the area, whether

---

6   Federal Democratic Republic of Ethiopia Population Census Commission, 'Summary and Statistical Report of the 2007 Population and Housing Census: Population Size by Age and Sex', *United Nations Population Fund (UNFPA)* (Addis Ababa: 2008), p. 84.

7   Samson, 'Ethnic Language', p. 19.

8   As Samson put it, 'data obtained from interview and researchers' observation with school children show that there is no room for the use of Na'o language at all levels in school and out of school situations'; 'Ethnic Language', p. 12.

public or private, employ Naayi as medium of instruction. Learning in a language other than their mother tongue pushes children away from Naayi, while schooling contributes to normalising Kafinoono as the language of formal and informal interaction.

The cultural similarity between the Kaffa and the Na'o is another factor that weakens the Naayi language and culture, given that 'cultural dissimilarity between groups in contact favours maintenance whereas cultural similarity [...] may facilitate language shift'.[9] When it comes to the Kaffa and the Na'o, the two groups have 'very close marriage customs, funeral ceremonies, traditional rituals and religions among others'.[10] Adopting Kafinoono for cultural practices is not perceived as a radical cultural departure, facilitating the language shift. Despite such similarities, the Na'o people have retained their own folkloric features—from their own cultural ceremonies and their way of cooking food to their material culture and, more importantly for the scope of this chapter, their oral literature.

Almost all previous studies on the Na'o people have focused on language, and their scope has not stretched beyond documenting Naayi grammar.[11] Aklilu and Siebert, Samson, and Dessalegn have focused on the sociolinguistic situation of Naayi, whereas Andualem has provided a descriptive syntax of the language.[12] We have come across no study on Na'o culture.

---

9   Ibid., p. 17.

10   Ibid.

11   These include: Aklilu Yilma, 'Two Phonological Processes in Nayi: Palatalization and Labialization' in *Proceedings of the First National Conference of Ethiopian Studies*, ed. by N. J. Pankhurst et al. (Addis Ababa: Institute of Ethiopian Studies, 1990), pp. 433–448; Aklilu Yilma, 'A Phonological Comparison of Bench and Two Majoid Languages' in *New Trends in Ethiopian Studies. Papers of the 12th International Conference of Ethiopian Studies*, ed. by Harold M. Marcus (Lawrenceville: Red Sea. 1994), vol. 1, pp. 1053–1063; Aklilu, 'Nayi Grammar'; Lionel M. Bender, *Comparative Morphology of the Omotic languages* [LINCOM Studies in African Linguistics] (Munich; Newcastle: LINCOM Europa, 2000); Ephrem Dejene, *Verb Inflections in Nayi* (Addis Ababa University School of Graduate Studies: unpublished MA Thesis, 2007); Samson, 'Ethnic Language'; Dessalegn 'Verge of Dying'.

12   Aklilu Yilma and Ralph Siebert, 'Sociolinguistic Survey Report of the Chara, Dime, Melo and Nayi Languages of Ethiopia: Part 1', *Journal of Language Survey Reports 2002–2009*, Language Assessment, Sociolinguistics (2002), 1–11; Samson, 'Ethnic Language'; Dessalegn, 'Verge of Dying'; Andualem Adal Tessema, 'A Descriptive Syntax of Naayi' (unpublished PhD thesis, Addis Ababa University College of Humanities, 2020).

Folk Songs: Theoretical Approaches, Materials and Methods

Dorson categorizes folklore into four major genres: oral literature, social folk customs, material culture, and folk performing arts.[13] Oral literature—also called verbal art, expressive literature, folk literature, or oral tradition (see the Introduction to this volume)—can be subdivided into specific genres, such as songs, riddles, anecdotes, proverbs, folk songs, chants, tongue-twisters, folk tales, myths, legends, jokes, and many more.[14] Among the Na'o people, oral poetry and folk songs are widely performed, and therefore this study focuses on this genre in particular.

As described by Finnegan, 'oral poetry is of common occurrence in human society, literate as well as non-literate. It is found all over the world, past and present'.[15] Each oral genre can have many subgenres, depending on the culture and other contextual factors. Subgenres of folk songs include marriage songs, love songs, songs of war, shepherd songs, children's songs, child-rearing songs, cattle songs, work songs, funeral songs, and so on. In other words, each folk song subgenre is performed for a specific occasion, or in a specific socio-economic context. Songs are transmitted orally, so performers learn the songs through direct observation, imitation, and personal participation.[16]

Prominent scholars of African oral literature like Ruth Finnegan and Isidore Okpewho have pointed out the special role that oral poetry plays in most African rural communities, especially at peak agricultural times such as ploughing, weeding, harvesting, threshing, or when building new houses.[17] Folk songs play an important role in the daily life of the Na'o, especially when it comes to work, religious ceremonies, festive gatherings, and entertainment. Despite their importance in Na'o

---

13 R. M. Dorson, ed., *Folklore and Folklife: An Introduction* (Chicago: The University of Chicago, 1972), p. 2.

14 Ruth Finnegan, *Oral Poetry: Its Nature, Significance and Social Context* (Cambridge: Cambridge University Press, 1977); and *Oral Traditions and the Verbal Arts: A Guide to Research Practices* (London and New York: Routledge, 1992). Isidore Okpewho, *African Oral Literature: Backgrounds, Character and Continuity* (Bloomington: Indiana University Press, 1992), p. 4.

15 Finnegan, *Oral Poetry*, p. 3.

16 Peter van Kranenburg et. al, 'Collaboration Perspectives for Folk Song Research and Music Information Retrieval: The Indispensable Role of Computational Musicology', *Journal of Interdisciplinary Music Studies*, 4.1 (2010), 17–43 (p. 18).

17 Finnegan, *Oral Poetry*; Okpewho, *African Oral Poetry*.

life, little effort has been made to collect, document, or disseminate this important form of oral literature. Cultural diversity is essential to human heritage, and language and oral poetry are among the major components of this cultural diversity.[18] Apart from being a medium of communication, language conveys the wisdom of a community of speakers. For Wamalwa and Oluoch, the loss of any language is a loss for humanity in general and of unique cultural features in particular.[19] Unless studies are conducted and practical recommendations are given, this unique language, and the oral culture attached to it, will be lost. This study therefore contributes to the preservation of Na'o oral culture by collecting, interpreting, and documenting Na'o folk songs.

Dorson has identified twelve theories of folklore that can be applied to the study of oral literature in general and folk songs in particular: historical-geographical, historical-reconstruction, ideological, functional, psychoanalytical, structural, oral formulaic, cross-cultural, folk cultural, mass-cultural, hemispheric, and contextual.[20] Among these theories, we found the functional and contextual approaches to be most relevant to the present research. Our interest lies in mapping the relationship between text and context, so as to shed light on the role played by oral traditions in Na'o society at large. An exclusive focus on the words and style of the songs would fail to capture the performative nature of folk songs and their social function. Rather than just looking at the text, we approached folk songs as a socio-cultural event. This means that recording the lyrics of the songs on a tape recorder is not enough. One has to record the whole performance: the gestures of the performers, the tone of their voice, the reaction of the audience, the clothes worn by the participants, and the position of the singer vis-à-vis the audience are all constitutive elements of the genre. More broadly, looking at folk

---

18   UNESCO, *Language Vitality and Endangerment*, presented at the International
      Expert Meeting on UNESCO Programme Safeguarding of Endangered Languages,
      Paris: UNESCO Ad Hoc Expert Group on Endangered Languages, 2003.

19   Eric W. Wamalwa and Stephen B. J. Oluoch, 'Language Endangerment and
      Language Maintenance: Can Endangered Indigenous Languages of Kenya Be
      Electronically Preserved?', *International Journal of Humanities and Social Science*, 3.7
      (2013), 258–266.

20   Dorson, *Folklore and Folklife*.

songs as socio-cultural events foregrounds their ideological meanings and functions within the socialisation process of a particular society.[21]

Folk songs, like any other social phenomenon, cannot be analysed in isolation or in terms of only one set of social relations, because they are connected to the total social whole of a given society. A functionalist approach helps us to identify the specific roles that folk songs play in their social contexts, for example as transmitters of the past, as entertainment, as sanctions for established beliefs, attitudes, and institutions, or as a form of psychological escape from socio-political repression.[22]

In order to acquire in-depth knowledge, we employed a qualitative research methodology.[23] Folklorists like Ben-Amos, O'Reilly, and Dundes strongly recommend that researchers consult informants who are knowledgeable about their chosen topics.[24] Accordingly, we employed purposive and snowball sampling techniques to select both the research area and the informants to collect relevant data from the community. We started the data collection process from the culture and tourism offices of Kaffa Zone, whose staff members helped us identify knowledgeable Na'o informants and their addresses. Our key consultants, Takele Beyene and Banderasha Demisie Bongo, then helped us locate relevant individuals in Decha district, and we asked them to name other consultants who knew about folk songs and who were known as good performers.[25] We mainly conducted interviews, and combined them with observation. After collecting the folk songs, we transcribed them with the help of our informants; we then translated them, first into Amharic and later into English, and analysed them thematically. The following section presents the functions of Na'o folk songs according to their performance contexts.

---

21   Martha C. Sims and Martine Stephens, *Living Folklore: An Introduction to the Study of People and their Traditions* (Utah: Utah State University Press, 2005).

22   Dorson, *Folklore and Folklife*; see also W. Bascom, 'Four Functions of Folklore', *The Journal of American Folklore*, 67.266 (1954), 333–349; and Desta Desalegn, *A Functional Study of Tulama Oromo Oral Prose Narratives* (unpublished PhD thesis, Addis Ababa University, 2015).

23   See C. Marshal, and G. Rossman, *Designing Qualitative Research* (PLACE: Saga Publications Inc., 2006); J. W. Creswell, *Qualitative Inquiry Research Design: Choosing Among Five Approaches* (Thosand Oaks: Sage Publications, 2007).

24   D. Ben-Amos, 'Toward Definition of Folklore in Context', *The Journal of American Folklore*, 84.331 (1971), 3–15; K. O'Reilly, *Ethnographic Methods* (London: Routledge, 2005); Alan Dundes, *Interpreting Folklore* (Bloomington: Indiana University Press, 1980).

25   'Banderasha' is an honourable name.

Na'o Folk Songs: Texts and Contexts

The Na'o people employ folk songs to express their emotions, hopes, attitudes and worldviews. Folk songs help them express a sense of togetherness, personal qualities and desires, and love for their land or country. Love songs or *wokise wokaasa*, songs of sorrow or *haalaassee*, marriage songs or *iwassee*, harvesting songs or *kookee* each have their literary features, functions, and contexts of performance. Our collection showed that Na'o folk songs can generally be categorized into three major sub genres: work songs, songs of entertainment, and songs of sorrow.

This classification is not unique to the Na'o. In Chapter 7 of this volume, Tadesse Jaleta Jirata analyses Gujji Oromo's *gelelle* or work songs, whose function and performance style are similar to Na'o *kookee*. The themes of the ceremonial song or *qexala* that Tadesse analyses also have several parallels with the *iwassee* we discuss below. Both poems celebrate the local culture, listing important cultural attributes as a way to instil pride and forge a sense of unity and collective identity. Megersa has studied the folk songs performed by women in one district of Wellega, who create and perform oral poetry—such as the *tutu* songs presented below—when grinding maize with a mortar and pestle, churning milk or grinding *teff* on a stone mill.[26] The Amharic *Jiggiea* songs studied by Daniel Mengistie Yimer are performed during agricultural activities and have a similar function to Na'o *kookee*.[27] Therefore, although the Na'o oral repertoire is distinctive, their oral genres share themes, functions, and performance modes with many of their neighbours, offering productive possibilities for future comparative analysis.

Work Songs

Agriculture is central to the Na'o economy, and is the main source of sustenance. Na'o people carry out agricultural activities together, and

---

26   Megersa Regassa, 'Females' Voice through Oral Poetry Among Limmuu Oromo, Ethiopia', *Journal of Ethnic and Cultural Studies*, 4.2 (2017), 28–40. *Teff* is the annual grass species of crop that is native to Ethiopia and Eritrea.

27   D. M. Yimer, 'Jiggiea Amharic Oral Poetry in North Wollo: Social Functions and a Sample Analysis', *International Journal for Research In Social Science And Humanities*, 5.6 (2019), 1–21.

the work songs performed in these contexts aim to strengthen the workers' morale and boost their physical endurance. Folk songs are associated with specific agricultural tasks, such as ploughing, planting, harvesting, and so on. For instance, *kookee* is one of the songs farmers perform during harvest to encourage one another, and it is believed that they even forget hard work because their attention is fully on the performance. The following harvesting song or *kookee* is sung together by men and women, with some leading and others following.

[Kookee woo kookee]	[simply a starting melody]
Kooshumenie woo kookee	Plough plough,
Asheni neye woo kookee	Grow [crop],
Butis neye woo kookee	Clear it [i.e. prepare the land],
Wete neye woo kookee	Collect it,
Keti tsinye woo kookee	Weed it,
Ginine woo kookee	Plant it

For the sake of melody, the farming activities are not recounted in their correct order, though farmers obviously know which activities precede or follow which. First farmers prepare the land, starting by removing unwanted wild weeds [*butis neye*, clear it]; then they plough the soil [*kooshumenie*]; plant the seeds; grow the crops; remove unwanted weeds again [*keti tsinye*, weed it]; and finally harvest.

The next step is grinding the cereals using a mortar and pestle. This process, called *tutu*, is generally carried out by women in a group, as grinding is considered a female duty. Therefore, the following folk song is performed by Na'o women.

Ingiybezu sheshkis aa sheshkis	May my beer be good, be
Ingiyatene abtusis aa abtusis	good,
Itieshenta qanambie naa sheshtaa qakayie	may my beer make you
Itie tirqam baabie natie irqa kayo	drunk, you drunk.
	Who will be successful?
	No one will be beaten.

We can understand from the song that the women are grinding cereals to make traditional beer [*ingiya*], boasting that the beer will taste good and will make the men drunk [*abtusis*].[28] Brewing a good beer is considered a prized skill in a woman, and through the activity and the song the women are reinforcing this social norm, working hard to be accepted and valued. Women sing this song in their compound around home while grinding *teff*. While the first group says '*ingiybezu sheshkis*' [may my traditional beer be good], the rest reply by reaffirming the point, '*aa sheshkis*' [yes let it be good]. Singing helps women concentrate on the activity and forget the toughness of the task.

Songs of Entertainment

Songs of entertainment are popular among the Na'o. They are used to pay homage to their families, their household materials, their cattle, and their king.[29] The most common folk song for entertainment is *wookisee wookasaa* ['we sing this song during...']. *Wookisee wookasaa* are sung at weddings and in times of leisure. In this case the phrase '*wookise wookasaa*' helps as a melody, because it is repeatedly recited during the performance. In addition, folk songs of pleasure or happiness such as *iyyoo iwassee, baraa bakuwee* [the girl is ready for marriage] are also common. Here is an example of *wookisee wookasaa*:

Wookisee wookasaa—wookisee wookasaa	[opening refrain] We sing/sang this song when...
Eremashiteina naayimba—wookisee wookasaa	we sang when we became happy
Nungus Shaagin hinaayimbaa— wookisee wookasaa	we sang when she/he got married
Baaraagn keiysen hinaayimbaa— wookisee wookasaa	we sang when she left home
Eremashiteina naayimba—wookisee wookasaa	we sang when we became happy

---

28   Traditional beer [*ingiya*] is known as *tella* in other parts of Ethiopia. It is a popular Ethiopian traditional drink. The raw material varies from place to place due to availability, cost, the challenges of final production, and other criteria. Some of the most common raw materials for most *tella* production in Ethiopia are barley, dagussa, sorghum, *teff*, and maize in a different region. The Na'o community typically use *teff*.

29   Informants told us that in earlier times Na'o people were governed by their own king [*kiyas*].

This folk song has an element of self-referentiality, as it mentions past occasions in which the performers decided to sing. This song can be performed at weddings, for example when the bride leaves her family home (*baaraagn keiysen hinaayimbaa*, we sung when she leaves home). Another example of *wookisee wookasaa* has an even longer list of occasions that make the performers and the community happy:

Wookisee wookasaa—wookisee wookasaa	We sang this song when...
Baaraa keiysin hinaayimbaa— wookisee wookasaa	We sang when the 'tabot' came out,
Bergi paadin hinaayimbaa— wookisee wookasaa	we sang for the special day, we sang when we became happy,
Eremashiteina naayimbaa—wookisee wookasaa	we sang when the king celebrates, we sang for peace of our country,
Kiyas kiyaabxin hinaayimbaa— wookisee wookasaa	we sang during harvesting, we sang when we became free from poverty,
Tur shishkin hinaayimbaa—wookisee wookasaa	we sang when we became happy
Um potin hinaayimbaa—wookisee wookasaa	
Gayidu kaayin hinaayimbaa—wookisee wookasaaEremashiteina hinaayimba—wookisee wookasaa	

When Ethiopia was ruled by a king, the Na'o people were also ruled by a king, and this song was performed when he celebrated festive occasions with his people. It is now performed during local holidays or in moments of relative wealth for the community. This genre is among the most widely performed, since remembering joyful occasions lifts people's spirits. Singing the *wookisee wookasaa*, people reflect on how to keep their unity, solve their problems, respect each other, share what they have, obey social norms, teach their children, and so on. The song follows a call and response structure, and repeating '*wookisee wookasaa*', 'we sang this song when...' after every line confirms what was said before.

There are also love songs, performed as a dialogue between two individuals. In the following song, a man woos a woman he loves and

wants to marry by telling her he is rich enough to provide for her and
for their future family:

Yee woyee	O my dear,
Iiyo qone	please do not leave me alone,
Yee otnatise	I will give you cattle,
Gantis natese	I will give you an ox

If she stays with him, he will give her cattle and they will share what
he has and live happily. He sings the song as if she is listening. Indeed,
she may listen if she is around, and sing her own song as a response to
his request by refusing or accepting. A possible poetic response is the
following song:

Woyee woyee–woyee	As if you gave livestock to my dad
Maab ishootyaastima	As if you gave a bull/ox to my dad
Maab ishgaansyaatsima	My dad has a cow.
Maab otinbab	He has an ox,
Maab gaansus baab	he has cereals,
Maab gaawon baab	he has an ox whose name is 'gaawon'

The girl who sings this song is rejecting the man's advances, saying her
father is rich enough to maintain her, and she does not need anything
else. She is not interested in the man, does not want any of his cattle, and
might even have another person in mind to marry in the future.

Among the songs of entertainment are songs performed at weddings,
called *iiyoosee* or *iyyoo iwassee*. These songs start with the phrase *iyyoo
iwassee*, and the word *iwassee* is repeated after every line. This song is
mostly performed by those taking part in the wedding when a groom
and his party arrive at the bride's family home. The song reinforces the
community's sense of identity by listing all the things for which the Na'o
are famous.

Iiyyoo iwassee iyyoo iwassee	[the opening refrain]
Hinyaabe iwassee	Our people,
Otkiyaases iwassee	owners of cattle.
Onyaabe iwassee	Our society,
Ondoode iwassee	our youth,
Gantisabziene iwassee	breed oxen,
Otabzine iwassee	breed cattle.
Oohunqutsas iwassee	Our culture
Shuratin iwassee	now outshines
Garinayaas iwassee	members of 'kalicha' deity,
Goobinayaas iwassee	those living around Goba area,
Bara degnye iwassee	those girls
Kaasambaaye iwassee	who are playing,
Nyaakudodee iwassee	those boys
Ayaambose iwassee	who are singing.

The purpose of the song is to instil cultural awareness and cultural pride in the bride and the groom, as they will have the social responsibility of handing down the culture to the next generation. Those singing wish the bride and the groom a good life and at the same time remind the married couple of their duty to protect and preserve the culture.

Some Na'o folk songs, for instance those in which Na'o youth express their readiness for marriage, are accompanied by traditional musical instruments, like the *kamba* [drum], *kirar, imbilta,* and *golfa.* The *golfa,* made of twelve horizontal pieces of bamboo cut to the same size and stitched together horizontally, and played by twelve individuals at a time, is the most popular. One can hear different sounds from each individual player. While skilled individuals play the instrument, others sing along.

Funeral Dirges

The Na'o community are known for their *wookisee waakasaa,* the songs of entertainment, but they also have songs of sorrow for funerals and for grieving a beloved or respected person's death. These songs are commonly called *hallaassee,* and sorrow is known as *yefay.* Relatives and neighbours of the dead person, both men and women, show their sorrow by performing *hallaassee.* The *hallaassee* can be performed on the occasion of funeral rituals, and is accompanied by a musical instrument called *tuli*, made of bamboo like the *golfa* but with animal skin covering the outer part. Once a person has passed away, it is believed that it is important to pray for those who are still alive. In the beginning, a relative or intimate of the dead says *hallaassee* while others reply *iwooyee*. Then, some of the mourners say *hallaassee* while others say *shubush gube* [death], *mooyee kolee* [dear, in the feminine]. The song begins by blaming death for snatching away a community member.

Hallaassee iwooyee haalaassee	[the opening refrain]
Shibusgube hallaassee	Oh death,
Gayidushgube hallaassee	oh poverty,
Eshenteno hallaassee	it's not the right time.
Shibusgube hallaassee	Oh death,
Shubamboto hallaassee	no he/she should not die.
Shubush gube hallaassee	Oh death,
Mooyee kolee hallaassee	oh dear [feminine form],
Bushenteno hallaassee	you shouldn't have died,
Yerkotnisei hallaassee	God bless the remaining family.
Biyabusyab hallaassee	Oh aged woman,
Biyabusgube hallaasse	oh aged man,
Bara degigne hallaasse	oh young woman,
Gnaku dode'i hallaassee	oh young man

During a *hallaassee* song, people do not call the name of the dead person but instead refer to the dead as 'the old man', 'the old woman', 'the woman', 'the man', 'the gentle man' or with other epithets. A *hallaassee* is closed by the exclamation *'wulee wulee wulee wulee'*, an expression of sorrow meaning 'alas!' *Hallaassee* songs are performed by men and women together, but this closing line is performed by the men alone.

Conclusions

The Na'o community has a rich repertoire of folk songs which punctuate everyday activities as well as more special occasions. Common contexts include marriage, agriculture and related activities, and funeral rituals. The present study offers an introduction to Na'o oral culture in general and one of the endangered domains of their culture—folk songs—in particular. Naayi is an exclusively oral language, without a writing system and without a standardised grammar. The community pass down their culture and history from generation to generation verbally through oral genres such as folk songs, proverbs, riddles, and so on. The community use folk songs to express feelings, hopes, attitudes, and a cultural worldview. The folk songs therefore help them to express a sense of togetherness, valued personal qualities, wishes, and the love of their land. However, such cultural wealth is limited to the areas where Na'o elders are living, specifically in rural areas. More studies are needed to fully understand the complexity of this endangered heritage.

The linguistic context in which Na'o live is profoundly asymmetrical, mirroring asymmetrical demographic and economic relations between the Na'o and their Kaffa neighbours. Very few, if any, of the neighbouring Kaffa people have learnt Naayi and its oral traditions, while the vast majority of Na'o have had to acquire, willingly or by necessity, Kafinoono and its oral traditions.

In local schools, Naayi does not appear anywhere, and teachers are almost all native speakers of Kafinoono. Naayi played a role for a while in local Na'o customary courts and community meetings, but the increased penetration of state institutions has made these customary institutions redundant. The songs cited in this chapter are among the favourite cultural domains in which Naayi still survives, although the younger generations know songs in Kafinoono and other languages too. Even though the elders still sing folk songs for various purposes and on various occasions, today the younger generations have largely abandoned Naayi and only retain a passive understanding of the language and their oral traditions. If the current trends continue, the death of Naayi-speaking elders may mean that the next generation of Na'o will not have incentives to learn Naayi and its cultural practices, specifically their oral traditions. The lack of a written historical record makes it easier for Na'o people to assimilate to Kaffa culture and language and lose the record of their identity. This makes the work of documenting the Naayi language and Na'o oral heritage all the more urgent and important.

Bibliography

Aklilu Yilma, 'Some Notes on the Nayi grammar' in *Ethiopia in Broader Perspective: Papers of the XIIIth International Conference of Ethiopian Studies* (Kyoto 12–17 December 1997), ed. by Katsuyoshi Fukui, Eisei Kurimoto, and Masayoshi Shigeta (Kyoto: Shokado Book Sellers, 1997), pp. 601–618.

——, 'A Phonological Comparison of Bench and Two Majoid Languages' in *New Trends in Ethiopian Studies: Papers of the 12th International Conference of Ethiopian Studies*, ed. by Harold M. Marcus (Lawrenceville: Red Sea. 1994) vol. 1, pp. 1053–1063.

——, 'Two Phonological Processes in Nayi: Palatalization and Labialization'. *Proceedings of the First National Conference of Ethiopian Studies*, ed. by N.J. Pankhurst et al. (Addis Ababa: Institute of Ethiopian Studies, 1990), pp. 433–448.

Aklilu Yilma and Ralph Siebert, 'Sociolinguistic Survey Report of the Chara, Dime, Melo and Nayi Languages of Ethiopia: Part 1', *Journal of Language Survey Reports* (2002), https://www.sil.org/resources/archives/9049

Amha, Azeb, 'The Omotic Language Family' in *The Cambridge Handbook of Linguistic Typology*, ed. by Alexandra Y. Aikhenvald and R. M. W. Dixon (Cambridge: Cambridge University Press, 2017), https://doi.org/10.1017/9781316135716.026

Bascom, William R., 'Four Functions of Folklore', *The Journal of American Folklore*, 67.266 (1954), https://doi.org/10.2307/536411

Ben-Amos, Dan, 'Toward Definition of Folklore in Context', *The Journal of American Folklore*, 84.331 (1971), https://doi.org/10.2307/539729

Bender, Lionel M., *Comparative Morphology of the Omotic* (Munich; Newcastle: LINCOM Europa, 2000).

Creswell, J. W., *Qualitative Inquiry Research Design: Choosing Among Five Approaches* (Thousand Oaks: Sage Publications, 2007).

Dessalegn Gebeyehu, 'On the Verge of Dying: Languages in Ethiopia', *OGMIOS Newsletter, Foundation for Endangered Languages*, 52 (2013), ed. by Christopher Moseley, pp. 3–13.

Desta Desalegn, 'A Functional Study of Tulama Oromo Oral Prose Narratives' (unpublished PhD thesis, Addis Ababa University, 2015).

Dorson, Richard M., *Folklore and Folk Life: An Introduction* (Chicago: University of Chicago Press, 1972).

Dundes, Alan, *Interpreting Folklore* (Bloomington: Indiana University Press, 1980).

Ephrem Dejene, 'Verb Inflections in Nayi' (MA thesis, Addis Ababa University School of Graduate Studies, 2007).

Federal Democratic Republic of Ethiopia Population Census Commission, 'Summary and Statistical Report of the 2007 Population and Housing Census: Population Size by Age and Sex', Addis Ababa: 2008, United Nations Population Fund (UNFPA), https://www.ethiopianreview.com

Finnegan, Ruth, *Oral Poetry: Its Nature, Significance and Social Context* (Cambridge: Cambridge University Press, 1977).

——, *Oral Traditions and the Verbal Arts: A Guide to Research Practices* (London and New York: Routledge, 1992).

Kranenburg, Peter van, Anja Volk Jörg Garbers, Louis P. Grijp Frans Wiering and Remco C. Veltkamp, 'Collaboration Perspectives for Folk Song Research and Music Information Retrieval: The Indispensable Role of Computational Musicology', *Journal of Interdisciplinary Music Studies*, 4.1 (2010), https://pure.knaw.nl/ws/portalfiles/portal/473290/Kranenburg_JIMS_10040102.pdf

Marshal, Catherine, and Gretchen D. Rossman, *Designing Qualitative Research* (Thousand Oaks: Sage Publications, 2006).

Megersa Regassa, 'Females' Voice through Oral Poetry Among Limmuu Oromo, Ethiopia', *Journal of Ethnic and Cultural Studies*, 4.2 (2017), https://doi.org/10.29333/ejecs/72

O'Reilly, K., *Ethnographic Methods* (London: Routledge, 2005).

Okpewho, Isidore, *African Oral Literature: Backgrounds, Character and Continuity* (Bloomington; Indianapolis: Indiana University Press, 1992).

Samson Seid, 'Ethnic Language Shift of Nao', Endangered Languages Project (2012), https://www.endangeredlanguages.com/lang/2680/samples/7353

Sims, Martha C. and Martine Stephens, *Living Folklore: An Introduction to the Study of People and their Traditions* (Utah: Utah State University Press, 2005).

UNESCO, 'Language Vitality and Endangerment', Presented at the International Expert Meeting on UNESCO Programme Safeguarding of Endangered Languages, Paris: UNESCO Ad Hoc Expert Group on Endangered Languages (2003), https://unesdoc.unesco.org/ark:/48223/pf0000183699

Takele Firehiwat, 'The Noun Phrase in Nayi' (MA thesis, Addis Ababa University, 2001).

Tessema, Andualem Adal, 'A Descriptive Syntax of Naayi' (unpublished PhD thesis, Addis Ababa University College of Humanities, 2020).

Wamalwa, Eric W. and Stephen B. J. Oluoch, 'Language Endangerment and Language Maintenance: Can Endangered Indigenous Languages of Kenya Be Electronically Preserved?', *International Journal of Humanities and Social Science*, 3.7 (2013), https://www.ijhssnet.com/journals/Vol_3_No_7_April_2013/28.pdf

Yimer, D. M., 'Jiggiea Amharic Oral Poetry in North Wollo: Social Functions and a Sample Analysis', *International Journal for Research in Social Science and Humanities*, 5.6 (2019), https://www.gnpublication.org/index.php/ssh/article/view/974/762

7. Orature Across Generations Among the Guji-Oromo of Ethiopia

Tadesse Jaleta Jirata

Introduction

> We teach our children through storytelling. Our children play with each other through riddling and singing. That is our culture and way of life; our knowledge and values transmitting from generation to generation.

With these words, fifty-two-year-old Areri Roba reflected on the role of oral literature in connecting generations among the Guji-Oromo society.[1] As is clear from the statement, oral literature, understood as a culturally embedded and orally performed form of art that a society owns, is an integral part of social relationships across generations as well as within the same generation.[2] In broader terms, oral literature has been a central component of cultures across the whole African continent. Within Ethiopia, it embodies a relatively intact oral flow of information and everyday life experiences.[3] The Somali, Sidama, Hadiyya, and Borana peoples use oral literary forms to express their ideas, beliefs, and values,

---

1   Areri Roba, personal communication.

2   Tadesse J. Jirata, and Jan Ketil Simonsen, 'The Roles of Oromo-Speaking Children in Storytelling Tradition in Ethiopia', *Research in African Literatures*, 45.2 (2014), 135–149.

3   See Abreham Alemu, 'Oral Narratives as Ideological Weapon for Subordinating Women: The Case of Jimma Oromo', *Journal of African Cultural Studies*, 19.1 (2007), 55–80; Nicolas Argenti, 'Things that Don't Come by the Road: Folktales, Fosterage, and Memories of Slavery in the Cameroon Grassfields', *Comparative Studies in*

   https://doi.org/10.11647/OBP.0405.07

and communicate through their network of social relationships (see also Yenaleam and Desta in Chapter 6 of this volume).[4] A study of oral literature among the Nuer and Anuak peoples in the Gambela region of western Ethiopia helps us to understand their cultural practices and social organisation across generations.[5] Such wealth of oral traditions within Ethiopia is comparable with how Ruth Finnegan conceptualised oral literature as the heart of cultures and memories, in which local languages are used as vehicles for the transmission of knowledge and values.[6] Therefore, oral literature characterises the grand artistic lives of the African peoples and has a significant place in their social and cultural lives.

In all African cultures, the central feature that distinguishes oral literature from its written counterpart, and gives life to its artistic realisation, is performance.[7] According to Finnegan, oral literature is reliant on a person who performs it in a specific context.[8] Oral literature can only be realised as a literary product through performance. Without its oral realisation by a performer (singer or speaker), an oral literary form does not have a defined existence.[9] Performance gives life to different oral literary genres and allows them to be identified as myths, folk tales, folk songs, riddles, or proverbs.[10] This idea holds two meanings. Firstly,

---

Society and History, 55.2 (2010), 224–254; Isidore Okpewho, *African Oral Literature: Backgrounds, Character, and Continuity* (Bloomington: Indiana University Press, 1992).

4   Ulrich Braukämper, 'The Correlation of Oral Traditions and Historical Records in Southern Ethiopia: A Case Study of the Hadiya/ Sidamo Past', *Journal of Ethiopian Studies*, 11.2 (1973), 29–50; John W. Johnson, 'Orality, Literacy, and Somali Oral Poetry', *Journal of African Cultural Studies'*, 18.1 (2006), 119–136; and Sahlu Kidane, *Borana Folktales: A Contextual Study* (Indiana: Indiana University Press, 2002).

5   See Bayleyegn Tasew, 'Metaphors of Peace and Violence in the Folklore: Discourses of South-Western Ethiopia: A Comparative Study' (unpublished PhD thesis, Vriji University Amsterdam, 2009).

6   Ruth Finnegan, *The Oral and Beyond: Doing Things with Words in Africa* (Oxford: James Curry, 2007).

7   Eshete Gemeda, 'African Egalitarian Values and Indigenous Genres: The Functional and Contextual Studies of Oromo Oral Literature in a Contemporary Perspective' (unpublished PhD thesis, University of Southern Denmark, 2008); Wilfried van Damme, 'African Verbal Arts and the Study of African Visual Aesthetics', *Research in African Literature*, 31.4 (2000), 8–20.

8   Ruth Finnegan, *Oral Tradition and Verbal Arts* (London: Routledge, 1992).

9   Tadesse J. Jirata, 'Oral Poetry as Herding Tool: A Study of Cattle Songs as Children's Art and Cultural Exercise among the Guji-Oromo in Ethiopia', *Journal of African Cultural Studies*, 29.3 (2017), 292–310.

10 Clarunji Chesaina, *Oral Literature of the Embu and Mbeere* (Nairobi: East African Educational Publishers, 1997); Okpewho, *African Oral Literature*; Edward Sackey,

these literary forms are realised through the oral medium, for they are performed through a spoken language. Secondly, these oral literary forms are distinguished by textual form and performance style. The modality of performance also distinguishes oral literary genres across generations. As Jirata and Simonsen state, what we call children's oral literature and adults' oral literature derive their identity from different performance styles and contexts.[11]

These rich and profound oral literary forms have been constantly overlooked in world literary studies. Although oral literature has been an integral and popular repertoire of literary forms in Africa, it has not received global attention as a literary product and has rarely been considered as "literature proper" in global literary scholarships. It has seldom been taken as a sophisticated artistic product. It has been rather studied as a reflection of "authentic" culture or part of the "traditional" way of life, and on these grounds oral literature has been perceived to be less relevant in the context of modern literary production.[12] Oral literature has long been associated with illiterate societies, and is therefore considered a residual leftover of a pre-modern past that lacked literary quality. It has also been understood as a preserve of the elders and is perceived as opposed to the social and cultural dynamism of the contemporary world. As a result, oral literature has been pushed to the margin of world literary scholarship.

In this chapter, I argue against this supposition by showing that oral literature is a dynamic artistic phenomenon adaptable to changing social contexts and circulating not only between different generations but also within the same generation. Oral literature, this chapter shows, passes not only from adults to children but also from children to adults, as well as from children to children. From this perspective, I argue that oral literature has continued to be an integral part of both adults' and children's cultures. My argument addresses the following questions: 1) What genres does Guji-Oromo oral literature encompass? 2) How do the different forms of the Guji-Oromo oral literature circulate? 3) Which generational groups are more active in the performance and

---

'Oral Tradition and the African Novel', *Modern African Studies*, 37.3 (1991), 389–407.

11   Jirata and Simonsen, 'Oromo-Speaking Children'.

12   Okpewho, *African Oral Literature*; Sackey 'Oral Tradition'.

circulation of oral literature? By answering these questions, I will show that oral literature is a dynamic cultural phenomenon, in which intra-generational and intergenerational artistic performances adapt to changing social and cultural contexts.

Socio-Cultural Background of the Guji-Oromo

The Guji-Oromo are one of the Oromo ethnic groups living over a large territory in the southern part of Ethiopia. They speak the Oromo language and are known as the cultural cradle of Oromo society because indigenous Oromo institutions such as the Gada system (see below) are still intact among them.[13]

The Guji predominantly inhabit rural areas, and their population is estimated to be 2 million.[14] Guji land is bordered by the Borana-Oromo in the south; Burji, Koyra, and Gamo in the southwest; Arsi-Oromo in the east; and the Gedeo, Sidama, and Wolaita ethnic groups in the north.

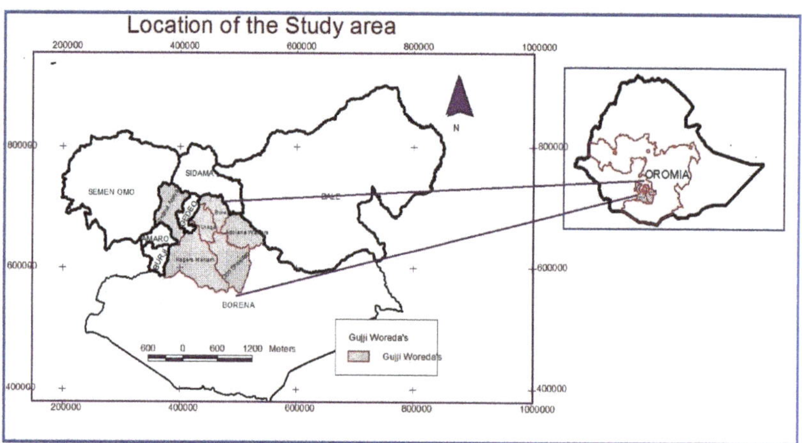

Fig. 7.1 Study area. Author's map.

13   Dejen N. Debsu, 'Gender and Culture in Southern Ethiopia: An Ethnographic Analysis of Guji-Oromo Women's Customary Rights', *African Study Monographs*, 30.1 (2009), 15–36; Tadesse J. Jirata, 'Folktales, Reality, and Childhood in Ethiopia: How Children Construct Social Values through Performance of Folktales', *Folklore*, 129.3 (2018), 237–253.

14   Federal Democratic Republic of Ethiopia Population Census Commission, 'Summary and Statistical Report of the 2007 Population and Housing Census: Population Size by Age and Sex' (Addis Ababa: UNFPA 2008), pp.1–113.

The Guji land consists of semi-highland and lowland areas with an altitude of 1500–2000 meters above sea level and less than 1500 meters above sea level respectively. The people who live in both areas subsist on mixed farming. They herd cattle and cultivate food crops such as *teff*, maize, and beans. Besides, they follow traditional methods of bee farming, through which they make money for their home expenditures.[15] The Guji-Oromo predominantly lead traditional ways of life in which oral communication plays a central role. Unlike neighbouring ethnic groups that are more internally uniform, the Guji contain three culturally similar clans: the Huraga, Mati, and Hokku. According to my informants, Huraga is the largest and most senior clan; Mati is the second largest and more junior; whereas Hokku is the smallest and most junior clan.[16]

The Oromo Gadaa system is the social structure that regulates and administers Guji society. It divides society into thirteen age groups or generational grades that succeed each other every eight years, prescribing progressive roles and social responsibilities.[17] These grades are known as Daballe (0–8 years), Qarree Xixiqa (9–12 years), Qarree Gurgudda (13–16 years), Kuusa (17–24 years), Raaba (25–32 years), Doorii (33–40 years), Gadaa (41–48 years), Batu (49–56 years), Yuba (57–64 years), Yuba Gudda (65–72 years), Jaarsaa (73–80 years), and Jarsa Qulullu (above 80 years). The Gadaa system organizes the social roles of the Guji-Oromo around these generational grades and assigns specific obligations as well as rights to members of each group.[18] The clans are mutually independent and have delegates in the Gadaa Council. However, the leader of the Gadaa grade (Abba Gadaa) is always from the Huraga clan.

---

15   Tadesse Beriso, 'The Pride of the Guji-Oromo: An Essay on Cultural Contact Self-Esteem', *Journal of Oromo Studies*, 11.1–2 (2004), 13–27.

16   Joseph Van de Loo, *Guji-Oromo Culture in Southern Ethiopia* (Berlin: Dietrich Reimer Verlag, 1991).

17   One Gadaa Council administers for eight years and hands over the baallii (authority) to the next Gadaa Council every eight years. See Abiyot Legesse, *Gadaa: Three Approaches to the Study of African Society* (New York: Free Press,1973); Van de Loo, Guji-Oromo Culture; Tadesse J. Jirata, 'Children and Oral Tradition among the Guji-Oromo in Southern Ethiopia' (unpublished PhD thesis, Norwegian University of Science and Technology, 2013); Beriso, 'The Pride of the Guji-Oromo'.

18   Van de Loo, *Guji-Oromo Culture*; Beriso, 'The Pride of the Guji-Oromo'.

The Gadaa system governs and shapes everyday life, cultural practices, and the value system of individuals, families, and clans. It regulates relationships between individuals, including prescribing the norms of parent-child relationships, adult-child relationships, and wife-husband relationships. It codifies the place of an individual in society and regulates the systems of political decision-making, power relations and power transfer, as well as the relations of the Guji with their neighbouring ethnic groups, with nature, and with supernatural powers.[19]

The Gadaa system structures beliefs, value systems, individual behaviours, responsibilities, social places, and cultural roles across every stage of a person's life. Accordingly, parents have the obligation to socialise their children, raise them in line with Guji norms and values, and teach them what is expected from them as children. Oral advice and reprimands are the major means of socialisation. Children are expected to be obedient, hardworking, and loyal. Children have a rich culture of play in which parents also participate.[20] Such participation on the part of the parents has two purposes. The first is providing evening entertainment in one's home before bedtime. The second is the socialisation of children. Not only members of a family, but also neighbouring (*olla*) families come together at someone's home or in a village compound to entertain each other. Oral literature plays a central role in these intra-generational and intergenerational relationships and social interactions.

Methodology

I carried out fieldwork among the Guji-Oromo in two phases, from July to December 2016 and from May to August 2017. To select appropriate locations for my fieldwork I made preliminary visits to rural districts where the Guji-Oromo reside in big villages. I then identified four rural villages where I would focus my fieldwork, namely Sorroo, Dhokcha, Bunata, and Samaro. These villages are far from each other, and were

---

19   Asebe R. Debelo and Tadesse J. Jirata, '"Peace Is Not a Free Gift": Indigenous Conceptualisations of Peace among the Guji-Oromo in Southern Ethiopia', *Northeast African Studies*, 18.1–2 (2018), 201–230.

20   Jirata 'Children and Oral Tradition'; Jirata, 'Oral Poetry as Herding Tool'.

chosen as representatives of the Guji-Oromo rural ways of life. The fieldwork involved ethnographic methods of data collection, including participant observation, ethnographic interviews (an informal interview that takes place in a natural setting as a part of participant observation), and in-depth interviews. I observed and recorded activities in the villages and homes of the Guji-Oromo, and oral performances in the collective customary practices known in Oromo as *jilaa*. Of these customary practices, the most relevant for this research were the *Balli Kenna*, a ritual through which power is transferred from the outgoing Gadaa generation to the incoming one at a sacred place called *Me'ee Bokko*; and the *Lagubasa*, an initiation ritual marking the younger generation's transition from childhood to adulthood at another sacred place called *Gadab Dibbedhogo*. Both are big traditional ceremonies involving three generational grades, the Raaba, Dori, and Gadaa. The *Lagubaasaa* is a rite of passage in which people in the Kuusa generational grade pass to the Raaba generational grade and gain the right to join the Dori and the Gadaa generations during ceremonial practices. These cultural events were marked and embellished by a vigorous and overwhelming performance of oral literary forms.

I also carried out participant observations among teams of people while they performed agricultural work and during social and cultural events in the neighbourhood, such as marriage ceremonies, extended family parties, and parties after cooperative work. I conducted unstructured interviews with adults at their homes and workplaces and children (in the age range between seven and fourteen) in the cattle-herding fields and in their school compounds.

My methods of data collection involved close interaction with Guji-Oromo adults and children in the places they normally frequent—their homes and neighbourhood, schools, workplaces, and cattle herding fields. I collected different oral literary texts, paying attention to the interplay between text, performers, and the social and cultural context of the performance. I later translated the oral texts from the Oromo language into English through a contextual translation method, and will present them in English throughout this chapter.

Oral Literary Traditions of the Guji-Oromo

The rich oral traditions of the Guji-Oromo convey and shape their ways of life and their knowledge system. Their individual and collective wisdom and verbal creativity are manifested through oral performances. Therefore, oral literature is an integral part of adults' and children's culture. The several cultural and social events that bring the Guji-Oromo together are always embellished by the performance of oral literary forms.[21] Based on the performance style, Guji-Oromo literary forms are often categorized as: *oduuduri* (myths and legends), *duriduri* (folk tales), *weedduu* (folk songs), *hibboo* (riddles), *mammaaksa* (proverbs) and *jechama* (sayings). Similarly, based on the contexts and purposes of performance, these forms are categorized as adults' oral literature, oral literature shared by both adults and children, or children's oral literature. In this sense, oral genres are already classified based on the different configurations of performer and audience. Defining these genres also includes the modality of transmission and circulation: who performs the oral text to whom and in which context. A genre is not only defined by its textual characteristics, such as meter or rhyme, but also by the social status of the performer and by the social context of the performance. For example, performances of oral songs by adults are characterized by audacity, vividness, tonality, the symbolic presentation of messages, conventionality, and a focus on artistic quality. Those by children involve creativity, captivating actions, playfulness, and interpersonal competitions. In both cases, literariness is created through a performance that encompasses verbal and non-verbal styles, including mimicry, artistic gestures, voices, and tones. The literariness of oral literature, then, lies in the text and performance which shows that it is both orature and literature. This rich oral literary tradition has contributed to the development of Oromo written literatures (see Ayele K. Roba in Chapter 3 of this volume). It is also a dominant literary form through which Oromo literary traditions can be represented in world literature. This implies that Africa can be part of world literature through its oral literary traditions.

---

21   Jirata, 'Oral Poetry as Herding Tool'.

Adults' Oral Literary Forms

This category includes the oral literary forms that are produced and performed by adults (a person becomes an adult at twenty-five years of age among the Guji people) for other adults. Its major literary forms are known in Oromo as *gerarsa, qexala, gelelle,* and *faaruu loonii.* Adults perform these oral literary forms either individually or addressing an audience, in different social and cultural contexts such as *Middaa* (social events to celebrate patriotism), *Jila* (ceremonial events), *Agooda* (cooperative work), and *Eebbisa Loonii* (rituals for honouring cattle). Only adults, both men are women, are legitimate participants in these events.

Events of this kind are not only common among Oromo-speaking people, but also among other Ethiopian groups such as the Amhara, Sidama, Gedeo, and Walayita peoples in different languages forms and under different names. For example, social events to celebrate patriotism are called *Middaa* among the Guji people, *qondala* among the other Oromo groups, and *Anbessa Geday* among Amharic speaking groups. Among the Guji and other ethnic groups, bravery is celebrated through the performance of these songs, and such cultural practices are perceived as honouring the heroism of an adult who managed to kill an elephant, a lion, or a buffalo. A person who killed one of these wild animals is considered a hero, acquires a high reputation in the eyes of all other men and women and is called *Abba Middaa* (meaning "a patriot"). Celebrations of such cultural practice are embellished through the performance of oral genres among all these different Ethiopian groups. Now, let us see these literary forms one by one.

The Gerarsa or Patriotic Song

The Guji-Oromo attach a deep value to bravery and reinforce it through singing the *gerarsa,* which is a popular praise genre. The genre is also to be found among the Amhara, Sidama, and Gedeo peoples in Ethiopia, albeit under different names. Among Amharic speakers, for example, the genre is called *qarerto,* though it shares many characteristics with the Oromo *gerarsa,* from performance context to style of delivery. Adult men sing the song in different social and cultural contexts, generally related to the accomplishment of an extraordinary achievement, such as killing a dangerous wild animal in a hunting expedition, killing an enemy during a war, producing large hectares of crops with a large herd of cattle, or enduring and surviving a difficult situation. Such accomplishments are seen as the outcome of bravery in Ethiopia, and the *geerarsa* promotes precisely the values of bravery, heroism, and physical prowess.

Men who accomplish such extraordinary achievements sing the song in the first person to tell the stories of their achievements and proclaim their heroism, generally as self-praise in front of others during social and cultural events. A *geerarsa* can also be sung about someone else, and in this case the performer honours a man in the audience. The *gerarsa* reflects the different level of honour attributed to individuals who accomplished heroic deeds. The level of honour varies with the achievement. For example, killing an elephant is considered more honourable than killing a lion. The elephant killer is called *mataa midda* (head of heroes) and is the first in the performance order. The patriots sing their own songs in turn, and the performance is embellished by ululations from the participants. The patriots sing the melody loudly while the participants (both men and women) appreciate and glorify them. The killer of an elephant takes the front stage and begins the performance by saying:

> Someone who killed a buffalo is cattle, for he eats grass
>
> Someone who killed a lion is a dog, for he eats flesh
>
> Someone who killed an elephant is a patriot, and can sing loudly.

These are verses that someone who killed an elephant always uses to open their *gerarsa*. Speaking these lines, the head of heroes (the killer of an elephant) asserts his superiority and calls for public attention. Men who only killed a lion or buffalo are bound to honour such men and strive to achieve the same. Similarly, men who participated in war against enemies sing about the deeds they accomplished during the military confrontation. In such a context, a hero performs the song to praise a brave man and reject a coward, and *gerarsa* is performed by one person at a time in the presence of an audience. While a person is performing, the audience listens and responds by shouting the word 'fight' (*lolee*) five times at given intervals. The following transcript of *gerarsa* can be observed as an example.

> *Attendants*: Fight (5x)
> *Singer*: When a stone at Gerceloo[1] rings (3x)
> A fool thinks it is a bell
> A brave has said Gerarsa
> And revealed what is in his heart
> He praised the brave and dismissed the coward
> *Attendants*: Fight (5x)
> *Singer*: When a man goes to war
> His mother gets sad
> When he comes back from war
> She is delighted.
> *Attendants*: Fight (5x)
> *Singer*: Death is inevitable
> One shouldn't be afraid of it
> One should fight and die
> *Attendants*: Fight (5x)
> *Singer*: A coward fears a shadow in the day
> A brave man shows a lion's eyelashes to his people

The word 'fight' comes at each break of the song and expresses the existence of a social consensus around the values of intrepidness, audacity, and military prowess. The last line in the first section of the song ('He praised the brave and dismissed the coward') and the last two lines at the end of the song ('A coward man fears a shadow in the day/A brave man shows a lion's eyelashes to his people') reveal the important function of *gerarsa* in promoting this conception of heroic masculinity. The brave man is praised and celebrated, while the cowardly man is ridiculed and defamed. The recurrent themes of bravery, fighting, and war allude to the tradition of warfare in the Guji-Oromo and showcase the role of oral literature in reinforcing such values. 'Brave' designates a warrior, 'fight' indicates the actions of attacking, killing, and defeating the enemy, while the third word 'war' represents the whole situation that involves the brave warrior and his actions. The frequent appearance of these words, therefore, situates the song within the broader theme of heroism. *Gerarsa* is good at arousing emotion, reflecting feeling, and communicating messages elegantly. That is why adults perform the *gerarsa* as an artistic expression, to reinforce and sustain bravery and patriotism. They use the song to push people towards better social and cultural achievements, and to discourage social and cultural weaknesses. Children grow up watching and listening to adults perform the song, but they are not eligible to sing it until they become adults. Through this song, adults perpetuate these values to the succeeding generation. As a text, *gerarsa* embodies symbolic and imaginative expressions conveying 'thick' messages about Guji cultural and gender values. As performance, it involves diverse tones and attractive melodies that shape its identity and engage the audience. This shows that, similar to the other genres of Guji oral literature, *gerarsa* is characterized by aesthetic complexity.

The Qexala or Ceremonial Song

The *qexala* or ceremonial song is another genre performed and cherished by Guji-Oromo adults. This form of oral literature is also popular among the Sidama and Gedeo peoples of Ethiopia. It is performed more frequently than the *gerarsa*. The cultural context in which *qexala* is performed is known as *jila* or ceremony, which is a popular event in which only adults participate. Although several minor *jilas* are available at different social occasions, there are four major *jila* in one Gadaa period of eight years. These are the *jila* of *Baallii kenna* or power transfer; the *jila* of *Laguubaasa*, in which members of the *Kuusa* grade pass from childhood status to adulthood; the *jila* of *Maqiibaasii* or naming children; and the *jila* of *jaarra utalli* or blessing. The central element of these ritual ceremonies is the performance of the *qexala*. Participants in the ceremonies sing the *qexala* in different styles, and no ritual and ceremonial practice of Guji people can be complete without such a performance.

Important elements that distinguish *qexala* from *gerarsa* are the performance style, content, and function of the two genres. In the performance of *gerarsa*, the expression *lolee, lolee* (fight, fight) is frequently recited by the audience at certain points of the song. The *qexala* also has a call and response structure, but the response is a different expression, *hoo, hoo* which is a deep and sober melody to signify humility and respect for the supernatural power. The song is performed by a chorus of senior, high-ranking men. The singers stand in a group facing the same direction and walk slowly while performing the song. One singer leads by reciting lines of the song, and the other participants then respond all together with their own line. The performance is characterised by the participants' gentle forward and backward movements, deep and homogenous melody, uniformity in clothing and gesture, as well as closeness and equality in group positions.

Fig. 7.2 Guji adults stand in a row singing a *qexala* song in a chorus. Author's photograph.

The *qexala* is performed by adults in the Raba, Dori, Gada, Batu, and Yuba generations as a means of reinforcing the values of solidarity and peaceful relationships between people; between people and the natural environment; and between the people and supernatural powers. At the beginning and end of a social or cultural event, adults in the generational grades come together and perform the song as a sign of opening and conclusion and to thank the supernatural power. Members take turns in leading the performance, since they all are considered well-versed in the performance of the song. The following is an example of a *qexala* song often performed during cultural ceremonies of the Guji-Oromo:

Lead singer:	Our custom, hoo
Chorus:	Our custom, our unity
Lead singer:	Our unity
Chorus:	Our custom, our unity
Lead singer:	Our symbol
Chorus:	Our custom, our unity
Lead singer:	My people, say 'we are happy'
Chorus:	Our custom, our unity
Lead singer:	Our symbol
Chorus:	Our custom, our unity
Lead singer:	Our custom is a symbol of our land.
Chorus:	Hoo
Lead singer:	Hoo, haa, hoo (2x)
Chorus:	Hoo
Lead singer:	Hoo, haa, hoo (2x)
Chorus:	Hoo
Lead singer:	Hoo, haa, hoo (2x)
	Our culture looks great
Chorus:	Hoo
Lead singer:	Hoo haa hoo (2x)
	It is in a great place
Chorus:	Hoo
Lead singer:	Hoo haa hoo (2x)
	Let us celebrate it
Chorus:	Hoo

The leader recites the lines while walking in front of the group, and they walk behind the leader and recite in unison 'hoo' and 'our custom our unity'. The performance is a demonstration of unity and cohesiveness between the leader and the group, as well as unity and cohesiveness within the group. It symbolises the value of solidarity and social harmony. The lyrics use phrases like 'our custom' and words expressing solidarity, unanimity, and peacefulness as key values of the Guji-Oromo society. 'Hoo' is recited in deep melody and signifies the honour and respect for supernatural powers.

The Gelelle or Work Song

The *gelelle* or work song of the Guji-Oromo is performed in the context of group work, known in Oromo as *agooda*. Working in a group is an important form of social networking and cooperation among the Guji-Oromo through which men create friendships and take turns at farming work. A group can consist of two to five men who perceive each other to be close friends. Members of a work group co-operate to enhance productivity and create a space for social interaction during planting, weeding, and harvesting. Men sing the *gelelle* when working in a group to motivate themselves to work harder. People believe that the *gelelle* is like an engine which fuels men to work quicker and longer. By using the song to praise each other, admire their surroundings and environment, and spur each other on, people revive their energies and build up endurance. The following is a *gelelle* song I collected on fieldwork. It is performed by an adult known as *wellisa*, meaning a clever lead singer. After each verse, the others shout 'Hee' to signify the agreement of the chorus with the lead singer. Like the 'Hoo' chorus cry in the Qexala, the 'Hee' cry in the Gelelle shows the chorus re-affirming the central and superior role of the higher powers in the social hierarchy.

Lead singer:	You boys, how are you my brave ones?
Chorus:	Hee
Lead singer:	Let me talk about you
Chorus:	Hee
Lead singer:	How are you, brave men?
Chorus:	Hee
Lead singer:	You would know your fame
Chorus:	Hee
Lead singer:	I shall talk about you
Chorus:	Hee
Lead singer:	Brave of braves, owners of coffee
Chorus:	Hee
Lead singer:	Ho, my men
Chorus:	Hee
Lead singer:	Men of great motivation
Chorus:	Hee
Lead singer:	How are you, my men?
Chorus:	Hee
Lead singer:	Men, defeated only by soil
Chorus:	Hee
Lead singer:	How are you, my men?
Chorus:	Hee
Lead singer:	Don't get tired, work hard

The song exemplifies the tradition of praising and energising one other through the performance of oral literature. Singing the *gelelle* encourages those engaged in agricultural work to build the endurance they need to survive through hardships. Here, oral literature serves as a tool to reinforce the values of physical resilience, labour, and productivity. It unleashes and sustains the moral stamina to work hard, reinforcing the importance of agricultural productivity for the people's livelihood.

Weedduu Loonii or Cattle Songs

Cattle have a special place in both the culture and livelihood of the Guji-Oromo.[22] They are respected and celebrated as valuable economic, social, and cultural assets. A household possessing many cows, bulls, and calves is identified in Oromo as *warra jiidha* (a wealthy household). Culturally, cattle are symbols of fertility and abundance and are part and parcel of many Guji cultural and spiritual practices. All ceremonies involve the ritual sacrifice of a bull (*qorma qala*), whose spilled blood symbolizes the cleansing of human sins. The ritual slaughter of a bull is therefore a symbolic way to communicate with supernatural powers. There are ceremonial occasions in which people sing songs to honour their cattle and express their love and respect for them. These celebrations involve drinking honey-beer and feasting with relatives and neighbours. The song, together with the honey-beer, raises the spirits of the participants and gives colour to the celebration. The cattle song is performed by any man and woman, usually during spring season as this is a time when the grass begins to grow and cattle become happy. Men and women sing the cattle song when they milk the cows, release cattle from shelter to the grazing field, lead cattle to the water pond, and lead cattle from the grazing field to shelter. When they lead cattle from shelter to the grazing field and from the grazing field to shelter, they sing songs such as the following.

> Lizards on mountains
> Cows of hundred calves
> Abundant in the field are my cattle
> They save me from trouble

---

22   Jirata, 'Oral Poetry as Herding Tool'.

> Those who love cattle are cheerful
> They are rich and plentiful
> Where cattle are abundant
> One's milking pot is always wet
> It is good to sing for cattle
> For it makes me humble

The song shows that the relationship between people and their cattle is based on a reciprocal exchange, with the people caring for cattle and the cattle providing the people with economic and cultural benefits. This oral genre celebrates the role of cattle in society, reinstates the importance of cattle husbandry, and transmits this value to their children.

In the performance of the genres of oral literature presented above, the performer manages the time, place, style, and purpose of the performance, which also differentiate one genre from the other. For example, the *gerarsa* is performed at events celebrating bravery that take place within homes or home compounds. The *qexala* is performed during the Gadaa ceremonies that take place at ceremonial places or *ardaa jila*, whereas the Gelelle is sung while working. Performances vary in tones, melodies, gestures, and messages across the genres. These features indicate the diversity and complexity in places, times, and styles of performance across the oral genres. The oral songs presented above are characterized by tonal variation, improvisation, whimsical facial expression, vivid body movements and gestures, repetition, and dramatic body movements. The literariness of the oral songs emanates from these qualities, which in turn contributes to the diversity and wide range of written literature, and clarifies the strong link between oral and written literature.

Oral Genres that Adults Perform with Children

Among the Guji people, childhood covers the *Dabballe* and *Qarre* generational grades, which span from birth to the age of sixteen. Among children, *oduuduri* (myths and legends) and *duriduri* (folk tales) are the two popular genres that involve the process of telling and listening.[23] The Guji people consider these oral genres a central component

---

23   Jirata 'Children and Oral Tradition'; Jirata, 'Oral Poetry as Herding Tool'; Jirata, 'Folktales, Reality, and Childhood'.

of their culture and a vehicle of the transmission of survival skills, customary practices, norms, and values from the past generation (the ancestors) to the future generation (children) via the present generation (grandparents and parents). Grandparents and parents, who are seen as the active generations mediating between the past and the future, play key roles in the transmission of oral literary forms.

This category represents oral literary forms that adults perform for children as a means of entertaining, socialising, and educating them. Oring and Tucker call 'folklore for children' all the different oral narratives (tales, songs, rhymes, riddles) that adults perform for children as part of generational knowledge transfer.[24] According to McMahon, these genres are produced by adults for children in order to develop the children's knowledge of their social world and to prepare them to become productive societal members in their adult lives.[25] Parents use oral narratives to equip their children with folk knowledge and to enable them to understand their social environment through entertainment.[26] The purpose of these narratives is therefore two-fold: socialisation and entertainment.[27]

Among the Guji-Oromo, the *duriduri* or folk tale is a popular oral literary genre that adults perform for children. Storytelling draws children and adults together. When adults tell folk tales to children, the children sit around them and listen to the tales with courtesy and curiosity. In such a context, children are learners and adults are teachers, and generally the performance has a didactic purpose. Storytelling at home is initiated by the children, as they are often the ones who ask their parents or grandparents to tell them a story. Parents or grandparents activate their memory and remember and reconstruct the oral tradition from their oral repertoire through performance. The children, on the

---

24   Elliott Oring, 'Folk Narratives' in *Folk Groups and Folklore Genres: An Introduction,* ed. by Elliott Oring (Logan: Utah State University Press, 1986), pp. 121–145; Elizabeth Tucker, *Children's Folklore: A Handbook* (New York: Greenwood Publishing Group, 2008).

25   Felicia R. McMahon, *Not Just Child's Play: Emerging Tradition and the Lost Boys of Sudan* (Jackson: University Press of Mississippi, 2007).

26   Nancy J. Schmidt, 'Collection of African Folklore for Children', *Research in African Literatures,* 2.2 (1971), 150–167.

27   Brian Sutton-Smith, 'Introduction: What is Children's Folklore?' in *Children's Folklore: A Source Book,* ed. by Brian Sutton-Smith et. al (Logan: Utah State University Press, 1995), pp. 3–10.

other hand, accept storytelling as a means of entertainment and listen attentively to their parents or grandparents, but also actively intervene to ask for clarifications at the end of the story. In such cultural interactions, adults hold real power and set norms for children.

The following extract is taken from my notes of participant observation at the home of Uddee Netere, a seventy-year-old man and a resident of Bunata Village. At Uddee Netere's home, I observed children initiating the storytelling session at night time. In the interval between coffee and dinner, Uddee Netere's ten-year-old grandson, Galchu, asked Uddee to tell him a folk tale. Galchu went to his grandfather and murmured in his ear, 'tell us the tale that you told us the other day'. The grandfather smiled and nodded his head to show his assent. Then, Galchu and his siblings gathered around their grandfather, who began by saying, 'Folk tales of the *maatti*, birds of the hill; it is the hill that cries and the fool that shies'. This is the expression the Guji people use to begin storytelling and call for the attention of listeners. Then Uddee continued:

> Once upon a time, a fox and a hawk were living together. One day, they were starving and they killed a rat to eat. However, the hawk decided to snatch the rat for himself and fly away to a big, tall tree. The hawk sat on the big tree with the rat in his mouth. The fox became very angry at the greedy act of his friend. He devised a trick to get back his delicious rat. He killed a small frog, went under the tree on which the hawk was sitting with the rat in his mouth, called to him, 'Hello Hawk, I have got a more delicious one, look at it', and showed him the frog from the ground. The greedy hawk was keen on the frog and opened his mouth to speak to the fox. When the hawk opened his mouth, the rat dropped down to the ground and the fox got it back. The hawk lost what he owned when he longed for something more, it was said.

The children responded to the tale with different actions and behaviours. Some of them smiled, others murmured as their grandfather spoke. At the end, the children laughed at the ignorance of the hawk and were surprised by the trickery of the fox against the hawk. The grandfather told them that the tale teaches that if you are too greedy, you will lose everything. In the performances of this tale, both children and adults acted as interlocutors but maintained distinct hierarchical roles. Parents are transmitters of norms and values and children learn these norms and values through their participation in the oral performances. In the context of storytelling, adults respect the interests and requests of their children. Children, in turn, respect adults and pay due attention to their instructions. They do what adults tell them to do and sit where adults tell them to sit. Through such performances, adults acquaint children with Guji ancestral knowledge, which includes harmonious relationships between adults and children as well as customary values, norms, and survival skills. Participation in such oral performances at home involves curiosity, respect, trust, appreciation, and affection. Children are curious to hear oral literary forms from parents, and parents are curious to teach their children through oral literature. Thus, children invest deep attention and value in the oral performance with adults, and adults use this opportunity as an occasion to equip their children with the cultural codes regulating intergenerational relationships.

Children's Oral Genres

Children's oral literature refers to the folk knowledge that circulates among two or more children, usually without or with limited involvement of adults.[28] It includes the folk tales, riddles, and songs that children produce and reproduce for one another in different social and cultural contexts. In these performances, children are the central agents who initiate, reproduce, and transmit oral literary forms. In other words, in the context of children's oral literature, children are both tellers and receivers of their folk culture.[29]

The concept of children's oral literature emerged at the end of the nineteenth century, in parallel with other significant changes in the way childhood was conceptualised. Children started being seen as social actors with their own culture as well as inhabiting the social world they shared with adults.[30] The interest in children's oral literature emerged within this paradigm, allowing us to see children not only as receivers of oral culture but also as producers and transmitters.[31] In the study of children's oral literature, children are understood as having their own

---

28   Tucker, *Children's Folklore*.

29   Jirata, 'Children and Oral Tradition'; Sutton-Smith, 'What is Children's Folklore?';
     Finnegan, *The Oral and Beyond*.

30   Tucker, *Children's Folklore*.

31   McMahon, *Not Just Child's Play*; Flemming Mouritsen, 'Child Culture- Play
     Culture' in *Childhood and Children's Culture*, ed. by Flemming Mouritsen and Jens
     Qvortrup (Denmark: Denmark University Press, 2002), pp. 14–42.

collective traditions. Within their group, children create an interactive fabric of activities out of their immediate social and natural environments with minimal involvement from adults.[32] These group traditions importantly foster children's social and cognitive development. In short, children's participation in the performance and circulation of oral genres is significant, allowing us to see children themselves as literary creators. Oral literature or orature is not, therefore, the preserve of adults alone. Nor are children always passive receivers of oral narratives imparted by their elders, but can be pivotal agents in the creation and transmission of orature. Among the Guji-Oromo, *duriduri* (folk tales), *hibboo* (riddles), and *weedduu* (folk songs) are the most important forms of children's oral literature. These oral literary forms are performed in the social contexts pertaining to children and young people: family time at home, herding cattle in the fields, and playtime at school and in the neighbourhood.

Fig. 7.3 Guji children performing storytelling in a cattle herding field. Author's photograph.

---

32   Shumirai Nyota, and Jacob Mapara, 'Shona Traditional Children's Games and Play, Songs as Indigenous Ways of Knowing', *Journal of Pan African Studies,* 2.4 (2008), 189–202; Robin Mello, 'The Power of Storytelling: How Oral Narrative Influences Children's Relationships in Classrooms', *International Journal of Education and the Arts,* 2.1 (2001); Donna Eder, *Life Lessons through Story Telling: Children's Explorations of Ethics* (Bloomington, IN: Indiana University Press, 2010).

In these dynamic contexts of work, study, and play, children form peer relationships and perform the different genres of oral literature as part of their culture of play. Children may learn a folk tale from their siblings or parents and then share it in the cattle-herding fields and school compounds. They may also learn a folk tale from children in the fields or school compounds and then share it with their siblings at home. Playtime at home gives children the opportunity to learn a variety of folk tales as it involves siblings who participate as tellers, listeners, and interpreters. Parents can also be involved as audience members, inverting the common hierarchy of storytelling that sees parents as storytellers and children as their audience. For example, I witnessed Roba, a ten-year-old boy, telling the following folk tale to his siblings and parents. He had learned the tale from his peers at school:

> Once upon a time, a cat's child and a rat's child were friends and used to play with each other. One evening, the mother cat asked her child, 'My child, where did you stay during the day?' The child replied, 'I was playing with rat's child'. The mother said to her child, 'Rats are delicious food. Catch her and eat her'. The child replied, 'Ok, I will do that tomorrow'. The mother rat also asked her child, 'My child, where did you stay during the day?' The child replied, 'I was playing with cat's child'. The mother rat said to her child, 'My child, how can you play with your enemy? Cats are our enemies. They eat us. Don't do that again'. The next day, the cat's child went to the playground early in the morning and was waiting for the rat's child. When she came out of her house, the rat's child saw the cat's child waiting for her. The cat's child called her, 'Come, let us play'. Then, the rat's child replied, 'My mother has told me what your mother told you. Now we know each other'. After saying this, the rat's child went back inside her home, it was said.

In this way, children share oral literature at home, in the cattle-herding fields, at school, and in village neighbourhoods. Even though adults tell folk tales to children with didactic purposes, the children comprehend and express them in their own ways when it is their turn to re-tell them. Roba told this story to his siblings and parents vividly, creatively and in a captivating manner. His siblings listened attentively, interrupted him to ask questions, and responded to the story with smiles and sounds of surprise. This shows that, in their performance of folk tales, children take liberties in relating the events, names, moods, and actions of characters, and react freely to what is being told to them. They say what they want to say, act in the way they want to act, behave in the way they want to behave, sometimes laugh loudly, sometimes stand up and shout, sometimes stop the teller and correct him/her, sometimes help him/her when he/she forgets the order of events or fails to remember specific stories. Children's performance of folk tales differs from that of adults in the styles used by the performer. Storytelling by adults entails complete opening terms like 'once up a time', the closing term 'it was said', candid mimicry, vivid gestures and intonation, which make the tale imposing and meaningful. By contrast, children often begin telling a story without the opening term 'once upon a time' and the closing term 'it was said', and the mimicry, gestures and intonation in their performance are more creative and artistic than those of adults. This shows the diversity and complexity in in the local oral literary forms which, in turn, contribute to the richness of world literature.

These days, children also have the opportunity to listen to storytelling and songs from mass media sources such as radio and television. My encounters in a remote rural village testify to this new trend in oral literature circulation. I approached a group of children performing a song in a grazing field and asked what they were singing. The children told me that they were playing *wadeb*, which is the name of a song popular with Tigrinya-speaking children in the northernmost part of Ethiopia. I asked the children to perform the song again, and they agreed. One of the children performed the song with a loud and smooth melody:

Wadeb, wadeb	Wadeb, wadeb
Wadeb Ahadu	Wadeb, one
Wadeb Kilitte	Wadeb, two
Wadeb Seliste	Wadeb, three
Wadeb Arbate	Wadeb, four
Wadeb Amishite	Wadeb, five
Wadeb Shidishite	Wadeb, six

I was surprised that the song was in Tigrinya, a language spoken very far away from the land of the Guji. I asked the children what the language of the song was, and they did not know. I also asked how they had learned the song, and they replied that they had learned from each other. I continued to investigate how the children had come across the song and learned that, sometime in the past, a child from the village had gone to a nearby town and watched the song on television. The child came back to his village and shared the song with his friends. The song was later circulated among the children in the village and became part of children's repertoire of oral literature. This instance shows the role of mass media in the circulation of children's oral literature, including across languages. In other words, this example demonstrates that children's oral literature from the northern part of Ethiopia was learned by children in the southern part of the country through television broadcasting. Television allowed Oromo-speaking children to learn the oral traditions of Tigrinya-speaking children. This reality reflects the new ways in which oral literature can cross different cultures and geographies, bypassing adults and language barriers. This trend may bring children from different cultures and geographies together and allow them to transmit their knowledge and values across long distances. Mass media, like schools and workplaces, helps children share their oral traditions and use them as a means of understanding each other's skills, knowledge, and experiences, and learning about the presence of different cultures and languages in the country.

Conclusion

Among the Guji, mastery of oral genres depends on age and on personal skills. Children become versed in the performance of *duriduri, hibbo,* and *wedduu,* and when they grow up, they learn how to perform the *gerarsa, qexala, weeddu loonii,* and *jecha.* Within this broad generational distribution of oral genres, individuals partake in oral literature based on their personal talents and inclinations. Some people can perform folk songs better than they do folk tales and riddles, others are better at performing folk tales and riddles than folk songs. Some people may remember many folk tales but not as many folk songs, others may have memorised an extensive repertoire of folk songs but be less versed in folk tales. During performances of these oral literary forms, people who do not have adequate knowledge and performance ability sit or stand by the side, watching the performance and learning from it.

Oral literature, as this chapter has shown, has both an intra-generational and an inter-generational circulation. Different oral genres are shared either among adults only, among children only, or across generations. Contrary to the widespread assumption that oral traditions are the preserve of the elders, this chapter has shown that children are active agents of oral circulation and preservation. They acquire oral literature from adults and then share it with other children, or they learn it from other children and then share it with adults. As a result, oral literature reflects the culture, values, and social practices not only of adults but also of children. It is not a static and fixed repository of cultural authenticity, but a dynamic, modern, and aesthetically complex tool of communication and knowledge sharing. It is memorised, circulated, and performed not only by elders, but also by children. Through these forms of artistic expression, adults teach one another and learn from one another, and children also learn from one another and teach one another. Children have a significant literary influence on the adults around them, encouraging them to memorise certain oral texts, thus connecting adults with children's culture. The oral literary forms that children and adults perform together serve as mutual socialisation into each other's culture. Inter-generational exchanges are as rich as intra-generational ones: adults educate children, but also learn from them, and children learn from adults, but also teach them. Studying oral literature helps us capture the dynamic nature of the relationship between adults and children among the Guji, and how it has changed and keeps changing based on broader processes of social and economic transformation.

By producing and reproducing different oral genres, children contribute to the continuity of oral traditions. In fact, the socio-cultural contexts in which adults perform oral literary forms, such as family playtime and neighbourhood social events, are slowly disappearing; some significant forms of oral literature are no longer lived culture for adults as a result but become part of what can be called a 'culture of memory'. This implies that people connect themselves to their past cultural practices through memory. But if some forms of oral literature may partly or fully disappear from people's everyday practices and become remembered as a culture of the past, such change is less observable in the culture and everyday lives of children. In the past, there was no distinction between the vibrancy of the oral practices of adults and children, but these days, folk performances are receding among adults and are instead retained by children. For example, folk tales, riddles, and cattle songs continue to be active elements of children's play culture. This is because children have alternative access to forms of oral literature through school books, mass media (mainly children's programs on radio and television), and because of an emerging interest in integrating oral literature with learning practices in schools.[33] Therefore, if we want to look for orature in Guji society, we need to look at children's social interactions.

This located study has helped to make children visible as agents and producers of oral literature. It has drawn attention to the importance of inter-generational as well as intra-generational transmission. Through a located ethnography of Guji-Oromo oral genres, it has highlighted its multiple channels of access and transmission, as well as processes of adaptation showing how oral literature is dynamic, adaptable, and able to evolve across changing social and cultural contexts. Today, several socio-cultural milieus that are the basis for the performance of oral literary forms are undergoing change. For example, children's spaces of play interaction with adults are decreasing, as the division of labour by age—which sees children work in different spaces from adults—has become common. Following the expansion of schooling in rural areas, children's time for play and peer interaction in cattle-herding places has also become shorter. Oral traditions among the Guji are set to continue for generations, but we may witness a change in transmission and circulation. Children's increasing access to school, children's television and radio programmes, and new media (like Facebook and digital games) may make the circulation of oral literature increasingly the responsibility of children and younger generation. As a result, the top-down, hierarchical transmission patterns from adults towards children may decline in importance, leaving more room in the coming years for intra-generational transmission among children and bottom-up inter-generational transmission from children to adults. Such contexts may ensure the wider circulation of oral literature and give rise to new forms that appeal to children's mediated lived experiences. As a result, oral

---

33   Abebe Yeseraw, Tadesse Melesse & Asrat Dagnew Kelkay, 'Inclusion of Indigenous Knowledge in the New Primary and Middle School Curriculum of Ethiopia', *Cogent Education*, 10.1 (2023), https://www.doi.org/10.1080/23311 86X.2023.2173884

literature can be considered as a primary literary culture that contributes to the delocalisation, sophistication, and dynamism of world literature.

Bibliography

Alemu, Abreham, 'Oral Narratives as Ideological Weapon for Subordinating Women: The Case of Jimma Oromo', *Journal of African Cultural Studies*, 19.1 (2007), 55–80, https://doi.org/10.1080/13696810701485934

Argenti, Nicolas, 'Things that Don't Come by the Road: Folktales, Fosterage, and Memories of Slavery in the Cameroon Grassfields', *Comparative Studies in Society and History*, 55.2 (2010), 224–254, https://doi.org/10.1017/S0010417510000034

Beriso, Tadesse, 'The Pride of the Guji-Oromo: An Essay on Cultural Contact Self-Esteem', *Journal of Oromo Studies*, 11.1–2 (2004), 13–27, https://oromostudies.org/wp-content/uploads/jos/JOS-Volume-11-Number-1_2-2004.pdf

Braukämper, Ulrich, 'The Correlation of Oral Traditions and Historical Records in Southern Ethiopia: A Case Study of the Hadiya/ Sidamo Past', *Journal of Ethiopian Studies*, 11.2 (1973), 29–50, https://www.jstor.org/stable/41988257

Clarunji Chesaina, *Oral Literature of the Embu and Mbeere* (Nairobi: East African Educational Publishers, 1997).

Debelo, Asebe and Tadesse J. Jirata, '"Peace Is Not a Free Gift": Indigenous Conceptualisations of Peace among the Guji-Oromo in Southern Ethiopia', *Northeast African Studies*, 18.1–2 (2018), 201–230, https://doi.org/10.14321/nortafristud.18.1-2.0201

Debsu, Dejen N., 'Gender and Culture in Southern Ethiopia: An Ethnographic Analysis of Guji-Oromo Women's Customary Rights', *African Study Monographs*, 30.1 (2009), 15–36, https://repository.kulib.kyoto-u.ac.jp/dspace/bitstream/2433/71111/1/ASM_30_15.pdf

Eder, Donna, *Life Lessons through Story Telling: Children's Explorations of Ethics* (Bloomington, IN: Indiana University Press, 2010).

Federal Democratic Republic of Ethiopia Population Census Commission, 'Summary and Statistical Report of the 2007 Population and Housing Census: Population Size by Age and Sex' (Addis Ababa: UNFPA, 2008), https://www.ethiopianreview.com – 2007 Census

Finnegan, Ruth, *Oral Tradition and Verbal Arts* (London: Routledge, 1992).

——, *The Oral and Beyond: Doing Things with Words in Africa* (Oxford: James Curry, 2007).

Gemeda, Esthete, 'African Egalitarian Values and Indigenous Genres: The Functional and Contextual Studies of Oromo Oral Literature in a Contemporary Perspective' (unpublished PhD thesis, University of Southern Denmark, 2008).

Jirata, Tadesse, J., 'Folktales, Reality, and Childhood in Ethiopia: How Children Construct Social Values through Performance of Folktales', *Folklore*, 129.3 (2018), 237–253, https://doi.org/10.1080/0015587X.2018.1449457

——, 'Oral Poetry as Herding Tool: A Study of Cattle Songs as Children's Art and Cultural Exercise among the Guji-Oromo in Ethiopia', *Journal of African Cultural Studies*, 29.3 (2017), 292–310, https://doi.org/10.1080/13696 815.2016.1201653

——, 'Children and Oral Tradition among the Guji-Oromo in Southern Ethiopia' (unpublished PhD thesis, Norwegian University of Science and Technology, 2013), https://ntnuopen.ntnu.no/ntnu-xmlui/bitstream/handle/11250/269081/638430_FULLTEXT02. pdf?sequence=2&isAllowed=y

Jirata, Tadesse J. and Jan Ketil Simonsen, 'The Roles of Oromo-Speaking Children in Storytelling Tradition in Ethiopia', *Research in African Literatures*, 45.2 (2014), 135–149, https://doi.org/10.2979/reseafrilite.45.2.135

Johnson, John W., 'Orality, Literacy, and Somali Oral Poetry', *Journal of African Cultural Studies'*, 18.1 (2006), 119–136.

Kidane, Sahlu, *Borana Folktales: A Contextual Study* (Indiana: Indiana University Press, 2002).

Legesse, Abiyot, *Gadaa: Three Approaches to the Study of African Society* (New York: Free Press,1973).

McMahon, Felicia R., *Not Just Child's Play: Emerging Tradition and the Lost Boys of Sudan* (Jackson: University Press of Mississippi, 2007).

Mello, Robin, 'The Power of Storytelling: How Oral Narrative Influences Children's Relationships in Classrooms', *International Journal of Education and the Arts*, 2.1 (2001), n.p., http://www.ijea.org/v2n1/

Mouritsen, Flemming, 'Child Culture- Play Culture' in *Childhood and Children's Culture*, ed. by Flemming Mouritsen and Jens Qvortrup (Denmark: Denmark University Press, 2002), pp. 14–42.

Nyota, Shumirai and Jacob Mapara, 'Shona Traditional Children's Games and Play, Songs as Indigenous Ways of Knowing', *Journal of Pan African Studies*, 2.4 (2008), 189–202, https://www.jpanafrican.org/docs/vol2no4/2.4_ Shona_Traditional_Children.pdf

Okpewho, Isidore, *African Oral Literature: Backgrounds, Character, and Continuity* (Bloomington: Indiana University Press, 1992).

Oring, Elliott, 'Folk Narratives' in *Folk Groups and Folklore Genres: An Introduction*, ed. by Elliott Oring (Logan: Utah State University Press, 1986), pp. 121–145.

Sackey, Edward, 'Oral Tradition and the African Novel', *Modern African Studies*, 37.3 (1991), 389–407.

Schmidt, Nancy J., 'Collection of African Folklore for Children', *Research in African Literatures*, 2 (1971), 150–167.

Sutton-Smith, Brian, 'Introduction: What is Children's Folklore?' in *Children's Folklore: A Source Book*, ed. by Brian Sutton-Smith, Jay Mechling, Thomas W. Johnson, and Felicia R. McMahon (Logan: Utah State University Press, 1995), pp. 3–10.

Tasew, Bayleyegn, 'Metaphors of Peace and Violence in the Folklore: Discourses of South-Western Ethiopia: A Comparative Study' (unpublished PhD thesis, Vriji University Amsterdam, 2009).

Tucker, Elizabth, *Children's Folklore: A Handbook* (New York: Greenwood Publishing Group, 2008).

van Damme, Wilfried, 'African Verbal Arts and the Study of African Visual Aesthetics', *Research in African Literature*, 31.4 (2000), 8–20.

Van de Loo, Joseph, *Guji-Oromo Culture in Southern Ethiopia* (Berlin: Dietrich Reimer Verlag, 1991).

Yeseraw, Abebe, Tadesse Melesse and Asrat Dagnew Kelkay, 'Inclusion of Indigenous Knowledge in the New Primary and Middle School Curriculum of Ethiopia', *Cogent Education*, 10.1 (2023), https://doi.org/10.1080/23311 86X.2023.2173884

8. Sephardi Orature and the Myth of Judeo-Spanish *Hispanidad*

Vanessa Paloma Elbaz

Introduction

Moroccan Sephardim, the Jews who came from Spain in the years following the mass conversions of 1391 and the expulsion of 1492, initially settled in Fez, and then in urban enclaves across the northern coast of Morocco: Tetuan, Tangier, Asilah, Chefchauen, Larache and Ksar el Kebir. The Jewish community of Northern Morocco speaks Haketia, a language based on medieval Castilian, with words of Hebrew and Moroccan Darija (colloquial Arabic) in its spoken form. Haketia's main form of transmission has been through songs, jokes, and stories: these are part of a rich and valuable orature that was core to expressing local specificity, belief, and gender norms. The Judeo-Spanish repertoire is rich and varied, including romances (*romanceros*), ballads (*cantares*), paraliturgical poems in rhyming couplets and triplets (*coplas*), humorous songs, historic songs, and children's songs, amongst others.[1] What was once a vibrant tradition, and formed a central part of daily communal sonic life, was drastically reduced over the last century due to modernisation, emigration, and secularisation of the community. Today, few older singers are alive, though the repertoire is undergoing a revival through the professional performances of singers

---

1   See Vanessa Paloma Elbaz, 'Jewish Music in Northern Morocco and the Building of Sonic Identity Boundaries', *Journal for North African Studies*, 27.5 (2021), 1027–1059.

    https://doi.org/10.11647/OBP.0405.08

from the diaspora who often turn to archival recordings and scholarly transcriptions as sources.

Many of the songs from this oral tradition have texts linking back to pre-expulsion texts. This facilitated a slippage between local Sephardi culture and Spanish hegemony. In fact, most early philological scholarship focused on the romances and the *romancero* tradition, foregrounding the connection between the Sephardi communities of the Mediterranean and Spanish literary history. The *romance* appeals to Spanish cultural hegemonic ideals of its global 'highbrow' contribution.[2]

But the Sephardi oral repertoire of northern Morocco is much larger and includes many more genres, including paraliturgical *coplas*, life-cycle songs, humorous songs, and liturgical songs. Notwithstanding the preponderant hispanist trend in world literature, scholars like Shoshana Weich Shahak, Judith Cohen, Oro Anahory Librowicz, Messood Salama, and myself have explored Judeo-Spanish children's songs, life-cycle orature, comedic local-historic songs and *romances* as expressions of local women's spirituality.[3] This wider repertoire often includes light-hearted aspects and is sung in mixed settings in semi-public spaces alongside food, laughter, and movement. Even romances were in fact mainly used as repertoire for quotidian contexts, with some specific examples being sung during life-cycle events. *Cantares del ciclo de la vida,*

---

2 See Karolina Watroba, 'World Literature and Literary Value: Is "Global" The New "Lowbrow?"', *The Cambridge Journal of Postcolonial Literary Inquiry*, 5.1 (2018), 53–68.

3 See Shohana (Susana) Weich-Shahak, 'Migration in the Twentieth-Century Sephardic Song Repertoire', *European Judaism*, 44.1 (2011), 136–150; Judith R. Cohen, '«Ya salió de la mar»: Judeo-Spanish Wedding Songs among Moroccan Jews in Canada' in *Women and Music in Cross-Cultural Perspective*, ed. by Ellen Koskoff (Westport, Connecticut: Greenwood Press, 1987), pp. 55–67, and 'Musical Bridges: The Contrafact Tradition in Judeo-Spanish Songs' in *Cultural Marginality in the Western Mediterranean*, ed. by Frederick Gerson and Anthony Perceval (Toronto: New Aurora Editions, 1990), pp. 120–127; Judith R. Cohen and Oro Anahory Librowicz, 'Modalidades expresivas de los cantos de boda judeo-españoles', *Revista de Dialectología y Tradiciones Populares*, 41 (1986), 189–209; Messod Salama, '"Yo, Señor, He nacido Hebrea/ y Hebrea Tendré que Morir": Forced Conversion, Religious Conflict, and Female Martyrdom in the Judeo-Spanish Ballad Sol la Saddika' in *Proceedings of the Twelfth British Conference on Judeo-Spanish Studies*, ed. by Hilary Pomeroy and Michael Alpert (Leiden: Brill, 2004), pp. 129–140, and 'Judeo-Spanish Romancero as a Source of Women's Spirituality' in *Languages and Literatures of Sephardic and Oriental Jews*, ed. by David Bunis (Jerusalem: Misgave Yerushalayim, 2009), pp. 362–379; Vanessa Paloma Elbaz, 'De tu boca a los cielos: Jewish Women's Songs in Northern Morocco as Oracles of Communal Holiness', *Hesperis-Tamuda*, 51.3 (2016), 239–261, and 'Jewish Music'.

or life-cycle songs, were mainly performed during the relevant event, or as an index for a moment in someone's life, to evoke a belief, an event, or a memory. Paralitugical *coplas* are songs relating to a specific Jewish holiday or tradition, and often have a large density of Hebrew words. But often a 'woman's' song would be sung as a melody in the liturgical service within the synagogue, as a reminder of the singer's female family members who, because of religious laws, could not participate vocally in the liturgy. This local, popular repertoire has not reached the status of a canonized 'literary contribution': it lies outside the repertoires accepted by literary elites and has been confined to anthropological and ethnomusicological study.

Quoting examples from sixteenth- and seventeenth-century printed *romanceros* and the extant oral tradition in Spain, the Spanish link can seem undeniable. However, this chapter argues, the reality of what Sephardim sing, conserve, and transmit is a layered interweaving of local, multilingual oral repertoire built over traces of historic material gathered by the community throughout its migrations, plus newly adapted pieces from current cultural influences. Their orature forms the bedrock of the cultural specificity of this localized community within its cities of origin and their diasporas, creating a continuum between the ancestral land, ritual, and traditions, usually transmitted through the maternal line. Whereas romances address concerns relating to group boundaries, *cantares del ciclo de la vida* usually deal with fertility, and paraliturgical *coplas* deal with sanctification—these, my research suggests, are the three preponderant concerns running through all the repertoire from northern Morocco.[4]

This chapter therefore disentangles the local-specific elements that developed in Morocco, showing how what was a repertoire originating in a culture of contact was slowly transformed into an indigenous and highly localised form of expression and sociality. It then goes on to analyse the ways in which Moroccan Sephardim have viewed and interacted with their orature compared with the way western scholars, and particularly Hispanists, have written about it, and the consequences of the power asymmetry between them. The colonial imprint, literary hierarchy, and nationalist appropriation by Spain are a thread weaving through the study, publication, and performance of these materials.

---

4   See Elbaz, 'De tu boca a los cielos' and 'Jewish Music'.

What's in a Name?

All of the Jewish repertoire in Haketia, often referred to within the Jewish community as the *cantares antiguos de Castilla,* plays a semi-sacred role within communal life, establishing communal rules for moral behaviour and expounding narratives of danger and life challenges. These *cantares* are most frequently sung by women in a variety of rituals, spaces, and contexts, thereby foregrounding women's voices and the concepts contained within their song in the semi-public spaces of extended communal networks, whether of a pilgrimage or a festive meal during a Jewish holiday. Messod Salama has summarized the profound sacrality this repertoire holds within the Jewish community by stating that:

> the singing and communal performance of such *romances,* together with their association with a ritual and a melody which was perceived as religious music, gave these particular ballads a sacred dimension [...] in some ways these *romances* are the feminine counterpart of the *piyyutim* sung by men in the synagogue and during public religious festivals.[5]

In other words, Jewish women's songs in vernacular Judeo-Spanish fulfilled a sacred role, just as liturgical poetry in Hebrew did for Jewish men. This sacred functionality moves their orature's centre of gravity from Spain squarely into the heart of local Jewish quarters, and even more intimately into Sephardi homes themselves.

To complicate matters, however, the names Jews themselves give to the repertoire show the connection between the oral traditions of northern Moroccan Jews and the long arm of history. The name *Los cantares antiguos de Castilla,* or ancient songs from Castile, shows how Moroccan Sephardim perceive their repertoire as a direct link to Castile and pre-expulsion life. Another name, *Los cantares del tiempo de la Reina Isabel la Católica,* songs from the time of Queen Isabel the Catholic, relates in a dramatic turn the core local repertoire to the time of the expulsion ratified by the Catholic monarchs, specifically naming Queen Isabel la Católica, and connecting northern Morocco to pre-expulsion Spain through what they perceive as an unruptured transmission of sonic material. The third name, *Los cantares de las judías antiguas,* or the songs of the ancient Jewish women, exemplifies the ownership of the repertoire by older Sephardi women: even though to

---

5   Salama, 'Judeo-Spanish Romancero', pp. 373–374.

an outsider they may appear as Spanish songs, within the community they are considered an expression of women's Jewish identity. These three classifications show the ongoing preoccupations within the Jewish community of northern Morocco with an element of place (represented by the mythical evocation of Castile); with temporality (represented by the reification of the traumatic period of the Catholic monarchs and the rupture they created for this community); and finally with a perceived unbroken transmission from older Jewish women to the younger generations. *Las judias antiguas*, the older Jewesses, serve as repositories of the community's oral traditions and local northern Moroccan Jewish cultural specificity. These names, then, play on a nuanced fluctuation between a sense of continuity and of traumatic rupture: historical continuity in the stable oral repertoire maintained by the community, and rupture because of the violent expulsion from Spain, which forced the community to rethink its history and identity and to modify its oral culture.

The Anxiety of Transmission

My own research has focused on understanding the inner use of this repertoire and the reasons why the community invested in and maintain its transmission. After fifteen years of in-depth fieldwork while living in Morocco, interviewing older Moroccan Jewish women and men, their children, cousins, and neighbours, I gathered over 120 songs.[6] After detailed analysis and comparison between community narratives and core themes of this repertoire, jokes, and proverbs, I discovered that the central theme of each song narrative was a core concern for the singers and their descendants. This thematic core was connected to other criteria, such as context of performance (daily, weekly, annually, or relating to the life cycle) and dynamic societal mechanisms. Considering theme, context and temporality of performance together allowed me to find symbolic functions. The main theme of each song justified its symbolic function and its continuous use for those who knew about it. In other words, the texts, their meanings, and themes are always central to women's discussions around the songs, though the melody is not. One of the reasons that the texts are especially central for women is the

---

6   Elbaz, 'Jewish Music'.

function of these songs within the encoded communication that Jewish women use within this highly patriarchal society, which Marie-Christine Borne-Varol has described as 'discours médiatisé', a mediated discourse, ideal for women's spaces:

> In a highly hierarchical patriarchal society where one could not easily challenge the father's authority or that of older brothers, the *romance* constituted a privileged mode of mediated communication. One only has to listen to a woman singing to know her emotional state or her opinion. In-between the biblical and profane themes, Judeo-Spanish *romancero* presents all sorts of possible transgressions within the social order. [...] For this reason, it's one of the forms of mediated communication most used within the home.[7]

Melodic identification may follow a division according to gendered musical spaces. For men, text is central, and they may sing it to different melodies. Jewish men may take the 'female' melody of a well-known *romance* or *copla* and include it within the Hebrew liturgy as a contrafactum, in order to remember a female ancestor.[8] Because these were the songs *de las judias*, they are performed within the synagogue, creating a judeo-hispano-moroccan specificity within traditional Hebrew liturgical texts in the space of the synagogue.[9] For women, a melody is intrinsically connected to a certain text, and when it is sometimes used for other texts it is with the underlying understanding that it "belongs" to the original text. Well-known melodies reappear and are reused with various texts throughout the textual repertoire in a repeated contrafactum.[10] What is most important is to transmit the community message which is embedded within the lyrics. As Alexander and

---

7 Marie-Christine Bornes-Varol, 'Les Judéo-Espagnols de Turquie et le discours indirect' in *Hommage à Marthe Westphal*, ed. by Raúl Caplan, Marie-Lucie Copete and Isabelle Reck (Nancy: Université Nancy 2, 2001), pp. 151–179 (p. 170). Translations are mine unless specified.

8 Contrafactum refers to the use of a known melody with a different textual underlay, such as the American song 'My country 'tis of thee' to the melody of 'God Save the Queen'; this is a musical technique that has been used for centuries, and is often thought to carry hidden meanings with reference to the index of the original melody.

9 Vanessa Paloma Elbaz, 'Judeo-Spanish Melodies in the Liturgy of Tangier: Feminine Imprints in a Masculine Space' in *Musical Exodus: Al-Andalus and its Jewish Diasporas*, ed. by Ruth Davis (Lanham: Rowman & Littlefield, 2015), pp. 25–43.

10 A repeated example I have found is the melody sung to Rahel Lastimoza, which appears throughout paraliturgical songs such as *Mose subio a los shamayim* and others.

Bentolila argue with reference to Jewish proverbs from northern Morocco,

> they are unequivocal keys to identity. Behind the proverb is not just the personal identification of the person speaking, but especially the association to the collective. Transitional phrases in conversations with proverbs include, 'we used to say', or 'I heard this phrase from my mother who had heard it from hers', which underline this issue. In addition to this, the speaker tries to show that the proverb comes from a common experience and reflects a collective experience.[11]

Once I understood the centrality of this orature to the establishment of gendered sexual and social boundaries within the community, my main interest became the function and context of performance, so as to understand (and help others understand) the relationship of this community to its sonic world. Focusing on repertoire functionality, and not exclusively on texts or melodies as Hispanists have done in the past, allowed me to analyse all the repertoire and its functions that are necessary for the community's social stability. The symbolic functions of the whole repertoire, and the foundational dynamics that prompt their continued performance, are concentrated on three principal themes: 1) identity construction through Judaism; 2) maintenance of group boundaries; 3) celebration of fertility.

The first and second functions point to the importance of this oral corpus for defining Sephardi identity. The third symbolic function rests mainly with the women's voices, confirming that these songs cannot be understood outside a gendered perspective. All those who have studied this corpus philologically, or for its liturgical value, are missing out on a key element of the tradition. Ignoring the role of women in this corpus creates a flawed misunderstanding of what the corpus is about and the functions it plays.

The primary function of this repertoire is as guardian of the group, which is why I have placed this function at the heart of the concentric circle in Figure 8.1. One of the most significant points about identity transmission within this group is that it is often performed through elements derived from cultures of contact, with an oscillation between the exclusively 'internal' repertoire and the repertoire of the 'external'

---

11 Alexander-Frizer Tamar and Yaakov Bentolila, *La palabra en su hora es oro: El refrán judeoespañol en el Norte de Marruecos* (Jerusalem: Instituto Ben-Zvi, 2008), p. 7.

world.[12] Examples include the use of Sephardi-identifying melodies for sung jokes about Manolete the Toreador, or a Spanish Christmas carol or *villancico* for a song about culinary preparations for a Jewish wedding. These elements are often gendered, with men singing both 'internal' and 'external' melodies during specific moments of the liturgy and women singing 'external' music from the cultures of contact with children during moments of great intimacy, such as when putting children to sleep, often using 'internal' lyrics, but sometimes not.

This is why a repertoire that is viewed by outsiders as 'Spanish' or 'Hispanic', the *romancero*, is identified for insiders with exclusive judeo-hispano-moroccan cultural specificity. It is also trans-national, connecting them to Sephardim throughout the world, while being fiercely local because of its local-specific melodies.

This repertoire marks the end of a process of 'assimilation' from general Spanish culture, in the pre-expulsion and post-expulsion periods, to fully being identified from within the Jewish community as belonging to the Sephardim. The process may have begun soon after Jews arrived in Morocco after their expulsion from the Iberian Peninsula in the fifteenth century. Other contemporary repertoires, which I classify as miscellaneous (Israeli, French, Spanish), can be found in the soundtrack or soundscape of the community, often during moments that teach listeners about the multiple elements that make up Jewish Moroccan identity. They therefore stand as an educational sonic embodiment of diversity and complexity.

An example of Sephardi hybridity through its songs can be sampled in a composition by a woman in Casablanca who had grown up in Ksar el Kebir. She took a well-known melody of Arabo-Andalusian music called *btaihi ghribt elhssine*, which is also sung in the synagogue during the song about the Passover story when the Jews left Egypt after crossing the Red Sea. Using this melody, she wrote a text for the Saturday night service concluding the sabbath, and called it *Eliyahou HaNabí*, after Elijah the Prophet, invoking the Prophet Elijah to come as a harbinger of the Messiah. The singer, my informant's mother, chose a moment charged with blessing to unify three identity markers: Moroccan, Jewish and Judeo-Spanish. The final lines talk about blessing her children with the blessing of the moment and the immanent presence of the Prophet.

---

12   For a detailed explanation of this see Elbaz, 'Jewish Music'.

Na, na, na-a, na na na na na Eliyahu Hanabi
El Dió me le hadée
A mi hijito que se llama Pinhas
El Dio me le hadée
A mi hijo que se llama Pinhas (claps)

Na, na, na-a, na na na na na Eliyahu Hanabi
God should protect him [from the Haketia verb *hadear*] for me
My little son called Pinhas
God should protect him for me
My little son called Pinhas (claps)

Na-na-na is a typical Arabo-Andalusian syllabification used for vocal fills of melismatic sections, with the voice imitating an instrument. Including the saying 'El Dio me lo hadée' as a main element indexes a common blessing that mothers, aunts and grandmothers utter about their offspring in the Jewish community, using the familiar Haketia turn of phrase: *me lo hadée*, which indicates intimate familial protective love.

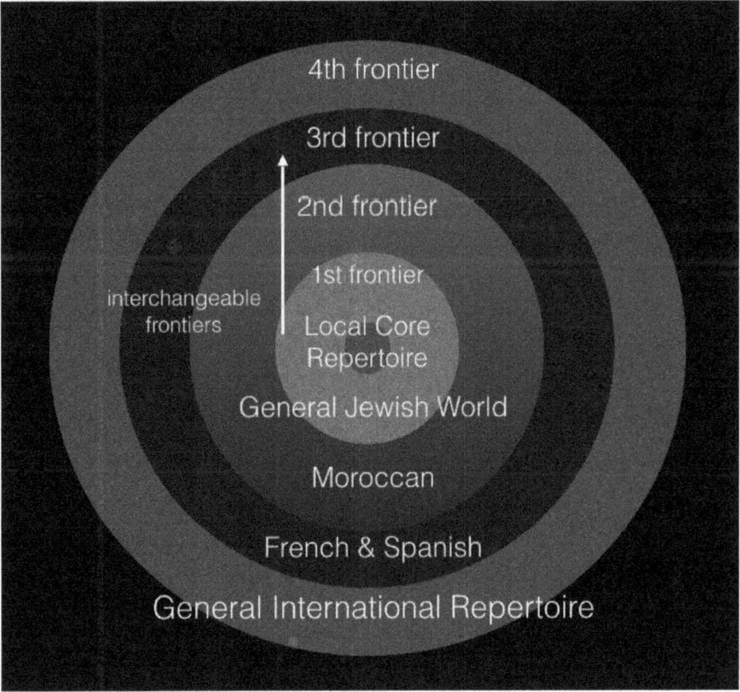

Fig. 8.1 Graphic depiction of the simultaneous and oscillating sonic bands of multilingual belonging performed in quotidian, cyclical and context-specific situations. Image by the author.

This graph demonstrates the simultaneous coexistence of the multiplicity of languages, repertoires, and affiliations that Jews in Morocco are consistently negotiating. At the heart of the graph sits the local core repertoire, in Judeo-languages and often connected to geographical or familial lineages. After the first frontier comes the often-liturgical repertoire that connects them to the wider Jewish world; this is followed by the second frontier repertoire, which is Moroccan, while the third frontier is French and Spanish. These three frontiers I have found to be interchangeable in their positioning in relation to the local core repertoire. Their placement shifts according to the person, their circumstances, and the context of performance. Finally, the general de-territorialised repertoire confirms that the local Jew is a part of a cosmopolitan network of repertoire circulation, while maintaining a rootedness to local geography, language, and meanings.

In the rest of this chapter, I trace the history of the recovery of the Sephardi repertoires from northern Morocco. This includes fieldwork collections of Judeo-Spanish oral repertoires undertaken by Spanish military personnel, such as those carried out by Tomas Navarro Tomás under the direction of Ramón Menéndez Pidal (in 1915–1916), and by the military musician Antonio Bustelo Basadre.[13] By contrast, Sephardi women were involved in two recording projects undertaken in the Moroccan diaspora in the early 1930s, one at the *Residencia de Señoritas* in Madrid and the other at Columbia University in New York, led by Zarita Nahón under the mentorship of Franz Boas.

Spanish Philology and the Colonial Project

Already with the rise of philosephardism in the nineteenth century, philologists began to play a crucial role in Spanish nationalism. From the time of the Spanish-Moroccan War of 1859–1860 until Moroccan independence, Spanish colonial writers and politicians pointed to Spain's interfaith past as evidence that the country was ideally suited

---

13   Antonio Bustelo Basadre notated the romances in Manuel Ortega's 1919 volume
      on *Los hebreos de Marruecos*; see Paloma Díaz-Mas and Elisa Martín Ortega,
      'Romances y Canciones Sefardíes en la colección de partituras en la biblioteca
      Tomás Navarro Tomás' in *Actas del XVIII Congreso de Estudios Sefardíes*, ed. by Elena
      Romero, Hilary Pomeroy and Shmuel Refael (Madrid: CSIC, 2017), pp. 55–74 (p.
      59).

to lead the European colonisation of North Africa.[14] Late nineteenth-century philologists studied Sephardi oral literature as a vestige of Spanish medieval memory, 'frozen' in time after the expulsion of the Jews in 1492, while early-twentieth-century Spanish intellectuals began a public discussion regarding the cultural loss of the Moroccan Jewish community.

The Judeo-Spanish repertoire from northern Morocco came to light in the early twentieth century through the work of the philologists José Benoliel and Ramón Menéndez Pidal. Benoliel, a Jew from Tangier, was an early supporter of Menéndez Pidal's project of tracing the Sephardi *romancero* or narrative ballad and linking it in a straight and unique line to Spanish literary culture, establishing an unbroken link between Sephardi culture and Spanish literary nationalism.[15]

By then, French culture and the Alliance Israélite Universelle (AIU) schools were well established in Morocco. The Alliance schools began

---

14   Eric Calderwood, 'Moroccan Jews and the Spanish Colonial Imaginary,1903–1951', *The Journal of North African Studies*, 24.1 (2019), 86–110.

15   In fact, the earliest written trace of *Moroccan* Judeo-Spanish repertoire is from a songbook from Gibraltar written in 1761 by the Tetuani Abraham Israel. The songbook included two paraliturgical songs within a collection of popular Spanish and a handful of English songs. Scholars have written extensively about the traces of medieval and renaissance romances found in the material collected in field recordings and handwritten Jewish songbooks throughout the Mediterranean basin; see Ramon Menéndez Pidal, *Los Godos y la Epopeya Española: 'Chansons de Geste' y Baladas Nórdicas* (Madrid: Espasa Calpe, 1956) and *Estudios sobre el Romancero* (Madrid: Espasa-Calpe, 1973); Paul Benichou, *Romancero Judeo-Español de Marruecos* (Madrid: Editorial Castalia, 1968); Manuel Alvar, *Endechas judeo-españolas* (Madrid: Instituto Arias Montano, 1969 2nd ed.) and *Cantos de boda judeo-españoles* (Madrid: CSIC, 1971); Samuel Armistead and Joseph Silverman, *Romances judeo-españoles de Tánger recogidos por Zarita Nahón* (Madrid: Cátedra-Seminario Menéndez Pidal, 1977), *El romancero judeo-español en el Archivo Menéndez Pidal (Catálogo-índice de romances y canciones)*, 3 vols. (Madrid: C.S.M.P., 1978), *En torno al romancero sefardí (Hispanismo y balcanismo de la tradición judeoespañola)* (Madrid: Seminario Menéndez Pidal., 1982), and *Judeo-Spanish Ballads from Oral Tradition, I. Epic Ballads* (Berkeley: University of California Press, 1986); Hilary Pomeroy, *An Edition and Study of the Secular Ballads in the Sephardic Ballad Notebook of Halia Isaac Cohen* (Newark, Delaware: Juan de la Cuesta, 2005); Susana Weich-Shahak, *Cantares Judeo Españoles de Marruecos para el Ciclo de la Vida* (Jerusalem: The Jewish Music Research Center, 1989), 'Canciones acumulativas sefardíes y congéneres hispánicas', *Revista de Dialectología y Tradiciones Populares*, 50.1 (1995), 73–91, *Un Vergel Vedre* (Zaragoza: Ibercaja, 1995), and *Romancero sefardí de Marruecos* (Madrid: Alpuerto, 1997); Paloma Díaz-Mas María Sánchez Pérez, *Los sefardíes y la poesía tradicional hispánica del siglo XVIII: el Cancionero de Abraham Israel (Gibraltar, 1761-1770)* (Madrid: CSIC, 2013), among others.

in Tetuan in 1860, as a response by French Jews to the danger of Jewish children's conversion to Christianity in Spanish Franciscan schools. One of their main proposals was to teach secular subjects in French, thus laying the linguistic ground for the cultural intimacy Jews would eventually enjoy with the French colonisers from 1912.[16] Through the system of the Alliance Israélite Universelle schools, France played a major role in the secularisation of Moroccan Jews. The schools—which taught French culture, academic subjects such as science, mathematics, and literature as well as Jewish religious subjects and the Hebrew language—furthered the influence of French culture without promoting assimilation. Moroccan Alliance students saw themselves as a 'Modern manifestation of Moroccan Jewry'.[17]

At the exact moment when the AIU was establishing a foothold in Morocco, Spain was reconsidering North Africa as the next step in its colonial expansion. In 1908, at the Second Africanist Congress in Zaragoza, D. Wenceslao Orbea affirmed:

> We must counter the influence of French schools that so assiduously support the 'Alliance Universelle' and in parallel, the Spanish government should create schools in Tangier, Tetuan, Larache, Rabat, Mogador, Safi, Casablanca and wherever it should be necessary. In this manner we will be able to enhance our influence, attracting both Moors and Hebrews who today are going off the path [forgetting their Spanishness] because of the education they receive in foreign schools [...]. I suggest that we create a National League for the spread of Spanish in all of North Africa, where thousands of families maintain with affection the language that their ancestors gave them.[18]

The 're-discovery' of Judeo-Spanish prompted an explosion of studies to 'recapture' the 'lost' literature of Spain's rich history. In 1919, Ramón

---

16   For further information on the AIU in Morocco see Michael Laskier, 'Aspects of the Activities of the Alliance Israélite Universelle in the Jewish Communities of the Middle East and North Africa: 1860–1918', *Modern Judaism*, 3.2 (1983), 147–171; Frances Malino, 'Prophets in Their Own Land? Mothers and Daughters of the Alliance Israélite Universelle', *Nashim: A Journal of Jewish Women's Studies & Gender Issues*, 3 (2000), 56–73; Jessica Marglin, 'Modernizing Moroccan Jews: The AIU Alumni Association in Tangier, 1893—1913', *The Jewish Quarterly Review*, 101.4 (2011), 574–603.

17   Marglin, 'Modernizing Moroccan Jews', p. 575.

18   In Manuel L. Ortega, *Los Hebreos en Marruecos* (Málaga: Algazara, 1994), p. 272 (originally published in 1919).

Menéndez Pidal described popular poetry as coming from a deep national wellspring cultivated by the populace before being 'refined' by the cultured classes. Popular indigenous material was therefore presented as the basis of every literary production of a country. As early as 1919, Menéndez Pidal stated that 'the subtleties found in a penetrating study [of literature] will find popular aspects almost always deeply embedded within personal and refined artworks'.[19] Menéndez Pidal had been collecting Sephardi romances as early as 1896.[20] Thanks to Angel Pulido's correspondence with Sephardim throughout the Mediterranean basin, Menéndez Pidal's collection of Sephardi romances could demonstrate the evolution and continuity of a grand Hispanic literary tradition, at home and in the diasporas.

The Spanish colonial project used this tradition and its *hispanidad* to buttress their colonial expansion in various geographic locations, most notably in northern Morocco. In November 1940, Franco established the 'Consejo de la Hispanidad' and established a cultural policy of *hispanidad* where 'Spain's cultural contributions would be extolled; public education advocated; anti-Semitism denounced and a conscious pro-Semitism practiced'.[21] I find it most significant that it was Sephardi women's orature that was used to support the ideology behind the Spanish colonial project and the connection of Sephardim to *Hispanidad*.

Spanish colonialism engaged mostly with Sephardim from the Muslim Mediterranean, and not those in the London, Amsterdam, or Florence, possibly because Mediterranean Jews were distant enough to provide an exotic buffer without being a local threat. (Jews were considered foreign in peninsular Spain, but indigenous in the Spanish enclaves of Northern Morocco.[22]) The connecting points between

---

19   Ramon Menéndez Pidal, 'La primitiva poesía lírica española', *Estudios Literarios* (1919), 255–344 (p. 256).

20   The first seems to have come from Salomón Levy from Oran, soon published by 1904 in Angel Pulido's book; see Paloma Díaz-Mas, 'Ramón Menéndez Pidal y la cultura sefardí' in *Lengua y Cultura Sefardí Estudios en Memoria de Samuel G. Armistead,* ed. by Nicolás Asensio Jiménez and Sara Sánchez Bellido (Madrid: Fundación Menéndez Pidal, 2015), pp. 179–2010 (p. 186).

21   See Bailey W. Diffie, 'The Ideology of Hispanidad', *The Hispanic American Historical Review,* 23.3 (1943), 457–482 (p. 458). Pro-Semitism seems like quite an exaggeration, as one of the publications of *Hispanidad*, the Colombian *Revista de Indias* in 1941 (5) called Roosevelt a Jew as an anti-American slur.

22   Maite Ojeda Mata, *Identidades ambivalentes: Sefardíes en la España contemporánea* (Madrid: Sefarad Editores, 2018), p. 159.

the Spanish and the Sephardi community were mostly Sephardi economic elites. Maite Ojeda Mata's *Ambivalent Identities: Sephardim in Contemporary Spain* presents Spanish studies that were instrumental in rebuilding European relationships with Jewish Mediterranean communities in colonial times.[23] The rest of this chapter discusses four elite Sephardim from Tangier and Tetuan and their relationships with Spanish officials and scholars between 1904 and World War II, in order to show how their work was received and employed by the Spanish academic establishment to root the Moroccan Judeo-Spanish oral tradition in the Spanish literary corpus.

José Benoliel, Sephardi Philologist from Tangier

In the early years of the twentieth century, Ramón Menéndez Pidal recruited Sephardi notables from around the Mediterranean to help him in his project of retracing Spanish literatures dispersed with the Sephardim after the expulsion.

José Benoliel (1888–1937) was born in Tangier, Morocco. He travelled extensively and studied in France and Palestine. He later moved to Portugal, where he worked as a Professor of Romance philology at the National University in Lisbon. In 1922, he moved back to Tangier and published his ground-breaking work on Haketia or Moroccan Judeo-Spanish, as well as serving as the President of the Jewish community and Head of its Rabbinic Yeshiva.

Within his papers are a series of letters from 1904 from Angel Pulido, who went on to publish *Españoles sin Patria y la Raza Sefardí* in 1905 ('Spaniards without a Nation and the Sephardi Race') using some of the material Benoliel had sent him.[24] On 23 May 1904, Angel Pulido wrote to José Benoliel while the latter still lived in Lisbon ask him to help Menéndez Pidal find Moroccan Judeo-Spanish *romances*. Benoliel became a key middleman. His contacts in Tangier helped gather over one hundred *romances* from northern Morocco which formed one of the foundations of Menéndez Pidal's Judeo-Spanish *romancero* project, laying the ground for the lengthy investigation by Spanish scholars

---

23 Ibid.
24 Angel Pulido's letters to José Benoliel are found in Special Collections of
    University of California Los Angeles Library. Collection 1625, Box 13, folder 2.

of the Moroccan Judeo-Spanish repertoire in the twentieth century.[25] Menéndez Pidal's work can be seen to link the *romances* to Spanish Krausism, that movement named after the German philosopher Karl Christian Friedrich Krause that in late-nineteenth and early-twentieth Spain was connected to *regeneracionismo* and sought to remedy Spain's decline through the richness of its past cultural empire.[26] In this context, it was the hispanicity of Sephardi repertoire, and not its local value, that mattered.

Benoliel's engagement with Menéndez Pidal's project, and the subsequent engagement of various Sephardi intellectuals from the elite with Spanish philological projects, demonstrate how each used the repertoire and their relationship around it, for different purposes. For Spain, it was about intellectual colonial expansion, whereas for Sephardim, it brought their most intimate orature into a European intellectual canon, thus appearing to elevate their community's status.

In another letter to Benoliel a few months later, Pulido wrote,

> For now I am trying to establish personal connections with all the populations that have Spanish Israelites: later I will formulate that questionnaire which you so discretely indicated, and which I have been thinking about. Do you have any friends in Sofia, Argentina, the Holy Land (Jerusalem, Tiberias…) Spanish Israelites? I would appreciate any personal indication.

Pulido's second letter shows the project of using the materials to link Sephardim and their culture throughout the Mediterranean to Spain becoming more apparent, while his claim to be 'a humble lover of humanity, of my country and the fraternal spirit between peoples' shows Pulido's desire to use pan-Hispanic Sephardi materials as part of the Spanish political project.[27]

Benoliel himself moved back to Tangier in the early 1920s, after his wife Paloma's death soon after childbirth, where he wrote his seminal volume on Moroccan Judeo-Spanish, *Dialecto judeo-hispano marroquí*

---

25   These romances are still at the Archivo Menéndez Pidal.
26   See Francisco Abad Nebot, 'La escuela de Menéndez Pidal y la tradición del krausismo español', *A distancia*, 1 (2008), 207–211.
27   Antonio Pulido, UCLA Special Collections, Collection 1625, Box 13, Folder 2.

o hakitía (1926–1928, 1952).[28] This philological study on its grammar and history included lists of proverbs, blessings, curses, and songs. I wonder if it was the sudden pain from his encounter with mortality that propelled him to focus on his own community's women's oral traditions, instead of the Portuguese poetry and Hebrew liturgical poetry that had occupied him until then. In his personal papers there is a series of letters from his mother telling him about the difficulty of handling his brother's violent outbursts related to his poor mental health, and others to his brother describing his pain at his wife's sudden death. Soon after he moved to Tangier, a few letters surface with declarations of love to his niece, whom he hoped to marry, despite the gaping age difference between them, after his wife's death. This triangle of relationships with women that comes through his letters, the decision to leave Lisbon for Tangier after Paloma's premature death, the difficulties of his mother's personal life, as well as his desire to remarry to have a mother figure for his infant are windows into the generally silent world of intimate family life in Northern Morocco and the central role of women in the foundation of nuclear and extended families. This connection of women to the core of the community's identity comes through clearly in the introduction to his volume on Haketia, where Benoliel clearly highlights the role of women's unification of both rabbinic and Moroccan voices through their melodies, inflections, and themes.

> We can't deny that Haketia has its own, unmistakeable tonality, but it is true that within it two different musical modes predominate. One is Arabic, because most people exercise their activities in commerce or different professions [in it]; the other is the Rabbinic, more restricted but no less important, which literally gives the note (its own, distinctive note that comes from the manner of reading, singing and explaining or discussing Talmudic texts) to a whole social class dedicated to studying and to Rabbinic letters. A foreigner to both, the Jewish woman is the one who has best conserved the musical tradition of the Haquitino dialect, and even if I cannot appreciate the general melodic value of her singing, I can appreciate that it is extremely rich and original in the variety of its tonalities.[29]

---

28   Benoliel's original publications were in a Spanish philological journal and spanned
      many years. Only in 1977 did the Instituto Arias Montano publish his book as
      a stand-alone volume; see José Benoliel, *Dialecto judeo-hispano marroquí o hakitía*
      (Madrid: Instituto Arias Montano, 1977).
29   José Benoliel, 1922, UCLA Special Collections, Collection 1625, Box 10, Folder 1, p. 45.

Benoliel, the first Moroccan Jew to write about Haketia and its oral traditions, explicitly states that it is women who have been able to hybridise both aspects of Moroccan Jewish life—the Arabic and the Rabbinic—within spoken Haketia, which has a Spanish medieval base. His focus on melody and tonality clarifies that it is not only textual material that carried on the vital transmission, but the inflections, the tone and all the many non-verbal elements that happen during speech and song.

The materials collected by Benoliel and his informants, and later Tomás Navarro Tomás' interviews with Sephardim in Larache and Alcazarquivir in 1915–1916, classified each item according to the Catálogo Menéndez Pidal (CMP) in relation to a Peninsular ur-text. This established Spain as the central source of all canonical texts, whether Sephardi or not.

Yet Benoliel's position vis-à-vis the attempts by Spanish scholars to claim the Sephardi heritage as their 'own' and to justify Spanish colonialism in Morocco appears fraught with contradictions. Or, more to the point, to coincide with a maturing of perspective. Towards the end of his life, once he was back in Morocco living within the Tangerine Jewish community, which was at its height during those decades, Benoliel seemed to resist such attempts by claiming a cultural specificity for the Sephardi oral tradition (he does not say it is Spanish; he says it is 'Arab-Rabbinic'). His work from 1922, only eventually fully published posthumously in 1977, shows a Sephardi countering the Spanish attempt to claim Sephardi heritage as their own. Benoliel, who as a member of the Sephardi cultural elite collaborated with these Spanish attempts while he lived in Europe, revisited this approach with his own publication.

Sephardi Women as Singers and Collectors

Tetuan, the capital of the Spanish Protectorate between 1912 and 1956, was home to an active Jewish community, after a group of Judeo-Spanish speaking Jews, following the expulsion from Spain, chose to settle there in 1530 instead of Fez, where a Judeo-Arabic majority had been living for centuries. Those who settled in Tetuan did so to preserve the traditions of the *Megorashim de Castilla*—those who had been expelled from Castile. They were concerned with the survival of their language, their specific liturgical rites and the laws regarding marriage and ritual slaughter of meat. Their connection to the oral traditions that Sephardi women sang was characterised by this anxiety of preservation.

Under the direction of Ramón Menéndez Pidal, Tomás Navarro Tomás included a collection of seven *romances* from the Sephardi community of northern Morocco in a recording project between 1931 and 1933. The *romances* were once again classified under the umbrella of Spanish literature, and were sung by two students from the women's section of the *Residencia de Estudiantes* in Madrid, the *Residencia de Señoritas*, Estrella Sananes and Yochebed Chocron, both from Tetuan. In the recording, Estrella and Yochebed sang the *romances* in unison, as would have been common in the Tetuan's Jewish quarter in the early twentieth century. These recordings take Sephardi women's voices out of their judería-specific context and ownership and stamp them, at the height of the Spanish Protectorate, with the imprimatur of hispanicity and Spanish literature. Both young women later became schoolteachers in the Spanish school system in Morocco and helped gather further romance texts for a Spanish philological project.[30]

If Estrella and Yochebed assisted with and sang for someone else's recording project, Zarita Nahón herself became a collector and a scholar. From an elite family in Tangier, Zarita Nahón studied at Columbia University and had finished her degree before the mid-1920s. Her parents lived in Tangier, and she is found on passenger lists of ships sailing from Gibraltar to New York.[31] Nahón studied Romance philology under anthropologist Franz Boas, a remarkable achievement for a young Sephardi woman from Tangier in that period. Boas encouraged his students to study their own cultures, and in 1929 Boas urged her to document the *romances* of her home community, as he himself was Sephardi and knew that, because of the the activities of the Spanish Protectorate, some of the traditions would be rapidly changing in future decades. Before finalizing the decision and embarking on this project, Boas and Nahón consulted Menéndez Pidal, who by that time was recognised as the world leader on the study of *romances*.

---

30   Paloma Díaz-Mas, 'Cuadernos de *cantares* du recueil des *romances* séfarades du Maroc de Tomás García Figueras' in *Cuadernos de Cantares comme technologies de transmission: Revue Yod*, ed. by Vanessa Paloma Elbaz (Paris: Presses de l'INALCO, forthcoming in 2025).

31   I must thank Noam Sienna for his help in identifying this aspect of her life.

Nahón took a leave of absence from her job as a high school teacher and travelled back to Tangier for six months and reconnected with much of her community, thanks to her mother's help in securing the customary rules of hospitality which then elicited collaboration from the 'best singers of these *romances*'.[32] During this period, Nahón collected a significant number of traditional songs from the repertoire on typewritten letterheads and in her own hand. Back in New York in 1930, Nahón asked her sister Simi Nahón de Toledano to sing a collection of *romances*, wedding songs, lullabies and even a short dialogue in Haketia for a recording, the first ethnographic recording of Jewish music in the Americas.[33]

Nahón's agency as an early elite conduit of global circulation for the safeguarding of her community's feminine oral traditions went against ideas of Spanish ownership of the Sephardi canon, establishing Sephardi culture as more transnational and cosmopolitan, weaving local narratives and needs through the framework of what had come through to them from a distant Spanish history, and evoking the external ring of the graph present earlier in the chapter (Fig. 8.1). This parallel pole of ethnographic musical interest in the work being done in Europe became 'a trend that positioned the folk song in Judeo-Spanish at the center of the musical bounty transferred by the Jews of Islam to America'.[34] However, Nahón was a student of Spanish philology, which practically, if not semiotically, ultimately tethered her project to the framework of *hispanidad*.

The Sephardi elite women from Tangier and Tetuan, the 'pearls' of Northern Morocco's Sephardim discussed in this section, presented their contributions to 'Spain's intellectual history' by committing their oral traditions to contemporary technology. Their voices, considered within their community as the continuation of the voices of their ancestors who were expelled from Spain in 1492, were co-opted by Spanish nation building in the decades in which fascism took hold in Europe and tried to delete their presence. Their contribution to a newly-minted

---

32   Armistead and Silverman, *Romances judeo-españoles de Tánger*, p. 22.
33   Israel Katz, 'The Sacred and Secular Musical Traditions of the Sephardic Jews in the United States', *American Jewish Archives*, 44.1 (1992), 331–356 (p. 335).
34   Edwin Seroussi, 'Third Diaspora Soundscapes: Music of the Jews of Islam in the Americas' in *Mazal Tov, Amigos! Jews and Popular Music in the Americas*, ed. by Amalia Ran and Moshe Morad (Leiden: Brill, 2016), pp. 208–236 (p. 211).

philo-sefardism that celebrated Spain's historical *convivencia*, lost with the Reconquista and the expulsion of non-Catholics, is especially poignant because of the fragile nature of oral traditions, and the fact that they were traditionally preserved by women, who have often been erased from the official narratives. The added element of femininity to the disappearance of oral traditions adds to their vulnerability to co-optation.

The Fashioning of an Anti-Fascist Sephardi Anthem

With the rise of fascism in the 1930s, the philo-sephardism of the nineteenth and early twentieth centuries gave way to rising levels of antisemitism. Sephardi Jews, whose heritage had been celebrated as part of a 'greater Spain', now fell victim to discriminatory accusations of being part of communist, Masonic, and anti-Catholic groups that threatened stability. In pre-World War II Paris, an unlikely composer, German-Jewish refugee Wolf Simoni, composed 'Avraham Avinu' (Abraham our Father), which later became the self-proclaimed musical anthem of Sephardi Jews. Israeli singer Yehoram Gaon recorded it in 1969 using Simoni's arrangement from 1937, and the song became an international hit.[35] However, to complicate matters, the original text of this paralitugical *copla* is found in a manuscript originating in Bosnia in the eighteenth century.[36] Notwithstanding the fame of the song and its lasting and ubiquitous presence in performances in Spain, Morocco, Paris, Israel, and the Americas, the exact origin of the melody remains unidentified. According to ethnomusicologist Edwin Seroussi, who has written extensively about the origin and transformation of this piece,[37] it most probably hails from Northern Morocco's Jewish communities, and he surmises it may be a *zarzuela* melody that came across the strait

---

35   Wolf Simoni, also known as Louis Saguer, was German Jewish refugee of Italian origin who moved to Paris in 1929 and studied composition with Arthur Honneger (1892–1955) and Darius Milhaud (1892–1974).

36   The manuscript was thoroughly studied, notated, and published by leading Spanish philologist Elena Romero from the CSIC; Elena Romero, *Coplas sefardíes. Primera selección* (Córdoba: Edicones El Almendro, 1988), pp. 43–50)

37   Edwin Seroussi, *Ruinas sonoras de la modernidad. La canción popular sefardí en la era post-tradicional* (Madrid: CSIC, 2019), pp. 107–110.

with the Spanish protectorate's cultural diplomacy efforts in the early twentieth century.

A cryptic message by Wolf Simoni within the score of the melody that set the song on its transnational life points to hidden political resistance. His arrangement of Abraham Avinu, the fourth of a set of four Sephardi art songs, was dedicated to the young non-Jewish Spanish composer Gustavo Durán Martínez. Before moving to Paris, Durán had been a member of Spain's *Generación del 27*, a friend of García Lorca, Dalí, Buñuel and Alberti, and had lived in Madrid probably at the elite *Residencia de Estudiantes* (the male version of the hostel attended by the two young Tetuani women a few years later). In the 1920s Durán composed four romances for voice and piano in Judeo-Spanish that he entitled *Romances Castellanos de los Balcanes*, each romance embodying a Sephardi city—Salonica, Sofia, Belgrade, and Constantinople. The musical gaze toward Sephardi cities by a young non-Sephardi composer from the *Generación del 27* demonstrates the broad influence of the musical philosephardi movement that Ramon Menéndez Pidal's *romancero* project had launched in the first decade of the 1900s. But by the time Simoni published his arrangement of Avram Avinu in 1937, Durán had abandoned composition and enlisted in the republican army to fight Franco's fascism. The anthem of Sephardism, then, does not stem from *Hispanidad*, nor does it hark back to the pre-expulsion age. Abraham Avinu, sung worldwide to connect Sephardim from diverse backgrounds, was moulded in anti-fascist Paris from a Bosnian Judeo-Spanish text with a probable late-nineteenth-century *zarzuela* melody taken to Spain by a Jew from northern Morocco. There it was published after being notated and arranged by Simoni, and dedicated to an anti-fascist Spanish military man (whom Simoni may have known during their overlapping Paris years) commanding battles against fascism at the time of publication. To cap it all off, Duran is a Spanish-Jewish family name, meaning that this Spanish composer who became a Republican lieutenant colonel, and later a political strategist for the FBI and eventually a diplomatic representative to the United Nations, could have been a descendant of Crypto-Jews, outwardly Catholic people whose ancestors were forced to convert but who secretly maintain knowledge and/or practice of Judaism.

Epilogue

On many occasions, Sephardim throughout the Mediterranean basin have maintained repertoires no longer extant in the Iberian Peninsula. As the previous section has shown, these diasporic *romances* began to cement a nationalistic idea of a greater Spain with members spread around the world. This idea of a 'greater Spain' remained central throughout the twentieth century. For example, the back cover of a 1989 LP issued by the *Archivo de la Palabra*, which included romances performed by two students from Tetuan recorded in 1932 by Tomas Navarro Tomás, described the recordings as preserving 'something so important for Spain's intellectual history.'[38]

At the same time, contemporary philologists and even some ethnomusicologists are quick to describe local variants of Sephardi romances that stray from the textual model established by Menéndez Pidal and his school as 'truncated,' 'contaminated' or 'incomplete', whether in content or form.[39] Such an approach establishes the 'correct' and 'complete' versions as coming from historic and canonised Spanish sources, legitimizing the complete ownership of the repertoire by Spanish intellectual and literary history. For example, the Romance *Una Hija Tiene el Rey* (The King has a daughter), collected in Oran, Tetuan, and Cuba, is often described by scholars as *La Princesa y el Segador* (The princess and the reaper), and a collapsing of two romances into one. Additionally, Menéndez Pidal's catalogue numbering system is still the only one in use today for Sephardi romance studies. Counter to Menéndez Pidal's own view that the romance 'lives in variants' and its repertoire is 'formed by variants itself' because of its oral foundation, the romance repertoire became canonised as an ossified repertoire. Instead of being a supple, constantly evolving repertoire, incorporating shifts as part of its intertextuality and social commentary, it became positioned in the past of a Spanish imaginary.

---

38   'estas grabaciones que preservaron algo tan importante para la historia intellectual de España'; *Archivo de la Palabra: voces de la edad de plata*, 3 records [trabajos realizados en 1931 por Tomás Navarro Tomás; libro con introducción de] Carlos Alberdi', Madrid: Publicaciones de la Residencia de Estudiantes, 1998.

39   See for example Armistead and Silverman, *Judeo-Spanish Ballads*; Pomeroy, *An Edition and Study of the Secular Ballads*; and Weich-Shahak, *Cantares Judeo Españoles de Marruecos*.

The Jews from northern Morocco who emigrated to the Americas, Spain, and Israel after 1956 have kept their oral traditions, part of a sonic collapse of time and space that connects them to their life in their cities of origin in Morocco. One example is a song written by Lucy Garzón, who emigrated to Venezuela and now lives in Miami, collected and analysed by Susana Weich Shahak.[40] This song in Haketia, about the Moroccan holiday of Timimona, on the day after the end of Passover, is full of multilingual references and uses a contrafactum on the melody of *El Relicario*, made famous by Sarita Montiel in the 1957 film *El último cuplé*. As Sephardim have done for centuries, using Spanish culture as a base to establish not a link to their *hispanidad* but a local attachment to their daily experiences, this example relates to the specificity of mid-twentieth-century Tetuan, allowing us to conclude that the idea of *hispanidad* as the driving impetus behind Sephardi oral traditions is misguided.

> *Un día de Timimona a visitar la familia fuí,*
> *en toa la calle no había un mancebo que me dijera be esh'hal Jolí.*
> *Unos se fueron a la Argentina, a Venezuela o al Brasil,*
> *otros se fueron a Palestina,*
> *diremos Bilbao, pa mor de los goyim.*
> *Y me quedé con mis amigas entre jilaba, Mohamed y Ali.*
> *Patalea Simi, patalea Tamo,*
> *que pa' vestir sefer en Tetuán vamos a quedar,*
> *porque los cuatro que aquí quedaban*
> *pa 'kadearlos se los llevaron los Benalal.*[41]

On a day of Timimona I went to visit the family
In the whole street there was not one young man that would say hello Jolí.
Some went to Argentina, Venezuela or Brazil,
Others left for Palestine,
We'll say Bilbao, for fear of the goyim.
I stayed with my friends between djellabas, Mohammed and Ali.
Kick around, Simi. Kick around, Tamo,
That we'll stay in Tetuan to dress Torah scrolls
Because the four who are left here
On top of it all were taken by the Benalal.

---

40   Shahak (2011), NSA Y6446a/8.
41   Ibid.

The tendency to claim Sephardi heritage as 'Spanish' has lasted until the present day, with the Spanish state again attempting to appropriate this heritage for political reasons—in the nineteenth century, to legitimise their colonisation of Morocco; in the present, to forge closer political and economic ties with the Israeli state. In 2015, Spain offered the descendants of those who suffered expulsion the possibility to apply for Spanish citizenship. Thousands of Sephardim applied, as well as Crypto-Jews from the Americas and Israeli Sephardim who wanted another passport to travel easily to non-Israel-friendly countries. Soon after, in October 2019, the *Real Academia Española* voted to create an Academia Nacional del Judeoespañol based in Israel. This Academy joins twenty-three other similar academies based in countries where Spanish is spoken, establishing Spain as the central hub and 'mother' country for their linguistic and literary culture. The Academia Nacional del Judeoespañol seems to frame oral heritage as text and lyrics rather than performance, which gives an impoverished picture of the tradition. It voted in as president emeritus Professor Ora Schwarzwald, a linguist, thus closing the circle of establishing philology as the way of claiming Sephardim as Spanish cultural subjects, even in the Holy Land.

The latest step in the institutionalisation of Sephardi orature into hispanist scientific study in Spain was in 2022, when a Spanish specialist of Judeo-Spanish orature, Professor Paloma Díaz-Mas, was voted into the Real Academia Española. Interestingly, her inaugural lecture in November 2022 did not relate to poetry and songs of oral tradition, to which she has dedicated most of her career, but to a 120-page medical and scientific text in Judeospanish: *Ciencia en judeoespañol*. This choice, explained by Prof Díaz-Mas with reference to the previous holder of her place in the Academia, a biologist, symbolically implies a hierarchical dissonance between 'real' Spanish literature and Sephardi orature— Sephardi orature cannot simply strut into the most hallowed hall of Spanish science but must slide in surreptitiously, after a non-fictional opening written by sixteenth-century men of science. Women's songs will come later. What was considered a valuable voiced contribution from the community's tradition to a larger body of literary and recording scholarship has been lost in almost complete anonymity until the present day.

However, evidence from Sephardi performers themselves shows that this oral heritage is a way to create or preserve their distinctive group identity in the face of diaspora and persecution, and not to reiterate a long-standing allegiance to Spain. Women's tenacity in the transmission and reinvigoration of this tradition has been neglected and forgotten as the oral–written continuum of the *romancero* tends towards the hegemony of the written over the oral. This exclusion, which I believe carries a heavily gendered bias, is an example of the gendered power relations that regulate both literary scholarship and the transnational circulation of oral and written literary texts. Tropes of *hispanidad* as the literary undercurrent of Sephardi women's orature contradict the lived experience of these local repertoires, which are often firmly tethered to a woman, a family, a city—and never to a nation or political nationalisms, contradicting hegemonic models of world literature and their canonical hierarchical approach towards intimate repertoires.

Bibliography

Abad Nebot, Francisco, 'La escuela de Menéndez Pidal y la tradición del krausismo español', *A distancia*, 1 (2008), 207–2011.

Aflalo, León, *Los muertos de Roni: Crónicas confusas y antiguas, soñadas y verdaderas, de dos familias judías, entre Tánger y Tetuán* (Madrid: Hebraica Ediciones 2004).

Alexander-Frizer Tamar and Yaakov Bentolila, *La palabra en su hora es oro: El refrán judeoespañol en el Norte de Marruecos* (Jerusalem: Instituto Ben-Zvi, 2008).

Alvar, Manuel, *Endechas judeo-españolas*, 2nd ed. (Madrid: Instituto Arias Montano, 1969).

——, *Cantos de boda judeo-españoles* (Madrid: CSIC, 1971).

Archivo de la Palabra: voces de la edad de plata, 3 records [trabajos realizados en 1931 por Tomás Navarro Tomás; libro con introducción de] Carlos Alberdi'. Madrid: Publicaciones de la Residencia de Estudiantes, 1998, http://datos. bne.es/edicion/Miso0000243724.html

Armistead, Samuel and Joseph Silverman, *Romances judeo-españoles de Tánger recogidos por Zarita Nahón* (Madrid: Cátedra-Seminario Menéndez Pidal, 1977).

——, *El romancero judeo-español en el Archivo Menéndez Pidal (Catálogo-índice de romances y canciones)*, 3 vols. (Madrid: C.S.M.P., 1978).

——, *En torno al romancero sefardí* (*Hispanismo y balcanismo de la tradición judeoespañola*) (Madrid: Seminario Menéndez Pidal, 1982).

——, *Judeo-Spanish Ballads from Oral Tradition, I. Epic Ballads* (Berkeley: University of California Press, 1986).

Bénichou, Paul, *Romancero Judeo-Español de Marruecos* (Madrid: Editorial Castalia, 1968).

Benoliel, José, *Dialecto judeo-hispano marroquí o hakitía* (Madrid: Instituto Arias Montano, 1977).

Borne-Varol, Marie-Christine, 'Les Judéo-Espagnols de Turquie et le discours indirect' in *Hommage à Marthe Westphal*, ed. by Raúl Caplan, Marie-Lucie Copete and Isabelle Reck (Nancy: Université Nancy 2, 2001), pp. 151–179.

Calderwood, Eric, 'Moroccan Jews and the Spanish Colonial Imaginary, 1903–1951', *The Journal of North African Studies*, 24.1 (2019), 86–110, https://doi.org/10.1080/13629387.2018.1459261

Cohen, Judith R., '«Ya salió de la mar»: Judeo-Spanish Wedding Songs among Moroccan Jews in Canada' in *Women and Music in Cross-Cultural Perspective*, ed. by Ellen Koskoff (Westport, Connecticut: Greenwood Press, 1987), pp. 55–67.

——, 'Musical Bridges: The Contrafact Tradition in Judeo-Spanish Songs' in *Cultural Marginality in the Western Mediterranean*, ed. by Frederick Gerson and Anthony Perceval (Toronto: New Aurora Editions, 1990), pp. 120–127.

Cohen, Judith R., and Oro Anahory Librowicz, 'Modalidades expresivas de los cantos de boda judeo-españoles', *Revista de Dialectología y Tradiciones Populares*, 41 (1986), 189–209.

Díaz-Mas, Paloma, 'Cuadernos de *cantares* du recueil des *romances* séfarades du Maroc de Tomás García Figueras' in *Cuadernos de Cantares comme technologies de transmission: Revue Yod*, ed. by Vanessa Paloma Elbaz (Paris: Presses de l'INALCO, forthcoming in 2025).

——, 'El Romancero, vínculo entre sefardíes y españoles' in *Rostros judíos del occidente medieval* (Pamplona, Gobierno de Navarra, 2019), 29–52.

——, 'La literatura oral sefardí: balance del pasado y perspectivas de futuro' *BLO*, 1 (2017), 79–109.

——, 'Ramón Menéndez Pidal y la cultura sefardí' in *Lengua y Cultura Sefardí Estudios en Memoria de Samuel G. Armistead*, ed. by Nicolás Asensio Jiménez and Sara Sánchez Bellido (Madrid: Fundación Menéndez Pidal, 2015), pp. 179–2010.

——, 'Las mujeres sefardíes del Norte de Marruecos en el ocaso de la tradición oral', *El Prezente: Studies in Sephardic Culture*, 2 (2008), 255–266.

Díaz-Mas, Paloma and Elisa Martín Ortega, 'Romances y Canciones Sefardíes en la colección de partituras en la biblioteca Tomás Navarro Tomás' in

Actas del XVIII Congreso de Estudios Sefardíes, ed. by Elena Romero, Hilary Pomeroy and Shmuel Refael (Madrid: CSIC, 2017), pp. 55–74, http://hdl.handle.net/10261/160564

Díaz-Mas, Paloma and María Sánchez Pérez, *Los sefardíes y la poesía tradicional hispánica del siglo XVIII: el Cancionero de Abraham Israel (Gibraltar, 1761-1770)* (Madrid: CSIC, 2013).

Diffie, Bailey W., 'The Ideology of Hispanidad', *The Hispanic American Historical Review,* 23.3 (1943), 457–482, https://doi.org/10.2307/2508538

Elbaz, Vanessa Paloma, 'Judeo-Spanish Melodies in the Liturgy of Tangier: Feminine Imprints in a Masculine Space' in *Musical Exodus: Al-Andalus and its Jewish Diasporas,* ed. by Ruth Davis (Lanham: Rowman & Littlefield, 2015), pp. 25–43.

——, 'De tu boca a los cielos: Jewish Women's Songs in Northern Morocco as Oracles of Communal Holiness', *Hesperis-Tamuda,* 51.3 (2016), 239–261.

——, 'Jewish Music in Northern Morocco and the Building of Sonic Identity Boundaries', *Journal for North African Studies,* 27.5 (2021), 1027–1059, https://doi.org/10.1080/13629387.2021.1884855

Frenk Alatorre, Margrit, *Las Jarchas Mozárabes y los comienzos de la lírica románica* (Guanajuato: El Colegio de México, 1975).

Katz, Israel, 'The Sacred and Secular Musical Traditions of the Sephardic Jews in the United States', *American Jewish Archives,* 44.1 (1992), 331–356, http://americanjewisharchives.org/publications/journal/PDF/1992_44_01_00_katz.pdf

Laskier, Michael, 'Aspects of the Activities of the Alliance Israélite Universelle in the Jewish Communities of the Middle East and North Africa: 1860–1918', *Modern Judaism,* 3.2 (1983), 147–171.

Malino, Frances, 'Prophets in Their Own Land? Mothers and Daughters of the Alliance Israélite Universelle', *Nashim: A Journal of Jewish Women's Studies & Gender Issues,* 3 (2000), 56–73.

Marglin, Jessica, 'Modernizing Moroccan Jews: The AIU Alumni Association in Tangier, 1893—1913', *The Jewish Quarterly Review,* 101.4 (2011), 574–603.

Menéndez Pidal, Ramón, 'La primitiva poesía lírica española', *Estudios Literarios* (1919), 255–344.

——, *Los Godos y la Epopeya Española: 'Chansons de Geste' y Baladas Nórdicas* (Madrid: Espasa Calpe, 1956).

——, *Estudios sobre el Romancero* (Madrid: Espasa-Calpe, 1973).

Ojeda Mata, Maite, *Identidades ambivalentes: Sefardíes en la España contemporánea* (Madrid: Sefarad Editores, 2018).

Ortega, Manuel L., *Los Hebreos en Marruecos* (Málaga: Algazara, 1994). Originally published in 1919.

Romero, Elena, *Coplas sefardíes. Primera selección*, with an introduction by Iacob M. Hassán (Córdoba: Edicones El Almendro, 1988).

Pomeroy, Hilary, *An Edition and Study of the Secular Ballads in the Sephardic Ballad Notebook of Halia Isaac Cohen* (Newark, Delaware: Juan de la Cuesta, 2005).

Pulido Fernández, Angel, *Españoles sin Patria y la Raza Sefardí* (Madrid: E. Teodoro, 1905).

——, Letters to José Benoliel, Special Collections of University of California Los Angeles Library. Collection 1625, Box 13, folder 2.

Salama, Messod, '"Yo, Señor, He nacido Hebrea/ y Hebrea Tendré que Morir": Forced Conversion, Religious Conflict, and Female Martyrdom in the Judeo-Spanish Ballad Sol la Saddika' in *Proceedings of the Twelfth British Conference on Judeo-Spanish Studies*, ed. by Hilary Pomeroy and Michael Alpert (Leiden: Brill, 2004), pp. 129–140.

——, 'Judeo-Spanish Romancero as a Source of Women's Spirituality' in *Languages and Literatures of Sephardic and Oriental Jews*, ed. by David Bunis (Jerusalem: Misgave Yerushalayim, 2009), pp. 362–379.

Seroussi, Edwin, 'Third Diaspora Soundscapes: Music of the Jews of Islam in the Americas' in *Mazal Tov, Amigos! Jews and Popular Music in the Americas*, ed. by Amalia Ran and Moshe Morad (Leiden: Brill, 2016), pp. 208–236, https://doi.org/10.1163/9789004204775_015

——, *Ruinas sonoras de la modernidad: La canción popular sefardí en la era posttradicional* (Madrid: CSIC, 2019).

Watroba, Karolina, 'World Literature and Literary Value: Is "Global" The New "Lowbrow?"', *The Cambridge Journal of Postcolonial Literary Inquiry*, 5.1 (2018), 53–68, https://doi.org/10.1017/pli.2017.41

Weich-Shahak, Susana, *Cantares Judeo Españoles de Marruecos para el Ciclo de la Vida* (Jerusalem: The Jewish Music Research Center, 1989).

——, 'Canciones acumulativas sefardíes y congéneres hispánicas', *Revista de Dialectología y Tradiciones Populares*, 50.1 (1995), 73–91, https://doi.org/10.3989/rdtp.1995.v50.i1.301

——, *Un Vergel Vedre* (Zaragoza: Ibercaja, 1995).

——, *Romancero sefardí de Marruecos* (Madrid: Alpuerto, 1997).

——, 'Migration in the Twentieth-Century Sephardic Song Repertoire', *European Judaism*, 44.1 (2011), 136–150, https://doi.org/10.3167/ej.2011.44.01.14

9. Two Tracks

Stories of the Destinies of Two Performative Oratures

Sadhana Naithani

Introduction

The relationship between orality and writing is an enigmatic one. It is generally assumed that oral narratives, songs, and other creative texts do not have anything to do with writing unless they are 'collected' and 'textualized' by folklore collectors and scholars. All modern folklore collectors have perpetuated this image ever since the brothers Wilhelm and Jakob Grimm published their collection of German folk tales in 1812. In Grimms' depiction, oral narratives were like plants that had weathered many storms over the ages and finally, through the work of the Brothers, had come to find a new life in print. This process of transformation was then repeated in many countries and everywhere it unleashed a cultural process with political overtones. In the second half of the nineteenth century, this process of collecting orality and textualizing it became the core of the cultural politics of the British Empire. Textualized orality became the key to understanding, controlling and representing the colonized without reference to the processes of collection and translation themselves. In the process, orality became inextricably connected with tradition, while writing was connected with the modern. This perception still holds. It would not be wrong to say that, in the popular perception, orality belongs to an age gone by or that

    https://doi.org/10.11647/OBP.0405.09

it is only to be found in some far-flung areas and among peoples not yet touched by modernity. This chapter concerns itself with two oratures that defy these popular perceptions about orality and its relationship with writing and tradition, and allow us to propose that they are part of world literature. Both are contemporary because they are regularly performed, and both have their separate histories of performance. I consider them 'oratures' because of their unique relationship to writing and to textuality. In the first case, people believe that its text originated in writing, but the written text got lost. The second case is based on well-known texts that were written down long ago, but its identity comes from the oral performance.

The first orature—*Pandun ke Kade* (Stories of Pandavs), performed by Muslim Jogis of Mewat—is based on research I carried out in 2009–2010 and on continued contact and communication with the performers. The primary research was undertaken in collaboration with film maker Sudheer Gupta and is encapsulated in a documentary film titled *Three Generations of Jogi Umer Farukh*, which should be seen as an audio-visual reference to this chapter.[1] There are many videos of the performers available on the internet; I recommend watching the TedX presentation by Omer Mewati (Umer Farukh) and a performance titled 'Bhapang Jugalbandi'.[2] My research for the second orature, *dastangoi* (storytelling), started in January 2019 and is ongoing. The information here is mainly based on conversations with performers Mahmood Farooqui and Poonam Girdhani in New Delhi. Both performers have several videos on YouTube and on social media. These should also be watched for an independent appraisal of my analysis.[3]

Oratures, Performance, and Folklore

Methodologically, I study oratures and their changing history of performance. The study of performance is an established field in

---

1   Sudheer Gupta, *Three Generations of Jogi Umer Farukh*, film, 54 minutes (New Delhi: Public Sector Broadcasting Trust and Doordarshan, 2010); the links for this and other documentary films and video recordings are given in the Bibliography.

2   TedX *Shekhavati Omer Mewati, Saving Rajathan's Legacy*, April 6, 2011; 'Bhapang Jugalbandi, Strange and Amazing Musical Instrument by Umer Farooq' (2015), YouTube.

3   I recommend the 2014 RSTV Documentary *Dastangoi* by Varun Mehta.

several disciplines, but I derive my perspective and method from the field of folkloristics. While the study of folklore was always aware of 'performance'—because there was no other way of collecting folklore except through performance—analysis remained centred on the texts. For nineteenth-century folklorists, performance was something they viewed, but they were unable to bring it to their readers. Edwin Smith and Andrew Dale were two British collectors of folklore in Northern Rhodesia in the late-nineteenth and early twentieth centuries who were sensitive to the loss of performance details in the printed versions:

> In order to hear these folk-tales effectively, one must hear them in their native setting. [...] Overhead is an inky-black sky dotted with brilliant stars, a slight breeze is moving the tops of the tress, and all is silent save the regular gurgling noise of the calabash pipes, as the men sit or lie around the numerous camp fires within the stockade. Then the narrator will refill his pipe, and start his story: 'Mwe wame! (Mates!)', and at once they are all attention. After each sentence he pauses automatically for the last few words to be repeated or filled in by the audience, and as the story mounts to its climax, so does the excitement of the speaker rise with gesture and pitch of voice [...]. To reproduce such stories with any measure of success, a gramophone record together with a cinematograph picture would be necessary. The story suffers from being put into cold print, and still more does it suffer in being translated into the tongue of a people so different in thought and life.[4]

Today, we have left the gramophone and cinematograph behind, and the audio-visual documentation of performance has become easy and necessary. The history of technology has deeply influenced the study of performance, but folklorists recognize that performance includes more than just the performers. It is a 360-degree study of the performance, the performers and the audience, and the performed text is yet another dimension that defines the performers and the audience. Since the 1970s, the study of folklore performances has grown tremendously. As Richard Bauman puts it,

> The foundations of performance-oriented perspectives in folklore lie in the observations primarily of folktale scholars who departed from the library- and archive-based philological investigations that dominated

---

4   Quoted in Sadhana Naithani, *The Story-Time of the British Empire: Colonial and Postcolonial Folkloristics* (Jackson: University Press of Mississippi, 2010), p. 39.

folk narrative research to venture into the field to document folktales as recounted in the communities in which they were still current.[5]

Several approaches have emerged since the beginning of the nineteenth century. From the romantic notions of people as 'natural performers' to seeing the performance as 'deep play' in anthropology, to current studies of performance of erstwhile oratures as located in contemporary reality, the study of performance has matured in many ways.[6]

I understand oratures as oral texts with well-defined and stable poetic structures and an equally well-established and well-defined genre of performance. This implies that, while being oral, they have maintained structural and narrative continuity. On the one hand, the concept of orature brings them closer to literary texts, but on the other hand their fluidity and adaptability to different contexts and audiences are also recognized. Additionally, such texts have always travelled and changed their appearance according to their location. In several cases they made their transition to written texts long ago. All these features make oratures part of world literature.

I therefore propose a study of oratures that is multi-medial and inter-disciplinary. It needs to be multi-medial because oratures are no longer only oral, performed in face-to-face settings. They are increasingly disseminated through technology, and even face-to-face performances are recorded on camera and then circulated via the internet as edited or unedited shows. This shift does not merely change the mode of communication, but creates new networks of communications between performers, performance, performance-texts, performance-contexts and the audience. These new networks of communication require to be studied separately. As a correlate, world literature cannot only concern itself with the historical folklore or written oratures and their circulation in print, but needs to include the other networks and technologies within its broader imagination of texts and circulation.

---

5   Richard Bauman, 'Performance' in *A Companion to Folklore*, ed. by Regina F. Bendix and Galit Hasan-Rokem (Chichester, UK: Wiley-Blackwell Publishing, 2012), pp. 94–118 (p. 95).

6   For the point about 'natural performers', see Bauman, ibid.; for 'deep play', see Clifford Geertz, 'Deep Play: Notes on the Balinese Cockfight', *The Interpretation of Cultures* (New York: Basic Books, 1973), pp. 412–453.

The study of oratures must be interdisciplinary, as its texts require linguistic and philological approaches, while the performance is conditioned by social and historical factors. We will see in the following how the integrity of performers and performance-text is rendered tenuous by historical conditions, and change cannot be merely explained away as dilution or corruption of a traditional paradigm.

Pandun ke Kade and the Muslim Jogis of Mewat

The first orature under discussion here is the heritage of a Muslim community of performers called Muslim Jogis, who belong to the Mewat region of the state of Rajasthan in India. By several accounts, the community has a history that spans five to six centuries.[7] Interestingly, the oratures they perform are rooted in the epics and religious lores of the Hindus. *Pandun ke Kade* is a shorter version of one of the two major Indian epics, the *Mahabharata*. While it is not possible to give a definite answer as to how Hindu texts came to be performed by Muslim performers, it can perhaps be explained as a liminal tradition between Islam and Hinduism in India.[8] The conversion to Islam in medieval Rajasthan produced such alignments at various levels. In the case of performers, one may surmise that they adopted a new religion but continued their professional practice. The Muslim Jogis of Mewat perform two kinds of texts: narrative songs about the relations between Hindu god Shiva and his spouse Parvati, and an epic. The epic they perform is called *Pandun ke Kade* and it is known to have been composed by a local Muslim poet of the sixteenth century called Saidullah. This composition was a written text, which became popular through the oral narrations by the Jogis. In other words, the written text was entrusted to memory, and slowly its written documentation disappeared. The text itself did not disappear, though, as it continued to be performed. In fact, an entire tradition grew around it, raising the questions: at which time

---

7   See G. D. Gulati, *Mewat: Folklore, Memory, History*, Delhi (Dev Publishers and Distributors, 2013).

8   See Dominique Sila-Khan, *Crossing the Threshold: Understanding Religious Identities in South Asia* (London: IB Tauris, 2004); and Mukesh Kumar, '"The Saints Belong to Everyone": Liminality, Belief and Practices in Rural North India' (unpublished PhD thesis, University of Technology Sidney, 2019).

of the year it will be performed, who will sponsor the narration, who will hear it, and, of course, who will perform it?

The Jogis gained a monopoly over the right to perform *Pandun ke Kade.* We do not know whether their right was ever contested, whether the poet wrote just for them, or whether they emerged as a group once they received this text. Whatever the process, the sixteenth-century poet passed away but his text continues to exist. And not only the text, but reference to the written document, the orature, is also continuously made orally, although it is not to be found anywhere. It is a classic case of orality making the written redundant, instead of the other way around. The community of Jogis gained a professional identity through the text and its performance: they became known as the group of people who play a one-stringed instrument called *bhapang* and perform in villages and temples in the region. They continued to pass the text on to the next generation through memory.

The Jogis' social identity was that of performers who earned their livelihood through performance. For that, they were dependent on the village folk, farmers, and landlords. The landlords were seen as sponsors, patrons, and mentors, because they could organize performance on a village scale. This is a hierarchical relationship, and the performers were placed near bottom of the social scale. Educated, modern and urban scholars have christened such performers 'folk performers'. However, they remained largely out of the purview of modern patrons and audiences until the second half of the twentieth century, when changes in the pattern of rural social structure influenced the lives of these performers in ways that have yet to be documented. At the time when modern scholars and institutions started characterizing these performers as folk performers, popular cinema became all-pervasive. While there is no causal connection between social change, scholarship, and mass entertainment provided by cinema, yet they are contemporaneous and influence each other.

In independent, postcolonial India of the 1960s, community life as well as the performance of Muslim Jogis had to contend with new challenges. Although located in the specific context of postcolonial India, these processes can be seen in other societies as well, particularly in postcolonial societies where independence from colonial rule was followed by the creation of a civil society and where performance traditions belonged to pre-colonial social structures that had been damaged, destroyed, erased and re-evaluated in colonial times. These postcolonial societies had to contend with tradition, and critique of tradition, to be able to evolve into independent nations. For example, the critique of the caste system in India led to the formulation of a constitution that negated the caste system as a defining element of social structures. Folk performers and their patrons related to each other within the caste system; its negation opened up new possibilities, but also took away its former security. This complex process can be illustrated by the history of a family of Muslim Jogis, told here in the form of a parable.

Jogi Zahoor Khan had *bhapang* in his blood. He played it even when he was sent to school. He went to school, but did not go very far in his studies. As a young man, he started to play his *bhapang* and sell cigarettes and *bidis* outside the cinema hall of his small town to supplement the meagre and dwindling income he received from traditional performance in the village. Hindi cinema, on the other hand, was drawing huge crowds, and any business outside the cinema hall would thrive. One day a film premiered there and the film crew came all the way from Bombay. Outside the cinema hall they heard the *bhapang* of Jogi Zahoor Khan and saw this cigarette seller playing a musical instrument. The music caught their attention and they asked the performer to come along with them to the tinsel town of the film industry—Bombay, now Mumbai. And off he went, on a course that would break all hitherto existing boundaries of fame.[9]

No matter how far the fame of a folk performer spreads, it still remains local, while fame earned through the film industry knows no boundaries. No wonder, then, that the hit songs in which Jogi Zahoor Khan's *bhapang* was heard across the nation also came back to his village. Until now, people of his generation and those younger than him remember the elation they felt as he reached unprecedented heights. This elation had a logical extension—the realization of the possibility that their art could find new vistas.

---

9   See Malini Nair, 'The secret ingredient to Bollywood's funny songs was a unique drum played by a distinctive man', *Scroll.in, 30* August 2023; the *bhapang* can be heard in the song 'De Data Ke Naam Tujhko Allah Rakhe', *Ankhen* (dir. Ramanand Sagar), music by Ravi, lyrics by Sahir Ludhianvi (1968).

What was happening in Zahoor's life was more than his personal success: two historical periods, two technologies and two art forms had collided with each other. Zahoor standing outside a cinema hall and playing the *bhapang* is an image that may show his powerlessness and cinema's power, but that is only the view on the surface. Zahoor and his art were actually exceeding the limitations of tradition, and the events that followed demonstrate the implications of this exit for the orature of the Jogis.

Popular cinema had used his musical instrument and his ability as a player, but not the songs and stories that the *bhapang* accompanied. The musical instrument was disconnected from the stories and the songs, and from the community of brothers and cousins who narrated or sang them. The oral epic was left behind in the village, too. It is as if the modern disjunction between tradition and the self was executed through the life of Zahoor Khan. The text did not travel to the film industry, not because there was no place for it there, but because that place was occupied by the classical version of the epic. The twists and turns in Zahoor's life are moments in India's cultural history that otherwise remain invisible to the naked eye.

Around the same time, a few years later, an urban, educated folklore enthusiast emerged as a new local patron for folk performers in Rajasthan, Komal Kothari. Along with his friend and writer Vijaydan Detha, Kothari founded Rupayan Sansthan in Borunda village to document Rajasthani folklore.[10] Zahoor Khan and his growing son, Umer Farukh, were some of the folk performers he patronized. On the one hand, then, the performers were experiencing a disjunction from tradition. On the other hand, almost simultaneously a folklorist came and evaluated the wholesomeness of the tradition and wanted to present it to the world as 'traditional folklore'. As if acknowledging the irony, young Umer sang a song in a private gathering at Kothari's house about the influence of fashion on young Jogis and their desire to abandon their traditional profession and become urbane and educated.[11]

Despite the opportunities in the film industry, or the possibility of becoming a symbol of traditional culture through identification by

---

10 For a profile of Komal Kothari and his work, see Rustom Bharucha, *Rajasthan: An Oral History. Conversations with Komal Kothari* (New Delhi: Penguin India, 2003).

11 See Gupta, *Three Generations*, 00:40–01:40.

a folklorist, the disjunction between the community and individual, between patrons and performers, between texts and sounds, and between music and musical instrument could not be contained. This was not intended: the disjunction had been caused by a combination of circumstance and chance within the larger frame of history. The performance at Kothari's home shows the transformation that was taking place within the community wherein youngsters were, in any case, feeling attracted to other, more urban lifestyles and professions.

The song that Zahoor's young son Umer Farukh was singing about 'fashion' in society was his own composition. The song itself is a record of social change, including the change in the self-perception of Jogis— that Jogis youngsters want to become 'gentlemen' and not performers. Indeed, awareness about school was spreading, and education was seen as a way to move out of caste-based professions and raise one's social and economic status. Umer himself was going to school. His father and uncles were mainly performers of the epic and songs, and he was exposed to them too, but he was also realizing the need to create texts that would work with wider audiences. Living between two worlds, Umer graduated from college and joined a clerical position (*naukri*) in the government. But he left his *naukri* soon to continue his life as a performer. Like his father, Umer also started playing on public radio, where there was a policy decision to create space for folk music. In this he was exemplary, as many of his community were lured by the promise of a small but stable income, certainly more than that which came from performance.

Another new phenomenon emerged for Umer's generation: around the 1970s, the world of festivals—national festivals, folk festivals, regional arts and crafts festivals, etc.—started. These were new venues for performance, drawing new kinds of audience. In these new venues, a fissure between text and performance inevitably developed, for the text was limited by language while the performance and music were not. As a result, the performance of the text remained more important in the local and traditional venues, but in new venues the universal language of the performer's style and music became the centre of attention.

New venues demanded 'traditional yet modern' performances, for which Umer Farukh had the talent. He combined the old with his own new creations: he knew the epic, the songs, but could also create new songs, fusing them with the contemporary discourse of a democratic society.[12] He was a success, perhaps bigger than his father as he was not dependent on another industry. Festivals became more international, and Umer, his uncles and cousins started roaming the world. He remained active in this circuit and carved out a small-town life for his family. His son Yusuf went to school, and after completion was trained in computers and wanted to change his profession, while also documenting his granduncles on a video camera that my film maker husband presented to him. Destiny had other plans, and Umer Farukh suddenly passed away in 2017 during a performance.

This brought his son Yusuf back to performance, as a stable income was already carved out by his father and he was familiar with all the circuits of this profession. For the last three years or so, Yusuf has taken on the role of his father as the lead singer of the group made up of his uncles and grand uncles. He not only looks increasingly like his father and sings his compositions, but also uses all the stage tricks, jokes, and commentaries that his father used. Decades of stage performance and the experiences of two generations before him have certainly increased the group's self-awareness as performers and as members of civil society. Yusuf's original additions are two: his engagement with the technology of his time—the new media—and establishing newer forms of community building. He is very active on Facebook, where he not only posts pictures of his every performance and of every newspaper article mentioning him, but also keeps in touch with each and every 'patron' that has appreciated his father, for example the officials of the public and private cultural institutions that have ever supported them, or people like Sudheer and me who became friends while researching the Jogis.

Yusuf's performances now include members of other performing communities. This cutting across community lines is a new phenomenon that has emerged, once again, due to several factors. On the one hand, performers do not really have large communities any more as most of the community members have moved on to other professions, and quite

---

12 See the song Umer Farookh and his *bhapang* group perform for a festival in Gupta, *Three Generations*, 03:00 onwards, where Umer also explains about being a Muslim Jogi and his relationship with the *bhapang*, and mentions the film song 'Data de' for which his father had played.

often the performers function as several families combined. On the other hand, festivals often create spaces that never existed in reality, bringing performers of different genres on the same stage in one evening. Urban audiences also expect 'variety' in cultural events. In the process, the performers have realized that they can themselves create new styles by coming together, and gain more traction and bargaining power with the sponsors as a result. One may either lament such changes as the loss of wholesome tradition, or one may come to the realization that folk performers have always responded creatively to the challenges of their times, because their art form is also the source of their livelihood. The coming together of performers of different communities also breaks down barriers of caste, religion, and gender, and as such is certainly a feature of civil society.

In orature of this kind, learning is mimetic, and it is over time that a performer makes his individual mark. Yusuf's grandfather made a mark by rising up to the occasion that sheer chance presented him with. His father made his mark by his ability to perform in traditional as well as non-traditional circuits of national and international festivals, which required more than just artistic ability: it required developing successful public relations among the educated, governmental, and international sponsors for which the tradition had not exactly prepared him. Yusuf is presently functioning within the networks established by his father, but will have to establish an independent relationship with the times in which he is living.

Dastan and Dastangoi: A Revival

The second orature that I want to discuss is called *dastangoi*, literally 'storytelling'. Rooted in various traditions of narrating stories in Iran and connected with forms of storytelling in Afghanistan, *dastangoi* is an Indian tradition of narrating stories that emerged in Mughal India and found its expression in the Persian-Urdu-Hindi languages. It is essentially a multi-lingual tradition whose exact contours are determined by the geographical location and defined by its style. *Dastangoi* flourished in both the courts and the streets of Mughal India.[13] A single individual,

---

13   See Frances W. Pritchett, *The Romance Tradition in Urdu: Adventures from the Dāstān of Amīr Hamzah* (New York: Columbia University Press, 1991) and website.

sometimes accompanied by one more, would narrate stories to small groups of listeners. They might also do so by invitation for a family. Both men and women have been known as narrators or *dastango* (*dāstān-go*), as they are called. We need only think of Sheherazade of the Arabian Nights, who is also a storyteller.

Unique to this style of storytelling is that the human voice is the only medium of communication. The dastango was not accompanied by any musical instrument. As a result, it is the play of language and modulation of voice that communicated the stories. And what did the dastangos narrate? They depended on repertoires of Persian origin, most famously the *Dāstān-e Amīr Ḥamzah*, which is a quasi-epic containing hundreds of stories revolving around Amir Hamza, believed to have been the uncle of the Prophet Muhammad. This style of stories is rooted in oral traditions of wondrous tales akin to the style of the Arabian Nights, with fantastic stories full of marvel, partly history, partly imagination. Several dastan texts became available in print in the nineteenth century, like the monumental, multi-volume *Dāstān-e Amīr Ḥamzah* (1881–1906) published by the famous Naval Kishore of Lucknow. The vibrant tradition of *dastangoi*, however, came to an end in the early twentieth century, and after 1928 no one is known to have participated in the tradition.[14]

After a complete break of many decades, the late-twentieth-century Indian scholar Shamsur Rahman Faruqi, inspired by the work of his American colleague Frances Pritchett, started researching the Urdu *Dastan-e Amir Hamza* and the tradition of *dastangoi*. His work inspired his nephew Mahmood Farooqui to think further. Mahmud Farooqui is a postcolonial Indian with school- and university-level qualifications, and in the 1990s he was pursuing higher studies in history at Oxford and Cambridge. As he himself told me, his knowledge of the Urdu language was minimal at that time. He had had some interest in theatre, but not at a professional level. Yet, inspired by the stories about the storytelling tradition of *dastangoi*, back in India he decided to experiment with it. Frances Pritchett had scanned the available sources and written in some detail about the *dastangoi* tradition in late-nineteenth and early-twentieth centuries.[15] The practice was liveliest in four cities: Delhi, Lucknow,

---

14   See ibid.
15   Ibid., p. 3.

Akbarabad (Agra), and Rampur. Each city claimed to have a unique style, but Lucknow's was perhaps the most vibrant. Yet, the available details related to a dastango are those of Mir Baqir Ali of Delhi. Born in 1850, he lived until 1928 and is the last known dastango. Dastangos were famous for narrating one story over days, weeks, or even years. At Mir Baqir Ali's house, people gathered every Saturday evening, and the narration went on until late in the night. Pritchett summarises from the available accounts that:

> a few basic devices of oral dastan recitation can be pieced together: mimicry and gestures, to imitate each dastan character; insertion of verses into the narrative; recitation of catalogues, to enumerate and evoke all items of a certain class as exhaustively as possible; maximum prolongation of the dastan as an ideal goal. Moreover, the association of dastan-narration with opium is mentioned in so many contemporary accounts that it should not be overlooked. If both dastan-go and audience were slightly under the influence of opium, they might well enjoy the long catalogues and other stylized descriptive devices, which slowed down the narrative so that it could expand into the realms of personal fantasy.[16]

This gives us a glimpse of the art of *dastangoi*, but the information is at best 'fragmentary'.

Pritchett then felt that 'dastan-narration as an oral art is essentially beyond our reach. We are several generations removed from the last expert practitioner, and the secrets of his art died with him. No folklorist ever made a transcript—much less, of course, a tape recording—of an oral dastan performance'.[17] In the late twentieth century, one was dependent on fragments of information about the art of dastangos and on the published repertoire of *dastangoi* tradition. Still, Mahmood decided to give it a go, and in 2005 he began to narrate dastans. Before that, however, several decisions had to be made.

The study of this process is a study of what it means to revive a tradition. Mahmood could not have revived the intimate, small group setting of the *dastangoi* tradition. Therefore, he could not have revived the place of the narrator sitting at the same level among the listeners, nor can today's sessions last interminably. With his interest in theatre,

---

16   Ibid.
17   Ibid.

he immediately imagined it as a stage performance. What he took from the *dastangoi* tradition were the costume of the narrator, the text, and the human voice as the only medium of communication. He started narrating selections from the Amir Hamza repertoire as dastangos used to do.

Right from the beginning it worked with the audience as authentic *dastangoi*—people were willing to listen to a story being told by a person sitting on stage and believe that they were experiencing the historical form of *dastangoi*. There was perhaps some cultural memory that helped the performer and the audience in subconscious ways. Media reports were favourable enough, and Mahmood could continue his experiment. He started realizing that while the form of storytelling is attractive to contemporary audiences, traditional texts have their limitations: they cannot be appreciated by everyone because of their linguistic style and because of the content of their stories, which sometimes clashes with contemporary sensibilities. So, he decided to compose his own stories, and thus emerged stories located in the Indian context: stories about the partition of India, about Buddha, about characters from the epic Mahabharata. Then came stories from international literature, like *Alice in Wonderland* or *The Little Prince*. More people joined him and the style started evolving. Then a woman called Poonam Girdhani, also a trained theatre actor, approached him and said 'will this remain just a male tradition?'. Mahmood included her in the group, and today she is another senior member. In fact, today there are even younger women in the group.

Easy as it sounds, many complexities are involved in this revival: of language, religion, region and politics. Traversing them requires considerable engineering. I have watched Mahmood Farooqui's narration of the story of Karna from the Hindu epic *Mahabharat*.[18] Karna, the illegitimate son of the heroes' mother Kunti, was wronged by the laws of Hindu society right from his birth. He was abandoned by his mother; he was born upper caste but grew up in a lower caste family; he disguised himself as a Brahmin because he wanted to learn archery from the master who only taught Brahmin caste boys and was discovered and cursed; finally, a very generous and righteous Karna joined the

---

18   For a brief extract, see Dastangoi, 'Dastan-e-Karn az Mahabharat'.

villains. Mahmood Farooqui narrates the travails of this character from the perspective of a secular and post-modern artist. He is certainly not limited within the bounds of traditional *dastangoi*. Stylistically, Mahmood takes from other narrative traditions rooted in styles practiced by Hindu narrators, and he mixes languages; Sanskrit, Hindi and Urdu. At times, he begins his performance by saluting the Hindu and the Muslim divinities. In a way, this is not a completely unknown style, since all classical musicians, including Muslim musicians and singers, start their performance by praying to Hindu gods and goddesses. What we see in Mahmood Farooqui's performance is a continuity of cultural nuances, but also a postcolonial form of *dastangoi* infused by ideas of Indo-Islamic syncretic traditions and post-independence constitutional secular discourse.

Tradition, Orature and World Literature

This brief description of two traditional oratures and their contemporary existence allows us to reflect upon three categories and their relationship to each other: tradition, orature and world literature. The two performative traditions were originally the product of the contact between Persian-Islamic and Indian-Hindu traditions of texts and performance. The Muslim Jogis of Rajasthan are located along the route through which the Sultans, Sufis, and traders brought Islam to India. They and their traditional patrons—the farmers and landlords—converted to Islam over the past millennium but continued to hold on to the stories of their Hindu epics, gods and goddesses. Although it has not been ascertained by any research, it is well worth asking the question whether Jogis were already professional narrators who earned their living by telling stories of the epics and of God Shiva, and conversion just made them Muslim Jogis. While they are practicing Muslims, other Jogis in the same region are Hindu, and each has its own specific, generally religious, repertoire. Their professional and religious identities could peacefully co-exist until the end of the twentieth century, but became problematic with the rise of religious fundamentalisms as both Hindus and Muslims started objecting to this happy combination. Their performative tradition continues, but the need to reinvent is also acute. While the musical instrument, music, and style of performance communicate with contemporary audiences, the audiences are not educated in the textual tradition. Performance venues have also changed in spite of themselves. These venues have emerged in the context of international discourses on heritage and its preservation by governmental and non-governmental organisations, both nationally and internationally. In the case of *dastangoi*, a conscious revival effort has been made. Here too, it was more feasible to revive the performance style than the traditional texts, and the textual repertoire had to be reinvented.

The geographies of performance have changed for both oratures, as their current venues of performance are not traditional—totally non-traditional in the case of *dastangoi*, and increasingly non-traditional in the case of the Muslim Jogis. Despite the differences in the context and identity of their performers, the two oratures are clearly proceeding on two tracks that share many similarities in the abstract.

These two ethnographies allow us to theorize about the form and content of oratures. The forms and contents of oratures may travel long distances, that is, they may have come from places far away from where they are found by the researcher. They may not even have any existence in the so-called place of origin. Their full growth may have been achieved in an unprecedented form in the place where we find them. For example, *dastangoi* must be seen as an Indian orature, although its texts may be rooted in a foreign landscape. On the other hand, the historical context of people may change and yet their orature may remain connected to a pre-existing tradition, as in the case of the Jogis. The relationship of form and content may change further in connection with historical time, as reflected in the contemporary forms of the two oratures discussed in this chapter. Processes of entextualization and recontextualization are visible throughout. Based on these two examples, one can say that the form and content of oratures are independent of each other. Content, meaning the texts, stories, language, and reception, is rooted in socio-historical context. Form, meaning the style of performance, music, and costume, is timeless and can take on new content. When the form takes on new content, as when *dastangos* start performing *The Little Prince* or *Alice in Wonderland* or when the Jogis start singing new compositions, the orature gains a new child that is genetically connected to its older self but has a life of its own. In both the oratures discussed above, the performers feel the need to change the content of their oratures or to create new texts for the form in which they are trained as part of a tradition, or for the traditional form which they choose to adopt and adapt after a historical break in the tradition. At the core of the oratures and their performance is communication between performers, performance texts, audience, and context.

The relationship between tradition, orature and world literature is reflected in the two performative traditions discussed in this chapter. Although they have different trajectories of existence, yet there are many processes that are comparable. In their traditional forms, they were performing texts that were international in their spread. The *Adventures of Amir Hamza* performed by the dastangos was a story known across Asia, particularly West and South Asia, and it was also translated in several European languages.[19] The epic composed by a Muslim poet for the Jogis in the sixteenth century was a retelling of the epic *Mahabharat*, also well-known across South, South-east and West Asia, and also translated into many European languages and acclaimed as a classic of world literature. Since these texts were essentially orally transmitted, they crossed several geographic, linguistic, religious, and cultural boundaries over a long time. In their travels they influenced several communities and cultures, and they themselves been influenced and reshaped by the communities and cultures with which they came into contact. They have existed as written and as oral texts; they have been read and they have been performed. Before the differentiation between folklore and literature was articulated in the early nineteenth century and then carried over to other continents in the context of colonialism, these oratures held a place similar to literature in their cultural contexts. The modern differentiation came about mainly based on the medium of communication—oral versus written. This differentiation was not even valid in several cultural contexts. For example, in India, classical arts and learning were also transmitted largely orally, although written and authored texts existed and were written and read. It is well-known that, in the colonial contexts, prioritising writing as symbolic of cultural superiority was advantageous to the colonizers as the colonized countries of Africa, Asia, Latin America, Australia, and Canada were predominantly oral cultures.[20] By implication, written literature became

---

19   See Pritchett, *The Adventures*.
20   See Naithani, *The Story-Time*; Briggs and Naithani, 'The Coloniality of Folkloristics'.

superior to oratures, and the latter could be kept out from world literature. By further implication, the list of world literature texts will be dominated by European literature. Postcolonial theory would see this as continuance of colonial paradigms, or what Walter D. Mignolo terms 'coloniality'.[21] It compels us to challenge this division between folklore and literature.

Orality as the medium of communication and the absence of an identifiable individual author are not weaknesses of oratures; they are their strengths that give them the dynamic energy to adapt to changing times, to metamorphose, and to experience revival after long historical breaks. The important thing is whether oratures are in circulation, whether they are still valuable, and whether, if no longer in circulation, they have historical value. The oratures behind these performative traditions continue to circulate across the world in many different forms and at many different levels, and each new technology, be it print or cinema or new media, attracts performers who are drawn to present these oratures according to its aesthetic capabilities.

To sum up, the relationship between tradition, orature and world literature is a dynamic one, as opposed to the common perception of it as static. This relationship keeps changing with reference to local and global history. It demands the expansion of the definition of world literature, from being a canon of unchanging written texts to include creative oral texts that have taken from and given to world cultures. A changed definition and the inclusion of oratures in world literature would also help in the preservation, revival, evaluation and dissemination of long-standing oratures, of which the versified oral epic *Pandun ke Kade* and the many *dastans* are examples.

Bibliography

Baumann, Richard, 'Performance' in *A Companion to Folklore*, ed. by Regina F. Bendix and Galit Hasan-Rokem (Chichester, UK: Wiley-Blackwell Publishing, 2012), pp. 94–118.

Bharucha, Rustom, *Rajasthan: An Oral History. Conversations with Komal Kothari* (New Delhi: Penguin India, 2003).

---

21   Walter D. Mignolo, *Local Histories/Global Designs: Coloniality, Subaltern Knowledges and Border Thinking* (Princeton: Princeton University Press, 2000).

'Bhapang Jugalbandi, Strange and Amazing Musical Instrument by Umer Farooq' (2015), https://www.youtube.com/watch?v=U9FywkzWERQ

Briggs, Charles and Sadhana Naithani, 'The Coloniality of Folkloristics: Towards a Multi-Genealogical Practice of Folkloristics', *Studies in History*, 28.2 (2012), https://doi.org/10.1177/025764301348

Dāstān-e Amīr Hāmzah (Lucknow: Naval Kishor Press, 1881–1906).

Dastangoi, 'Dastan-e-Karn az Mahabharat', https://www.youtube.com/watch?v=8S-puxBzIGA

'De Data Ke Naam Tujhko Allah Rakhe', *Ankhen* (dir. Ramanand Sagar), music by Ravi, lyrics by Sahir Ludhianvi (1968), https://www.youtube.com/watch?v=b9m-TMNbRCs

Geertz, Clifford, 'Deep Play: Notes on the Balinese Cockfight' in *The Interpretation of Cultures* (New York: Basic Books, 1973), pp. 412–453.

Gulati, G. D., *Mewat: Folklore, Memory, History* (Delhi: Dev Publishers and Distributors, 2013).

Gupta, Sudheer, *Three Generations of Jogi Umer Farukh*, film, 54 minutes (New Delhi: Public Sector Broadcasting Trust and Doordarshan, 2010), https://cultureunplugged.com/storyteller/Sudheer_Gupta

Kumar, Mukesh, '"The Saints Belong to Everyone": Liminality, Belief and Practices in Rural North India' (unpublished PhD thesis, University of Technology Sidney, 2019), http://hdl.handle.net/10453/134150

Mehta, Varun, *Dastangoi*, RSTV Documentary (2014), https://www.youtube.com/watch?v=_GFsOa2a3Q4

Mignolo, Walter D., *Local Histories/Global Designs: Coloniality, Subaltern Knowledges and Border Thinking* (Princeton: Princeton University Press, 2000).

Nair, Malini, 'The secret ingredient to Bollywood's funny songs was a unique drum played by a distinctive man', *Scroll.in*, 30 August 2023, https://scroll.in/magazine/1045905/what-made-bollywood-songs-funny-a-unique-drum-played-by-a-distinctive-man

Naithani, Sadhana, *The Story-Time of the British Empire: Colonial and Postcolonial Folkloristics* (Jackson: University Press of Mississippi, 2010).

Pritchett, Frances W., *The Romance Tradition in Urdu: Adventures from the Dāstān of Amīr Hamzah* (New York: Columbia University Press, 1991). For an augmented translation, see: http://www.columbia.edu/itc/mealac/pritchett/00litlinks/hamzah/index.html

Sila-Khan, Dominique, *Crossing the Threshold: Understanding Religious Identities in South Asia* (London: IB Tauris, 2004).

TedX *Shekhavati Omer Mewati, Saving Rajathan's Legacy*, 6 April 2011, https://www.youtube.com/watch?v=4ObtOH_wPRs

10. Morocco's Popular Culture Powerhouse

Darija and the *chaabi* music of Nas El Ghiwane

Karima Laachir

This chapter shows, through the example of the Moroccan musical group Nas El Ghiwane, how contemporary *chaabi* (popular) music has reinvented the literary language of Darija, the spoken form of Moroccan Arabic. Nas El Ghiwane was established in 1970 and is credited not only with revolutionising the aesthetics of Darija and pioneering a new genre of popular music (*Ghiwanian* song) but also with initiating a popular social and political movement towards freedom in the 1970s and 1980s, an era popularly known in Morocco as 'the years of lead' and marked by brutal political oppression. Despite singing in vernacular Darija and drawing on localised aesthetics and politics, Nas El Ghiwane attained regional and global fame.

The name Nas El Ghiwane refers to the 'new Dervishes'.[1] The Ghiwane were an ancient Sufi sect of wandering musicians who sang throughout Morocco, entertaining the popular classes and transmitting religious knowledge and wisdom. In fact, the group's use of storytelling through

---

1   The name comes from a *malhun* poem: 'I asked the jasmine about you / I asked the rose / I asked the friends of Ghiwane about you' (Ghiwane meaning 'love' or 'passion'); Elias Muhanna, 'Folk the Kasbah: A Conversation with Omar Sayyed, Leader of Nass El Ghiwane', *Transition*, 94 (1993) 132–149 (p. 143).

     https://doi.org/10.11647/OBP.0405.10

song draws heavily on Morocco's popular Sufi poetry and performative traditions of folk tales and proverbs, as well as the sounds, rhythms, and repertoire of *Gnawa* (African-Moroccan) music. The group elevated a plural literary Darija and promoted forms of music that cut across regions and social classes.[2] Their subtle and sophisticated lyrics spoke directly to a nation in search of its soul at a time of political upheaval and rapid social change. Nas El Ghiwane's music shows that although Darija is co-constituted with Arabic Fusha (formal, literary Arabic) and Tmazight (a language of the indigenous people of the region), as well as with other languages in Morocco, it has its own literary imaginary that has been a powerhouse of Morocco's popular oral culture.

The success and trajectory of Nas El Ghiwane point to the ways in which intensely local oral vernacular cultural forms can come to have broader national, regional and global resonances, expanding our notions of what constitutes world literature. The group's global reach draws attention to the 'need to shift the dominant understanding of "the world" in world literature beyond "world-system" macro-models that assume a universally shared set of literary values and tastes with Europe and the US at the centre'.[3] It highlights the importance of aesthetics and values that may appear other and marginal, but that travel widely and circulate globally.

Why Vernacular Darija?

The oral and written cultures of Morocco have been profoundly shaped by the country's long history of multilingualism. Vernacular languages such as Darija and Tmazight, which are in fact the mother tongues of the vast majority of Moroccans, have traditionally existed alongside Arabic

---

2   As Morocca. critic/scholar Muhammad Hannun put it, 'We became open, through [Nass El] Ghiwane, to the truth of their message –that our colloquial Arabic has its words and its images, and their ability to rise to beauty and the construction of it, as well as the [ability to] capture what we did not believe it could capture', quoted in Melanie Magidow, 'Trending Classic: The Cultural Register of Moroccan Malhun Poetry', *The Journal of North African Studies*, 21.2 (2016), 310–334 (p. 326), https://doi.org/10.1080/13629387.2016.1130943

3   Further examples and discussion on this point can be found in Karima Laachir 'The Literary World of the North African Taghrība Novelization, Locatedness and World Literature', *Journal of World Literature*, 4 (2019), 188–214 (p. 11), https://doi.org/10.1163/24056480-00402004

Fusha—the modernised form of classical or Quranic Arabic taught in schools across the Middle East and used in print culture, media and religious affairs—as well as Judeo-Arabic and Judeo-Spanish.[4] With the arrival of the French and Spanish colonial powers in the early twentieth century, the linguistic landscape of Morocco was further complicated. The imposition of French as the exclusive language of education and administration during the period of French colonialism (1912–56), had a deep and lasting impact on Moroccan culture.[5] In the aftermath of independence in 1956, the Moroccan state's ambiguous politics of Arabisation did not succeed in dislodging the French language from the public sphere. To the present day, French has retained its status as an urban language of the educated middle and upper classes, even if in recent decades it has been partially supplanted by English as the language of trade and business.

Morocco's multilingual society is fragmented along lines of class, regionalism, ethnicity and, particularly in recent decades, ideology. Languages have come to embody the ideological identity of those who wield them. As such, a linguistic divide maps over widening ideological rifts within the Moroccan intelligentsia and Moroccan society more broadly. Arabic Fusha, Darija and French have each, respectively, come to be associated with particular political, social and cultural orientations. Such arbitrary oppositions between the diverse languages of Morocco have acted to obscure political, cultural, and linguistic nuances and complexities. Arabic Fusha, for instance, is widely held to be the language of so-called regressive or Islamist forces. French, by contrast, is imaginatively linked to the progressive, the secular, the democratic and the western. In some circles, Arabic Fusha is viewed as '*la langue de bois*', a 'wooden language' that does not allow cultural or literary creativity. As such, it is allegedly responsible for the crisis in Morocco's educational system. This is an allegation that betrays both an internalisation of orientalist tropes with respect to Arabic and an ignorance of the failures of the postcolonial state to implement viable multilingual strategies in

---

4   Moha Ennaji, 'Aspects of Multilingualism in the Maghreb', *International Journal of the Sociology of Language*, 87 (1991), 7–26, https://doi.org/10.1515/ijsl.1991.87.7; and *Multilingualism, Cultural Identity, and Education in Morocco* (New York: Springer Science + Business Media, 2005).

5   Spencer D. Segalla, *The Moroccan soul: French education, colonial ethnology, and Muslim resistance, 1912-1956* (Lincoln: University of Nebraska Press, 2009).

education that would accommodate Tmazight, Darija, Fusaha as well as French and English.[6]

This disdain towards Arabic Fusha—sometimes viewed as the Latin of Arabic— and the flawed argument by which it is held responsible for the manifold problems within the Moroccan education system, has seen calls made to replace it with Darija in public schools. Notwithstanding such calls, and despite the rich oral cultural heritage of Morocco's vernacular languages, both Darija and Tmazight have been relegated to the margins. Neither language is imbued with any sort of symbolic, cultural, or economic prestige.[7] 'In post-independence Morocco (1960–1980s)', Catherine Miller notes, 'several important journals (either francophone like *Souffle, Lamalif, Intégral* or arabophone like *Afāq, al-Asās, al-Thaqāfa al-jadīda*) acted as fora for the Moroccan intelligentsia/artists and addressed the issue of what should be the 'Moroccan national culture, the role and place of language, education, oral literature, popular culture, arts, etc.' Yet the attitude of these intellectuals toward Darija was just as ambiguous.[8] While current debates on the respective merits of Fusha and Darija have pitted the two languages against each other, the relationship of Arabic Fusha to Darija or spoken Arabic (also called 'Amiyya) is in fact complex and, across the Arabic-speaking world, intersects with intense anxieties around education, socio-economic shifts, and changing understandings of national selfhood. Arabic Fusha is perceived in most postcolonial Arabic-speaking nations as the emblem of their 'decolonised' Arab national identity and as a cosmopolitan, trans-regional, and symbolic language that represents a rich and prestigious cultural heritage. Its coexistence with the vernacular spoken forms of Arabic, which are almost invariably perceived as inferior, has long been the subject of fierce debate across the region. Moroccan vernacular oral literature does not precede to Arabic written literature; rather, it has its own complex aesthetics and a wider audience and reception within

---

6   This view also exposes a disdain for the vast body of literature written in Arabic in Morocco and in the wider Arabic-speaking world and, at best, reveals an ignorance of the avant-garde trends in the politics and aesthetics of contemporary Arabic literature.

7   Kees Versteegh, *The Arabic Language* (Edinburgh: Edinburgh University Press, 2017).

8   Catherine Miller, 'Contemporary dārija Writings in Morocco: Ideology and Practices' in *The Politics of Written Language in the Arab World: Writing Change*, ed. by Jacob Høigilt and Gunvor Mejdel (Leiden: Brill, 2017), pp. 90–115 (p. 93).

Morocco. However, vernacular oral literature is not recognised in the Arabic literary field and is often studied as a form of folklore from an anthropological perspective. It is not deemed sufficiently 'literary', but is instead perceived as a genre for the 'lower' classes, namely working-class peoples and peasants, despite the fact that it effectively cuts across various classes. However, as Marilyn Booth argues, in the case of Egypt,

> If literary forms associated with colloquial Arabic have often been dismissed by the cultural and political establishment as inferior – implicating forces of distinction that maintain lines of political and economic dominion in the society – that very dismissal can act as a positive mark of collective identity out of which political resistance is born.[9]

The incorporation of non-elite tastes and aesthetics into literary narratives in the Arabic speaking world is still a challenge, as 'elite institutions of cultural judgement' continue to consider vernacular writing as secondary to Arabic Fusha and 'a sign of lack, an admission of inability to master the "literary" language—an accusation that continues to haunt colloquial poets'.[10]

What is often lost in this debate is the fact that most people in the Arabic-speaking world move daily between the two languages. In the cultural field, oral and written literature remains a vibrant place for the practice of multilingualism and for the crossing of linguistic borders, as writers incorporate various literary models and genres, including local oral narrative forms. This incorporation stems from a lived experience of multilingualism and its wider practices of reading and writing that go beyond linguistic and ideological divides to expose the degree to which the oral and the written are intertwined.

---

9   Marilyn Booth, 'Beneath Lies the Rock: Contemporary Egyptian Poetry and the Common Tongue', *World Literature Today*, 75 (2001), 257–266 (p. 259).

10   Booth (Ibid.) adds that 'Indeed, it is a marked feature of contemporary colloquial poetry that genealogies of colloquial poets become part of the poetic lexicon. Perhaps, as practitioners of an art so often pushed to the literary margins, poets who compose in the colloquial feel especially anxious to document a pedigree of excellence, determination, and commitment even as they question that past's relevance to their own voice'.

Darija is one of Morocco's most vital artistic languages.[11] Regionally diverse in terms of vocabulary and idioms, and varying also between rural areas and urban centres, it is nonetheless understood by most Moroccans, who are able to communicate in it across regions. Darija is therefore the language that reaches the widest audience, and it can effectively embody popular concerns, aspirations, modes of thought, and activism. At the same time, Moroccan Darija is quite different from other forms of vernacular Arabic in the Levant and the Arabian Peninsula and is not easily understood outside Morocco and the Maghreb.

Moroccan Darija has a rich oral and performative literary repertoire and heritage.[12] Its sophisticated and popular literary imaginary and vocabulary has persisted across centuries of literary production in forms as diverse as *zajal,* a strophic poetic form 'with no set rhyme scheme or meter',[13] and various genres of Sufi poetry; *halqa* performances (see Fatima Zahra Salih in Chapter 5 of this volume);[14] *malhun* and *gharnati*

---

11 In fact, both Darija and Tmazight have a long and rich cultural heritage and have been used in the production of poetry, proverbs, legends, stories, and music.

12 As Elinson puts it 'Although it is important not to overstate the extent to which dialectal Arabic was accepted in the Arabic literary and cultural canon in the pre-modern period, the fact that it was included and discussed is significant. That the giants of the Arabic cultural tradition such as Ibn al-Khaṭīb and Ibn Khaldūn accepted and praised works in dialect points to a certain level of ambivalence between the use of Standard Arabic and colloquial in writing in the fourteenth century'; 'Writing Oral and Literary Culture', p. 191.

13 *Zajal* is oral strophic poetry in the vernacular. Mohamed El Fassi produced twelve volumes between 1986–1991, *Maalmat al-malhun* (Encyclopaedia of malhoun) (Rabat: Publications de l'Académie du Royaume du Maroc) showing the importance of this vernacular poetic tradition that extends centuries back through Moroccan history and the wider region. Alexander Elinson argues that, 'Although there is a continuity of sorts from the pre-modern zajal form to the contemporary period, the contemporary Moroccan zajal as a written poetic form with no set rhyme scheme or meter is a free verse form closely related to similarly free verse in fusha, and it is a much more recent phenomenon that, I would argue, emerged out of a particular context of linguistic change in Morocco where proponents of expanding the use of dārija in the written realm have been challenging standard language ideologies that would prefer to preserve the fusha/darija – Standard/ non-Standard division of labor in the Arabic language'; 'Writing Oral and Literary Culture: The Case of the Contemporary Moroccan zajal' in *The Politics of Written Language in the Arab World: Writing Change,* ed. by Jacob Høigilt and Gunvor Mejdell (Leiden: Brill, 2017), pp. 190–211 (p. 194).

14 A Moroccan-specific genre of performances that take place in the open air in popular markets or streets. It is usually led by one person called a *Lhlaiqi,* whose improvised performance may include stories, songs, acrobatic arts, and popular and religious wisdom, depending on the interests of the audience present.

music;[15] as well as modern performance genres across theatre, music, cinema and television.[16] A number of prominent Moroccan intellectuals, like Abdou Filali-Ansari, Abdellatif Laabi, Abdallah Laroui, Mohamed Achaari and Abderrahim Youssi, have promoted the idea of two languages, linked semantically and in terms of vocabulary but different in terms of syntax, structure and imagery.[17] They perceive Darija not as a mutilated form of Arabic Fusha, but as a language with deep roots in Moroccan local cultures, shaped by the spoken Arabic of the tribes who migrated to North Africa and incorporating historical Punic and Tmazight influences.

It is only in the 1980s that Darija started to be valorised, and particularly over the past two decades various initiatives have sought to give Darija its due place in society. Newspapers or magazines in Darija have been launched with some success, like the weekly news magazine *Nichane* that circulated between 2006 and 2010, and novels written in Darija.[18] Moreover, Darija is the dominant language of performances, television shows, dramas, films and popular music and poetry. Plays written in Arabic Fusha and French get translated into Darija when performed for the public, to ensure a wider circulation.[19] Arguably, it was Nas El Ghiwane who lay the groundwork for Darija's reinvigorated role in popular culture in the 1970s.

---

15   *Malhun* is a form of sung poetry in colloquial Arabic that has a long history in Morocco; *gharnati* is a regional form of classical music that originated in Algeria and spread to Morocco in the twentieth century.

16   See Elinson 'Writing Oral and Literary Culture', pp. 190–211; also Catherine Miller, 'Contemporary dārija Writings in Morocco: Ideology and Practices' in *The Politics of Written Language in the Arab World: Writing Change*, ed. by Jacob Høigilt and Gunvor Mejdel (Leiden: Brill, 2017), pp. 90–115.

17   See for example Abdou Filali-Ansari in *Maroc: La guerre des Langues*, ed. by Kenza Sefroui (Casablanca: En toutes lettres, 2018), pp. 41–55 and 155–59.

18   Examples include Muhammad Barrada's (Mohamed Berrada), *Lucbat al-Nisyan* (*The Game of Forgetting*) and *al-Daw' al-Harib* (Fleeting Light); and Yusuf Fadil's (Youssef Fadel), Hashish (Hashish) and Mitru Muhal (A Meter Tall? Unlikely); see Alexander E. Elinson, 'Dārija' and Changing Writing Practices in Morocco', *International Journal of Middle East Studies*, 45.4 (2013), 715–730, http://www.jstor.org/stable/43304009

19   Cleo Jay, 'Performing Change? Contemporary Performance Practices in Morocco' (unpublished PhD thesis, SOAS, University of London, 2017).

Why Chaabi Popular Music?

The post-independence Moroccan state, in accordance with a broader pan-Arabist trend, promoted 'modern song' and classical Andalusian music, which were both dominant forms of cultural production at the time. As we have seen, Arabic Fusha was perceived in most postcolonial Arabic-speaking nations as a symbol of their 'decolonised' Arab national identity, both national, trans-regional, and cosmopolitan, and was therefore heavily promoted, whereas vernacular forms of Arabic, such as Moroccan Darija, were dismissed as parochial. Chaabi music, with its associations to vernacular Moroccan Darija, was not considered sophisticated enough to be elevated as representative of Moroccan culture.

Chaabi music, however, has deep roots in Moroccan society and is representative of the richness of popular culture. For example, the *aita* genre,[20] sang in Darija and Tmazight across different regions of Morocco and dominated by women singers, is embedded in local popular traditions of healing: singers known for their strong vocals call on their local *wali* (saint) and intercede with God to heal them and solve their problems. Chaabi music is connected to the genres of *malhun* and *zajal* vernacular poetry, which have flourished in Morocco for centuries and have come to be written down and valued as poetic forms of expression from the people and for the people.[21] *Aita* songs even played a role in the anti-colonial struggle. The famous late-nineteenth century *aita* pioneer singer and poetess Kharbousha, who came from the region of Abda, composed songs around themes of fighting both colonialism and the tyranny of the ruler at the time, Aissa Ben Omar.

---

20 *Aita* means call, lament, or cry; *aita* groups are composed of mixed male and female singers and dancers with a lead singer who is usually a woman; the women signers are called *sheikhates*, a term which is sometimes used in a derogatory way to refer to 'loose women'. Despite their sophisticated vocal, poetic, and musical skills, then, these women artists are not always well perceived in traditional Moroccan society; see Hassan El Bahrawi, *Fann al-ayta fil-maghreb* (The Art of aita in Morocco) (Rabat: Union des Écrivains Marocains, 2003); and Hassan Nejmi, *Ghina al-Aita* (Aita songs) (Casablanca: Toukbal, 2003).

21 Elinson argues that 'the fourteenth century saw a flourishing of zajal and other colloquial forms [of poetry] in the official realm in al-Andalus and medieval North Africa' but their popularity did not mean that these vernacular forms of poetry were easily accepted as 'legitimate poetic forms' by some critics and scholars, and its 'popularity waxed and waned'; 'Writing Oral and Literary Culture', p. 190.

While it originated in rural Morocco, *aita* moved to urban cities with the mass migration of peasants to big urban centres for work from the 1950s onward. It links the village to the city with songs that represent the difficulties facing peasant men and women in their new environments, translating the pain of exile, alienation, love, sorrow, and the lure of alcohol, as well as calling on local walis to sustain them in their daily struggle. Nas El Ghiwane's blend of soul and Sufi music draws on this rich repertoire of *aita* from the various regions of Morocco.

In 'Notes on Deconstructing "the Popular"', Stuart Hall explains why popular culture 'matters'. Hall proposes that people en masse may be inspired by popular culture to act as an oppositional political force. Popular culture 'is one of the sites where this struggle for and against a culture of the powerful is engaged: it is also the stake to be won or lost in that struggle'; in other words, popular culture 'is the arena of consent and resistance'.[22] Oral and aural expressions of culture attract large audiences and garner wide engagement. This is particularly the case in a society like Morocco where illiteracy rates have traditionally been high. Oral popular culture is also important in cementing a 'sense of belonging and community'.[23] As Ziad Fahmy puts it: 'Cultural productions, in any form, are not socially relevant unless they are communally and socially activated; they must be discussed, breathed and animated in the routine of everyday life'.[24] By employing imagery and metaphors that drew on a shared Moroccan heritage, and in a language accessible to the vast majority of Moroccans, the music of Nas El Ghiwane created a sense of togetherness.

The Phenomenon of Nas El Ghiwane

The popular musical group Nas El Ghiwane is sometimes referred to as the 'saviour' of the Moroccan nation. The group formed in the 1970s in a context marked by heightened political oppression under

---

22   Stuart Hall, 'Notes on Deconstructing "the Popular"' in *Foundations of Cultural Studies*, ed. by David Morley (Durham: Duke University Press, 1981), pp. 347–361 (p. 239).

23   Joke Hermes, *Re-reading Popular Culture* (Malden: Blackwell Publishing, 2005), p. 136.

24   Ziad Fahmy, *Ordinary Egyptians: Creating the Modern Nation through Popular Culture* (Stanford: Stanford University Press, 2011), p. xiii.

the reign of King Hassan II. They quickly became the voice of popular discontent. Their music combined deep existential meaning while simultaneously mobilising resilience and hope. They sang against corruption, disillusionment, and oppression, but also expressed hope for a better Morocco, particularly for the working classes.[25] They were a phenomenon, insofar as they were extremely popular across all social classes in Morocco. Nas El Ghiwane's music draws from diverse sources, including the rich popular repertoire of *aita* music from Morocco's plains and plateaus; the tradition of *malhun* music,[26] an urban working-class genre of music associated with craftsmen's guilds; and the trance music of religious fraternities such as the Gnawa, which has strong Moroccan and trans-Saharan roots.

Sufism, as a branch of Islam, is known for its embracing of music and sounds as tools to free the soul and bring it closer to God. Music is used for *dhikr* or remembrance of God and is often used simultaneously with dance to awaken the soul and its spirituality. Diverse Sufi *tarikas* (or brotherhoods) use basic musical instruments such as the flute and the *bendir* (a frame drum common in the Maghreb region) to produce repetitive and rhythmic tones that lead the listeners to a state of trance or mystical elation that can heal the soul. Sufi popular music is often used to conjure up spirits in healing ceremonies, and Nas El Ghiwane lyrics and music are embedded in this tradition of informal popular religious practices. The group uses traditional instruments such as the *tbila* drum of Sufi brotherhoods, the *harrazn* (cup-shaped drums) of itinerant musicians and beggars, and the *gembri*, the percussive bass of the Gnawa musicians, which gives it a trance aesthetic that moves listeners in a way similar to the Sufi rituals of healing through music.

---

25   As Lhoussain Simour puts it, 'These concerns inform the poetic diction of the group and remain at the genesis of the social, political, and cultural inequalities that have plagued postcolonial Morocco for decades', *Larbi Batma, Nass el-Ghiwane and Postcolonial Music in Morocco* (Jefferson: McFarland & Co, 2016), p. 3.

26   According to Abbès Jirari, *malhun* has deep roots in Moroccan history starting in the fifteenth century in the south of Morocco as a regional genre but then moved later to urban centres and male craftsman guilds to become a 'national' genre that represents in contemporary times, Moroccan 'authenticity'; Abbès Jirari, 'Al-Zajal fi l-Maghrib: al-Qasida /Zajal in Morocco' (unpublished PhD thesis, University of Rabat, 1970). Magidow claims, 'Since the Nass El Ghiwane cultural movement of the 1970s, malhun has come to appeal to most Moroccan publics, including audiences fluent in French and/or in Amazigh languages'; 'Trending classic', p. 316.

Their vernacular lyrics are rooted in local proverbs and storytelling as well as the religious imagery of *zawiyas* and popular Sufism. They were inspired, for example, by the rich repertoire of famous Moroccan Sufi vernacular medieval poets Sidi Abderhmane Al Majdub and Sidi Boualam Al Jilali, infusing this zajal poetry with courageous directness and social relevance. One of Nas El Ghiwane's earlier songs, *'Allah ya Mawlana'* (God our Master), has a strong Sufi theme of supplication. Its rhythmic music moves the listeners to a state of trance, but the song also engages with ideas of disillusionment and the loss of hope in postcolonial Morocco. At the outset, the song uses metaphors associated Sufism, referencing attempts to reach God:

> Oh God our Lord, God our Lord
> Surely Alive, my One God
> Glory be to God, be generous with us
> With you, I filled my streams with water
> And my bee is protected in your blossom
> Don't let me be miserable
> A servant coming to you through the Sufi path.

In the middle of the song, however, there is a shift of register as the lyrics dwell on contemporary social realities:

> Enough of crying, my eyes
> Enough of calming the situation
> Time cheated me and threw me away
> I have no hope.

Another canonical song is *'Gher khuduni'* (Just Take Me) which was released in 1974. Like *'Allah ya Mawlana'*, the song combines a Sufi tone with an overt political engagement with the turbulence of the era. At a time when many political activists and dissidents, particularly of the Left, were imprisoned or disappeared, the song's lyrics defy the fear being instilled in the Moroccan population:

> For you, I would give up my soul
> Just take me
> My friend is gone...
> Show me the way to God
> I am bereft over those who went...
> I am bereft
> Shackles in the hands of a blacksmith

> I am bereft
> The blood of those betrayed won't be in vain
> The rights of those wronged won't be overlooked
> You who stabbed me in the back
> It's only one death
> Just take me, oh God just take me.

Nas El Ghiwane constituted a social movement that mobilised large audiences, and offered Moroccans hope and optimism at a time when the country was going through significant political and social changes marked by tyranny and lack of freedoms; they sang the people's fears, aspirations and dreams as well as expressing their defiance of the growing tyranny of the postcolonial regime at the time. The group originated in the biggest slums of Casablanca, built specifically to accommodate rural migrants in Al Hay Al Mohamadi in the late 1960s and early 1970s. None of the members were formally trained in music except Allal Yalla, the master of banjo and oud.[27] Leftist intellectuals and artists in Morocco in the 1960s to 1980s called for the reinvention of traditional popular and vernacular culture as a fundamental element of a decolonised national identity. The well-known Moroccan theatre director Tayeb SidiqTayeb Sidiqi devoted his career to reinventing Moroccan theatre, drawing heavily on popular and traditional genres of performance such as the *halqa* or oral storytelling. Nas El Ghiwane performed and sang in the 1970s in several of his avant-garde plays and performances.

Nas El Ghiwane is credited with revolutionising Darija's cultural heritage, by synthesising the old traditional forms with new popular trends. In the process, they produced over twenty albums and have significantly influenced other *chaabi* musicians.[28] Drawing heavily on the oral poetic tradition of *zajal* poetry in their lyrics has enabled the group and their lead poet Larbi Batma to reinvent Darija in a way that appeals to all classes and regions in Morocco. As contemporary Moroccan poet Driss Messnaoui states in reference to the importance of *zajal* tradition to Darija 'a language without the garment of zajal remains a naked and

---

27   The group was made up of five musicians: Larbi Batma (d. 1997), Omar Essayid, Boujemaa Ahagour (d. 1974), Allal Yalla and Moulay Abdelazziz Tahiri, who left and was replaced by Abderhman Paco in 1974.

28   The cultural movement created by Nas El Ghiwane gave birth to other popular groups such Jil Jilala, which w rose to prominence in the 1970s; it also heavily influenced Algerian Raï music.

poor language'.[29] Elinson points out that *zajal* served in the 1970s and 1980s as 'a vehicle for political critique ... the product of a particularly heated political moment in Morocco and the rest of the Arab world when Marxist/leftist movements sought political and social change under autocratic postcolonial rulers, and expressed solidarity with the Palestinian cause'.[30] Indeed, the sung poetry of Nas El Ghiwane is a genre of *zajal* that is committed to social causes and deeply rooted in the masses aspirations but without compromising the aesthetics of the literary language of Darija and while contributing to its valorisation as a poetic language.[31]

Their lyrics, mostly composed in Darija by their charismatic front man, the poet Larbi Batma (d.1997),[32] express ordinary people's fears and aspirations in a language that is rooted in popular imagery, using rich traditional metaphors and proverbs to express dissent and to overcome censorship. According to Hassan Najmi, the group is not just a phenomenon but 'the testing centre that came out of history in order to reconstruct history'.[33]

Nas El Ghiwane's fusion music draws on the repertoire of the peasants and the dispossessed in a new form that aims at healing and mobilising people. The Moroccan maternal heritage is always present

---

29   Translated from Darija and cited by Miller in 'Contemporary dārija Writings in Morocco', p. 95.

30   Elinson, 'Writing Oral and Literary Culture', p. 198.

31   It is important to note Elinson's division of contemporary *zajal* into two main categories: 'zajals composed with an "oral mentality", i.e. drawing from Moroccan oral culture and meant to be performed orally': these includes *malhun*, *aita* and the sung poetry of Nas Al Ghiwane and other popular groups; and 'zajals that are composed with an intellectual or "writing mentality" that draw from all manner of world intellectual culture – philosophical, religious, literary, historical, etc.' The latter type is less accessible to the masses and requires education to be appreciated unlike the first category; Elinson, 'Writing Oral and Literary Culture', p. 200.

32   With the death of the group's poet and lead singer Larbi Batma in 1997, the group practically ceased to exist or create new songs. When he was diagnosed with cancer in 1993, Batma published a sequence of two books that document his life and his artistic itinerary with Nas El Ghiwane and how they come to embody the aspirations of generations of young Moroccans; the first one is called *Araheel* (Departure; Casablanca: Manshuraat Araabita, 1995) and the second one *Al'alam* (The pain; Casablanca: Dar Toubkal, 1998). Batma also published his zajal poetry under the title *Hawd Ana'na'* (Mint basin) (Casablanca: Dar Toubkal, 2013). One of the group members, Omar Essayid, published their lyrics in the volume *Kalām al-Ghiwane* (The poetry of Al-Ghiwane) (Casablanca: Matba'a al-Najāh al-jadida, 2007).

33   Simour, *Larbi Batma*, p. 3.

in their well-versed vernacular poems with proverbs coming from the depth of Moroccan oral culture. The song *'Tabni wa taali, tamchi wa tkhali'*, takes its title from well-known Moroccan proverb meaning, 'You may build towers, but in the end, you will leave them behind'. The song directs its criticism to the corruption and greed of the elites; it obliquely references the misuse of public funds to accumulate huge wealth by some elites, at the expense of further impoverishing the poor. In the same vein, their song *'Mahmouma'* (Careworn) expresses, in an eloquent Darija, the burdens of the working classes and the way they are crushed by the system in contrast to the few elites who run the country and live a life of luxury.

The group uses the *mawwal* (plural *mawawil*), a traditional form of solo vocalisation, before the song begins that relies heavily on the voice of the singer, common in many other Arab countries. In the case of the Nas El Ghiwane, it was the powerful voice of Larbi Batma who is well known for his Ghiwanian *mawawil*. Batma's *mawawil* highlight the beauty of Darija, as in the song *'Wanadi ana'* (I call you) in which rich metaphors are used to express the turmoil of the time and the fate of dissidents who disappeared without a trace:

> Impossible for my heart to forget him; impossible my heart as you
> love him
>
> Ah my heart, I came alone; ah my heart I came from a far
> Impossible for my heart to forget him;
> Oh my heartache, its tears and heartbreak
> Winds and clouds drizzled over me, and a dense murk took over me
> And loved ones are gone, I am alone and all depend on me
> Oh eyes that heal, hearts that know
> Oh mountains that stand and winds that blow
> This is a new generation without master and slave.

As Rachid Adnani puts it, 'If there were a soundtrack for what Moroccans call the "years of lead", a large part of it would be comprised of their songs'.[34] Nas El Ghiwane did not participate in politics openly through protests or political parties, but their project was shaped by the sufferings of the masses in postcolonial Morocco and the disillusionment with the

---

34   Rachid Adnani, 'Beyond Rai: North African protest music and poetry', *World Literature Today*, 80 (2006), 21–26 (p. 25).

notions of national liberation and independence. Their songs and music provided a powerful critique of the regime's tyranny and corruption, using a language understood by all Moroccans. One of their canonical songs *'Assiniya'* (Moroccan tea tray) has strong cultural and social connotations in Morocco. It reflects on solidarity, unity, togetherness, hospitality, and generosity: the principles that Nas El Ghiwane has tried to transmit in its songs.

One of the most celebrated songs of the group, *'Fin ghadi biya akhuya?'* (Where are you taking me brother?), is a critique of the regime of Hassan II. Using camouflaged language, it reflects on the alienation experienced by Moroccan migrants abroad while underlining the tyranny and lack of opportunities that drive people to leave their homeland:

> Where are you taking me brother?
> Blow after blow, who will stop the misery?
> O people, don't blame us then for living in exile

The group also produced songs in support of pan-Arab causes such the Palestinian cause with their series of songs called *'Felistiniyat'* (in 1972 and 1974). Their song *'Ya bani el-insan'* (Oh human being) tackled the question of tyranny and oppression in the Arabic speaking world. In 1995, they produced a very popular song in solidarity with the African countries and the various wars and conflicts plaguing the continent after independence, called *'Ya dem sayel'* (Spilled blood), denouncing the neo-colonial policies in Africa and the corruption of the ruling elites.

Nas El Ghiwane gained international appeal in the 1970s–90s. They were recognised not only as an engaged popular music group working in solidarity with the oppressed and the marginalised in Africa and the Middle East, but also as an originator of new trends in popular music that have influenced various other local and regional groups. Within Morocco, the group laid the ground for the establishment of other popular groups such as Jil Jilala and Lem Chehab, as well as igniting interest in the genres of *malhun* and *aita*; regionally it inspired Raï singers such as Cheb Khalid and others in Algeria. It has also inspired the many genres of engaged social and political music in the wider Arabic-speaking world, such as the work of the Lebanese musician Marcel Khalifa. Martin Scorsese used one of Nas El Ghiwane's song *'Ya sah'* as the soundtrack of his film *The Last Temptation of Christ* (1988). And in

2007, Scorsese, with the help of the World Cinema Foundation, restored an old musical documentary made about the group in 1981 by the Moroccan filmmaker Ahmed El Maanouni. El Maanouni's film called *El Hal* (Trances) followed the steps of Nas El Ghiwane in composing their lyrics and music as well as in their popular tours across the country, and in Tunisia and France.

Conclusion

Oral literary genres have a long, rich history in various Arab countries. *Nabati* poetry in the Gulf, *zajal* in the Maghreb and Levant, and the oral epic, known as *sira*, across the Middle East are prime examples of this rich and diverse oral literature. Some oral literary traditions have been recorded in written form for centuries, others remain almost exclusively in the realm of the spoken word.[35] Vernacular popular oral culture is still largely under-researched in Morocco in comparison with Egypt, for example, where there is a considerable scholarship on pioneering vernacular poets like Ahmed Fouad Najm, Bayram al-Tunisi, Abderahmane Al Abnudi, Salah Jaheen, Sayyid Darwish and others (see also Virginia Pisano in Chapter 11 of this volume).[36] Despite this neglect, Moroccan Darija has a rich cultural heritage, and the Chaabi music of Nas El Ghiwane is an important example of that reworking of that heritage to powerful effect.

Nas El Ghiwane's music offers an accessible language of social and political critique that is shared across Morocco and that transcends class and regional divisions; it overcomes the obstacles of illiteracy to offer ordinary Moroccans a language they can use to critique the oppression

---

35   For example, in North Africa the *taghrība* ('western mgration') or *sira* of Banu Hilal is still a living oral tradition performed by professional storytellers and singers, it is seen as 'the national folk epic of the Arab Maghrib'; see H. T. Norris, 'The Rediscovery of the Ancient Sagas of the Banū Hilāl', *Bulletin of the School of Oriental and African Studies*, 51 (1988), 462–481 (p. 463).

36   See for example, Marilyn Booth's *Bayram al-Tunisi's Egypt: Social Criticism and Narrative Strategies* (Exeter: Ithaca Press, 1990); Kamel Abdel-Malek's *A Study of the Vernacular Poetry of Aḥmad Fu'*ād Najm (Leiden: Brill 1990); Anastasia Valassopoulos and Dalia Said Mostafa, 'Popular Protest Music and the 2011 Egyptian Revolution', *Popular Music and Society*, 37 (2014), 638–659; and Ziad Fahmy's *Ordinary Egyptians: Creating the Modern Nation through Popular Culture* (Stanford: Stanford University Press 2011).

of the state and the rapid social changes engulfing their communities. This could not have happened without the power of Darija and its specific imagery and forms of expression, which are rooted in centuries of oral cultural heritage. Nas El Ghiwane's reinvention of Darija shows the language's capacity for creativity.

In fact Darija, this chapter has argued, is the powerhouse of popular culture in Morocco, with *chaabi* music a fundamental part of that culture. However, there is a need to document and write its richness, as it remains largely an oral culture. Darija's vernacular literariness is embedded in the cultural heritage of stories, proverbs, legends and music. Therefore, instead of opting for the flawed equation of 'either or', as per the current debates in Morocco on the relative merits of Fusha and Darija, it is preferable to enrich and nurture Morocco's multilingual landscape of oral and print languages and cultures that are not only co-constituted but also marked by their own literary specificity and locality.

Nas El Ghiwane's music is inspired by both localised and transregional Sufi popular religious practices and music, which is viewed as 'cathartic' and having an ability to 'heal' and mobilise. This calls for research to be conducted on the intersection between popular forms of Islamic practices of peasants and poor people with genres of music. This oral vernacular music also calls for a rethinking—and a re-opening—of the extant discussion on world literature. The music of Nas El Ghiwane clearly demonstrates how, far from being untranslatable and untransferable, localised aesthetics and politics can take a global turn.

Bibliography

Adnani, Rachid, 'Beyond Rai: North African protest music and poetry', *World Literature Today*, 80 (2006), 21–26, https://doi.org/10.2307/40159129

Batma, Larbi, *Al'alam* (The pain) (Casablanca: Dar Toubkal, 1998).

Batma, Larbi, *Araheel* (Departure) (Casablanca: Manshuraat Araabita, 1995).

Batma, Larbi, *Hawd Ana'na'* (Mint basin) (Casablanca: Dar Toubkal, 2013).

Booth, Marilyn, 'Beneath Lies the Rock: Contemporary Egyptian Poetry and the Common Tongue', *World Literature Today*, 75 (2001), 257–266, https://doi.org/10.2307/40156525

El Bahrawi, Hassan, *Fann al-ayta fil-maghreb* (The Art of *aita* in Morocco) (Rabat: Union des Ecrivains Marocains, 2003).

El Fassi, Mohamed, *Maalmat al-malhun* (Encyclopaedia of malhoun) (Rabat: Publications de l'Académie du Royaume du Maroc, 1986–91).

Elinson, Alexander, 'Darija and Changing Writing Practices in Morocco', *International Journal of Middle East Studies*, 45 (2013), 715–730, https://doi.org/10.1017/s0020743813000871

—, 'Writing Oral and Literary Culture: The Case of the Contemporary Moroccan zajal' in *The Politics of Written Language in the Arab World: Writing Change*, ed. by Jacob Høigilt and Gunvor Mejdell (Leiden: Brill, 2017), pp. 190–211, https://doi.org/10.1163/9789004346178_010

Ennaji, Moha, 'Aspects of Multilingualism in the Maghreb', *International Journal of the Sociology of Language*, 87 (1991), 7–26, https://doi.org/10.1515/ijsl.1991.87.7

—, *Multilingualism, Cultural Identity, and Education in Morocco* (New York: Springer Science + Business Media, 2005), https://doi.org/10.1007/b104063

Essayid, Omar, *Kalām al-Ghiwane* (The poetry of Al-Ghiwane; Casablanca: Matba'a al-Najāh al-jadida, 2007).

Fahmy, Ziad, *Ordinary Egyptians: Creating the Modern Nation through Popular Culture* (Stanford: Stanford University Press, 2011), https://doi.org/10.1515/9780804777742

Filali-Ansari, Abdou, *Maroc: La guerre des Langues,* ed. by Kenza Sefroui (Casablanca: En toutes lettres, 2018).

Hall, Stuart, 'Notes on Deconstructing "the Popular"' in *Foundations of Cultural Studies*, ed. by David Morley (Durham: Duke University Press, 1981), pp. 347–361, https://doi.org/10.2307/j.ctv11cw7c7.20

Hermes, Joke, *Re-reading Popular Culture* (Malden: Blackwell Publishing, 2005).

Jay, Cleo, 'Performing Change? Contemporary Performance Practices in Morocco' (unpublished PhD thesis, SOAS University of London, 2017).

Jirari, Abbès, 'Al-Zajal fi l-Maghrib: al-Qasida Zajal in Morocco' (unpublished PhD thesis, University of Rabat, 1970).

Laachir, Karima, 'The Literary World of the North African Taghrība Novelization, Locatedness and World Literature', *Journal of World Literature*, 4 (2019), 188–214, https://doi.org/10.1163/24056480-00402004

Magidow, Melanie, 'Trending Classic: The Cultural Register of Moroccan Malhun Poetry', *The Journal of North African Studies*, 21 (2016), 310–334, https://doi.org/10.1080/13629387.2016.1130943

Muhanna, Elias, 'Folk the Kasbah: A Conversation with Omar Sayyed, Leader of Nass El Ghiwane, *Transition*, 94 (1993), 132–149.

Nejmi, Hassan, *Ghina al-Aita* (Aita songs) (Casablanca: Toukbal, 2003).

Norris, H. T., 'The Rediscovery of the Ancient Sagas of the Banū Hilāl', *Bulletin of the School of Oriental and African Studies*, 51 (1988), 462–481, https://doi.org/10.1017/s0041977x00116465

Segalla, Spencer D., *The Moroccan Soul: French education, colonial ethnology, and Muslim resistance, 1912-1956* (Lincoln: University of Nebraska Press, 2009).

Simour, Lhoussain, *Larbi Batma, Nass el-Ghiwane and Postcolonial Music in Morocco* (Jefferson: McFarland & Co, 2016).

Valassopoulos, Anastasia and Dalia Said Mostafa, 'Popular Protest Music and the 2011 Egyptian Revolution', *Popular Music and Society*, 37 (2014), 638–659, https://doi.org/10.1080/03007766.2014.910905

Versteegh, Kees, *The Arabic Language* (Edinburgh: Edinburgh University Press, 2017).

11. Dissenting Voices of Cairo

Sheikh Imam, Ahmad Fu'ad Negm, and their Legacy in the Contemporary Music Scene

Virginia Pisano

Introduction

This chapter analyses the work of Egyptian singer and *'ud* player Sheikh Imam (1918–1995) and poet Ahmed Fu'ad Negm (1929–2013), together with the songs of young Cairene artists who have been inspired by the duo. Sheikh Imam and Ahmad Fu'ad Negm's songs are symbols of Egyptian popular culture in terms of musical aesthetics and poetics.[1] And they were still aesthetic referents for collective struggle during the demonstrations of January 2011 in Tahrir Square.

It was while in Cairo in 2010 that, following the suggestions of a Palestinian researcher and activist friend based in Berlin, I decided to work on Sheikh Imam and Ahmed Fu'ad Negm. Born as I was in a family of music-loving Italian political activists who took part in the May 1968 movement, it was inevitable that my research topic would revolve around the relationship between arts and politics. Because of the

---

1   Marilyn Booth, 'Exploding into the Seventies: Ahmad Fu'ad Nigm, Sheikh Imam, and the Aesthetics of New Youth Politics', *Political and Social Protest in Egypt, Cairo Papers in Social Science*, 29.2–3 (2009), 19–44. All translations from the songs are mine unless otherwise indicated.

     https://doi.org/10.11647/OBP.0405.11

decline of political songs in Egypt during Mubarak's time, I had initially decided to focus on the 1970s and on the myth of the 'committed singer'. But between January and April 2011, I found myself involved in the protest movement and began interviewing musicians who were giving concerts in Tahrir Square.[2] Therefore, I decided to include in my enquiry the experiences and views of these young artists on the artistic and political heritage of the 1970s. My research topic took shape between interviews conducted in the stairwells of buildings where people were taking shelter during street clashes, and outdoor concerts unthinkable until a month earlier.[3]

The core of this chapter is devoted to my analysis of Imam-Negm's songs. The first part considers the songs in relation to modern Egyptian vernacular poetry, while the second reads them as representatives of the collective imaginary. I then assess the songs relation to censorship and evaluate their diffusion and popularity, within and outside Egypt. The final section revolves around contemporary—musicians, singers and a theatre and choir director—selected because of their proximity to Imam-Negm's style and their interest in keeping his heritage alive. The dissenting songs in Cairo, I argue, do not necessarily draw inspiration from imported genres, such as rock and rap, or from folk music—as some scholars and journalists tend to highlight[4]—but can be the product of indigenous forms of music and poetry (see also Laachir in Chapter 10 of this volume). I end the chapter with a few considerations on the circulation of the 'Arab artist' label in the post-2011 period, inspired by my personal experience as a researcher and curator.

Imam-Negm's Songs as Products of Egyptian Popular Culture

Imam Mohammed Ahmad 'Eissa was born in 1918 in a poor family of the Giza area, Ahmed Fu'ad Negm in 1929 in the Egyptian Delta province of Sharqiya to a police officer and a housewife. They spent

---

2   This research was carried out between Autumn 2010 and Spring 2011. Cairo today is in a much less hopeful state, waiting for the release of its 40,000 political prisoners. Chants and screams have become whispers; paranoia and depression have taken the place of the thrilling energy of 2011.

3   See for example the event *Al fan midan*; Silvia Mollicchi, 'Al-Fan Midan Brings the Arts to the Streets', *Egypt Independent*, 10 May 2011.

4   See e.g. Mark LeVine, *Heavy Metal Islam* (New York: Three Rivers Press, 2008).

their childhood as colonial Egypt declined and grew up artistically in a politically charged cultural environment. It was an epoch marked by a shift from elitist Oriental music to national Egyptian music, with theatre director Salama Higazy (1852–1917) and the great composer Sayyed Darwish (1892–1923). Musical theatre became a major cultural tool of resistance against British occupation; Darwish played an important role in creating the national sentiment that became a central element of the struggle against the British rule, and his social and patriotic songs won him the sobriquet of the father of Egyptian modern music.[5] Indeed, till the mid-twentieth century the main grievances voiced by Egyptian songs of dissent concerned nationalist demands and independence from British rule.[6]

A few decades later, under the Egyptian political establishment of, first, Gamal 'Abdel Nasser and later Anwar Sadat, political songs became 'state-commissioned and government-orchestrated patriotic songs'.[7] A few political songs did remain genuine songs of protest, however, Sheikh Imam and Ahmad Fu'ad Negm's compositions among them. Their dissenting songs were political songs that used literary and musical elements of Egyptian popular culture to provide a social and political critique along the lines of the left-wing opposition to the regime.[8] The duo was at the forefront of an underground cultural movement that, from the end of the 1960s, denounced the social problems in the country and derided the Egyptian—and international—political establishment.

This cultural movement was led by poets such as Salah Jahin (1930–1986), Fu'ad Haddad (1927–1985) and Abderrahman Abnoudy (b. 1938), who challenged official mainstream Fusha (classical Arabic) poetry by composing poems in colloquial Egyptian. By using idioms and words belonging to everyday life, these poets dealt with topics that

---

5   Habeeb Salloum, 'Sayyed Darwish: The Father of Modern Arab Music', *Al Jadid Magazine*, 7.36 (Summer 2011); R. El Maliki, 'Political Songs in Egypt', *Egypt Today*, August 2008.

6   El Maliki, 'Political Songs in Egypt; Booth, 'Exploding into the Seventies'.

7   Salah Eissa, editor-in-chief of *Al Qahira Weekly*, speaking for a documentary on Sheikh Imam on *Al Jazeera*; 'Cheikh Imam'.

8   The UK-based Centre for Political Songs defines political songs as 'music providing social commentary and supporting a historical narrative, traditional songs and political parodies functioning to sustain a campaign, to express discontent, to generate support, to motivate, to console, to provoke, to educate or to mock'; http://www.gcu.ac.uk/politicalsong/

had been hardly treated before and raised 'controversial issues about the responsibility of cultural producers, the political roles of poetry in a neo-colonial context, the boundaries of community/nation and the meanings of marginalities'.[9]

The process had started even earlier, in the 1880s, with the poet of the Urabi revolt, 'Abdallah Nadim (1844–1896). He was followed by Bayram Tunsi (1893–1961), who brought the pre-modern tradition of *zajal* poetry to new heights.[10] Tunsi's poems addressed a popular audience, both in the sense of as wide a public as possible, including all strata of the population, and of the public as an agent opposed to the centres of power.[11] Their main targets were British domination and corruption and the quarrels among Egyptian nationalist politicians. Nadim and Tunsi's poems were dismissed by the members of the cultural establishment, who considered colloquial literature to be inferior to classical Arabic literature. Curiously enough, one of their critics was the writer of the 'Egyptian street' Naguib Mahfouz, who called colloquial Egyptian a pernicious social disease needing urgent treatment.[12]

Marginality and dismissal made this genre of *zajal* poetry a valuable tool for political resistance. A broader community of writers and readers than the ruling educated elite was created, and the poems asserted a separate, specific identity, and proclaimed a distance from the nation and subverting the message of the regime.[13] Nevertheless, in some cases *zajal* poetry was co-opted by the regime and its official opposition as a tool to talk to the masses. Under Nasser, for instance, *zajal* poems for workers and peasants were published as booklets (like *Ikhtarna li al-fallah*, We have Chosen for the Peasants), or in the journal of the official opposition party, *Hizb al-Tagammu* (Socialist Party).[14]

---

9   Marilyn Booth, 'Beneath Lies the Rock: Contemporary Egyptian Poetry and the Common Tongue', *World Literature Today*, 75. 2 (Spring 2001), 257–266 (p. 257).

10   The Urabi revolt was an uprising led by Colonel Ahmed Urabi between 1879 and 1892 challenging the Khedive and European influence in Egypt. *Zajal* (plural *azjal*) is a form of colloquial poetry composed in prescribed meters and rhyme schemes that was introduced in the Middle Ages in Arab Spain (see Laachir in Chapter 10 of this volume).

11   See Booth, 'Beneath lies the rock'.

12   Quoted in Kamal Abdel-Malek, *A Study of the Vernacular Poet Aḥmad Fu'ād Nigm* (Leiden: Brill, 1990), p. 2.

13   See Joel Beinin, 'Writing Class: Workers and Modern Egyptian Colloquial Poetry (*zajal*)', *Poetics today*, 15.2 (Summer 1994), 191–215.

14   Ibid.

Negm's Poetry and Its Subversive Power

Although Negm already wrote poems in *zajal* form, his encounter with the poetry of Bayram Tunsi while in prison was a turning point in his life and career.[15] Indeed, according to Dalia Said-Mustapha, Negm was not an innovator but a biting observer of his time who inherited the tradition of Egyptian vernacular poetry.[16] His collection of *zajal Images from life and prison* won the prize sponsored by the Supreme Council for the Promotion of Arts, Literature and Social Sciences in 1964. The main theme of this collection is social injustice, viewed as inequality and domination rather than class struggle:

> I am the people, marching and making my way
> My struggle is my weapon and my resolve is my friend
> [...]
> My children will defeat every oppressor.[17]

In 1962 Negm met Sheikh Imam, who had started singing his compositions in local cafés, accompanying himself with the *'ud* (lute). While Negm was a self-educated member of the working class—he had worked in the British army camps and was fired for organizing workers' demonstrations—Imam was born in a poor family. After training as Qur'an reciter, Imam had learnt the basics of music and *muwashshah*[18] singing from Sheikh Darwish el-Hareery, a prominent musical figure in Cairo of the time. He then started singing at weddings and circumcision ceremonies, and played in Zakarya Ahmad's ensemble before his phase of political engagement. In the words of the poet Nizar Qabbani, the collaboration between the pen and the *'ud* became 'an alliance to fight for the cause of the masses whose tongue was tied'.[19] In the *zajal 'Shayyid*

---

15   In an interview, Negm states that Tunsi's poetry was responsible for his artistic and political awakening; Booth, 'Exploding into the Seventies', p. 24.

16   Dalia Said-Mustapha, 'Negm wa al Sheikh Imam: su'ud wa uful al ughnyia al siyasyya fi Masr' (Negm and Sheikh Imam: the rise and the decline of political song in Egypt), *Alif: Journal of Comparative Poetics*, 21 (2001), 128–160.

17   Ahmad Fu'ad Negm, *Suwwar min al-hayat wa al-sign* (Images from life and prison) (Cairo: al-Majlis al-a'la li-ri'ayat al-funun wa al-adab wa al-'ulum al-igtima'iyya, 1964); Negm-Imam, 'Anā al-sha'eb'.

18   'A genre of pre-composed art song with roots in Andalusian Spain'; Marcus L. Scott, *Music in Egypt* (Oxford: Oxford University Press, 2007), p. 100.

19   Abdel-Malek, *A Study*, p. 19.

qusurak' (Build your palaces), Negm and Imam name the actors of collective resistance:

> We know our minds and we have joined together
> Workers, peasants and students.[20]

After the Arab defeat of 1967 in the war against Israel, the duo became renowned among students and the leftist intelligentsia, and their songs became the leitmotiv of strikes and demonstrations during Nasser's and Sadat's rule. In the late 1960s, the duo moved to the lower-class neighbourhood of Khosh Qadam, which later became an important centre of political and cultural activism. In 1968, with the song *'Gifara mat'* (Che Guevara is dead) their popularity among the leftists increased, even abroad. The song is a call to workers and ordinary people to come together against the establishment:

> O workers and dispossessed
> Chained from head to toe
> Enough!
> You have no way out
> But guns and bullets.[21]

Although this was hardly a realistic strategy for workers and peasants, who had just resumed mobilizing at the end of the 1960s after a period when collective resistance had abated, such inflammatory calls were severely punished by the regime. The duo was jailed several times between the 1960s and the 1980s.

Most of Imam-Negm's songs re-interpreted oral stories, proverbs, and vernacular poems. While I return below to a more detailed analysis of their popularity, it is important to stress this link to popular culture as one of the reasons for their success among a wide range of audiences.[22] Indeed, according to Dalia Said-Mustapha, Imam-Negm's compositions are a product of the Egyptian popular culture that emerged onto the official cultural scene in the twentieth century.[23] The songs could be understood and sung also by illiterates, which is why they became

---

20   Negm, 'Shayyid qusurak' (Build your palaces), quoted in Beinin, 'Writing Class', p. 212.
21   Negm-Imam, 'Gifara mat'.
22   Booth, 'Exploding into the Seventies', p. 39.
23   Said-Mustapha, 'Negm wa al Sheikh Imam'.

threatening tools of social protest.[24] As *'ud virtuoso* Mustafa Said puts it, 'they were the only ones to convey the thoughts of the street'.[25]

Yet, despite their Marxist view and radical political programme, Negm-Imam rarely drew attention to the differences among these social categories in terms of class, demands and objectives. Their project—like Bayram Tunsi's—was conceived in collective popular-national terms. Their *zajal* were tools for creating a popular-nationalist discourse that could challenge dominant cultural and political norms.

Expressing Resistance Through Music

Popular culture played as much a role in the lyrics written by Negm as in the music composed by Sheikh Imam. Take the song *'Baqaret Haha'* (Haha's cow), written by the duo as a response to the defeat of 1967. According to Said-Mustapha, Negm-Imam filled with political content the skeleton of a song that was already popular among the people of the *rif* (countryside):[26]

> Outsiders came in and sucked all the milk
> The cow called out and screamed 'My Children'
> But the children of shame were fast asleep.
> The cow was oppressed, she was overwhelmed
> She fell into the well; bystanders asked
> 'Well, why did she fall?'
> She fell from fear
> She fell because of hunger and rest.[27]

The helpless cow represents Egypt, suffering because of its defeat in the Arab-Israeli war and inability to resist American interference. The song has a circular rhythm often used in popular ceremonies like the *zar*.[28] It is easy to follow and creates a sense of ordinary ecstasy. The choir is an important element in the song and builds a dialogue with the singer by repeating the word *'Haha'* on a higher pitch.

---

24   Ibid.
25   Personal interview, Cairo 6/05/2011.
26   See Said-Mustapha, 'Negm wa al Sheikh Imam'.
27   Negm-Imam, 'Baqaret Haha' (Haha's cow). Translation by Walaa' Quisay.
28   Ceremonies with music, singing and dance, organized mainly in the countryside in order to heal illnesses.

Many scholars consider Negm-Imam to have been largely inspired by the famous Egyptian composer and theatre director Sayyed Darwish.[29] In fact, Negm-Imam's aim comes close to Darwish's: composing songs of social interest that could be easily understood and appropriated by the people, and performing them on any kind of stage, from factories and streets to theatres and universities.

Negm-Imam's songs are very essential: the music is minimalistic, with few embellishments; the rhythms are basic, there is no virtuosity, and the lyrics appear to be more important than music. Almost all songs start with a *muqaddimah*, an instrumental introduction in the main *maqam* or melodic mode of the song. The choice of only the *'ud* and sometime the *riqq*, a frame drum, as accompaniments to his voice, as well as the important presence of the choir, show the link with medieval *zajal*, which in the Andalusian tradition was performed by a poet/minstrel accompanied by percussion, flute, and choir. This style lends itself to be easily received by the audience, and its simplicity is in contrast with the style of the popular songs of the time, in which the orchestra played a central role and which left no place for audience participation.[30] According to the virtuoso *'ud* player Hazem Shaheen, Sheikh Imam sang 'collective songs': this feature differentiates them from the typical style of Egyptian singers of the time like Umm Kulthum and Abdel Halim Hafez, whose performances were conceived only to be listened to.[31]

Returning to the song *'Gifara mat'* (Che Guevara is dead), it is possible to identify different parts. The song starts with a military march beat that announces an important message, repeated by the choir on a low, serious pitch:

> Guevara is dead
> Latest news, on the radios
> In the churches
> In the mosques
> In the alleys
> On the roads
> And in cafés and bars

29　E.g. Booth, Said-Mustapha, El Maliki, 'Abdel Malek.

30　See Virginia Danielson, *The Voice of Egypt: Umm Kulthum, Arabic Song and the Egyptian Society in the Twentieth Century* (Chicago: University of Chicago Press, 1997).

31　Hazem Shaheen, personal interview, 4/06/2011.

Imam then switches to an ironic tone, the music becomes lighter, and the voice pitch higher. This part is addressed to the 'unheroic' local politicians and military leaders whose practices contrast those of Guevara:[32]

> What do you think?
>   You, with your wealth and your *antikat*[33]
>   All dressed up and fed
>   All warmed up.
>   You and your new-age stylish struggle
>   In the floaters[34]
>   What do you think?
>   You, with your wealth
>   Guevara is dead.

Following this ironic part, the song moves to the rhythm and musical phrases often used by mourning women in the Egyptian countryside and in poor urban neighbourhoods:

> Guevara is dead
> No humming
> No propaganda
> In his moment of demise
> With none of his comrades to bid him farewell
> His screams ascended to the heavens
> Shouting, but who would listen?

The final part of the song is characterised by a severe tone that suggest an idea of seriousness to the audience. The poem becomes a declaration of armed struggle, at the time of the first real challenge to Nasser's regime:

> Guevara's screams! You slaves!
> In any homeland and every place
> There is no alternative
> And no other way.
> Get the armies ready
> Or tell the world
> This is the end.

---

32 See Booth, 'Exploding into the Seventies', p. 32.

33 By '*antikat*', Negm means the members and supporters of the regime; he defines them as the old generation.

34 The reference is to Abdel Nasser. At the time left-wing intellectuals criticized him for the Six-Day War.

In this as in other songs the choir plays a central role. Indeed, Sheikh Imam staged participative performances in which the choir involved the audience impromptu in the performance. In this specific example, it functions as an echo of the singer, a collective reply in a descending tonal line, mourning the dead hero.

In summary, two main features characterise Imam's songs: the use of familiar poetic structures and diction, and a musical language that evokes and encourages popular oral performances and collective life. Negm's use of the *mawwal*,[35] the heroic epic, children's games, jokes, and storytelling creates an unapologetic political vocality that is recognizable as part of oral popular culture. Likewise, the style of Sheikh Imam's compositions, with is musical rhetorical strategies of repetition, refrain, and dialogue, draws on both popular secular songs and on Qur'anic recitation. According to El Maliki, they have become part of the collective memory of the Egyptian people.[36]

Representing the Collective Imaginary

Imam-Negm's songs embed a form of collective imaginary that is based on three elements: a typification of Egyptian society, a pungent use of humour and satire, and a set of themes and targets. [37] The main characters they depict are the *fellah* (pl. *fellahin*) or peasant, the *afandi* or bureaucrat, representing the educated elite, and the *ibn al balad* or son of the country, who represents the working class. Two groups above these categories—the indigenous ruling class and the *khawagat* or foreigners— are perceived as the oppressors. The dialectical narrative of these songs

---

35   The *mawwal* is a genre of vocal art music improvises melodically while singing
       poetic texts; see also Laachir in Chapter 10 of this volume.
36   El Maliki, 'Political Songs in Egypt'.
37   See Abdel-Malek, *A study*. During my fieldwork, I experienced what Bruno Nettl
       describes in his chapter 'You Will Never Understand this Music: Insiders and
       Outsiders' (in *The Study of Ethnomusicology: Thirty-Three Discussions*, University
       of Illinois 2015 [1983], 157–168). After being told by his teacher of Persian chant
       that he will never understand Persian music as Persians instinctively do, Nettl
       reflects on the different approaches of outsiders and insiders to musical heritage.
       Likewise, many interviewees explained to me that it would be almost impossible
       for me to understand the humour of Sheikh Imam and Ahmed Fu'ad Negm as it
       was 'typical Egyptian humour'. Yet even though some allusions or nuances are
       difficult to catch for a non-Egyptian, many 'outsider' researchers have managed to
       identify the main features related to humour and satire in these songs.

depicts Egyptian social forces in a perpetual 'struggle of opposites': rich/poor, urbanized/rustic, ruler/ruled, native/foreigner.[38]

In his song *'Ya'ish ahl baladi'* (Long live the people of my country), written one year after the 1967 defeat, Negm uses irony to portray the Egyptian social pyramid with the rich at the top and the poor masses at the bottom.[39] The following stanza shows the poet's critique of Nasser's slogan of social alliance:

> The people of my country live
> Not knowing one another
> No bond among them
> To allow the 'alliance' to live on.

Although Negm-Imam's songs were popular among left-wing intellectuals, the song does not spare them from ironic critique:

> Long live the intellectual,
> Pedantic, slippery, chatty.
> He lacks experience
> He dislikes the crowd,
> With one empty word here
> And a hollow term there,
> He quickly fabricates solutions.

Poor people, and particularly the *fellahin*, are the heroes of Negm-Imam's songs.[40] Many of them celebrate the peasants and portray the *rif* as the breeding ground of talented and honest people.[41] The song *'Ya Baheyya'* ('O Baheyya'), which became very popular thanks to the movie *Al 'asfur* (The sparrow, 1976) by Youssef Chahine, describes Egypt as a poor peasant woman who looks modest but whose beauty is concealed:

> Egypt
> Mother Baheyya
> Clad in scarf and in galabeyya
> Time has turned senile
> You are still youthful
> Time is moving back
> You are coming forward.

---

38   Abdel-Malik, *A Study*, p. 31.

39   Negm-Imam, 'Ya'ish ahl baladi'.

40   Said-Mustapha, 'Negm wa al Sheikh Imam'.

41   Salah Eissa in 'Cheikh Imam'.

The song also celebrates the peasants:

> Poor of this country
> *Fellah* and labourer
> You are the lubricant of the waterwheel
> The coal of the factory.[42]

This idealization of the poor may lead us to consider Negm-Imam's songs nationalistic or even populist rather than dissenting. Yet their use of humour and satire undercuts this idea and sets these songs in opposition to the apologetic public discourse of the regime. Indeed, while the regime tried to offer an abstract and romantic image of the homeland to distract the impoverished masses from the wretchedness of their life,[43] Negm–Imam challenged this representation, offering instead a critical nationalism. As a result, their songs were seen as anti-patriotic by the establishment, a view represented by the lyricist and *Al Ahram* columnist Mostafa al Damarani: 'this attitude is destructive. What are they criticizing? The Egyptian civilization is the root of all human progress and we should try to build, not destroy by being offensive.'[44] Nonetheless, their song *'Bahebbyk ya Masr'* (I love you Egypt) is a pure ode to the homeland:

> I love you Egypt
> At night and in the morning
> I swim with your love,
> It is my rescue
> [...]
> Even if they jailed me and hung me
> And thought about driving me out
> By torturing me
> I would come closer to you.
> I cannot flee.[45]

Irony, derision, mockery, and jokes are all important elements in Imam-Negm's songs. The musical parody of Imam gives to his songs a performative punch, and his hilarious tone does not soften the political critique, but rather it intensifies it. Verbal imagery and musical and

---

42   Negm-Imam, 'Ya Baheyya'.
43   El Maliki, 'Political Songs in Egypt', interviewing Salah Eissa.
44   Quoted Ibid.
45   Negm-Imam, 'Bahebbyk ya Masr' (I love you Egypt).

spoken tonalities are employed in parodies that criticize the official rhetoric of populism and to attack the rulers—whether Nasser, Sadat or Mubarak—and its foreign allies.[46] The first song to earn the artists a prison sentence—from 1967 to 1971—was *'Al hamdullillah khabbatna takhti bitatna'* (Thanks to God we bat under our armpits),[47] which directly attacked Nasser. The establishment saw this critique of the 1967 defeat as an insult to the military, as it directly attacked the regime's attempt to improve its image before the masses and contain their anger:

> How nice to watch our soldiers
> Come back empty-handed
> From the line of fire.
> The battlefield of Abdel Gabbar[48]
> Will ruin everything.
> Thank God for the state of Egypt
> Drowning in lies, the people confused
> Slogans praising and scraping
> Even before the traitor.
> God willing, He will destroy everything of Abdel Gabbar. [49]

After a concert at 'Ain Shams University in 1977, Negm spent one year in prison for 'insulting the president' and for imitating the president's voice.[50] The reason for this charge was the song *'Bayaan ham'* (Important announcement), in which Negm derides President Sadat and his alliance with the United States and Israel:

> This is an announcement
> Radio station 'Splendor of the past'
> From Cairo to Kurdufan
> And from Venezuela and Iran,
> And from any home
> And brutalized land
> Because of Yankee tourism.
> [...]
> On this great occasion (to which you're not invited)

---

46   See Booth, 'Exploding into the Seventies', p. 38.

47   The image recalls the movement of soldiers marching.

48   Abdel Gabbar means the servant of the Fearsome as opposed to 'Abdel Nasser which means the servant of the Victorious.

49   Negm-Imam, 'Al hamdullillah khabbatna takhti bitatna'.

50   Janet Stevens, 'Political repression in Egypt', *MERIP Reports*, 66 (April 1978), 18–21 (p. 21).

> We present to you Shehata[51] the stoner
> Unrehearsed
> The chief broker in our developing nation
> Bribing the card dealers before each game of poker
> Sabotaging the farmland and selling its crops.
> Now he's a prince of the army too
> You cannot deny
> And say you don't know
> Nor can you say you've never heard of him.

The phase of Imam and Negm's production following the 1973 war engages in social and political criticism against the peaceful resolution of the Arab-Israeli conflict.[52] Take the song *'Valery Giscard d'Estaing'*, which attacks Sadat's alliance with the West by deriding the French president, who visited Egypt in 1975:

> Valery Giscard d'Estaing
> Along with his madam
> Will catch the wolf by its tail
> And feed all the hungry
> The poor will eat sweet potatoes
> And walk around haughty and proud.
> Instead of naming their kid Shalata[53]
> The poor folk will name him Jean.
> All of this thanks to our friend
> The romantic d'Estaing. [54]

Another popular song of the time is *'Nixon baba'* (Papa Nixon), which derides the US policy in Egypt and the American president, who visited the country in 1974. The song displays Sheikh Imam's typical style of declaiming improvised phrases soaring above the rhythm:

> Pleased to meet you papa Nixon
> The boy of Watergate,
>
> They loaded you
> With many honours
> The sultans of beans and oil.

---

51   A typical Egyptian name, it carries an assonance with Sadat; translation by Walaa Quisay.
52   See Okasha, 'Prince of Disillusionment'.
53   A common Egyptian name.
54   Negm-Imam, 'Valery Giscard d'Estaing'.

> They put the red carpet under your feet
> From Ras el Tin to Mekka
> And they say you have done the pilgrimage.[55]

Imam's satirical verses also targeted social issues such as malnutrition and hunger. The song *'Al ful wa al lahma'* (Beans and meat) addresses the lack of nutritious food in a country that imports 40% of the food it consumes:

> As for the question of beans and meat
> An alleged source has decreed
> That medicine has advanced greatly
> And that Dr Mohsin says:
> The Egyptian people are better off eating beans
> Instead of meat.
> And eating Egyptian beans
> Makes you strong as an ox
> And that such proteins
> Cannot be found in any other food.[56]

Imam-Negm's verses contain many slogans of the left-wing opposition movement, which reached its climax with the bread riots of 1977. However, the singer Azza Balbaa', who married Negm in 1975 and later sang with Sheikh Imam, states that the two artists were not completely convinced by the slogans of the left movement but 'felt a kind of gratitude to the left because it embraced the whole experiment.'[57] Their parody of *Umm Kulthum* is an interesting example of this attitude: according to Azza Balbaa', Negm-Imam used to criticize the diva's alignment with the regime before the leftist bigwigs and their revolutionary audience, whereas in private they told Balbaa' that she 'should learn from this great artist and her style'.[58] The song *'Kalb el sitt'* (The lady's dog) refers to Umm Kulthum, who was called *'el sitt'* (the lady), and the use of her artistic and social charisma to the detriment of the poor people. Elsewhere, Negm-Imam target state-sponsored and co-opted artists, singing that, 'The state is submerged with lies/ but everything is OK

---

55   Negm-Imam, 'Nixon baba' (Papa Nixon).
56   Negm-Imam, 'Al ful wa al lahma' (Beans and meat).
57   Azza Balbaa' interview in Okasha, 'Prince of Disillusionment'.
58   Ibid.

as long as the damned masters are happy / because of the poets who fill their stomach with poems.'[59]

In terms of social and political critique, the years 1975-1981 marked the height of the Negm-Imam phenomenon. This was the time when students called for armed struggle against Israel and imperialism, while President Sadat's economic policy (*Infitah* or opening to the free market) forced him to improve diplomatic relations with Israel and the US. Particularly after the Camp David accords of 1977 and the first *Intifada*, demonstrations and strikes in Egypt spread to all social strata, from students and members of the opposition to workers. Negm-Imam targeted the populist approach and the hypocrisy of the ruling class and the bureaucrats, who were only interested in amassing personal wealth.[60]

The themes and targets of Negm-Imam's songs vary according to the historical moment, this section has shown. They include war and defeat, the Arab-Israeli conflict, social struggle, social and artistic critique, the Palestinian issue, corruption, love for the homeland, the harshness of people's life, and the celebration of revolutionary heroes. Their three main targets include social injustice, political figures such as Nasser, Nixon, Sadat and their foreign allies, and state-sponsored artists like Umm Kulthum and Abdel Halim Hafez.

Other themes are present, too. The songs *'Mamnu'at'* (Bans) and *'Sign el 'ala'a'* (The citadel's prison) deal with the impossibility of living everyday life, particularly because of the tension between personal freedom and state control:

> Banned from travel
> Banned from singing
> Banned from speaking
> Banned from longing
> Banned from discontent
> Banned from smiling.
>
> Oh Egypt, my love, you are a boat
> Longing but imprisoned
> With an informant in each corner
> A police in every port.[61]

---

59   Quoted in Michael Slackman, 'A Poet Whose Political Incorrectness is a Crime,' *New York Times*, 13 May 2006.

60   See Okasha, 'Prince of Disillusionment'; Clement, 'Worker Protests'; and Booth, 'Exploding into the Seventies'.

61   Negm-Imam, 'Mamnu'at' (Bans), transl. Walaa Quisay.

And in *'Sign el 'ala'a'* they sang:

> The devotees gathered in the castle's prison[62]
> The devotees gathered in Bab Al-Khalq[63]
> And the sun is a chant, rising from the prison cells.
> And Egypt is a chant, rising from the throat.
> The devotees gathered in the cell.
> No matter the length of imprisonment; no matter the oppression
> No matter the despotism of the jailer
> Who could ever dare imprison Egypt?
> [...]
> The liar landed informants at my door
> And the informants let loose their hungered vicious dogs.
> They gather the devotees to the prison cell. [64]

Sounds of Power: Censorship and Diffusion

'With noise is born disorder and its opposite: the world.
With music is born power and its opposite: subversion.'[65]

Negm-Imam's songs were never publicly broadcasted in Egypt, and no official cassettes, LP or CD were ever recorded. It was in France that *Le Chant du Monde* recorded a LP in 1976 that reached platinum with one million copies. Even today, there is no official recording in Egypt, and the cassettes that circulate originate from other Arab countries, mainly Lebanon and are considered valuable items, though nowadays their songs can be easily downloaded from the Internet. In other words, Sheikh Imam's songs have been living in the memory of people and in underground or private recordings of very poor quality. As the next section will show, the situation has slightly evolved since the overthrow of Hosni Mubarak in February 2011. Yet, as theatre director Salam Yousry put it, 'they are not on radio, nor on television, they are still in prison!'[66]

In Egypt, these songs circulated only through underground unofficial cassettes and through live concerts that took place in universities, during demonstrations, at the headquarters of *Hizb al-Tagammu* (Socialist Party),

---

62   During Anwar El Sadat's presidency, the underground room in the citadel of Saladin in Egypt was turned into a political prison.
63   A court that dealt with political prisoners.
64   Negm-Imam, 'Sign el 'ala'a' (The citadel's prison).
65   Attali, *Noise,* p. 6.
66   Salam Yousry, personal interview, 17/01/2011.

or in private houses, often advertised by word of mouth.[67] By 1975, 200 songs were recorded on cassettes and distributed in the underground market. Performances were a way of challenging the attempt by the state to control sites of mobilization and they constituted occasions for encouraging collective participation to the public sphere. After a brief appearance on state television and radio early on in Imam and Negm's careers, the regime immediately understood that co-optation could not work with them. As already mentioned, the duo was imprisoned several times and systematically censored. As Negm said: 'We do not fear prison which has become a constant duty of any person in Egypt with self respect'.[68] Unlike contemporary musicians, they seem to have hardly experienced forms of self-censorship.

For Attali, music is an attribute of power in all its forms. 'Eavesdropping, censorship and surveillance are weapons of power. [...] to listen, to memorize, this is the ability to interpret and control history, to manipulate the culture of people, to channel its violence and hopes'.[69] His ideas about censorship and state control under totalitarian regimes apply to the Egyptian case: the state has become a 'gigantic eavesdropper' that seeks to silence subversive noises and dissenting voices in search of cultural autonomy.[70] As far as control over recordings is concerned, the Egyptian case is twofold. On the one hand, censorship represents a pure exercise of power with the aim of preventing the masses from accessing dissenting songs. On the other hand, censorship prevented Negm-Imam's songs from becoming part of the music industry, and as a result it kept their consumption collective, as songs were consumed before the invention of recording machines. When Marylin Booth asked Sheikh Imam in an interview if he would have accepted to cooperate with official media channels, replied: 'I would still refuse unequivocally. My mass media are the masses'.[71]

---

67   Booth, 'Exploding into the Seventies', p. 21.

68   Negm-Imam, interviewed by Janet Tucker, 'While Sadat Shuffles: Economic Decay, Political Ferment in Egypt', *MERIP Reports*, 65 (March, 1978), 3–9, 26 (p. 9).

69   Attali, *Noise*, p. 7.

70   Attali goes even further, arguing that recording has always been a mean of social control, beginning with the Tables of the Law. He quotes Hitler's *Manual of German Radio*: 'without the loudspeaker, we would never have conquered Germany'; Ibid., p. 87.

71   Booth, 'Sheikh Imam the Singer', 20.

Negm-Imam were the voice of the leftist movement. If to say that the left co-opted them is probably too strong, it is important to stress that it only the regime but also the left-wing opposition movement involved artists in their political project. At the same time, it was thanks to their affiliation to the movement that the duo gained a broader audience and sponsored sets for performances. In Negm's words: 'We have slept for years in those prisons, but we have been able to continue singing to the people as members of the Egyptian nationalistic intellectual movement, that wishes to build an advanced humanistic culture.'[72] If music was an instrument of the Egyptian regime, for Negm, too, 'Songs are weapons'.[73]

Popularity and Decline of Sheikh Imam's Songs

Issues of censorship and diffusion have played a part in the popularity and decline of Sheikh Imam's songs are related. When, during my fieldwork in Cairo in 2011, I asked artists and audience members to estimate Negm-Imam's popularity among Cairenes in terms of class and generation, many argued that their songs had been popular among leftist intellectuals and students in the 1960s and 1970s.[74] According to Marylin Booth, 'to this day, these songs circulate in the memories of 1960s activists and onlookers'.[75] Indeed, most academics and journalists think that Negm-Imam's popularity in Egypt remained confined to activists, intellectuals and students, mainly members of the Socialist Party.[76]

---

72 In Tucker, 'While Sadat Shuffles', 9.

73 Said-Mustapha, 'Negm wa al Sheikh Imam'.

74 I prepared three different questionnaires, one for the artists, one for the older generation of listeners, and one for the younger members of the audience, in order to evaluate the popularity of Sheikh Imam and Negm's songs in Cairo. I also interviewed listeners, most of whom belong to the habitual audiences of performances by the artists selected.

75 Booth, 'Exploding in the Seventies', p. 21.

76 See Abdel-Malek, *A study*; El Maliki, 'Political Songs in Egypt'; Okasha, 'Prince of Disillusionment'; Said-Mustapha, 'Negm wa al Sheikh Imam'. Professor Francesca Corrao of Naples' Orientale, who was personally involved in the left wing political and cultural environment of 1970s' Cairo, concurs that Sheikh Imam was and is mainly diffused among the Cairene intelligentsia. In the past only wealthy people could afford recorders, and today they alone have access to these songs on the Internet. She points out that it is very difficult to perform a quantitative analysis of the popularity of Sheikh Imam, however, particularly because of the changes that

While their popularity among intellectuals and students shows the strong presence of popular culture among educated people, it also implies that the popular strata were unconcerned or could not access these songs, which as we have seen were hardly available since they were censored and banned from the official market. However, several of my interviewees stated that the lower strata of the population also knew, and still know, them. When I interviewed the young daughter of a member of the Islamist opposition movement who was active in the 1990s, she declared that her father raised her with Negm-Imam's songs and that part of the Egyptian Muslim Brotherhood shared a passion for these songs with the left-wing movements.[77] While stressing that this is the personal view of the interviewee, it shows that the struggle against a common target could make cultural tastes of activists with different backgrounds converge. Perhaps Sheikh Imam's training in Qur'an recitation made him appear *halal* to the moderate stream of the Islamist movement. It is not by chance that he was called 'the red sheikh'.

Negm often declared his mistrust towards the Islamist approach to social injustice and criticized the local Muslim Brotherhood, declaring that the sheikhs are corrupted and that religious ideologies are responsible for the poor's resigned acceptance of class inequalities.[78] At the same time, in 1979 he published a collection of poems in praise of the Iranian revolution.[79] In one of them, Ayatollah Khomeini is called '*gamid giddan*', a very strong man, and is praised for exacerbating relations with Israel and the US. As Negm put it: 'I wrote these poems as the Iranian revolution was on the threshold of victory. I dedicate these poems to Iran, to revolution everywhere and to Egypt'.[80]

Many activists who were involved in the January 2011 uprisings in *Tahrir* Square told me that when young artists sang Negm-Imam's songs in the square, people from different classes and backgrounds started singing along: many knew the songs though not necessarily the singer. Other interviewees affirmed that most people belonging to the lower

---

Cairo has undergone in the last three decades in terms of demography, migration and social mobility; personal interview, 23/05/2011.

77   Personal interview, 17/01/2011.

78   Interview with Al Naqqash.

79   A. F. Negm, *Ughniyat wa ash'ar lil-thawra* (Songs and poems for the revolution) (Beirut: Dar al Kalima, 1979).

80   Quoted in Abdel-Malek, *A Study,* p. 58.

social strata, and in particular those who were never involved in any political activity, do not know their songs. According to Mustafa Said, the new generation knows these songs better than the old one because of YouTube, though he adds that Sheikh Imam was more famous with the 1960s generation.[81]

For some, Negm-Imam's songs were more famous abroad—in other Arab countries like Iraq, Syria, Lebanon and Palestine—than in Egypt, largely because in Egypt they were censored.[82] For Said Mustapha, Sheikh Imam was not as famous as Umm Kulthum or Abdel Halim Hafez because he sang provocative songs linked to the political and social context of the time and did not sing about everyday life topics such as love, pain and passion.[83] By contrast, for Zohair Sabbagh, a Palestinian professor of sociology at Birzeit University, 'despite the politics of obscurity, oppression, blockade and banishment which followed the Camp David Accords [...], it is clear to us that amongst the people, the poems of Ahmad Fu'ad Negm and the songs of Sheikh Imam were widely disseminated in Egypt, in our land and throughout the Arab world of silence'.[84]

So were these popular songs or songs of the elite? Negm himself stated that, 'I frankly admit that in my estimation I have not succeeded in becoming the poet of the Egyptian people... a poet who can reach all the Egyptians despite the conspiracy of silence by the state mass media. The reason for this is that our audience is limited to those of the middle-class who listen to our ballads because they can afford to own recording machines.'[85]

For Said Mustapha, these dissenting songs declined from the beginning of the 1980s until the early 2000s mainly because of the disappearance of left-wing political movements.[86] For Corrao, the memory of Sheikh Imam was lost until the birth of new left-wing political movements, and especially until the spread of the Internet. With the rise of the Islamist movement as the main political force—schizophrenically both repressed and co-opted by the regime—the left-wing opposition

81   Mustafa Said, personal interview, 5/05/2011.
82   See interviews in 'Sheikh Imam'; also F. Corrao, personal interview.
83   Said-Mustapha, 'Negm wa al Sheikh Imam'.
84   Quoted in Barbara Harlow, *Resistance Literature* (London: Methuen & Co., 1987), p. 64.
85   Abdel-Malek, *A Study*, p. 23.
86   Said-Mustapha, 'Negm wa al Sheikh Imam'.

was dismantled, until the birth of *Kefaya* (Enough), the coalition of intellectuals from different ideological backgrounds founded in 2004 that called for the end of Mubarak's regime.[87] Since the leaders of this movement were former students involved in the 1970s uprisings, Sheikh Imam's legacy resurfaced, a view with which artists and audiences I interviewed generally agreed. A few members of the older generation, such as the activist Alaa' el Sheikh, went further and argued that the decline of political movements and of these dissenting songs was related to the fact that the generation born in the 1980s did not grow up in 'the culture of the revolution'.[88] According to Mustafa Said, instead, if this genre of protest songs declined after the 1980s, today there is a renewal of political songs in any style, from classical Arab songs to rap, hip-hop and heavy metal.[89] This takes me to the final section of this chapter, which deals with the influence of Negm and Imam's songs on activists and musicians involved in the 2011 uprising. I argue that a new generation of artists has inherited Sheikh Imam's legacy and still perform his songs, either keeping the same aesthetic features or introducing innovations.

The Legacy of Sheikh Imam and Ahmed Fu'ad Negm in Tahrir Square

According to all the artists I interviewed during my fieldwork in Cairo in 2011 and who participated in the demonstrations, Sheikh Imam's songs could be heard everywhere in Tahrir square.[90] Many concerts were held, particularly thanks to the engineer and businessman Mamdouh Hamza, who financed the material for these performances. Despite the tightening of censorship in the last years of Mubarak's regime, all these artists could perform in public places and got resonance in the media, especially on Egyptian newspapers in English language and some private television channels.

I decided to conduct focused interviews in particular with two contemporary artists who were involved in the Tahrir events and were

---

87 See al-Sayyid M. K., '*Kefaya* at a Turning Point', *Political and Social Protest in Egypt*, 29.2–3 (2009), 45–59.

88 Alaa' el Sheikh, personal interview, 6/05/2011.

89 Mustafa Said, personal interview, 5/05/2011. See also Levine, *Heavy Metal Islam*.

90 See also Antoon, 'Singing for the Revolution'.

close to Sheikh Imam's style: Salam Yousry, the director of the theatre company *Al Tamye* (The Silt) and the project *Mashru'a Kural* (The Choir Project); and the *'ud* player Mustafa Said. I prepared a questionnaire that covered their social and political background; censorship and self-censorship; channels of diffusion; the aesthetic features of their works; humour and satire; old and new issues in their songs; their audiences; their motivations and political involvement; disappearance and renewal of songs of protest.

Salam Yousry: Al Tamye Theatre Company and The Choir Project

Theatre and choir director Salam Yousry founded *Al Tamye* Theatre Company in 2002, which performed the show *Al Tamye wahed wa al shagar alwan* (Same mud, different trees) from 2003 to 2009.[91] The show was a tribute to Sheikh Imam and built on songs chosen from Imam's repertoire. These included *'El ful wa el lahma'* (Beans and meat), *'Bayan Haam'* (An important announcement), *'Shayyd Qusurak'* (Build your castles), and *'Kelmeteen le Masr'* (A few words for Egypt).[92] While the bare and humourous lyrics remained the same, the songs were deconstructed, stretched into longer acts and developed into parodic sketches following the style of composer Sayyed Darwish. The instruments were the same as in Sheikh Imam's performances, namely an *'ud* and percussions, with solo voices alternating with long parts sung by the choir. The performance was carried out by twenty-five singers/actors and a choir, which played a central role.

Most of *Al Tamye*'s members are former students of the faculty of fine arts—Salam Yousry himself is a painter and the son of artists—and are part of the upper-middle class. Some professional musicians and actors joined the company. Most members were born to parents who were themselves involved in political activities in the 1970s and used to attend Sheikh Imam's concerts. Likewise, the audience of *Al Tamye*'s performances consists mainly of upper-middle class students, activists, the sons and daughters of the generation who used to demonstrate in Tahrir Square in the 1970s.

---

91   See http://www.altamye.com/
92   Mahmoud, 'Act of Parody'.

When I asked Salam Yousry about censorship and self-censorship, he replied that finding subtle ways of getting around them can sometimes stimulate artistic creation. He also added that the *mukhabarat* (secret service) always try to intimidate associations and venues hosting this kind of performances—in Cairo the most important ones at the time of this research were *Al Saqya* cultural centre, *Rawabet* Theatre and the Townhouse Gallery. The internet is the main tool of advertisement, especially Facebook. According to him, the show, initially very light, became politically charged and challenging, mainly after the Gaza bombing in 2009.[93]

Concerning the themes of the songs, Salam Yousry argues that the social issues treated by Imam are still contemporary, and even 'Bayram Tunsi's poems still concern living matters'. However, some themes and targets—like revolutionary heroes, political figures, and the war against Israel—have changed or are out of date. Interestingly, when I asked him about the link between Sheikh Imam's songs and Egyptian nationalist ideology, Yousry replied that he lost interest in performing this show because many verses are too nationalistic and distant from his beliefs. This is why he started creating new shows and later developed the Choir Project.

The *Masru'a Kural* or Choir Project is the other 'child' of Salam Yousry.[94] Born in 2010 as The Complaints Choir in Cairo—on the model of the one created by Kalleinen and Kochta-Kalleinen in Helsinki in 2005—this is a participatory project involving non-professional and professional singers and musicians.[95] Project participants write the songs during workshops lasting a few days and then perform in different venues; the themes are chosen from everyday problems in Cairo, such as traffic, pollution, as well as from issues of national interest, like unemployment, corruption, religious extremism.

I consider this project an important example of contemporary dissenting music. In fact, it is possible to find similarities with Sheikh Imam's songs, particularly for what concerns the songs' aesthetic features and political and social commitment: the music is minimalistic, though several instruments are played (an *'ud*, a *daf* or large-sized frame

---

93   Salam Yousry, personal interview,17/01/2011.
94   See http://www.choirproject.net/
95   See http://www.complaintschoir.org/

drum, an accordion, a melodica; a guitar and a *ney* reed flute were recently added); the melodies are simple and easy to memorize, and the lyrics are far more important than the musical compositions. Take the following extract:

Workers are not heard,

Factories have been sold
The wheat we eat is American
Our natural gas is sent abroad.
I am a stranger in my own country
My rights are trampled on
Banks in place of green spaces
All sense of justice gone.[96]

As Salam Yousry points out, these songs, like Sheikh Imam's, challenge the regime because they are collective, easy to memorize and increase people's social and political awareness and their involvement in the social sphere. This choir gives the participants an experience of collectiveness and of what collective action without leadership means. This is no doubt the main reason why Salam Yousry is persona non grata to the regime.

Mustafa Said

Mustafa Said is a young virtuoso *'ud* player and composer from Egypt who teaches the *'ud* at Antonine University in Beirut. During our interview, he stated that Sheikh Imam was the only musician who conveyed the thoughts of the street, and that his songs, after a decline due to the dissolution of left-wing political movements, have reappeared in the last six-seven years. Said is the only musician I met who is not from an upper-class background; he gained his first musical experiences in the Sufi circles of Tanta, a city between Cairo and Alexandria. Although he does not usually sing Sheikh Imam's songs, I decided to include him in my research because of the song he composed for the revolution and performed in Tahrir Square in February 2011.

---

96   See 'Cairo Complaints Choir, May 2010, Part 1'.

The song's title is *'Ya Masri hanit'* (Oh Egypt this is only a few days away), with lyrics by the Palestinian-Egyptian poet Tamim Barghouti.[97] In a BBC broadcast, Said was interviewed along with Ahmad Fu'ad Negm: this is a revealing image that presents Said as the heir of Negm-Imam, though he has his own personal style that draws more from erudite music than from popular Egyptian style.[98] The way Said uses his voice in this song sometimes reminds one of Qur'an recitation: his pitch rises and descends fast with many embellishments, the *'ud* is a strong presence and is not only used as accompaniment but almost as a proper voice with an 'angry' tune. Unlike Negm-Imam's songs, there is almost no humour, and the dominant feelings in the song are pride and anger. This is an extract:

> Oh Egypt this is only a few days away
> Our day will be dewy
> And the day of the villain is gone.
> There is nothing left of the regime
> Other than a few batons,
> [...]
> O people there is no ruler
> Except in the imaginary of the ruled
> And those who will stay at home will be like traitors,
> Would be as if they handed the rest to the police
> Or told about where they live.
> [...]
> O Egypt we have become prisoners
> Dead and alive
> So those who stay at home are impossible to understand
> And those who go out will be protected by God.[99]

Aside from the song and his relationship with Sheikh Imam, Mustafa Said's music can be considered as the most interesting expression of his dissent, since it touches the core question concerning the Western cultural colonial heritage in Egypt. Along with his ensemble Asil and the foundation Amar (Arab Music Archives and Research) based in Beirut, Mustafa Said has managed to inject new life into the Arab music

---

97   Mustafa Said, 'Ya Masri hanit' (Oh Egypt this is only a few days away)', http://www.youtube.com/watch?v=p7l26PsSF6Q

98   BBC News Arabic, https://www.youtube.com/watch?v=gZqtLDWA5ng&t=74s .

99   Transcribed from the video at footnote 97.

heritage of the early twentieth century, the music that existed before the Cairo Congress of 1932, when Western musicologists set the canon of modern Arab classical music. According to Said, the music before the Cairo Congress was deleted on purpose as a result of cultural colonisation from the West. According to Mustafa this colonial approach is still poisoning the image of Arab music in Europe nowadays.[100]

Conclusions

This chapter has shown how lyrics written in a vernacular language and their musical arrangements have been tools for challenging the establishment and mainstream culture throughout twentieth century Egyptian history. A common thread links the compositions and poetry of Sayyed Darwish and Bayram Tunsi to those of Sheikh Imam and Ahmad Fu'ad Negm and the work of contemporary artists. An analysis of the latter's music and lyrics highlights how Imam-Negm's songs were composed according to musical idioms and poetics rooted in the Egyptian popular culture, embedding a collective imaginary in terms of popular themes and the role of humour. An analysis of the audiences and diffusion of these songs shows that despite their involvement in political struggles, Imam and Negm were—and still are—mainly popular among middle- and upper-class intellectuals and students, though their popularity did traverse social and ideologically boundaries.

As to the duo's influence on contemporary artists, this chapter has argued that, even though today some of their themes and language have become outdated, Imam-Negm's songs still represent an aesthetic reference for collective struggle. This living heritage is the product of a century-long tradition of vernacular resistance poetry put to music, connecting the grievances of several generations of Egyptians.

In fact, the evolution of dissenting songs offers a tool for analysing colonial cultural relations and twentieth-century Egyptian history from political, social, musical, and literary perspectives. Highlighting the renewed popularity argues and influence of Negm-Imam's song in Tahrir Square and with contemporary artists in 2011, this chapter has shown that old and new dissenting songs of Cairo do not necessarily

---

100 See 'Medinea Meetings 2015'.

draw inspiration from imported genres, such as rock and rap, and that they can be the product of renewed local forms of music and poetry. 'Innovation' in art production is not necessarily the integration of western patterns into 'a' supposedly conservative Arab culture.

This leads me to my final point. A decade after my fieldwork and the uprising of 2011, I want to end this chapter with a few reflections on some of the consequences of the intensified circulation of Arab artists in the French and British cultural scenes after the upheaval of 2011 in Egypt, reflections that are directly relevant to the question of global circulation that is at the heart of world literature as well as world music.

After I returned to France in summer 2011, a number of cultural organizations suddenly manifested an interest in my research. Meanwhile, projects led by 'young revolutionary artists' were produced, and major festivals and cultural organizations across Europe began to programme them.[101] This enthusiasm provoked intense questioning about how 'Arab cultures' in general—and the Egyptian 'revolutionary experience' in particular—get represented in European institutions. Many researchers started reflecting on how the 'revolution' and its main actors were becoming part of the international institutional machinery. Ilka Eickhof noted how the 'Arab springs' have been an important catalyst for international interest in the Arab art scene and for foreign intervention.[102] And according to Richard Jacquemond, the post-2011 period is marked by a re-organisation of the 'Arab cultural space' that includes an accelerated circulation of artists and intellectuals between Arab countries and Europe, and between Arab countries themselves, producing a 're-conceptualisation of the Arab cultural space and a shifting in the transnational dynamics.'[103] But, as Laura Gribbon argues, 'the game of the international artistic market tending to promote a post-orientalist and post-2011 version of the rebellious Arab artist started to push local actors to conform to the representations of themselves

---

101   See for example the event 'A night in Tahrir' organised within the first edition of Shubbak Festival.

102   See Ilka Eickhof, 'My friend, the Rebel. Structures and Dynamics of Cultural Foreign Funding in Cairo', *Arab Revolutions and Beyond: Change and Persistence*, Berlin: Working Paper, 11 (2014); and Ilka Eickhof, 'All that is Banned is Desired: "Rebel Documentaries" and the Representation of Egyptian Revolutionaries', *Middle East - Topics & Arguments*, 6 (2016).

103   Richard Jacquemond and Frédéric Lagrange, eds, *Culture pop en Egypte: entre mainstream commercial et contestation* (Paris: Riveneuve, 2020).

that circulated abroad or, at a minimum, to negotiate with these representations.'[104]

The sudden interest of French cultural organizations in my research topic enabled me to start working in the autumn of 2011 as a cultural operator and project curator. But if the possibility to make European ears hear voices from the alternative Egyptian artistic scene filled me with satisfaction, the enthusiasm shown by cultural institutions and audiences for the Egyptian 'revolution' and its protagonists left me with a voyeuristic and neo-colonial aftertaste. Despite my best intentions, I started feeling uncomfortable in my professional environment, especially given the ways in which some important French cultural institutions framed and presented artistic projects led by Arab artists. The institutional machinery, I felt, was transforming these artists into guinea pigs, just as the Canadian Lebanese artist Jayce Salloum had shown in his 1993 video project on the impact of the European glaze on narratives of the Lebanese civil war.[105] Simply put, the narrative of the 'heroes of the resistance' that emerged in the immediate post-2011 period builds on two alternative clichés: artists are either depicted as the heirs to a mythical tradition that is frozen in the past and requiring preservation (rather than being invented and constantly renegotiated); or else the same artists are represented as symbols of a (neo)colonial model of modernity and encouraged to adopt European dominant tastes and artistic norms.[106] As a result, artists seem to embody what the Egyptian poet Tamim Barghouti calls the 'false dichotomy of innovation versus heritage, where innovation means westernization, and heritage means backwardness and reactionary behaviours'.[107] This is why, in order to counter this tendency, I decided to focus on musicians who are part of a transnational community that defines itself as the 'alternative Arab artistic scene' and draws inspiration from local aesthetics and

---

104 Laura, Gribbon, 'New Coat, Same Colors: Ilka Eickhof on Funding and Cultural Politics', *Mada Masr, April* 7 (2014).

105 See Jayce Salloum and Walid Ra'ad's video 'Tal3een al janub' (1993), in particular the interview at min. 57.11.

106 Richard Jacquemond, 'Un mai 68 arabe? La révolution égyptienne au prisme du culturel', *Revue des mondes musulmans et de Méditerranée*, 138 (December 2015).

107 Tamim Barghouti, excerpt of the text 'Circulation of Heritage and Innovation, on Both Sides of the Mediterranean', commissioned by Festival d'Aix for the Medinea Meetings 2015.

music forms.[108] Mustafa Said, with whom I later collaborated, represents a perfect antidote to the false dichotomy mentioned above.[109]

Following a conference that I curated in 2015, I started enquiring into how institutional discourses and curatorial approaches on the 'Arab artist' label have evolved in the last ten years, and how the postcolonial repositioning in arts production and dissemination is affecting the collaboration between European organisations and Arab artists.[110] Indeed, in the last three or four years, some important European cultural institutions have started questioning the 'Arab culture' or 'African culture' labels by staging debates and activities gathering professionals, artists and researchers around this question. For example, BOZAR organised the symposium 'Race, power & culture: a critical look at Belgian cultural institutions' in Brussels in May 2019, and Les Bancs Publics held an event on 'Post-migrant creation in Europe' at La Friche de la Belle de Mai in Marseilles in September 2017.[111]

London's Shubbak festival, with which I have worked, has also been very active in this regard. In July 2019 we organized four events, among which a talk on 'Programming contemporary Arab culture: a critical look at institutional discourses and practices',[112] attended by established artists and professionals, and a roundtable on 'Working with European institutions' involving mainly young artists from the Middle East invited by Shubbak.[113] The events framed the issue so as to show that the 'Arab

---

108 See the work of artists Kamilya Joubran, Tamer Abu Ghazaleh, Abdullah Miniawy; researchers Youssef El Chazli and Ali Charrier have written expensively on this topic.

109 See Mustafa Said's interview on this issue at the 2015 Medinea Meetings organized by the Festival d'Aix in Marseilles; 'Medinea Meetings 2015'.

110 Ibid.

111 https://www.bozar.be/en/activities/149228-symposium-race-power-culture; and https://www.lafriche.org/evenements/creation-post-migratoire-en-europe/

112 Invitees included the Syrian-French Paris-based arts manager and cultural thinker Jumana Al-Yasiri, British-Egyptian Artistic Director of Battersea Arts Centre Tarek Iskander, Moroccan artist Younes Atbane, Lebanese Programs and Editorial Coordinator at Mophradat Brussels Marie-Nour Hechaime, Lebanese artist, activist, theatre maker Hanane Hajj-Ali, British Director of The Mosaic Rooms Rachel Jarvis, and Egyptian Country Director of Drosos Foundation Wessam El Beih.

113 Invitees included Moroccan dancer Youness Aboukaloul, Jordan theatre maker Amal Raphael Khouri, Lebanese actress and director Tamara Saade, Egyptian-Dutch spoken-word artist Samira Saleh, Tunisian dancer Mohamed Toukabri, Egyptian cartoonists Mohamed and Haithem El Seht, Egyptian arts journalist

culture' label created and used by European cultural institutions is a contested one, often co-opted by different political agendas. The main critique revolved around the fact that if this label has helped some up-and-coming Arab artists to create a niche in a very competitive British artistic environment, it has also forced these artists to conform to institutional requirements in terms of topics, formats, and aesthetics to adopt. One speaker interestingly summed up the general picture by highlighting its contradiction: 'If, on the one hand, a number of European cultural organisations supporting Arab artists ask these artists to comply with their expectations and those of their audiences, on the other hand, the same institutions are in search of 'authentic' artistic projects that represent different visions of the world.'[114] Other artists pointed out that many colleagues have started rejecting these requirements and proposed new mobilisation strategies against what they called the 'NGO-ization' of the arts, and to reverse this domination. For example, some suggested avoiding 'hot' issues disseminated by mainstream media and recurring in the programmes of British organisations showcasing Arab artists, such as migration, war, religion, freedom of expression, cultural preservation, and so on. A participant raised the question of how to adapt the aesthetics of art projects created for audiences in European capitals to a local Egyptian audience (and if it makes sense to do so).

Navigating between my experiences of researcher and curator, in the last ten years I have begun to understand how the intensified circulation of Arab artists in European cultural institutions after 2011 has created patterns of mutual influence. Despite the contradictions implied by the adoption of the 'Arab artist' label, the increased attention and resources allocated by European institutions to promote artistic creation from Arab countries have allowed the creation of spaces for open debate involving artists, professionals, and researchers. Discussions have revolved around how institutional narratives and modes of production impact artistic work, and what strategies artists and professionals can adopt to respond to this tendency. These debates have opened up unexpected positive evolutions in the field and are contributing to reframing the relationship between the actors involved in the artistic market.

Ismail Fayyed, Egyptian playwright Sara Shaarawi, Palestinian director of theatre Samar Khalil, and Moroccan cultural operator Mehdi El Azdem.
114   Tarek Iskander.

Bibliography

'A Night in Tahrir', *Shubbak Festival*; https://www.aljazeera.com/features/2011/8/7/london-art-festival-questions-arab-identity

Abdel-Malek, Kamal, *A Study of the Vernacular Poet Aḥmad Fuʾād Nigm* (Leiden: Brill, 1990).

Antoon, Sinan, 'Singing for the Revolution', www.aljadaliyya.com, 31 Jan 2011.

Al Jazeera, *Al Sheikh Imam*, http://www.youtube.com/watch?v=6nr29wcvsdI

——, *Political Songs in Egypt*, http://www.youtube.com/watch?v=Aycgmoj_29U

Al-Sayyid, Mustapha Kamel, '*Kefaya* at a Turning Point', *Political and Social Protest in Egypt, Cairo Papers in Social Science*, 29.2–3 (2009), 45–59.

Attali, Jean, *Noise: The Political Economy of Music* (Minneapolis: University of Minnesota Press, 1985).

Barghouti, Tamim, 'Circulation of Heritage and Innovation, on Both Sides of the Mediterranean', text commissioned by Festival d'Aix for the Medinea Meetings 2015.

Beinin, Joel, 1994, 'Writing Class: Workers and Modern Egyptian Colloquial Poetry (*zajal*)', *Poetics Today*, 15.2 (1994), 191–215, https://doi.org/10.2307/1773164

Booth, Marilyn, 'Sheikh Imam the Singer: An Interview', *Index on Censorship*, 14.3 (1985), https://journals.sagepub.com/doi/pdf/10.1080/03064228508533890

——, 'Colloquial Arabic Poetry, Politics, and the Press in Modern Egypt', *International Journal of Middle Eastern Studies*, 24.3 (1992), https://www.jstor.org/stable/164623

——, 'Beneath Lies the Rock: Contemporary Egyptian Poetry and the Common Tongue', *World Literature Today*, 75.2 (2001), 257–266

——, 'Exploding into the Seventies: Ahmad Fuʾad Nigm, Sheikh Imam, and the Aesthetics of New Youth Politics', *Political and Social Protest in Egypt, Cairo Papers in Social Science*, 29.2–3 (2009), 19–44.

'Cairo Complaints Choir, May 2010, Part 1', http://www.youtube.com/watch?v=CXkIq2QXF30&feature=relmfu

'Cheikh Imam', *Al Jazeera*, http://www.youtube.com/watch?v=6nr29wcvsdI

Clement, Françoise, 'Worker Protests under Economic Liberalization in Egypt', *Political and Social Protest in Egypt, Cairo Papers in Social Science*, 29.2–3 (2009).

Danielson, Virginia, *The Voice of Egypt: Umm Kulthum, Arabic Song and the Egyptian Society in the Twentieth Century* (Chicago: University of Chicago Press, 1997).

Eickhof, Ilsa, 'All that is Banned is Desired: "Rebel Documentaries" and the Representation of Egyptian Revolutionaries', *Middle East - Topics & Arguments*, 6 (2016), https://archiv.ub.uni-marburg.de/ep/0003/issue/download/157/10

——, 'My friend, the Rebel. Structures and Dynamics of Cultural Foreign Funding in Cairo', *Arab Revolutions and Beyond: Change and Persistence, Berlin: Working Paper*, 11 (2014), https://www.polsoz.fu-berlin.de/polwiss/forschung/international/vorderer-orient/publikation/working_papers/wp_11/WP11_Tunis_Conf

El Maliki, R., 'Political Songs in Egypt', *Egypt Today*, www.egypttoday.com, August 2008

Gribbon, Laura, 'New Coat, Same Colors: Ilka Eickhof on Funding and Cultural Politics', *Mada Masr, April 7* (2014), https://www.madamasr.com/en/2014/04/07/feature/culture/new-coat-same-colors-ilka-eickhof-on-funding-and-cultural-politics/

Harlow, Barbara, *Resistance Literature* (London: Methuen & Co., 1987).

Jacquemond, Richard, 'Un mai 68 arabe? La révolution égyptienne au prisme du culturel', *Revue des mondes musulmans et de Méditerranée*, 138 (2015), https://doi.org/10.4000/remmm.9247

Jacquemond, Richard and Frédéric Lagrange, eds, *Culture pop en Egypte: Entre mainstream commercial et contestation* (Paris: Riveneuve, 2020).

LeVine, Mark, *Heavy Metal Islam* (New York: Three Rivers Press, 2008).

Mahmoud, S., 'Act of parody', *Al-Ahram Weekly*, 924 (2008), www.weekly.ahram.org.eg

Marcus, Scott L., *Music in Egypt* (Oxford: Oxford University Press, 2007).

'Medinea Meetings 2015', https://www.youtube.com/watch?v=inu5cSQ8Kis

Mollicchi, Silvia, 'Al-Fan Midan Brings the Arts to the Streets', *Egypt Independent*, 10 May 2011, https://egyptindependent.com/al-fan-midan-brings-arts-streets

Negm, Ahmad Fu'ad, *Suwwar min al-hayat wa al-sign* (Images from life and prison) (Cairo: al-Majlis al-a'la li-ri'ayat al-funun wa al-adab wa al-'ulum al-igtima'iyya, 1964).

——, *Ughniyat wa ash'ar lil-thawra* (Songs and poems for the revolution) (Beirut: Dar al Kalima, 1979).

Negm-Imam, 'Anā al-sha'eb' (I am the people), http://www.youtube.com/watch?v=SbO55R33OHI

——, 'Bahebbyk ya Masr' (I love you Egypt), http://www.youtube.com/watch?v=v00-sr8AWdA

——, 'Baqaret Haha' (Haha's cow), http://www.youtube.com/watch?v=HCuHE-WQ6g8&feature=related

——, 'Bayaan ham' (Important announcement).

——, 'Al ful wa al lahma' (Beans and meat), http://www.youtube.com/watch?v=L026gxezEUM or http://www.youtube.com/watch?v=BbdAGwNmdvo

——, 'Gifara mat' (Guevara is Dead), http://www.youtube.com/watch?v=daybzy7v5tI&feature=related

——, 'Al hamdullillah khabbatna takhti bitatna' (Thanks to God we bat under our armpits), http://www.youtube.com/watch?v=kynIDEVns4E

——, 'Mamnu'at' (Bans), tr. Walaa Quisay, http://www.youtube.com/watch?v=6Lh7GIG0gLM *Mamnu'at,*

——, 'Nixon baba' (Papa Nixon), http://www.youtube.com/watch?v=bh4fiRgD38s

——, 'Sign el 'ala'a' (The citadel's prison), http://www.youtube.com/watch?v=7sJ1_qbvbOw

——, 'Valery Giscard d'Estaing', http://www.youtube.com/watch?v=1eE6r8nyehw

——, 'Ya Baheyya' (Oh Baheyya), http://www.youtube.com/watch?v=dYceV1LRzrY&feature=related

——, 'Ya'ish ahl baladi' (Long live my countryfolk), http://www.youtube.com/watch?v=3LuxdJy5wzc

Nettl, Bruno, *The study of ethnomusicology: thirty-one issues and concepts* (Champaign: University of Illinois Press, 2005).

Okasha, S., 'Prince of Disillusionment', *Cairo Times*, 21 June 2000, www.cairotimes.com

Said, Mustafa, 'Ya Masri hanit' (Oh Egypt this is only a few days away)', http://www.youtube.com/watch?v=p7l26PsSF6Q

Said-Mustapha, Dalia, 'Negm wa al Sheikh Imam: su'ud wa uful al ughnyia al siyasyya fi Masr' (Negm and Sheikh Imam: the raise and the decline of political song in Egypt), *Alif: Journal of Comparative Poetics*, 21 (2001), https://doi.org/10.2307/1350040

Salloum, Habib, 'Sayyed Darwish: The Father of Modern Arab Music', *Al Jadid Magazine*, 7.36 (Summer 2011).

Salloum, Jayce and Walid Ra'ad, 'Talaeen al janub' (1993), https://vimeo.com/81763753

Slackman, Michael, 'A Poet Whose Political Incorrectness is a Crime', *New York Times*, 13 May 2006, www.nytimes.com

Stevens, Janet, 'Political repression in Egypt', *MERIP Reports*, 66 (April 1978), https://www.jstor.org/stable/3011139

Tucker, Judith, 'While Sadat Shuffles: Economic Decay, Political Ferment in Egypt', *MERIP Reports*, 65 (March 1978), https://www.jstor.org/stable/3010875

Index

About the Team

Alessandra Tosi was the managing editor for this book.

Lucy Barnes and Hannah Shakespeare proof-read this manuscript; Rosalyn Sword indexed it.

Jeevanjot Kaur Nagpal designed the cover. The cover was produced in InDesign using the Fontin font.

Cameron Craig typeset the book in InDesign and produced the paperback and hardback editions. The main text font is Tex Gyre Pagella. The heading font is Californian FB.

Cameron also produced the PDF and HTML editions. The conversion was performed with open-source software and other tools freely available on our GitHub page at https://github.com/OpenBookPublishers.

Jeremy Bowman created the EPUB.

Laura Rodríguez was in charge of marketing.

This book was peer-reviewed by Frederico Fernandez, Annachiara Raia and an anonymous referee. Experts in their field, our readers give their time freely to help ensure the academic rigour of our books. We are grateful for their generous and invaluable contributions.

This book need not end here…

Share

All our books — including the one you have just read — are free to access online so that students, researchers and members of the public who can't afford a printed edition will have access to the same ideas. This title will be accessed online by hundreds of readers each month across the globe: why not share the link so that someone you know is one of them?

This book and additional content is available at
https://doi.org/10.11647/OBP.0405

Donate

Open Book Publishers is an award-winning, scholar-led, not-for-profit press making knowledge freely available one book at a time. We don't charge authors to publish with us: instead, our work is supported by our library members and by donations from people who believe that research shouldn't be locked behind paywalls.

Join the effort to free knowledge by supporting us at
https://www.openbookpublishers.com/support-us

We invite you to connect with us on our socials!

BLUESKY
@openbookpublish
.bsky.social

MASTODON
@OpenBookPublish
@hcommons.social

LINKEDIN
open-book-publishers

Read more at the Open Book Publishers Blog

https://blogs.openbookpublishers.com

You may also be interested in:

Oral Literature in the Digital Age
Archiving Orality and Connecting with Communities
Mark Turin, Claire Wheeler and Eleanor Wilkinson (Eds)

https://doi.org/10.11647/obp.0032

Tellings and Texts
Music, Literature and Performance in North India
Francesca Orsini and Katherine Butler Schofield (Eds)

https://doi.org/10.11647/obp.0062

Searching for Sharing
Heritage and Multimedia in Africa
Daniela Merolla and Mark Turin (Eds)

https://doi.org/10.11647/obp.0111